*Journals of The*

# EARTH

## GUARDIANS

### SERIES 2

# Journals of The
# EARTH
# GUARDIANS
## SERIES 2

L . C  W E B B

**To order additional copies of this book, contact:**
Xlibris
AU TFN: 1 800 844 927 (Toll Free inside Australia)
AU Local: 0283 108 187 (+61 2 8310 8187 from outside Australia)
www.Xlibris.com.au
Orders@Xlibris.com.au
818170

# CONTENTS

# The ~~Sergeant's~~ General's

## Rules of Combat

1. Always be prepared to fight *But don't go looking for one*

2. Never let down your defences. - Pain can be your friend. (But don't let it show)

   *Everyone is an enemy -until otherwise*

3. Never turn your back on the enemy.

4. Don't draw attention to yourself - you will get shot.

5. If your mission is going well - it's most likely a trap. Have a Plan B and C

6. Never show all of your cards. *Always work to better your cards*

7. Do your homework and study your enemy. *Treat your enemy as your friend*

8. Never let your feelings affect your actions. (~~Love~~ and Fear are weaknesses)

9. The enemy will take any opportunity to strike - as should you. *To extract information or time let them think they have the upper hand.*

10. Don't get caught. *the most important rule*

I - Lila Willows will live by these rules.

L. Willows

*Dodge your enemy to stay alive -*
*- Learn their moves - then strike*
*New Game - Shoulder Tap*

"When shadows constantly surround the light, what is the point in running"

# CHAPTER 1

# THE REALITY OF TRUTH

*Journal entry by Matt Winters*

*Several days have passed since Lila went missing and today was the day my sister Jane had arranged to return Danny and Ruby home.*

*Maxwell had kindly asked her to look after the children for a little while longer when Lila went missing. So that I could help in the search party. But there is only so long you can keep the truth from your children before . . .*

*The knock at the door echoed through the apartment as Jane walked in with Danny and Ruby behind her. The look on their little faces was filled with so much confusion when only I came to greet them, and as Ruby looked around the room she excitedly asked, "Where's Mummy?"*

*And I —— I couldn't —— I just started to tear up.*

*Thankfully Adela and Max were there as well, and they greeted the children with a comforting smile before they sat them down on the couch. Adela then went on to tell the story of how brave their mummy was, rescuing people she had never met and in doing so put* herself in danger. She explained to them how there was a fire and that Mummy has gone missing, but that they still had people out looking for her.

The way Adela told the story made Lila out to be the hero — and she was. She absolutely was. But it was also hard for me to hear.

It was so sweet though, because when the story was finished Danny just nodded, understanding Adela then went to hug his little sister and me as we tried to comfort each other.

We sat on the couch crying for a while, and I tried to distract them with cartoons but nothing would console them. All they wanted was their mum, and every time the front door of the apartment opened they were so hopeful that it was Lila, and that maybe she just got a little lost on her way home.

When they finally fell asleep, Adela helped me to quietly put them off into their beds, then we sat at the dining room table just talking about anything else — instead of what had happened.

I could see what Adela was attempting to do, and I was grateful for the attempt of the distraction, but it wasn't working. I couldn't stop thinking about her.

Several more days past and the family and the hotel staff still stayed in that hopeful mode — that at any minute Lila would walk through the lobby doors and greet us all with her beautiful smile. But for me the reality had started to sink in, and I feared that Lila was either locked in the deepest, darkest cage that these sick 'Collectors' have — never to see the light of day again, because of all the trouble she's caused —— or —— she's _dead_.

## Journal entry insert by Alex Woods

Every night I wake up in a panic from the nightmares, and it's getting harder and harder to shake them. I keep getting flashes of Lila in the national park surrounded by fire.

The worst one was last night when I woke up in a sweat looking around the room, and the strangest most unexplainable thing happened when I lay back down on the bed – I saw her – I saw Lila – She was lying on the bed next to me and she looked like she had been beaten, with cuts and bruises all over her. It was gut wrenching. I didn't know what to do or say and she looked right at me as I heard her echoing voice, "Alex... Alex, help me..." then she disappeared.

But then I really did wake up. – I looked around the room again and saw no evidence that she was ever there, but I know it was her – I know she's alive and I'm not going to give up on her.

I really do blame myself for what happened to Lila – I should have known better and I should've paid closer attention to everything that was happening.

But something still wasn't adding up for me – I needed Matt to tell what happened to him. I needed to know how long he'd been working for Darkman, and how and why he did what he did. I also needed to know if he was still working for the enemy or if he was just pretending like he had claimed.

It sucked because I had so many questions that needed answered, but it was the middle of the night and I can't just barge into Matt's apartment and start interrogating him.

So, I waited until morning and knocked on Lila's apartment door only to be greeted by Adela, who had accidentally fallen asleep on Matt's couch – again. And that was suspicious.

I told Matt I needed to talk to him and quickly checked to make sure the kids were still sleeping before I sat down at the table to ask him my many questions.

It was very interesting though, because Adela seemed way too quick to jump to Matt's defence. I tried to explain to her that I really needed to know, if we had any hope in finding Lila. But Adela didn't listen, she just demanded I get out – of Lila's apartment.

–What the hell.

Matt stood up to calm Adela down, and he understood why I was asking the question so he very helpfully explained, "It happened just after Max's birthday party, that guy. . . Terrence was waiting for me in the elevator. . . I thought he was just a hotel guest until he grabbed me. . . I remember waking up in my bed the next day. . . but I had slept most of the day away. Lila was worried about me and assumed that I had drunk too much at the party . . . but she instantly picked up that something was wrong . . . Apparently, I did something that gave me away. Before she cured me though. . . she asked me everything she needed to know and then filled in the pieces for me afterwards. . . She kept the knowledge a secret and used that opportunity to feed bad intel back to the 'dark man' or lead us to any clues."

Damn, that was actually a really good idea – If it had actually worked.

Our information session was interrupted by Adela's phone ringing. It was Jessica letting us know about the search party. Most of the team were still out searching the national park and had apparently found something.

I was excited and quickly stood to my feet grinning, "What are we waiting for let's go."

But Matt looked surprisingly unexcited and unhopeful as he sighed, "I can't, the kids are still sleeping."

Again, Adela chimed in wanting to help and offered to stay and look after Danny and Ruby while we went to look for their mother.

I'll admit – I'm not overly used to Adela being so caring. She used to be a bit of a snob before Lila saved her. Maybe I'm just being sceptical or severely lacking sleep.

When we got to the national park, I decided to ask how Matt was coping. I was also a little worried at the surprisingly large amount of time Adela and he were spending together. I mean she's stayed at Lila's apartment almost every night since her disappearance.

But when I asked Matt about it, he just shrugged it off explaining that Adela had been helping get the house in order and keep him company, then added, "I know it's weird. . . I'm just not used to being in an empty home and Adela's being really helpful."

Alright this is the hard part for me – because we had reached the dreaded spot where we last found Lila running through the fires looking for us, and shouting our names before getting hit with tranquillisers and disappearing forever. It was really hard to bear. And I still couldn't shake that horrible feeling of guilt. I had to stop and couldn't move, almost short of breath.

"Hey, are you okay?" Matt asked, thankfully breaking me from my nightmaring trance.

I nodded and kept walking up to where Maxwell and his search party stood. When we got to the group, they were all standing around a large hole in the ground filled with broken tree roots and branches. It was as if someone had tried to cover it up – but maybe that's just false hope for me.

Chase had jumped down into the hole to inspect it and stated, "It's roughly two meters long and it was in the shape of a cocoon until someone smashed it from the outside."

I then excitedly interrupted explaining how I had seen it before, "That's what grabbed Lila when she was running from the fire."

Chase stared up at me with a worrying look before he pointed to the dried blood in the cocoon, "Do you think Lila might have hid in here to escape the fires?"

After that, the conversation began to sound very pessimistic with some reminding us that there is a possibility that Lila might be dead, and I was really struggling to listen at that point.

Then it happened – I heard Lila's voice clear as day, saying my name. I looked around to see her but instead I just saw Matt asking me if I was okay. -- Again.

"Yeah. . . I'm fine," I replied. But Matt didn't believe me. And I turned around again as I heard Lila's voice calling to me.

I kept looking around nervously, until Matt grabbed me by the shoulders and demanded, "Alright now, I know you're not okay. What's going on?"

Yep – because I'm seriously going to be the one to tell Matt that I can hear his wife's voice in my head and that I'm being haunted by her in my nightmares. Coz that's sane – not.

Luckily before I could answer with the words 'I'm fine', Jess received a text from Jennifer stating that they had found something in the east car park. So, the search team all started making their way towards the east car park instead.

But I didn't. I was still confused and convinced I was losing my mind, and I rushed over to the lake to splash some water on my face then sat down leaning against one of the burnt trees.

And it happened again – I heard Lila's voice. She called my name, only this time I got a vision of Lila in a dark concrete room, her hands were bound with metal chains hanging from the ceiling. And she was covered in blood with cuts and bruises everywhere, and burn blisters from where the chains held her.

I saw a dark shadow of a man in the room walking towards her and she cringed in pain as he tortured her. And I couldn't take any more of the vision, fearfully pulling away from the trees in terror looking around the park, only to see Matt trying to calm me as I screamed Lila's name.

Yep – I was definitely losing my mind.

"Alex! . . . What is it?" Matt asked.

But honestly, I didn't know what it was either, and I just looked at him still muddled and answered, "I don't know" then ran away from him at full speed up to the east car park.

# Original journal entry continued by Matt Winters

Alex has been acting really strange ever since Lila disappeared. And I was beginning to worry that the thought of losing Lila was too much for him.

The problem is, as Lila's husband, I'm not entirely sure how to show sympathy for him.

I did ask him if he was alright but he seemed evasive, and rudely left me on my own in the middle of the national park. So I had to make my own way up to the east carpark.

By the time I got to the car park the search party had already arrived and was discussing what each had uncovered. We did however, have a small hiccup that Max was attempting to handle.

One of the police officers was a detective named George Nell; he took a very keen interest in this case because he and Lila were in the same class together in high school. But I'm beginning to worry that George was suspecting foul-play and probably noticed that we were not being entirely honest with the situation, because he kept asking Max for the truth. Only to have Max answer with a half-truth and play ignorant.

Still Gorge persisted, "Mr Eden, this situation has gone from bad to horribly worse. So, far I've got a suspicious fire, a missing woman, an abandoned tranquilliser gun and some government officials trying to take over the case. And now I've just received word that the media have gotten a hold of this story . . . Is there anything you are still not telling me about this case?"

When I heard the detective mention the tranquilliser, I became excited and rushed to Alex to confirm, "We were right she didn't get shot. They really were tranquillisers . . . That means she's alive."

*Unfortunately, George over heard me and started asking me the questions instead, "What do you mean alive? And shot by who?"*

*Whoops.*

*Thankfully Max played it smart and deflected the question back to George, "Mr Nell, you mentioned something about a government official, who do you mean?"*

*But before George could answer that, a black BMW pulled up into the car park and Alex unexcitedly answered, "Speak of the devil. . . here he comes."*

*I suddenly got this horrible knot-like feeling in my stomach as Agent John stepped out of the car and walked towards the group, introducing himself to the detective. He had a practiced smile and he arrogantly greeted us before he announced to the search party and the remaining police officers, "Attention please, I would just like to personally thank all of you for putting in such valuable time and effort in searching for any clues to the whereabouts of Ms Winters. . . But my team has been asked by the missing woman's parents to take over from here. . . and we request that you all kindly make your way back to cars and head home. Thank you."*

*That did not sit well with Lila's team and they all started quietly grumbling, except for Alex who instead, loudly questioned, "Wouldn't it be faster if we all helped?"*

*John then moved closer to the group and quietly replied, "No. . . they'll only get in the way. . . Besides I'll need you and your team to go back to Mission control for a debrief."*

*I got a very strong suspicion that absolutely no one from Lila's team were planning on doing that either, and continued to quietly grumble. Chase, especially did not like John and I noticed him* giving John the death stare. Maybe it was something Lila said to him.

The other problem we had though, was that George overheard John's orders and questioned him about Mission Control, "I'm sorry did I miss something?"

To which John smugly and rudely replied "No . . . oh except for the part where I need you and your men to get your gear and leave. . . You're contaminating the scene."

As he said that a white media van pulled into the car park and John didn't look too pleased to see them, "Great, who alerted the media? You know what, never mind. I'll deal with the news crew. You guys head on home and get some rest."

I watched as John went to speak to the media and began to realise why Lila didn't like him. If she really could sense the nature of a person, she would have known that John is a real arse.

Either way, the team was sent packing and Chase drove us all home. But while we were driving home Maxwell started discussing ideas and options with the team. We were all in agreement that we were not giving up on the search and that we would not be telling Agent John anything about what really happened.

But since the media was involved, the Guardians of the group would have to be a lot more discreet with their abilities. Making things a lot more difficult for us.

## Journal entry insert by Maxwell Eden

I had suggested it might be a good idea for Matt to take Danny and Ruby to visit Lila's mother and see how she was coping with the news, considering it was soon going to be on the news.

Matt tried to explain to Mrs Willows what he could about Lila's disappearance, while Danny and Ruby sat in her loungeroom and drew pictures.

Surprisingly, Hanna was handling it a lot better than I had thought, and for some reason she was convinced that her husband General Willows would fix this, and asked if I could check in with my team to see if there were any updates.

I agreed to her request and stepped into the loungeroom to check on Danny and Ruby and also make a phone call. While I did, Ruby showed me the picture that she drew of Lila surrounded by flowers and trees, "It's beautiful," I whispered as I phoned Jessica for an update.

When Jess picked up, her voice on the phone sounded both fearful and surprised as she explained, "Hey . . . Dad. Perfect timing . . .I'm assuming you're calling for an update and we've got major news. We've finally got hold of the security footage from the east car park, and we found an unmarked black car entering the car park around the same time as the fires, but the car didn't leave until after midnight. . ."

"Did you get a look at who's driving?" I asked.

But Jess responded almost unsteady, "That's the major part. I'm sending you a picture now."

Within seconds I received a picture and looked down at my phone at a grainy image of what looked like Ben, Lila's old cadet friend. I glanced up and studied the pictures around the room to see one of

General Willows with all of his cadets that included Lila and Ben. And I began to suspect that we may have missed something, and that Lila may have invited the wrong man into her home.

So I spoke softer to talk to Jess, "Try to keep this from Matt for me. . . at least until we have more information to go on."

I then hung up, grabbing the picture of the cadets and Lila, and slipped it into my pocket.

Very casually, I walked back into the dining room where Hanna and Matt were talking and curiously asked, "Mrs Willows, I was wondering if your husband was around? I was told he was the one who asked the government to take over the search for Lila. . . He might have some answers for us."

I sat down at the table to listen to Hanna's answer, and she was actually quite helpful for me and informed us that Richard had left for a mission a few weeks ago. But she also agreed to contact him for an update and disappeared into her bedroom to make the call.

As I sat at the table, I started getting all the wrong kinds of suspicions. And I got a little distant and distracted while Matt and I waited for Hanna to finish calling the General, then Matt asked quietly, "Any news from Jess?"

Since I didn't want to tell him any of my suspicions yet, I shook my head and responded, "No . . . we hit a dead end."

Hanna soon returned to the room after she tried several times to get in touch with her husband, but each time she got no answer. Eventually she decided she would be of better use at the hotel, helping to look after Danny and Ruby while we continued the search for Lila.

So, she packed her bags and came back to the hotel with us.

## Journal entry insert by Alex Woods

My frustrations were hitting a new level – and it was agonising just waiting around the hotel not doing anything, not knowing anything. And what was worse – was the feeling of losing my damn mind.

I felt like screaming, just sitting at Maxwell's desk looking at old security footage, while Jess was talking on the phone to one of the detective friends she met at the national park – George, I think.

But it happened again – I heard Lila's voice calling my name. I looked around desperately trying to find where the voice was coming from, but still I saw nothing, and when Adela walked in, I lost it.

I threw the keyboard in a fit of rage, screaming, "This is pointless! We're never going to find her this way!"

Adela tried to calm me down, but it was futile as I continued to rant, "We're never going to find her."

Then it happened again – I heard Lila's voice calling my name and I stopped my rant.

I was feeling really tired and I was really beginning to doubt my sanity. I knew looking around the room was probably pointless but I did it anyway and I still saw nothing.

Now clearly concerned for me, Adela asked me if I was okay.

But I wasn't – I was losing my mind – I was going freaking nuts.

Still Adela wanted an answer and concerningly stared at me. All I could think to do was nod my head and reply, "I'm fine. I think I just need some rest" as I stormed out of the room.

Something was definitely wrong with me – and as I paced back and forth in the elevator, I may have punched the walls a few times, trying to get control of my head.

What the hell is happening to me?

Then it happened again – I heard Lila's voice call my name but this time she appeared behind me. I wasn't sure if I was losing it or not, and I was a bit scared. Mainly because she was still covered in dirt with blood dripping from everywhere, and her hands were bound with chains. So either I'm imagining things – or I'm being haunted by her ghost.

Yep – I really think I'm losing my mind.

Not only that, I still didn't know what to do, and I stepped back into the corner of the elevator staring at her. But she followed my movements and looked straight at me as she spoke my name, and it echoed as if she were a ghost, "Stop fighting me, Alex."

– And what the hell was that supposed to mean?

I started to panic as I watched her fade away again and I screamed, "No!" as I tried to grab hold of her, but it was no use.

And unfortunately for me – the elevator doors opened at the worst time. -- Crap.

I looked up to see Matt staring at me, with Danny and Ruby behind him, and Maxwell carrying Mrs Willows bags for her. -- Double crap.

I'm not entirely sure how I really looked at the moment, but they all looked genuinely concerned for me as Matt asked again, if I was okay?

And again, with that question. – I was beginning to see why Lila hated it so much. I mean I wasn't overly sure what was happening to me – Was I really seeing Lila – is she even alive – or was her ghost really haunting me because I failed to protect her and let her die.

Can you honestly answer truthfully to that question if the answer was – 'I'm fine Matt, I'm just being haunted by your missing or presumably dead wife?'

Yep – Probably not.

So, still not knowing what to say I just smiled, and nodded my head as we rode the elevator in silence to our floor.

# CHAPTER 2

# I'M SO SORRY, LILA

## Journal entry by Terrence Connors

I failed her. I had originally invited Lila to come and hear my side of the story, and I stupidly led her straight into a trap. I don't know how they found out about the meet, but now, seeing Lila in this condition — it was agonizing.

When she was hit with the tranquillisers, she fell and hit her head and her hair was quickly soaked in blood from a head wound, which meant she wasn't stable enough to travel underground via the trees. So instead, I pulled her into the cocoon and waited for the coast to be clear.

But in the pitch black of night, they came, they dug down and broke open the cocoon to find me holding Lila and telling her it was all going to be okay — trying to keep her awake.

Her eyes were glassy as they slowly looked up to see Ben, one of General Willows's minions, but Lila didn't see it that way. She quickly pulled away from me and held onto Ben's arms as he lifted her out.

"Lila . . . No," I shouted, but I was too late, Ben had already injected her with the Neuritamine.

She stared up at Ben as if he had broken her heart, then fell unconscious into his arms.

I wanted to pull her away from him, but before I could Agent John walked up behind me with his congratulations, informing me, after the fact, that the General and my mother both agreed that it was a good idea to team up and acquire the target together.

All I could think to do was smile and play along, not wanting to draw suspicion to what I was really thinking, because I didn't want Lila to get hurt. And knowing exactly what the General has done to our kind before made me very uneasy.

So, I just followed John back to his car and said "Excellent plan, I'm happy for the assistance." All while Ben followed behind us carrying Lila's comatose body.

They've spent weeks now running test on her in one of the General's many hidden bases scattered around the world.

The General did ask me if I wanted to leave and return back to my master, but I played it smart and said "No," then sternly reminded him that I was the one who caught the asset, which meant she belonged to my master and not him.

He didn't seem too pleased with that, but I didn't care. I was more concerned about Lila. Mainly because some of the General's tests weren't exactly humane, and one in particular hadn't been used for some time — given that we had other methods for the test outcomes.

The test was designed to understand the guardian's natural healing response and recovery. And the general wanted it done on Lila because he was convinced that she was stronger than she was letting on.

I didn't want it done and I tried to object. But considering I was not in my master's facility all I could do was watch as the horrific procedure was performed on Lila by one of our doctors — without anaesthesia and still awake.

The doctor made deep incisions at certain points in Lila's body to ensure enough damage, and to bring her to the point of a slow death, usually due to the amount of blood loss.

Lila was very reluctant to cooperate with this test, even after the process of beating her to breaking point. But she didn't scream as they held her down, instead she stayed very quiet through-out the entire process. — She really was stronger than they expected.

And when the procedure was finished, they just left her on her cell floor to mend on her own.

I stood at the cell door and I couldn't breathe. Just seeing Lila lay on that cold, dark, bloodied floor, after watching the doctor mutilate her beautiful body. I was in tears because I knew this was my fault, and I couldn't take anymore.

I'm determined now more than ever to protect her, so I took the first opportunity I could, to convince my mother that the General's methods were ineffective and that I may be able to provide an alternative.

But I suspect my mother had her qualms about my allegiance to her because she hesitated — she even wondered why I was grinding my teeth so much.

Eventually she agreed to my request and arranged for a transport to her facility instead. The only downside was her methods weren't as kind to the new recruits either, especially when the Neuritamine wasn't taking any effect. But I knew that in having Lila there, I would have sway on certain tests being done to her.

As we travelled to Mothers facility, I carried Lila myself — ensuring no one else touched her. And I was very careful of the many wounds that were still healing and had not yet closed.

Her face was still pale from the blood loss — but I know she's a fighter.

It was very strange though, she was still unconscious as I cradled her in my arms, walking into the greenhouse where I spent most of my time, but as I was carrying her, she had her head resting on my shoulder, and she pulled closer to me nestling her bloodied face into the crook of my neck. And I sensed her relaxing in my arms.

I don't why, maybe she thought I was her husband — Matt, or her friend — Alex.

Either way, I stayed focused and carried her into — well my home.

I have a small log cabin that overlooks the coy pond in the middle of an enormous greenhouse, attached to one of Mothers many training facilities — it's the place where I stay when I'm not hunting. Mainly because Mother wants to keep an eye on me, but I know it's my prison. And I know she's not really my Mother, she's just my master.

I very carefully placed Lila down in the corner of the cabin and silently grunted to myself as I watched the guard's chain her to the wall. A place where I once sat.

When the guards left, I very gently placed a blanket over Lila, wishing I could do more for her — but I knew if I interrupted the General's last despicable test, he would have demanded it be done again. And I was never going to let that happen again.

In tears and still struggling to breath, I sat down next to Lila, and watched her as she remained unconscious leaning against the wall. I stayed and listened to her slow shallow breaths and the sound of her weakened heart beating, and drew comfort that she was still alive.

And I know she was sleeping, but I just had to say it, so in my tears, I carefully held her still healing and very bloodied hands and whimpered, "I'm so sorry Lila. . . I'm so, so sorry"

## Journal entry insert by Alex Woods

I walked into apartment 141 – my apartment. My very, very empty apartment, and lay down on my bed, exhausted from the lack of sleep and tried desperately to convince myself that I wasn't crazy.

But the image of Lila kept replaying in my mind – the part when she asked me to stop fighting her. – What the hell was that about?

I didn't understand it, but there was a lot about Lila that I never understood.

So, I sat in my room at the end of my bed and said to the empty room, hoping if Lila really was there, she would hear me, "Okay, I promise I'll stop fighting. . . Just let me see you."

I waited in the silence and looked around the room but saw nothing. So, I sighed and instead laid back down on the pillow and closed my eyes in the hopes of getting some small bit of sleep.

And that was when Lila appeared sitting at the end of my bed. She crawled up and leaned over me, gently brushing the hair from my face. I felt the soft touch of her hand, and I opened my eyes to see her amazing blue eyes looking down at me. I was both shocked and horrified to see her.

She was covered in more blood and dirt, and she looked pale – worse than before. It made me sick and I threw up at the sight of her. Especially seeing the dried blood in her hair.

Holy Mother of craps all over.

I didn't know what to say, so I blurted out, "Is it you? Are you really alive? What have they done to you?" I was close to tears, holding a bin of vomit, and wasn't sure if I wanted to know those answers, but I cried, "Please tell me this is real?"

"Alex . . ." she interrupted, almost out of breath, then touched the tear on my cheek and smiled, "Don't cry Alex . . . you need to focus. I don't have much time, John . . ."

But something interrupted her, and she cringed in agony with electrical sparks surrounding her as she disappeared before my eyes. I shrieked Lila's name as I woke up in a fright, sweating and panting.

I scanned the room again, looking for her. Looking for any signs that she was actually there, but again I found nothing.

Still, I was positive that it was her, and that I wasn't going crazy and in an angry confusion and whispered, "John."

## Journal entry insert by Lila Winters

I didn't know where I was when I woke up again. It looked like some kind of log cabin with my hands chained to the wall, sitting in a pool of my own dried blood.

Feeling a world of pain, I peered up to see Ben kneeling next to me holding a taser, and Richard standing in the doorway watching and glaring at me.

"Lila . . . are you okay?" Ben whispered, almost sounding concerned for my well-being as he helped me to sit up and offered me a drink of water.

"Ben?" I rasped, a bit groggy and confused, "What's happening Ben?"

But Richard didn't let him answer as he shouted, "That's enough!" and Ben stood to attention.

Richard then cautiously walked over to kneel down next to me and studied my wounds, smiling as he said, "Hey, Pumpkin. Welcome to your new home".

I wanted to punch him or hurt him, but I was too weak to break out of the chains. I tried to though. I stood up at full speed and tried to grab him, but Ben moved at full speed pulling him out of the way and pinned me up against the wall.

Then with a grin, Richard looked back at me, impressed and commented, "Well, it looks like her speed wasn't affected by the tests."

Memories of those test started to race through my mind as my eyes glowed a hue green. But Ben scowled at me and demanded, "No, Lila Don't do it!" and he pressed me harder against the wall. I looked back at Ben and shook my head in disappointment with tears rolling down my cheeks and sobbed, "Why?"

But he couldn't even look at me, instead he injected me with yet another tonic that made me feel even weaker, then placed me back down. Only this time he rested me on a stretcher bed and pleaded, "Don't fight me Lila, or you will die."

He actually sounded genuinely concerned for my life as he looked back at Richard and awaited his next orders.

I watched as Richard walked out of the cabin scowling at me, "Such a stubborn child. . . clean her up."

Ben then kneeled back down to speak to me, but I refused to look at him as he explained, "Lila, you're in a facility that is impossible to escape from and if you try to escape, they'll shoot you and anyone who failed to keep you under control. . . So please just cooperate with me."

He moved to unchain me from the wall and I wanted to escape but I didn't. I just sat there, refusing to look at him. He then quickly went outside and brought back in a bowl of water and a cloth. And now he had gained my attention, when I watched his hands glow a fiery red to warm up the water.

Well Frac – he's a Fire guardian – I should've clicked to that when I saw my bedroom plant on fire and him standing over my bed while I was trying to escape Terrence's nightmaring hold on me. – It was an obvious clue and I completely missed it.

Ben sat down next to me, and gently cleaned my wounds then rubbed an antiseptic gel on them before he applied the bandages. He did become particularly hesitant when he was tending to the wound where the darts hit. But they were nothing in comparison to the others.

After he was finished, he sat in silence, occasionally glancing at me, hoping I'd say something or even just look at him. So, I asked, "Did you know?"

He looked down at the floor in silence as I asked again, "Did you know?"

"Yes," he tentatively nodded.

I then looked at the cloth Ben was holding now covered in dirty blood and snickered, "After everything we've been through! How could you not tell me?!"

Holding back my tears, I stared at him, watching as his brows furrow, almost like if he was confused and he scoffed back defensively, "Like you were so open and honest about who you were."

"I was protecting you." I rebuked trying to defend my lies.

But Ben saw through that, "No. You were pushing me away like you always do."

I started to argue with Ben, and stood up to yell at him only to realise, he missed one of the wounds, quite a large gash on my upper thigh – from one of the many horrid experiments they did on me.

I stumbled a little from the pain of standing, and Ben tried to assist me and offered to tape it up for me – but I refused, pulling away from him, "So what is this . . . Revenge! For what? . . . Did I hurt your feelings . . . did I break your heart? What? . . . What did I ever do to deserve such deceit from you?"

He continued to follow me and tried to grab hold of me, beginning to tear up as he urged, "No, Lila I would never do this to you. This isn't me . . . I love you . . . this is the last thing I ever wanted for you."

But that was really hard to believe. I knew deep down he always loved me – that's why he always wanted to look after me and made sure I was okay after – Brody died – But I could never return his love – because all I could see in him was a soldier. – At least now I know why.

Either way, whatever love I did have for him was lost, and I wanted to make sure he knew, so I grunted through tears, "Love! You think this is love. . . No, Ben . . . you were just following orders. Like you always do."

I limped back and forth ignoring my pain, constantly trying to avoid him. But it did not help my injuries at all, it just made it worse. And when I began to stumble, Ben rushed at full speed to hold me up. But I didn't want him touching me and I lost my temper, pushing him back into the wall – way too hard, causing the wall to shake.

I was going to scream at him again, and tell him that he was a terrible friend and a liar, but the fight was interrupted as Richard stood back at the door, analysing the scene.

As usual, Ben quickly stood to attention but then he explained that it was his fault he got pushed and that it was just a simple misunderstanding. And that surprised the frac out of me – he was protecting me.

I don't think Richard believed him though, because he walked over and stood in front of me, all arrogant and smug, "Just a little warning for you, around here if you cause trouble, there will be severe and fatal consequences. . . Are we clear?"

I saw Ben in the corner of my eye and he looked almost scared for my life as he pleadingly whispered under his breath, "Please Lila, don't make this worse."

Was he fraccing serious – How could this get any worse – I've nearly died – more times than I can count, and my body feels like it's on fire as it slowly tries to heal itself from the all brokenness. – And yet he's pleading with me to not make this worse.

Now that I think about it – Richard really is a psychopath, so I'm pretty sure he could make this worse if he wanted to. And since I didn't want any more pain, I reluctantly nodded my head and replied, "Perfectly... Richard."

He then strutted out of the cottage, but before he left, he addressed me one more time, "From now on you will call me Sir."

And that was so <u>not</u> going to happen – instead I stood tall and contemptuous towards him, completely ignoring the pain and smugly replied, "I'd rather die."

I watched as he scowled at my still defiant attitude – and I knew full well that he was the one who tried to break me. But he never will.

Even so, Richard was determined and stupidly arrogant, and he replied, "That can be arranged," as he walked out the door with Ben following behind him.

I sat back down on the stretcher bed and sighed remembering the days when I was the perfect little soldier girl. – I think I was 15 years old running alongside Ben and two newbie cadets as we completed an incredibly difficult obstacle course, in the rain and covered in mud.

Richard was standing at the finish line timing us as we crossed the line, all puffed and out of breath. And I was shocked when he shouted at us, demanding us to do it again, and I shrieked back at him, "Sir, we've done the course twice already. . . We need to rest."

But Richard turned his stopwatch around, responding, "And twice now you were all too slow. . . Do it again."

I stood my ground not wanting to do it again and I knew the other cadets were struggling as well and shook my head, wheezing.

Again, Richard berated me for not following orders, then stood over me and jeered, "I did not raise you to be a quitter," insisting that I do it again.

That was when Ben tapped my shoulder and started running with me to redo the obstacle course, and as I ran, I mumbled, "You didn't raise me at all."

That was also the day I really started to doubt Richard's method and training. I was over being beaten, and I was over lying to doctors, and teachers, and anyone who saw me, about my broken arm or broken leg or broken anything. And I was definitely over wearing make-up to cover all the bruises that I received during my daily training. – And Oh Holy Frac.

Snapping out of the memory I sat back down on the stretcher bed, staring at the log walls of the cabin. And everything started to become clearer now, as I realised that all this time, I was fighting to save people from being collected, I didn't even realise that the General was a Collector and that I had already been collected.

## Journal entry insert by Alex Woods

I stayed up all night waiting for Lila to appear again. And I really tried to be calm and open to whatever the hell was happening to me. I was even trying to convince myself that I wasn't losing my mind, whispering, "You're not crazy. She's real and she's coming back."

I was struggling to stay awake and eventually I began to drift back off to sleep when Lila appeared again, sitting next to me and held my hand to wake me up, whispering, "Alex."

And oh, just hearing her voice made me doubt my sanity, but also made me want to cry.

I opened my eyes at the sound of her sweet voice, and worryingly asked, "Lila are you okay. . . I thought something happened to you."

She looked a little hesitant to answer, and cleared her throat, "I'm fine. . . I just got a bit of a shock."

"Where are you? Are you safe? Is he hurting you?" I asked.

I also wanted to pull her closer to me and hug her, but then took a minute to realise Lila's appearance had changed since the last time I saw her. She was still covered in dirt and dried blood, but it looked like someone had given her medical attention with dressings and bandages and what looked like antiseptic cream.

She also seemed confused when I asked if he was hurting her, so I asked again, "Lila is Terrence hurting you?"

She took a deep breath and shook her head, "No . . . but that's not who I came to talk about . . . it's John, you can't trust him. He was there when Ben was putting me in the car. . . Please you need to be careful."

I tried to interrupt her as I struggled to follow along, but still confused I mumbled, "John and Ben . . . But Terrence and . . . and Richard."

Her eyes darted to mine when I mentioned Richard, and she sighed looking very disappointed and almost in tears, "Yes Alex, General Richard is the one holding me here."

I wanted to hold her and comfort her, but I didn't know if that would hurt her further. Still, this conversation was also confirming a lot for me and I stood up and grinned, "This is huge. We have a lead . . . I have to go tell the team."

I rushed out of my apartment and down the hall, but Lila raced to stop me and begged, "No stop . . . you can't tell anyone about this. Please!!! I can't risk John or anyone else finding out that I can still contact you. . . It's far too dangerous and I need more time."

I felt her hands pressing against my chest, desperately trying to get me to understand – but I didn't. "Lila . . . I can't just sit here and do nothing!"

Lila whimpered, looking up at me with her teary and pleading eyes, "You're not doing nothing Alex . . . the fact that I can see you and talk to you is more than enough . . . but I also need you to be here for me . . . I need you to protect my family. . . please."

I stared into her eyes and watched as a tear rolled down her cheek as I nodded to her request, but then she became startled looking around and whispered, "Someone's coming . . . I have to go. I'll come back. I promise . . ."

She began to disappear again and I really didn't want her to – not again. And I tried to grab her as I shouted, "No wait! Lila . . . please."

But then I woke up again – only this time I was standing in the hallway outside Lila's apartment, just about to knock on the door. – What the hell is happening to me?

## Original journal entry continued by Terrence Connors

Yeah — I was right in assuming my mother had doubts in my allegiance because she had arranged for a swift reminder to be given. The beating lasted throughout the night and when the sun rose, they stopped to return me back to my prison cottage.

I was dragged semi-conscious into the greenhouse cottage by two of my mother's guards as they chuckled at my weak and demeaning state.

And as I laid on the cottage floor failing to hide the agonising pain I was in, I peered up though my swollen eyes to see Lila lying on the stretcher bed.

Someone had touched her while I was getting my reminder, they'd cleaned her wounds and I was really hoping that was all they did to her.

Lila started to stir awake when she heard the commotion, and stared at me confused. I think she was scared as she watched one of the guards add their little reminder, kicking me in the stomach and ribs one last time. But they were quickly brought to attention by Ben as he walked into the cottage.

Yet, Lila kept staring at me, completely ignoring Ben as she moved slowly to kneel down next to me and inspect my bruises. Then in a rage, she stood up shouting at the guards, "What the hell did you do to him?"

— Yeah Okay this woman's got no fear.

The guards just chuckled at her, "We just gave him what he deserved, for ever doubting his master."

One of the guards went to kick me again, and I braced myself for the pain but instead Lila stood in front of me. She raised her hands towards them, and tree roots sprung up just outside the cottage door, reaching in to grab hold of them and drag them out of the cottage, throwing them across the green house garden. And I heard their screams as they landed.

"Lila Stop!" Ben shouted as he grabbed hold of Lila's hands and pushed her back down on to the stretcher, completely disregarding her injuries.

— And so help me, if he ever touches her again I'm going to kill him.

I tried to move and stop him but I couldn't, I was in too much pain. She didn't struggle though, she just scowled at him — waiting for him to let go.

Eventually Ben slowly released his grip on Lila and pulled out a small rag from his pocket and, whispered, "Are you okay?"

But Lila didn't answer him. Instead she just stared at the floor and waited for him to leave. He placed the rag in her hand and as he did it jingled a little and before he left, he turned back to her, and sighed, "Happy Birthday Lila."

— Oh damn, it's her birthday.

I was really struggling to stay awake or even move. And I desperately wanted to, when I saw Lila trying to hold back the tears as she sat up and looked inside the rag to find her bracelet and a necklace, along with a note from Ben — I guess.

She read the note in silence as she put her jewellery back on then wiped the tears from her eyes. And I kept watching her as she pulled a seed from her bracelet and held it in both hands, then as her eyes glowed the seed grew into a beautiful white rose bud. Her eyes glowed again and the rose blossomed, changing its colour to blue.

I didn't know what Lila was doing, and she noticed me watching her as she looked at me then crushed the rose in her hand, dropping it into the cup of water that was left for her on the table along with a plate of bread — that had not been touched.

I was amazed at what Lila was doing, staring at her as she swirled the water and the flower petals inside the glass started glowing, turning the water light blue. She then sat down and drank a large sip of the water, cringing at the taste and clawing at her wounds in pain as they all started to heal.

Again, Lila held her screams back — and I found that both fascinating and impressive. Every beating and experiment she had received, she never let anyone hear her pain or see her fear — Grunted yes, but it lasted mere seconds before she went back to scowling at her torturers.

I continued to stare at Lila, and I tried to be brave and hide my own pain, watching as all of her open wounds started to close properly.

She then stood up removing the bandages and began to feel revitalised and healthy, even her colour was back. — And damn that was good to see.

But some of the wounds hadn't disappeared fully — they must have been the more severe ones, and the others left scars in their wake. — And that wasn't good to see.

I began to feel all my guilt return to me, and I looked up to see Lila staring me this time, watching as I struggled to stay awake and gasping in pain every time I moved.

Very slowly, Lila moved to kneel down next to me and held my hands. I didn't know what to do and it wasn't like I could stop her. But I also didn't want to stop her.

After a moment, she let go and started to study my injuries, dabbing some of the blue water onto the wounds on my face. I tried to be brave but the pain was quite severe and I cringed a little, but after a few seconds, some of the pain disappeared.

I was seriously confused by her actions, and I tried to sit up but as I did, I began to cough up blood, which filled me with an unsettling feeling as I held my torso and trembled.

Staying silent, Lila started unbuttoning my shirt to assess the large purple bruises covering my torso and back. She gently ran her hand across my wrist where the chains dug into my skin and burned, then she looked at her wrist to see similar markings.

"Why did they do this to you?" she puzzled, looking over the many wounds I had.

I struggled to talk, but I mustered up enough strength and rasped, "I made them angry."

Her actions became even more confusing to me when she handed me her glass of blue water and demanded I drink it. I was sceptic and suspicious, not knowing why she was acting so nice, after everything that had been done to her. But she just sat there and waited for me to drink, then two seconds later I was curled in a ball, screaming in agony.

The pain only lasted a few moments, passing as the bruises began to slowly fade. I then felt really tired, and struggled to move with quite a lot of injuries still yet to be healed, so I just lay there as Lila leaned over me to see if I was okay.

I had no idea why she was being so calm and nice to me, and I stared at her, trying to figure her out. But I felt my heart hurt a little when I realised the necklace that she had put back on was the one I gave her — the white oak tree of life pendant with the ruby stone in the middle. —— Did she remember me? Did she really know who I was?

With a weak smile, I looked up at her and I continued to stare at the pendant as I fell asleep.

---
## CHAPTER 3
---

# A DEADLY BIRTHDAY

*Journal entry by Lila Winters*

Today was moving very slowly as I sat and nursed Terrence's wounds while he slept.

Don't ask me why. I didn't fully understand why I was being nice to him either.

The blue-rose tonic had helped his wounds to heal and he was no longer coughing up blood but he still seemed delirious, drifting in and out of consciousness.

I tried to make him comfortable with a blanket and I let him use my leg as a pillow while he slept on the cold hard floor, I even pulled him away from the bloody corner – where all the chains and my blood was.

I must have frightened him though, when he finally came to, because he stood to his feet in a hurry and just stared at me. And now realising he was topless and only in his boxer shorts with blue-rose paste smeared onto all of his now healed bruises and closed wounds probably didn't help. — He almost looked embarrassed.

"What did you do to me?" he asked, trying to keep his distance.

I stood to my feet and rolled my eyes slightly, "I didn't look if that's what you're worried about . . . I just wanted to help." He then stared back at me in sheer confusion, and I irked at him, slightly annoyed at his rudeness, "A simple thank you will suffice."

But he didn't thank me, he was too busy trying to rub the blue-rose paste off his skin and instead asked, "Why?"

What the frac —— I just saved his life and he asked why.

"Fine next time, I'll let you die," I snickered, sitting back down on the stretcher bed and cleaning up the blue rose petals from the ground. All while he rushed to the dresser in the corner and found some non-torn pants for him to wear.

Eventually he turned around to see what was left of the blue rose paste sitting on the table next to his bloodied shirt, and picked up a rag covered in his blood then noticed the rags covered in my blood. All of a sudden, his demeanour changed and he became almost sad, and I sensed guilt in him again.

So, I placed the last of the blue petals on the table, and stood next to him biting my bottom lip then explained, "You were very close to death when they brought you back here. . . The rose water helped to heal your internal bleeding and some of your exterior wounds, but the damage was quite severe."

I also made sure I didn't look at him, just in case I got in trouble because he had yet to find a shirt. But Terrence then turned to me, pulling my face up to meet his gaze and held his hand on my cheek.

I could tell he was trying to read my nature and intentions. And his face almost looked happy when he glanced down at the necklace I wore, holding it in his other hand as he finally whispered, "Thank-you, I didn't know you could do that."

He started looking over some of the newly formed scars on my body, and somehow, I could sense his sadness as he gently ran his fingers over them. But I didn't want him touching me either, so I pulled away, unsure of him then watched as he wandered around the cottage.

He eventually found a top and began to stare out the window at the garden. And I was kind of still curious and thought it would be the best time to ask, "So why did they do that to you?" I know I'd already asked that question, but I needed to ask it again.

I stared at Terrence and waited for the answer, and he looked back at me and noticed I was twiddling with my finger and smiled before he answered, "I was being punished because I didn't do what I was told."

And Damn Fracs.

I cleared my throat, feeling a little uneasy as I realised the white lily I had used on him while he slept didn't work like I'd hoped. Most people under the influence of Neuritamine wouldn't have any memory after the substance was cleared from their bodies.

So either, he was never under the influence of Neuritamine and is just a very bad person or the white lily was no longer effective. Which did hinder my plans to escape.

Now slightly disappointed, I sighed as I sat back down on the stretcher bed, and surprisingly he respected the distance I had put between us as I continued to question him and learn as much as I could. – I was merely trying to see how cooperative he'd be after saving his life and all.

He was actually very forthcoming with me. Which again surprised the frac out of me, but there were moments when he diverted the question.

In the conversation, I learnt that Richard and his recruits were part of a wider network of organisations spanning across the globe, and that Richard worked with what is known as "The Board" which was all the CEO's and government officials that oversee the network's operations.

I had apparently gained the attention of several board members and there was a race to who could collect me first. – Aren't I popular?

The information Terrence was giving me, was actually helping me to understand why on my first day at the Eden Hotel I was visited by both Richard and John and why they were so insistent on recruiting me.

But my wonderful info-session was rudely interrupted by the arrogant man himself, as Richard walked into the cabin, smugly smiling at Terrence and commented, "Well would you look at that. . . Mr Connors lives. And has healed up quite nicely."

He then looked at me who had also healed a lot faster than the last time he saw me, and walked over to the table to inspect what was left of the blue-rose paste. But as he picked it up, my eyes glowed and the paste was destroyed, turning black and hard and broke apart like sand, and the blue petals withered away.

"Well what do you know, I raised you to be strong and smart," Richard sneered with a scowl back at me.

"Mr Connors mentioned before that you had developed a healing tonic . . . Apparently, the last time Mr Connors had the opportunity to capture you, you were all alone in the park crying."

With an evil grin he stared at me, showing absolutely no sympathy as he continued, "Ben tells me that it was your husband that made you cry. . . Do you want to tell me about it . . .? I'd be more than happy to have some stern words with him if you'd like."

I said nothing and instead glared at Ben, hating him even more for betraying my trust like that. — The night Matt threw me down a hill after parading me around like a trophy was actually a really hard night for me to cope with — and Ben was really comforting for me, letting me cry it out on his shoulder. I stupidly let him see my weaknesses because I trusted him.

But now instead of being my friend he's standing guard at the cabin door listening in – leaving me to question – Was ever really my friend?

Richard had obviously grown tired and impatient of standing around, and stood at the cabin door still grinning at me. "Well then, I have a surprise for you, Pumpkin . . . Follow me and don't try anything stupid."

He then led me out of the cottage that was in the middle of a large greenhouse with Terrence and Ben cautiously walking behind me.

The greenhouse was attached to what looked like a black ops site with training facilities, weapons room, sleeping quarters, and laboratories. There were a lot of what I assumed to be soldiers – well armed, wandering the building and some standing guard at a few closed doors.

I followed Richard into a large laboratory, where two lab technicians were waiting, typing away on their computers. They became very excited when I walked into the room, whispering to each other and glancing occasionally at my fresh scars and even tried to touch them.

The nerve of them, it was like I was an animal or some kind of science project to them.

But what was interesting, was before either of them touched me, Terrence stepped in front of me and glared at them as he sternly warned, "If you value your life. . . I strongly recommend you *not touch her.*"

The lab technicians then wisely, stepped away.

Richard however ignored the tense and uncomfortable moment, and signalled to Ben to retrieve a box from the refrigerator that had a birthday cake inside.

Ben was then ordered to stand in front of me, but looked like he didn't not want to be there, holding the cake.

No – What was he doing? Please don't do this.

I felt my entire body tense as Richard boasted saying happy birthday to me while lighting the candles. They then sang happy birthday to me and acted as if this was a normal and expectable thing to do to a prisoner.

All except for Terrence and Ben who just stayed quiet. But I did hear Terrence whisper under his breath the words, "I'm sorry Lila." And Ben whispered under his breath, "Me too."

Well that definitely shocked the Frac out of me.

When Richard and the Lab Techs finally stopped singing their horrible tune, I mustered up the best fake smile I could and gently blew out the candles.

## Journal entry insert by Alex Woods

The team was really struggling today of all days to continue the search for Lila. We all knew it was Lila's birthday and we knew – if she was alive – which only I knew she was – that it was not going to be a happy day for her. And team morale was really Lila's area of expertise.

I walked into the conference room and I definitely sensed an off vibe from the team, but they were taking it really well. Probably because they were distracting themselves with the search.

Matt, Adela and Jessica were looking over satellite and surveillance photos of the national park. And Jennifer, Henry and Katie were looking into the Bendigo warehouse where we had found the Neuritamine vials hoping to find a link to any other organisation.

Maxwell however, was nowhere to be seen, and when I asked where he was, the answer intrigued me. Apparently, John was down stairs demanding to speak with us but no one was interested in talking to him. – Except for me of course. Because I wanted to kill him – after extracting every piece of information I could from him.

I casually backed out of the conference room, and rushed down the stairs hoping to catch John and question him about his involvement, remembering what Lila had said. But by the time I got to the lobby, Maxwell and Chase were already in a heated conversation with him.

"Mr Eden, this is a government issue and does not concern you . . . I demand you let me speak to my agents immediately," John demanded arrogantly.

But Maxwell was undeterred by his rudeness and replied, "None of them are in the mood to talk to you. . . and I am not going to force them to comply with any of your demands. So, I suggest you compose yourself and leave quietly."

John started looking around at the other hotel guests who were gawking and being nosey then softly whispered, "If they're planning a rescue mission, I should be involved."

With a smug grin, Maxwell reminded John that it was him that had ordered the team to go home, and that he was supposedly the one in charge of finding Lila, so her family and friends could recover, then questioned, "Are you saying you are no longer able to continue the investigation."

That question seemed to have hit a nerve, because John angrily stormed out of the building grumbling to himself.

I was actually really impressed at the way Maxwell handled that, and he spotted me spying from the staircase and came over to greet me. We then walked back up to the conference room together to hold a 'staff, plus extras' meeting. So that we could all catch up on what we had found.

But I wasn't filled with a lot of confidence, because of what I knew and how I knew it. And the fact that it was asked to be kept quiet from the very person we were looking for, made me feel very uneasy. – So this meeting was going to be hard for me.

In the meeting, we all sat around the conference table as Adela and Maxwell explained what they had found.

"We have reason to believe that Lila's parent may have been compromised," Maxwell explained as he laid out the surveillance photos of Ben driving into the national park and then a picture of Lila and her cadet friends that Maxwell 'borrowed' from Mrs Willows' house.

Jess continued the explanation stating that all of the cadets in the photo had dropped off the grid shortly after they graduated cadet school. She then pulled out a picture of Brody and his death certificate and added, "Except for this boy, who suspiciously died while out on a supposed team-building exercise."

As Matt looked at the photo, he became very uneasy and shifted in his chair trying to find something to change the subject. He looked over at me and faked a cough to get my attention before he whispered under his breath, "Alex that's Lila's friend. Remember the story I told you?"

I guess Matt forgot that there was more than just me who had really good hearing because Adela interrupted, "What story?"

– Crap.

Again, Matt shifted in his chair, nervously chuckling and not knowing what to do or say until Maxwell pushed the subject further. "Matt, if we're going to have any chance in finding your wife. We need to know as much as possible. Do you know something about this boy?"

I glanced at Matt and he regrettably nodded to me, hoping I would tell the story. So, I explained, "Brody was one of Lila's friends . . . and his death while it may be suspicious . . . it was very much an accident." I stopped the explanation there hoping that the team would drop the subject, but they didn't. So, I continued, "It wasn't a team-building exercise . . . It was a graduation ceremony. . . Lila was matched up with Brody and they were sparring to prove they're abilities. She purposefully failed the test in the attempts to save Brody's life, but . . ."

I didn't want to continue anymore, because I knew this was a sore subject for Lila. And I was pretty sure she didn't want this kind of story revealed on her birthday.

Thankfully Maxwell quickly pieced together what really happened and chimed in, "Right. Well . . . we all know Lila would never intentionally kill anyone. . . So, we will just leave this as accidental and move on."

He quickly pulled Brody's photo off the table as Matt added, "That was the day Lila vowed never to work for Richard again. . . Don't get me wrong. He's tried on several occasion to recruit her. . . but every one of his messenger soldiers was sent back with bruises and a very wordy message of . . . No."

Adela excitedly gasped with a revelation and turned to me, "This may explain why Lila was one of the last of the guardians to be taken. . . Richard may have purposefully kept her file off any of the databases, so he could keep her close to him."

I really didn't know whether to be glad or not at Richards attempts to delay the inevitable. However, Maxwell interrupted wanting to add more to the revelation.

"I think there's more to it than that. . . I did a little digging into Lila background and found these." He then placed Lila's birth certificate on the table along with a photo of a man holding a baby girl and explained, "Lila's real parents were William Knight and Katherine Willows. . . Hanna Willows sister. . . Lila said they had supposedly died in a car crash the day after she was born on the drive back from the hospital. But there are no records or newspaper articles or even a police investigation to confirm that. I can't even find their death certificates. . . I think Lila's parents may still be alive."

Awe Crap – what does that mean?

Matt picked up the photo and shook his head, commenting, "This looks like my Ruby when she was born . . . I don't understand. . . Lila would have told me about this."

"Unless, she didn't know," I interrupted voicing my thoughts, "It's possible Hanna and Richard were keeping this from her for a reason."

With that information Matt stood up in a panic and rushed to the door, "I have to get Danny and Ruby away from Hanna."

But Maxwell rushed to stop him before he opened the door, "Don't worry Matt, I've already assigned Chase to protect Danny and Ruby. . . He's on his way to collect them from day care now. . . But we need to keep what we've learned a secret until we know more. The last thing we want to do is tip our hand too early and give whoever is behind this the heads up."

Matt took a moment to think but then agreed and sat back down as Maxwell began to assign new tasks for all of us. Adela and Jessica were tasked with tracking down Katherine Willows and William knight. Matt was tasked with keeping an eye on Hanna and work with Chase on protection detail. And I was tasked with filling in for Lila as head of security while we had nosey government agencies wandering around.

And as we began to walk out of the conference room, Katie looked over to her mother and jokingly said, "I sure wouldn't want to be the one to spill all this to Lila when we finally find her."

Double Crap – I cringed at thought of having to tell Lila, knowing that I was the only one in contact with her. And I jumped with fright when Matt tapped me on the shoulder and asked me if I was okay.

He then confessed to me, "You know this whole thing would be a lot easier to handle if I knew for absolute certainty that she was alive. I mean. . . What if this whole time we've been searching for her, I should have been grieving with my kids?"

I wanted to tell Matt so badly about Lila being able to contact me. But I couldn't. I didn't know who to trust anymore. I mean even John – the man I worked alongside with for years had betrayed us.

Instead I just nodded and grinned to Matt as I walked out of the room in a hurry.

## Original journal entry continued by Lila Winters

I was growing tired of this stupid charade of playing the part of a content birthday girl as Richard offered me a slice of cake. Instead I declined and irked, "Richard, what am I doing here?"

He didn't look happy to see me not playing along. "We need to run a few more tests on you before we start on our next project," he replied, finishing off his slice of cake.

"No" I scoffed, knowing it wasn't going to be as simple as that.

And it wasn't – Richard just evilly grinned at me again, "Now Pumpkin, you're not in a position to say No."

He turned and watched as my eyes glowed, and noticed the small potted plants the Lab Techs were experimenting on as the plants grew larger, wrapping its large tendrils around the Lab Techs necks and gently but firmly squeezing, lifting them off the ground.

Feigning disappointment, Richard sighed as he looked around at the scene and shook his head. "Now Pumpkin, do you honestly think I care about a couple of scientists. Everyone here is expendable to me." Then to prove his point, he pulled out his gun and shot Ben.

I screamed as I watched Ben collapse to the ground, struggling to breathe as his lungs filled with blood. And the

Lab techs were instantly dropped to the ground as the tendrils let go and I rushed to help him.

I held his head, sobbing and trying to stop the bleeding, and pleaded through my sniffles, "Ben! No . . . Please. Stay with me . . . Don't die . . . please don't die . . . Not today."

He looked up at me and smiled as his gaze became distant, then he held his blood-covered hands on my cheek, wiping my tears away and smearing his blood on my face as his hand became limp in mine, drawing his last breath.

The rage built inside me as I tried and failed to wake him up, calling his name, and staring into his vacant eyes.

Terrence then very cautiously knelt down next to me, and I could sense all of his sadness and guilt as he checked Ben's pulse, confirming to Richard that he was dead. And with that Richard callously boasted, "I told you Lila . . . when you cause trouble, there will be consequences. . . Consequences like these."

He blamed me for Ben's death. And now I was consumed with rage as I stood up glaring at Richard. My breathing was slow and I could feel every muscle in my body tense as my hair turned white and my eyes glowed a furious dark green, commanding the tendrils of the plants to rise up again. This time they attacked Richard with the tendrils wrapping around his body and squeezing tightly. And I very much enjoyed watching the fear fill his smug and pretentious little face.

I moved at full speed and snatched the gun from Richard and fired at him in a furious rage.

But before any of the bullets hit him, more of the plants grew and created a shield protecting him. Terrence then clutched my hands tightly, pulling the gun away from me and holding me.

"I saved your life and this is how you repay me," I seethed as I struggled to break free.

His grip grew tighter around me, pulling me closer to him, and spoke softly, trying to calm me down, "Ben may have been one of Richard's minions. . . but he was my friend too. So I know how you feel . . . but killing your father is not the answer. They will only send another to take his place."

He was right, killing Richard wasn't the answer — but he was very, very wrong when he called him my father — he's never been my father — not for a second.

I stopped struggling and stared up at Terrence. And he could see my watery eyes and the pain that filled them, so he pulled me closer, wrapping his arms around and hugging me in an attempt to console me.

The grief filled me, and I felt my body going numb but still Terrence held onto me, and I cried and broke down, screaming in frustration. I screamed so loudly that the windows in the laboratory shattered, and somehow the instrument caught fire and lights over-head blow up sending sparks flying.

But in all the chaos, Terrence just kept holding me, not to restrain me, but to comfort me.

And I held on to him so tightly, needing and longing for that sense of security that somehow he just gave, as I sensed his true nature.

Eventually I had stopped screaming and relaxed into Terrence arms, burying my face in the crook of his neck to muffle the sobs. And while still holding me, Terrence raised one of his hands and released Richard, who was still tied up in plants, struggling to break free in the midst of everything. He fell to the ground gasping for air, and watched as the room was filled with soldiers trying to douse the fires, and save the other lab instrument and computers.

Terrence then stood protectively, holding me in his arms and demanded Richard to stop this now. But Richard took one look at my now long white hair and the chaos I had created and sniggered, "No, this girl is more powerful than we had ever imagined. . . We need to find out what makes her tick. . . her strengths and her weaknesses. And I'm not stopping until we have them."

I could feel Terrence's grip tighten around me when he bickered, "But she's your daugh—." But I interrupted him before he could finish that sentence — because I am anything but his daughter. I pulled away from Terrence, looking around the room and I barked, "If you want to know exactly what I can do. . . then this laboratory clearly isn't big enough."

To that Richard greasied me suspiciously then turned to the exit, demanding I follow him.

Terrence remained very close to me as we were led out of the facility and into the large outdoor garden surrounding the entire facility filled with trees and shrubbery.

The two lab technicians then started attaching wireless probes on my head, chest and arms all while Terrence stood protectively near me, glaring at them. – And I don't know how but I also sensed him feeling very territorial.

I was beginning to doubt whose side of the chessboard he was playing on or who he was there to protect as I contemplated his previous actions. – He defended Richard but then also tried to protect and console me. – What is with this guy?

I looked around the garden and noticed several heavily armed guards all cautiously watching and waiting for me to make a wrong move.

"They're not going to shoot me again, are they?" I asked sarcastically to Richard.

"Only if you try to run, Pumpkin . . . And for the record it was Ben who shot you," he retorted as he watched from a cautious distance. Which right now was very smart move for him.

I clenched my fist anger, but Terrence held my arm and whispered so quietly to the point that only a guardian would hear, "Lila, don't give in to his games. He's goading you and you know it."

But honestly who gives two-fracs what reason I give for pummelling his arse?

Still, Terrence was right — So instead I waited until the Lab techs had finished attaching their science stuff. And as I walked to the centre of the garden, Richard chortled, "If it helps, I promise I won't shoot you."

I contemptuously smiled back to Richard and sneered, "I know you won't shoot me . . . because you need something from me . . . but when I finally do get my moment and I will . . . I'll very much enjoy watching you suffer."

I then very wryly glanced over to Terrence — happily ready to show him what a real nature guardian can do as I raised my hands towards the trees calling to the fallen leave, and pulling them forward, creating a vortex of leaves around me, slowly lifting me high up into the air, and flying off towards the tree line.

As I passed over the heads of the armed guards, tree roots grew from underneath them, trapping them where they stood and crushing their weapons in two.

The two Lab technician became nervous at this point, probably assuming that I was trying to escape and both pulled out their guns. But before they could fire a shot, I watched

Terrence move at full speed and remove all their weapons, including Richard's. – Well that was new.

"What are you doing?" Richard bellowed as he readied to fight Terrence.

But Terrence calmly replied, "If you kill her, your entire reputation with The Board goes up in flames and any deal you have with this facility or my master is reneged. So, I suggest you stand down . . . it's not like she can get very far."

Richard glared at him for a moment then stood back and turned to watch as I flew over the tree line and out of sight.

Huh – looks like Terrence was being forced to play nice with him – I wonder who his 'master' is.

It was actually very difficult to control the leaf platform and required more of my concentration, considering the last time I did it – I had help. Eventually, the platform stabilised as I flew around what I have now discovered to be an island. One of three, surrounded by water as far as the eye could see.

Oh, Frac and Fruit Cakes.

I started making my way back towards the facility but dipped down into the trees to collect more seeds then flew over the grassy grounds, scattering them across the open field.

When I landed at the tree line, I slowly walked back towards Richard and his thugs, still with wry grin and eyes glowing green. And using my super hearing, I listened to the Lab techs analysing the data they were receiving, and they commented,

"This is unbelievable" and "Sir, if this data is correct, she is one of the strongest guardians we have."

Well der – I could have told them that.

Now with a mild headache, I suddenly realised I had a nose bleed. And I very quickly and discreetly wiped the fresh blood from my lips and brushed it onto my pants near the waist, pulling my shirt over to cover the fresh stain. Hoping that no one would notice, as it blended in with the rest of the blood.

And when I stopped and stood next to Terrence again, Richard looked at me and seemingly unamused, questioned, "Is that's it?"

I deviously smirked with my eyes still glowing and with a flick of my wrist, they watched in terror as all the seeds I scattered grew quickly and ferociously, creating a jungle effect of trees and plants surrounding us and the facility.

I snickered a little as the two lab techs and Richard looked around in a slight panic and awe, shielding themselves from the debris of falling dirt and leaves.

But Terrence stayed standing next to me, completely undeterred with a slight peak at lips – it almost sounded like he was snickering too. – Maybe there's hope for him yet.

When the dust settled one of the lab techs shouted to his other partner, "That was . . . AMAZING! We have to run some more test and samples. We need samples of everything."

I shook my head, laughing at the scientist then turned to Richard and growled, "I thought you said you needed me for something. . . This is child's play and I'm getting bored."

I then briefly glanced back at the freshly grown trees and shrubbery and huffed "And I grow tired of these tests. . . Tell me what it is you want from me so I can be done with you."

In the corner of my eye, I noticed Terrence's grin widen as he crossed his arms and stared at me with a sense of pride him. – Ooh, I think he likes me and my stubbornness, and I don't think he likes Richard – which make me like Terrence just that little bit more.

I may have smiled a bit while I was waiting for Richard's response, as he gawped around at the freshly grown trees. And without even looking at me, he replied, "Fine. No more test . . . We'll start the next project at the end of the week. . . Until then Terrence will fill you in on what we need from you."

THE END OF THE WEEK – He's out of his Fracking mind.

I tried to rebut and demand we get this over with, but he silenced me and continued his speech, "...No buts, we have a process we must follow and because of you, I have a death to report. . . Now go."

I really, really <u>hate</u> this man – and one day soon, I will get my revenge on him and I will very much hope that it is slow and painful, just like all the pain he has caused me. – Although I doubt, he's strong enough to bear that pain or even live through it.

I glared at Richard before I turned in a huff to follow Terrence back inside, but one of the lab techs stopped us.

"Wait!" he demanded with slight fear in his voice, "We also need a sample of your hair, given that it's turned white and if you don't mind, can you tell us how you did it?"

I stayed quiet, leering at him then at half speed grabbed Richard's hunting knife, and stood threateningly in front of the lab tech. He didn't respond to courageously but took a sigh of relief when he watched me cut my long white hair to shoulder length with one fell swoop.

Then without an ounce of care, I dropped my hair and the knife to the ground in front of him as I followed Terrence back inside.

I just want it on the record that this is the worst birthday
I've ever had.

# CHAPTER 4

# K.I.S.S.I.N.G

## Journal entry by Terrence Connors

It's been 5 days now since Lila turned our outdoor training yard into a jungle, and I can't help but laugh as I watch the maintenance crew try to regain some of the area. — She really is damn good at what she does.

Lila was waiting for me when I walked into the greenhouse. I decided this morning that I'd bring her breakfast from the mess hall. You know to try and earn a little favour from her — I think she's starting to warm up to me.

Although when I placed both our breakfasts down on a flat rock, Lila caught me off guard and tried to punch me in the face. I quickly dodged her and fought back, but she was fast and managed to hit me several times, the most painful and memorable one was the kick in the lower backside — where she laughed at me. And there was one where she kicked me in the stomach, sending me flying across the garden and into the greenhouse glass doors.

But that was where the fun ended.

Lila had moved at full speed, pinning me to the ground with her knee on my back when four of the guards ran into the greenhouse to assist me, aiming their weapons at Lila as if she were a hostile and demanding, "Get down on the ground! Now!"

She did as she was told and lay on the ground with her hands face down and waited, while I quickly rushed to her defence and stood between her and the guards, commanding them to lower their weapons.

"Stand down! . . . We were just training. . . everything's fine . . . just put your guns down!"

"Sir, are you alright?" One of the guards asked as he lowered his weapon.

I nodded nursing the new bruise on my buttocks, "Yes, every thing's fine, just injured my pride that's all."

I could hear Lila chuckling to herself, and I helped her to stand before she walked with a swagger back to where I had placed our breakfast.

The four guards returned to their post all cautiously looking back as I followed to sit down next to Lila.

"Remind me next time I agree to train you . . . to let you win," she tittered, pouring the milk into her bowl of cereal then handing me the milk bottle.

"I'm Sorry, about that," I replied, "You fight really well and they were just doing their job."

We sat and ate breakfast in silence until I broke it, "So, you still haven't told me how you're able to fly on those leaves."

"And you still haven't told me where we are, so I guess we're even," she cheeked, then handed the empty breakfast bowl back to me and walked back inside the cottage.

Stubborn one, isn't she — But she had me there.

I can understand why she doesn't trust me. But I also know she appreciates my presence, especially every time I prevent her from getting shot. Not a lot of people here are confident in the amount of freedom I've given Lila over the last few days. And if it were up to them, she'd be in chains in a cold cell in the darkest part of the building being beaten and studied — And I think she knows that.

I followed her back into the cottage to find her pacing back and forth, playing with her fingers and biting her lip completely lost in her own thought. I stood and watched her unusual behaviour and eventually she asked, "Why are you here?"

"I'm your guard. I've been charged to make sure you don't escape or hurt anyone."

I thought that one was obvious — but she continued to pace and I won't lie seeing her bite her bottom lip did make me curious.

Then she asked again, "No, I mean why are you here being nice to me."

Ah Yeah — we hadn't really gotten to this conversation yet.

"Well you did save my life, so I kind of owe you there. . . and there's the fact we used to be friends once, a long time ago . . . but I guess you don't remember that," I replied, feeling a little — grim.

"Are you sure I'd want to remember?" she snapped, still pacing the floor.

Ouch — I sat down on the stretcher bed a little saddened by her comment and mumbled, "Probably not."

Finally, Lila stopped pacing but still bit her bottom lip as she stared at me for a long time as if she was studying me then let out a long breath as she sat down next to me.

"Okay . . . let's call a truce."

"What?" I gasped, struggling to believe what I had just heard and was shocked at the fact that this was her idea. For the last few days, all she'd doing was everything I asked while she dug around for information — with her many, many questions. The fact that she agreed to train me on how to fight like her, shocked me to no end — But I still always sensed an ulterior motive in her.

I stared at her — slightly suspicious, and she picked up on it, then slouched back leaning on the wall behind me. "Look Terrence. . . In order to get through whatever the hell this is . . . I'm going to need a friend. . . Someone I can trust. And you seem to be constantly surprising me . . . especially of just how protective you are of me . . . Now I don't know if that's because. . . if anything were to happen to me, you'd be in serious trouble or if there is actually a genuine concern for my wellbeing."

"A little of both." I butted in, shrugging my shoulders.

Still she just continued, "I propose a truce. . . I promise to still do whatever you ask of me and try to stay out of trouble . . . to keep you from getting into trouble. As long as you promise to be honest with me . . . to the best of your ability anyway. . . Terrence. . . I need you to understand that I'm putting a lot of trust in you . . . I'm exhausted. . . and I can't stay awake all night anymore worrying that you'll change your mind and start those horrid experiments on me again."

She started to tear up, playing with her fingers and I turned to her and urged, "Lila that wasn't me . . . I promise."

But she moved away using her super speed to stand to her feet and turned back to me, "You're promises don't mean anything to me. . . yet. But mine do. . . I've never broken a promise before and I'm not planning to start now."

She then nervously held her hand out, "I promise to do whatever you ask of me, as long as you never lie to me, and promise to never let me go back to the horrible place."

Her eyes were now filled with tears of desperation and fear and I could see why. I knew she lay awake at night scared of the dreams and memories. And I couldn't blame her if she was scared of me. I didn't torture her myself but I did let it happen.

But I also promised myself that I would never let it happen again — so I stood up and took a step towards her. Then in fear she stood back— with her hand out still, and begged, "Terrence, I need to hear you say it . . . that you will be my friend. Like you said you were a long time ago."

I felt a little short of breath hearing that she was asking for my friendship.

"Lila . . . It's my fault you're here. Why would you want to be friends with me?" I asked, a little cautious in my approach towards her.

She started to stutter in her reply, "Well yes, it's kind of your fault . . . But friends forgive each other and . . . trust each other. Which mean this friendship is only going to work if we're both completely honest and trust each other from now on. So . . . Terrence. . . would you like to be my friend?"

She then waited for me to agree or say something, but part of me was still apprehensive and took a few seconds to think. — I wanted nothing more than to be friends with her but not like this — not with fear looming around her. But she needed someone to trust and she also needed to sleep. So, I shook her hand to agree to the deal.

"Okay. . . I promise. But if we're really going to agree on this kind of truce, then we should do it properly." I then pulled my hand away from hers, placing it in the centre of Lila's chest, and Lila hesitantly did the same to mine. And as our hands and eyes began to glow green, I whispered, "Now we both know that our intentions are pure."

I felt a little bit happier — sensing that she really did want to be friends with me, and I also sensed that she was being honest when she said that she'd never broken a promise before, which made it easier for me to trust her.

So I had an idea that I thought she might like and pulled my hand away and smiled a little, "Come on, I want to show you something."

I held on to Lila's hand as I led her to the other end of the greenhouse to a large set of doors, guarded with a biometric lock with fingerprint and iris scanner. And when the doors opened, Lila just stood in amazement at the sight of a very large and very old Bristle-cone pine tree, that stood in the centre of the second greenhouse.

"It's beautiful," she remarked as she walked around studying the tree, "But what the frac did you do it? . . . It's dying."

— Um alright did she just say 'frac' — is that her way of swearing?

I really couldn't help but smile then, as I tried to explain, "That would be all the experiments and tests people have done to it. . . which is why they need you."

She shook her head, staring back it me confused. "Me? . . . What do you want me to do? This tree's too old. . . I can't heal it . . . I don't even think you could."

Yeah — she was right with that fact — I know I'm not as strong as Lila, not by a long shot — not after seeing what she did in the outside garden.

I followed her as she studied the tree and went on to explain, "Actually they want you to find a memory. . . This is a very special tree. The Guardians call it a Memoriae Arbor . . . a memory tree. This tree is connected with dozens of other trees around the world, creating a network of stored memories of the guardians that lived long ago. . . I've managed to sift through some of the memories. But I seem to have hit a dead end."

Lila quickly interrupted my explanation in an attempt to summarise what I was saying, "So, they thought two nature guardians would be better than one. . .," then asked, "What are they looking for?"

"They want us to find the first memory ever stored by this particular tree," I replied, leaning against the tree. I then told her the story of the nature guardian who was the protector of the memory trees.

"The Board . . . the people who run this whole organisation, found one of his journals and discovered that he had found or created a tonic that made whoever consumed it immune to anything . . . Which is why we're looking for his memory. . . It said in the journals that he and his family lived to be 283 years old. But because he was believed to be immortal, guardians and humans alike both feared and coveted this power. . . So, he fled with his family and came here to live out the rest of his days. . . And he planted this tree in order to continue his duty to protect the Memoriae arbors."

Lila leaned against the tree next to me as she took a moment to process then excitedly responded, "Okay, so how are we supposed to find this memory?"

Wow — I was shocked and in disbelief and questioned, "Wait that's it? I was expecting you to be a little . . . you know . . . sceptical or not believe me."

She chuckled at me then smiled, "Terrence, I have fought a century-old water dragon and her children, been rescued by a tree nymph, attacked by several trees, had many conversations with a tiny robotic bird and been held hostage by you, trapped in my own mind. This . . . this here is just another day at work for me . . . so please, just tell me what to do."

Yeah wow — she really did know how to keep an open mind, and with that response, I thought it might be a good idea to do a test run.

"Okay, it's not too hard. Just put your hand on the tree," I said, demonstrating.

But that's when she became hesitant, "Um hang on . . . I thought the General wanted us to wait until tomorrow . . . you know the process and all?"

I just laughed and grabbed her hand to place it on the tree next to mine. "Relax, we'll just call it a practice run. Now close your eyes and breathe."

Lila began to relax a little, but before she closed her eyes she said, "Okay, but if we get in trouble, I'm blaming you."

And while still laughing at her, I mumbled, "You always did," before I closed my eyes and pulled both of us into a meditative sleep. — Well, at least I got her to sleep.

When we opened our eyes again, we were standing in an old herbal shop in what looked like Sydney - Australia, in the late 19th century. We were in the back of the store, when Lila asked, "What the frac am I wearing?" pulling at the corset around her waist, "And why am I wearing a dress?"

We were soon interrupted by a man standing at the counter, holding the hand of a young boy, both wearing very dirty tattered farming clothes.

"Excuse me ma'am," the small boy said through his coughs and spluttering.

Lila then walked out to greet them. "Yes dear, how can I help?"

The man very timidly approached her. "I'm very sorry we've come in so early. I was just wondering if you had anything to help my son . . . he's very sick. And I don't know what to do."

I stayed at the back of the store and watched as Lila walked around the counter and knelt down next to the boy, who had sweat dripping from his pale forehead and had a chesty cough. She felt the boy's cheeks and asked to look at his tongue and throat. Then began to walk around the room picking out ingredients from boxes and jars that were displayed around the shop. She ended up with lavender — parsley — garlic — cinnamon sticks — eucalyptus leaves and a honey pot.

But while walking past the store window, Lila glanced at her reflection, which did not look like her at all. She was around the same age but had longer jet-black hair and a paler complexion.

She mumbled something under her breath as she walked back to the counter, crushing the lavender and Eucalyptus leaves into a paste and put it in a small pot before crushing the garlic, parsley and cinnamon sticks, then mixed the powder into the honey.

With a smile, Lila walked back to the man, "Okay, take one teaspoon of this honey twice a day for seven days and rub this paste on his chest at night until he stops coughing."

She held the pots out for the man to take, but the man shook his head, saying, "We can't afford all this" and he pulled from his pocket two silver coins and a broken necklace, "This is all I have."

Lila very kindly continued to smile and placed the pots of herbs in his hands along with his coins and necklace, whispering, "Don't worry about it, just make sure he gets plenty of rest."

The man grinned and left holding his son's hand, excitedly thanking Lila as he closed the door. And I walked out of the back of the store toward Lila as she commented, "Herbal medicine has really come a long way since . . . well, whatever time period this is."

I nodded to her as I created the exit portal then held Lila's hand as we stepped through, pulling her back out of the meditation.

Opening my eyes again, I was back in the greenhouse holding Lila's hand against the tree. But Lila didn't look too good as she opened her eyes. She held her head in pain and mumbled, "I feel . . ." but before she could finish her sentence, she fainted in my arms.

I placed her gently down on the ground and brushed the hair from her face to see if she was okay. But upon further inspection of the rest of her body, I discovered a fresh blood stain hidden under her shirt. It didn't seem to be as old as all the other blood stains she had received from her initiation phase. And I know I didn't let anyone else touch her after that.

"Where did this come from?" I whispered to myself as I lifted her shirt further to see if there were any fresh wounds.

But as I leaned in closer to inspect Lila's torso, she woke up to see my face very, very close to hers. And yet she said nothing, she just watched me looking over her and moving my hands along her skin, inspecting the scars on her for any signs of infection or new injuries.

Eventually I noticed her staring at me with a slight grin at her lips and again she was biting it. I moved away feeling a little anxious and unsure what conclusion she may have come to while she watched me putting my hands all over her body.

Not the best start to our new-found friendship — I suppose.

I cleared my throat trying to explain to her as I helped her to rise. "I found some blood on your waist. I was just checking to see if you were hurt."

"And am I?" she questioned with a wry smirk.

I shook my head, "No, but I'm still curious where the blood came from."

"Who knows . . .," she shrugged her shoulders, as if she wasn't worried, "You do realise you weren't the only one to be beaten half to death in these last months. Frac, for all I know it could be Ben's blood."

I noticed her trying to hold back the tears as she began to storm off towards the cottage, so I raced after her to apologise, "I'm sorry. . . you know it's my job to keep you . . . alive. I was just worried."

I could tell she wasn't being completely honest with me. But given everything that she had been through, I wasn't going to push it. She never promised to be honest with me, only to do as she's told. Instead, I offered Lila the chance to shower and a change of clothes.

Although I don't know how open she would be to a shower, given the set of conditions The Board has for prisoners.

She followed me through the corridors and into the locker rooms, where Adela's old locker was and I handed Lila a change of clothes, feeling a little guilty as I frowned. "These used to be Adela's. . . They should fit you".

I then needed to take a moment and kind of stood in a bit of an awkward silence for a few seconds before I hesitantly explained, "This may sound . . . um awkward . . . but I'm not actually allowed to leave you alone."

Lila choked back a laugh as things became really uncomfortable between us.

"You're right, it does sound awkward . . . can you at least turn around and promise not to look?"

It was a fair request, but there was another small problem. I also hadn't showered in weeks — and I was in no mood to lock her in the cottage with those chains on her. So, I made a counter-offer, "I'll make you a deal, because I wouldn't mind a shower after you. I promise I won't look at you . . . If you do the same for me and also not disappear?"

She giggled and bit her bottom lip, realising the ironic predicament then looked around in the shower room and came up with an idea that would benefit us both.

I watched as she fiddled with her bracelet and pulled a seed out, placing it on the floor under the middle shower head and waved her hand over it. — From that seed grew a small hedge that covered from one wall to the other so that all I could see was Lila's head and nothing more.

She peered back at me and smiled, "Now we can both shower and you won't be breaking any rules," then started to undress and threw her bloodied, torn clothes out on to the floor of the locker room and proceeded to shower.

And I was really beginning to appreciate this truce we had going — this is the first prisoner I've ever had that was willing to accommodate for my needs as well. So, I weighed up my options and readied myself to shower.

As we stood under the water washing away the blood and dirt, Lila began a conversation with me — which was not at all weird.

"Hey, Terrence, I have a few questions about the project."

"Fire away," I replied.

I may have also glanced over to make she was still there. — I will admit — I quite enjoyed the company.

But while she showered, something fascinating happened as she cleaned the dirt and blood from her very obvious white hair. It began to change colour again back to a dark golden blonde. — The hair colour she used to have when she was young.

I was beginning to suspect that her sudden change of hair colours was attached to her emotions, and that anger or rage was turning her hair white. I'm still unsure why though.

If that was true, it was actually comforting for me to know that she held no anger towards me or better still, felt comfortable around me.

There was a slight problem though, because while I was lost in my own thought observing her, Lila had actually asked me a question and was staring back at me, waiting for an answer.

She then kindly repeated the question again, "Back at the memory tree, I thought I saw my mother . . . the real one. . . I mean I've only seen one picture of her. . . but I know she not that old."

"It was most likely your great-great-great-grandmother," I replied.

In a slight shock, Lila looked back at me, "Wait, so you're saying my great-great-great-grandmother was a Nature guardian . . . why did you take me to that memory?"

"I didn't. . . Your genes did . . . your DNA acts as like a compass or a key that makes it easier to find certain memories in the tree."

"And how did my great-great-great-grandmothers memory end up in that tree?" she asked.

Yeah — Wow — she really does know how to ask the pointed questions, and I wasn't really sure how honest I should be. Until Lila so very sternly reminded me that our new-found friendship was based on honesty and that not answering the question was not helping my case. And it was a fair point.

When Lila turned off her shower, she wrapped a towel around her and waited for me to do the same. — ensuring not to break the rules and leave the shower room without me.

And I continued to reluctantly explain as we moved to the locker rooms, "The man who wrote the journals was one of your ancestors. . . And that is why they needed you. . . The Board thinks that someone in the same bloodline is more likely to find him faster."

"How do they know that I'm from the same bloodline as a man who lived hundreds of years ago?" she queried — with yet another pointed question.

This next part really caught Lila's attention though as I explained while starting to get dressed, "The Board has a database of guardians that dates back long before the Egyptian pyramids were built."

The problem was when I had finished my explanation and put on my pants, Lila had gone unusually quiet, but I heard her breathing become heavier.

I turned to see if she was okay, and to my surprise, it was actually her who was peeking this time and biting her bottom lip. She herself hadn't even finished getting dressed standing in just gym pants and a bra, still holding her top in her hands.

When she eventually realised that I had noticed her, she quickly stopped ogling me and continued to get dressed. She may have also seen me grinning back at her.

"My apologies, I was distracted in thought," she mumbled, trying to defend her actions.

Which I thought was quite amusing.

I walked slowly towards her, still grinning, "I'm sure you already know this, but Nature guardians are very good in sensing the nature of a person . . . their wants . . . and their desires."

I stood in front of her bare-chested then held her hand, and placed it on the muscles of my very defined abdomen. Knowing that it was exactly what she wanted.

She ran her fingers along the old scars I had received from my younger days — after the many tests. And I watched as she bit her lip again and her heart started racing as her eyes wandered. I then ran my hand across her chest and down across the muscles of her abdomen, and over the fresh scars she had, one in particular above her hip bone where I rested my hand.

She took a breath in an attempt to compose herself, miserably failing as I leaned in to kiss her. And just as our lips were about to touch and her breath was on mine, she breathed, "Stop."

I did as she asked but I also didn't move and stayed incredibly close, gazing into her amazing blue eyes, then I watched her run at full speed out of the locker rooms.

# CHAPTER 5

# CONFUSING EMOTIONS

*Journal entry by Lila Winters*

I didn't know how to feel. Terrence had given me so much information and I was about to hit information overload.

I was still grieving the death of my childhood friend Ben and his betrayal. I missed my family, especially my kids. And I was filled with constant worry that if I did anything stupid here, they would be the ones to pay for it.

While staring out at the waters, I sat at the very edge of the island at the base of a palm tree. And I cried, trying to suppress my fears when a man with sandy-blond hair, carrying a garden rake and wearing dirty coveralls startled me. He tapped me on the shoulder, saying in a very strong American accent, "Excuse me miss . . .are you okay?"

At that moment I was sure something bad was going to happen. By now Terrence would have reported to the General that I had disappeared, and the General would've order something horrible to happen to my beautiful children, just to spite me.

I quickly turned to the man and begged him not to hurt my family and apologised for running off. I even asked them not to hurt Terrence and explained that it was me who broke the rules, not him.

The man interrupted me and tried calm me down, handing me a handkerchief, "Actually I was just going to ask if you were okay?. . . I'm just the groundskeeper here. I don't know what you are and are not allowed to do . . . but if it makes you feel better, I won't tell anyone you were here."

I took a great sigh of relief but still worried that Terrence had already reported my disappearance.

"I'm still going to have to ask you if you're okay?" the man asked again.

I nodded, wiping the tears away with his handkerchief, "Yeah. . . I just miss my family."

"Oh . . . well, I'm not sure how to help you with your family, but I am told my hugs are magical, if you don't mind hugging a dirty gardener."

His offer was very nice, and I know generally it's frowned upon to hug strange men when you're stuck on an island with no means of escape. But I had already broken several rules today, so one more wouldn't hurt.

When Terrence finally did find me, he looked puzzled at the sight of me hugging the gardener, but also petrified from not knowing where I was for a full 10 minutes.

I stopped hugging the gardener and kindly shook his hand and introduced myself, "I'm Lila . . . Lila Winters."

The gardener then beamed with a smile as he replied, "Well, it's a pleasure to meet you Lila . . . my names William . . . William Knight."

He briefly glanced over at Terrence and nodded, "Well, that's my cue to get back to work. Good day, Miss Winters," then he trotted away, whistling.

At full speed Terrence darted toward and was in a fluster as he started to say, "Lila, I'm . . ."

But I cut him off before he got the chance to berate me, "I know what you're going to say, and I'm really sorry if I got you in trouble and I promise I'll go inside and do anything you ask. I just needed some air. . . and apparently a hug."

Then at full speed I ran back into the greenhouse cottage, still wiping the tears off my cheek, when Terrence ran into the cottage at full speed behind me and grabbed hold of my hand, demanding "Lila, would you just slow down for a second."

But I was still fraught with panic at the thought of my punishment for disobeying the rules being taken out on the people I loved and desperately whimpered, "I'm sorry . . . Terrence. I'm so very sorry. Please just tell me, they're going to be okay?"

He stared back at me in confusion, asking who and what I was talking about, but eventually he realised my fears. "Lila, I would never do that to you. . . The only person who knew you were missing was me. . . However, I was starting to get worried about your safety, I mean . . . that 10 minutes felt like a lifetime for me."

I let out a breath as I sat down on the stretcher bed, and started to feel helpless and relieved at the same time as I sobbed "I just miss them. . . a lot. And I wish I knew they were okay".

Listening to my cries, Terrence sat down on the stretcher bed next to me and sighed, pulling out his phone from his pocket. But before he unlocked it, he turned to me and very sternly spoke, "This must remain a secret between you and me. . . because if they find out. . . both of us will get a swift reminder of the rules and I won't be able to stop it. . . I also want you to know that I'm only doing this because I care very much for you as my friend . . .now I can't let you phone them because the others will find out, but there is something I can show you."

I nodded in nervous excitement, agreeing to his terms, continuing to wipe the tears off my face as he unlocked his phone and tapped on a bluebird icon.

The phone then displayed live video footage of my apartment from the balcony. I saw Hanna, serving dinner to Danny and Ruby, who were sitting at the dinner table. And in the background, Adela and Matt were drinking coffee and talking. Adela looked like she was trying to comfort him.

She really is a nice friend—when she's not hypnotised.

It was then I realised and angrily mumbled, "Bluey . . . you've been spying on me and my family."

Terrence turned to me, and very seriously whispered, trying to defend himself, "I'm not, Richard and John are . . . they don't know I've tapped into their surveillance systems yet."

I was livid, but I didn't know who to be mad at. And in feeling a surge of emotions I started pacing and stopped a few times to say something, but every time I stopped, I felt angrier and started pacing again.

Eventually I stopped, feeling so unsure of what to do next and did the only thing I knew of that was a positive release of my emotions—I hugged Terrence and began to cry.

And he just stood there holding me.

After a while and a long time of crying, I had eventually become extremely exhausted, just standing there hugging Terrence, and he could definitely tell I was falling asleep on him.

So, he carefully and quietly led me out into the greenhouse garden to yet another large tree, only this one wasn't as old.

He placed his hand on the tree and waited as one of the branches grew down to meet us and helped us to walk up to the top of the tree, to find in the middle of it was a large hollowed-out section that had been decorated with pillows and toys and superhero action figures that looked like they had been played with, a lot.

Terrence started to set up some pillows and a blanket, all while I continued to hold on to his hand, crying and refusing to let it go — and somehow, he just understood.

When he had finished, he sat me down next him covering me with the blanket, while I looked around the make-shift tree house, and commented, "This is beautiful."

Terrence then went on to describe how he used to play up here when he was a child and that it was his favourite spot on the island because only he could get up here.

He'd spent so long up here that he had developed a special bond with the trees because they protected him from all the bad people.

"You are actually the first person that I've brought up here," he whispered.

I pulled in closer to hug him again and thanked him, asking why if this place was so special to him that he would bring me up here.

And he replied, "Because this is the safest and most private place on the entire island . . . and I know there's something you have been wanting to do all week and haven't had the chance to yet." He then pointed down to the tree vine that had started wrapping around my hand. — I played ignorant, but it didn't work. — He just smilingly sighed, "I thought we agreed to be honest with each other . . . Look, I know if anyone can make you feel better right now. It's your friend Alex . . . so go . . . but make sure he knows not to tell anyone."

"You'd really let me do this?" I asked both shocked and excited.

He smiled back at me and nodded as he readied himself to leave, but I still didn't want to let go of his hand and asked him to stay with me. So, he sat back down next to me, getting comfortable, and continued to hug me as I fell asleep in his arms. But before I finally nodded off to sleep, I kissed his cheek and thanked him one last time.

# Journal entry insert by Alex Woods

I was sure I was starting to lose my mind, trying to distract myself with TV and hotel paperwork stuff, and security footage, and pretty much anything to keep me from worrying about Lila.

I mean, she promised me the last time I saw her that she would come back, but she hasn't and it's been days . . . I even started talking to the plant she gave me as a house-warming present in the hopes that she would hear me.

Then finally, just when I was about to lose all hope, she appeared sitting on the couch next to me. She looked beautiful and happy and healthy and clean now. – I may have briefly doubted that I was actually seeing her and that this wasn't just a dream but to be honest I didn't care.

She leapt into my arms and gave me the biggest and tightest hug I had ever gotten and didn't let go for a long time and again I didn't care.

I held onto her, so happy to have her in my arms and instantly bombarded her with questions one after the other like – Are you okay? – Are you hurt? – Why is your hair shorter? – Why is your hair blonde? – Have you turned evil yet? And lucky last – Can you tell me where are?

She then happily answered as followed, "Yes, no, I cut it because the A-hole of a scientist wanted a sample, I don't know about that one. . . but at one stage it turned white, I'm pretty sure no and . . . on an island possibly somewhere in the Indian Ocean given the temperature and the native wildlife, but again I'm not sure . . . I'm sorry if that doesn't help."

"Actually, just seeing you again helps a lot," I said, hugging her even tighter, "Although the white hair is an interesting twist."

Lila was so happy to see me and sat on the couch for hours, asking me about what was happening back here at the hotel. I told her as much as I could and even showed her some pictures that Danny and Ruby drew of her.

By the end of it, we were both half asleep snuggled up on the couch with Lila lying in my arms smiling. I even wished her a happy belated birthday, which for some reason struck a nerve and made her tear up a bit, hugging me tighter. But she didn't want to talk about it and I respected that.

"Alex," she sleepily whispered, "Thank you . . . I really needed this."

But our happy reunion was abruptly cut short as Terrence Connors appeared in my apartment in a panic looking for Lila.

"Lila, we need to go. Your dad's looking for us," he stated, grabbing hold of Lila's hand.

And confused, I questioned, "Wait what do you mean us? Which dad? What is he doing here?"

But Lila didn't answer any of my questions, she just hugged me one last time, sighing, "I'm sorry Alex, my times up . . . Look after Matt for me!" Then she disappeared – again.

I then woke up on the couch alone and in a fright as if I had just had a horrible nightmare again, but as I looked around the room, I noticed that the house-warming present Lila gave me was retracting and growing back into its original size.

Yes! – It wasn't a dream – She's alive and I'm not crazy!

## Original journal entry continued by Lila Winters

I swear the night went way too quickly and I woke up in a bit of a fright. But I was still holding Terrence's hand and he still had his arms wrapped around me, making me feel safe again, and I started to relax in his arms. But then we both heard Richard searching the greenhouse calling our names and quickly losing his patience.

Terrence's eyes peered across to mine and he smiled before he pulled his arms away.

And I – well, I really don't want to talk about it. But I quickly moved away and said, "You really need to stop doing that," as I let go of his hand and began to climb down the tree to greet Richard. Leaving Terrence confused, sitting there watching me and asked, "Doing what?"

We finally caught up to Richard waiting at the entrance way of the smaller greenhouse, along with his "Thing 1" and "Thing 2" idiot scientists, who very much liked to test my patience.

They were standing there, very eagerly holding all their probes and computers, and were even stupid enough to ask for more blood samples – because they didn't get enough the last dozen times they fraccing asked for it.

But out of respect for Terrence and our renewed friendship, I did as I was told. I even smiled nicely to the Lab technicians and helped to hold the blood vials for them.

I did cringe a little, struggling with my emotions when they were attaching the probes to my body, and I watched as they also attached probes to several large metal rods that had been drilled into the side of the very old, very fragile Bristle-cone Pine tree.

But again, I said nothing. I just held Terrence's hand, for emotional control, because I knew he could feel — how and what I was feeling, and exactly what I wanted to do to "thing 1" and "thing 2" — and the fact that I didn't react really ate me up inside.

I also think Richard came to the wrong conclusion when he glanced down to see me holding Terrence's hand because he smiled and asked nicely, "Are you ready, Pumpkin?"

And I have always hated that pet name.

"Well, it's not like we have a choice," I barked at Richard as both Terrence and I held onto the tree and pulled ourselves into a meditative sleep.

# Journal entry insert by Alex Woods

I was beginning to feel ecstatic as I showered this morning. I even sang and did a little dance. But my joy was quickly shut down as I answered the phone to hear the lobby receptionist explain that Detective George Nell and a group of policemen were waiting downstairs, and were hoping to have a word with me.

So, I rushed at full speed to get dressed and raced downstairs to meet them, hoping they had some good news to share with the team.

I found Detective George waiting for me, and for some reason he didn't look happy as I asked, "Hey, George, what's going on? Have you found anything on Lila yet?"

But as I asked that the two police officers that were with him pulled my hands behind my back and handcuffed me as George said, "I'm sorry, Alex . . . you're under arrest for arson, reckless endangerment of human life, vandalising public property, and the murder of Lila Winters."

"Murder? What? George, what are you doing?" I asked, but he wouldn't listen as he continued to read me my rights and place me into the back of a police car.

And what the hell just happened?

# CHAPTER 6

# DENIAL

## Journal entry by Alex Woods

I couldn't believe it. George arrested me. Now I'm sitting at the police station in the interrogation room in absolute disbelief. And there was no way they had any evidence of anything I was accused of. – Murdering my best friend – the nerve of them.

And it did not surprise me at all when instead of Detective George entering the interrogation room it was Agent John.

I dismally grunted as I sat back in my chair, thinking back on what Lila said to me. And John then sat down at the interrogation table and placed a manila folder down in front of me, and sighed, sarcastically greeting, "Hello Alex, getting into trouble again I see."

I was in no mood for sarcasm and got straight to the point, "What do you want, John?" However, the tone in my voice did not seem to mask the distrust I held for him.

"Whoa, so much hostility. . . You know it was only a few months ago we used to be friends, working on the same side . . . Tell me Alex, why the sudden change of heart?" he asked sarcastically again.

And yep – I really wanted to hurt this guy, but I just sat there quietly, remembering what Lila said, "John can't be trusted".

He opened the manila folder and started looking at photos, casually stating "So, you've been charged with arson and the murder of Lila Winters . . ."

"She's not dead . . ." I refuted, loudly.

John then placed an autopsy photo of a burned female body on the table in front of me, explaining without the sarcasm, "She was found late last night by one of our search teams."

I stared down at the photo but shook my head, "That's not her."

"Don't worry Alex, denial is a natural part of grief. . . We're just sorry it took so long to find her. . .," he stated, and in an attempt to push me further he added, "When we found her, it looked like some of the animals had had a little snack on her."

Yep – that caused me to slam my hands down on the table, standing up to tower over him and shouted, "She's not dead!"

But before John could say anything else, George walked in, escorting Max and one of his lawyers behind him.

Max looked at me devastated and sighed, "Alex . . . I just came from the morgue. Matt and Adela identified the body themselves."

No. No. and No.

He then placed a bag of Lila's personal belongings on to the table. And inside it was Lila's phone, what was left of her burned security I.D badge and her locket bracelet with little seeds falling out of one of the lockets, and what was left of her burned clothes.

No. No. No.

Still in disbelief, I shook my head, but what really topped it off was the photo George handed me of a strand of hair, apparently found on Lila's clothes as he explained, "We compared this hair's DNA with one we sourced from Lila's hairbrush . . . it's a direct match."

I really began to doubt my sanity then as George proceeded to show me more evidence that confirmed that the charcoaled female remains were indeed Lila's, and that the dreams that I had been having of Lila visiting me and trying to warn about all of these things was really just a dream.

That is until I analysed the photos closer. The clothes that the body was found in had not completely burned to ash and had very specific tears and blood stains on it that I recognised from when Lila first visited me in the dreamland.

She was very dirty at the time and her clothes were torn in the exact same places.

But here was the best part, the shining moment that lifted my spirits helping me to believe that she was still alive. The hair strand they used to confirm Lila's I.D was white. – And last night she told me, she cut her hair because it had turned white and they wanted a sample.

A wry grin appeared across my face when I looked at the photos, and Maxwell and George were very concerned for me, as Maxwell asked, "Alex. . . are you, okay?"

I broke my concentration long enough to nod, but then looked at John who was surprisingly calm, until George admitted that the evidence Maxwell's lawyers had provided and the eye witness testimonies that had been given, all confirming exactly what I was doing at the time Lila went missing, absolved me from all charges and then told me I was free to go.

My grin got even wider watching John become very disgruntled as he sat back in his chair and groaned – It was hilarious just watching his nostrils flare.

I stood up, towering over John and scowled, "These photos mean nothing. . . In fact, it just proves she still alive," then stormed out of the room, quickly thanking Maxwell for his help.

I marched out of the police station, but I became enraged. This was the worst thing that could have happened, and it only makes things more difficult. I got so mad that I kicked Maxwell's car, creating a hefty dent in the passenger side door.

-- Whoops.

Maxwell had rushed out to see me and witnessed my irrational outburst of emotions.

"Alex, you need to calm down"

But that's when I started really shouting, and while I do believe my emotions are justified, I could have handled it a lot better as I yelled, "Calm down!!! How can you ask me to calm down? Matt now thinks Lila is dead! . . . What now, are we just supposed to stop looking for her? All because of a few hair strands."

Because of my rage, I thought it was best for me to walk back to the hotel, but as I started storming off, Maxwell chased after me to stop me. "Alex just stop for a minute . . . please . . . Look, I know you loved her and that this grieving process is going to be hard for you . . . but . . ."

I grunted and interrupted what was probably going to be a very comforting speech and shouted again, "She's not dead! . . . I know she's not dead!"

"How? How do you know?" He asked, trying to get me to see reason, "They had her bracelet, Alex. . . You and I both know she was wearing it on the day. There's even a DNA match . . ."

"I've seen her," I explained, "I know it sounds crazy, but she visits me in the dreamland."

But he didn't believe me, and looked at me as if I wasn't sane anymore – Like he'd understand though he's just a human. And I know she's not dead.

I moved closer starting to speak quieter to ensure no one else heard. "Do you remember what we were doing the night before we went after Darkman . . . I mean, Terrence . . . Whatever his name is. . . Lila was complaining about not getting any sleep because Terrence kept invading her dreams . . . that's what she's been doing to me. I've seen her. I know she's alive."

Again, Maxwell still doubted me. "Alex . . . are you sure it wasn't just a hopeful dream?"

I shook my head, fuming that he still wasn't believing me and grunted, "No, it was real. She was real . . . and I'm not giving up on her," then I ran off at full speed back to the hotel and up onto the roof top garden.

I was irritable and really struggling to believe in anything right now.

– What if Maxwell was right? – What if I'm just seeing what I want to see? – What if losing Lila pushed me to the edge of breaking point, and I really am losing my mind?

I looked around at all the plants and the trees, and started talking to them in a hopeful attempt to communicate with them, and ask for help.

"Okay, I know I'm not a Nature guardian, but I need your help! I have to talk to Lila! Please. . . I need your help! Just help me find her! Tell me she's still alive."

I then held onto the branch of a tree and wished for something – anything to happen.

But nothing happened, so I tried it Lila's way and sat down to meditate, repeating to myself, "She's not dead . . . she's not . . . I know she's not."

## Journal entry insert by Lila Winters

Terrence and I had been searching through the memories stored inside the tree all day, and we're not getting anywhere. I also noticed Terrence was beginning to lose his patience and he was most likely worried that if we didn't get any results that one of us was going to get in a lot of trouble. – I think he was very worried that it was going to be me.

In one of the memories, we were walking through the village of an old castle. I was dressed in what seemed to be royal attire—with a tiara and a very uncomfortable dress, and Terrence was dressed as —I think a knight and was escorting me through the village. The townspeople even curtseyed as we passed them. But it still wasn't the memory Terrence was looking for.

"This is taking too long" he bickered.

I was getting tired and starting to feel my real body weakening, so I tried to get his attention, "Terrence . . . I really am starting to get tired. We've searched hundreds of memories now, with no success."

Then while scanning around I tried to find some where to sit, because I believed it was time to negotiate. "Alright Terrence, we'll try one more memory. But after that I really need to sit down . . . in the real world."

As I looked up to see what Terrence's answer would be, he noticed my nose was beginning to bleed and he looked concerned for me. But I was in a hurry and really didn't care, so I grabbed his hand, pulling him into the next memory, via a glowing portal.

We abruptly fell to the ground in the next memory. – And Frac that hurt.

And I groaned in frustrated pain, lifting my head to see that we were in the woods outside a quaint little cottage that overlooked a beautiful, shimmering lake. The scene really did look picturesque.

I peered down gazing at my reflection in the lakes-water to see a woman with pale skin and long dark-red hair, wearing a red hooded cape, and old maiden clothes. In disbelief I looked closer at the reflection and realizingly gasped, "Red . . ."

FRAC buckets – this memory was supposed to be a fairy tale. But unfortunately given my track record with myths and legends – fairy tales weren't that farfetched anymore.

"Terrence! . . . I have a really bad feeling about this one!"

I quickly stood to my feet searching around for Terrence, only to be greeted by a very angry, very big wolf, growling at me as it approached me from out of its hiding place amongst the trees.

"Yep, really bad feeling."

The wolf charged at me at a very fast speed, but when it got closer, I somehow threw a fireball at its feet, startling the wolf and most definitely myself – who's hand was for some reason was still on fire.

I screamed in a panic, "Argh. . . Fire guardian. I'm a Fire guardian," quickly smothering my hand with the cape, trying to put it out.

"Terrence?" I called, nervously looking at the wolf and backing away slowly. "Terrence if that's you in there, just try to remember . . . I'm your friend and we don't eat friends, okay... I think it's time we went back to the real world. So, just take my hand, okay,"

Very timidly I held my hand out hoping that if the wolf really was Terrence, he would cooperate. But he didn't, he tried to bite me instead, so I ran for it.

I ran at full speed around the lake, trying to get away from him, but he followed me, running at full speed as well and was very close to catching up.

Unfortunately, my nose began to bleed again and I became extremely dizzy, needing to slow down, and stopped to lean on a tree in the hopes that I had lost him.

Again, I realised I was wrong. Because when I turned to see if it was actually safe to stop, the wolf pounced on me, knocking me to the ground and leaving large gaping claw marks, that tore across the length of my abdomen. And as I screamed in horrifying pain, the wolf stood over me and bit my arm to stop me from inching away.

"TERRENCE! PLEASE! TERRENCE!" I shouted and pleaded, crying from the pain I was in, trying so badly not to let the fear show.

Eventually I found the opportunity to punch the wolf as hard as I could in the nose then grabbed hold of his neck as I created a portal directly beneath us, causing us to fall through.

## Journal entry insert by Terrence Connors

The last memory we visited was horrific. I had absolutely no control over anything I was doing, trapped in a wolf's body and attacking Lila. I felt powerless just listening to her scream my name, while watching her cry as I clawed and bit her.

When she finally managed to pull us out of the meditation, I opened my eyes and looked around relieved to be back in the green house. But my fear quickly returned to me as I looked at Richard and his scientist, panicking and yelling, "Somethings wrong" as they typed away on their computers.

My eyes darted over to see Lila's distant eyes staring back at me with blood trickling from her nose as she held her stomach trying to stop the blood from seeping through her shirt.

I could already see that her wrist was bleeding from what looked like a wolf's bite, and I dreaded the thought knowing what I had done. Then with short breathes I lifted Lila's shirt to see the large claw marks that spanned across her stomach. The wounds were deep, and she was losing a lot of blood — very, very quickly.

She started shivering and rasped my name through her trembling teeth as she collapsed, with her face becoming pale faster than before.

I cradled her in my arms and ran at full speed back into the cottage, gently resting her on the stretcher bed, and tore open her shirt to get a better look at the wound. — And It wasn't good. — I didn't hesitate and ripped her shirt right off to use as bandage for her wrist, then took off my shirt to use on her stomach wound.

I was so focused on Lila when Richard rushed in, yelling, "What the hell happened back there?"

So, I yelled back at him, "Get the chopper ready. We need to take her to the village!"

Then scooped Lila back up into my arms and rushed out of the cottage, yelling and cursing at the guards to get out of my way as I walked her out of the greenhouse toward the helipad.

I held onto her as the helicopter took off, refusing to let anyone else touch her, and as I stared down at Lila, I saw her pale skin and her hazy tear-filled eyes struggling to stay open, and I pleaded, "Stay awake Lila . . . don't fall asleep. Promise me. Promise me you won't fall asleep."

She didn't answer, so I pulled her closer to me, and I was in tears as I whispered in her ear, "I need to hear you say it Lila . . . Promise me you'll stay awake and not Die."

I stared at her and saw a glimpse of a smile as she breathed, "Okay. . . I promise I won't die."

She then stayed staring at me, while I focused on stopping the bleed waiting for the helicopter to land on one of the neighbouring islands. — We called it The Village and it had a hospital there that Mother uses for The Board's conditioning program and research.

So, if anyone knew how to save Lila, it was them.

# Original journal entry continued by Alex Woods

I sat on that roof top garden all night, trying to meditate, searching for anyone or anything that could help me. But nothing happened. And I got frustrated and vented, punching a fist size hole in the ground as I screamed, "Why isn't this working?"

Suddenly a small barn owl flew down, landing in front of me and chirped, "That is an interesting question . . . It could be because you do not know who you are calling for . . . or it could be because you are calling to all the spirits and all do not know how to answer. There are a number of reasons why it is not working . . . Alex Woods."

I jumped in fright and screamed – only a little – then asked, "Are you a spirit guide? Please tell me you're a spirit guide."

The owl then replied cryptically, "If that is what you call me, then that is what I am." He then looked at me weirdly as he turned his neck way too far my liking and explained, "You seek our help where we can-not provide it."

"What? Why not?" I asked, only increasing in my frustration.

He obviously picked up on my frustration, as he spanned his wings out before he answered, "In order to access another Guardian's dreamland, you must first be in the dreamland. You also require a connection point at both ends. Your friend was able to access your mind through the elements around you . . . but there are no animals where your friend is being held."

Yes! This is what I needed to hear.

"So, she is alive," I exclaimed, taking a breath of relief as I questioned, "Can you tell me where she is? Is she okay?"

But I didn't seem too happy when he replied, "No, I do not have that answer."

Well Damn it. This bird was as helpful as a pin in a nail box.

I really tried not to show my frustration and begged, "Well can you help me at all?"

But again, he answered cryptically, "Yes . . .follow your enemies and there a friend will be found" then he flew away, leaving me very confused as I yelled,

"What does that mean? Which enemy?"

I hadn't realised though, that Matt and Adela had walked into the garden and were standing behind me, when Matt asked "Alex, who are you talking to?"

Awe – Crap.

I jumped in fright again, then excitedly turned to explain, "Matt, you won't believe this, but it worked. I finally got to speak to a spirit guide, and they told me how to find Lila."

"Alex stop," Adela grunted, trying to interrupt me. But I just kept rambling,

"Now I don't know exactly where she is, but they did give me a clue, and I'll need you guys to help me decipher it."

Matt quickly lost it and yelled, "Alex enough! . . . Lila is dead. I saw the body myself. I just came up here to tell you about the funeral arrangement we've made . . . and to give you this."

He then handed me Lila's locket bracelet, still covered in soot and ash and — her blood as he explained, "She would have wanted you to have it."

I won't lie seeing the blood on the locket did make my stomach churn. And I felt short of breath, glaring back at Matt and Adela, shaking my head and urged. "No . . . she's not dead, I know she's not . . . she visits me in the dreamland and we've spent the whole night talking and—" My rant was interrupted when Matt punched me in the face before he stormed off inside.

I nursed my face as Adela angrily glared at me and questioned, "What is wrong with you? The man has just lost his wife and you carry on about how you dreamed about her . . . You dreamed about his dead wife."

My temper was hanging by a thread, and I yelled "She's not dead!"

But it seemed to fall on deaf ears as Adela yelled back at me, "Yes, she is! And you need to accept that and move on for Matt's sake and yours."

She tried to compose herself and take some calming breathes as I stood there quietly listening to her. "Now! . . . I have just finished talking with John, and he has kindly agreed to give the group a few weeks off to grieve and . . ."

That was it, that was the clue the bird had told me about. "John," I mumbled, getting excited with determination.

But Adela wasn't listening to me, she just continued her speech ". . . Matt was going to ask before you went off on your crazy rant if you could speak at the funeral next week?"

I wasn't really listening to her. I was actually scanning the skies to see the small barn owl flying past the hotel and replied, "Um, I'm not actually sure I can make it . . . I have to go out of town for a while . . . Right now, actually."

I then turned around, closing my eyes as I ran off the edge of the hotel building and as I fell, I transformed into a small barn owl – flying through the city.

I stalked John's car as he left the hotel and drove out of the city to the Essendon airfields where a private jet was fuelled and ready for him. I flew down onto the plane out of sight and morphed into a large green gecko, crawling along the side of the plane and into the cabin.

And right now, I'm really thankful that Lila had taken me to the zoo when she did, and helped me bond with all the animals— even the gross and slimy ones.

I very happily and quietly crawled up on to John's brief-case and rested as the plane took off. Now taking comfort in knowing that I was on my way to rescue Lila — or die trying.

# CHAPTER 7

# A WALK DOWN MEMORY LANE

Journal entry by Terrence Connors

43 hours —— that's how long it has been since Lila arrived at The Village hospital. She had slipped into a coma just before we got her to the hospital.

The doctor worked at full speed trying to stop the bleeding. But for some reason, Lila's stomach had to be stitched back together twice. I don't know why but her body kept vibrating at a ridiculous speed as she slept. I've never seen anything like that before.

The doctor even tried to sedate her further, and failed each time.

And I couldn't bear it, just watching while she lay in the hospital bed with all her wounds bandaged, blood bags leading into both arms and a breathing tube in her mouth.

I felt so guilty, because I did this to her, and all I could think to do was pray, — which is something I don't usually do.

Eventually, Richard walked into the room to see me holding Lila's hand, and it looked like he was pleased for a brief second before he asked, "Is there any change?"

I shook my head just as disappointed—if not more. Then he asked me if I knew how to make that blue healing paste that Lila used on me, but again I shook my head.

"Huh," he snickered, "all this time, we thought it was you who made the tree blossom 20 years ago. Now I'm starting to think it was all her."

He grimaced at me disappointingly as he walked out of the room holding Lila's medical chart. Probably to go berate the doctor for his incompetence.

Then suddenly I fell into a meditative state as I was pulled into the dreamland, where Lila was standing there waiting for me, looking around and admiring the forest trees.

I gazed at Lila, shocked and amazed. — She was getting good at sharing a meditation.

She looked so much better in the dreamland — still wearing her hospital gown and bloody bandages and pale from all the blood loss. But she smiled at me, and that was what made her look — perfect to me.

She walked towards me, and tittered, "I wouldn't let the General get to you that way. . . He's always been an arse."

She then waved her hand over the trunk of the tree and created a seat out of its lower branches, thanking it as she slowly sat down. I moved to help her and sat down next to her, watching as Lila held her stomach and winced in pain, trying to get comfortable.

"Are you okay?" I asked, loving the fact that she was resting her head on my shoulder — it made me feel like maybe she wasn't angry at me for doing this to her.

She grunted from the pain as she replied, "Yeah, even in my dreams I still feel the pain . . . I take it you guys didn't know that what happens to us here in the dreamland affects us in the real world as well."

I stayed silent, not wanting to answer. Remembering the last time I was injured in the dreamland, was when I confronted Lila and came out with some very nasty bruises and broken ribs. So yeah — I knew she'd get hurt. I just wasn't expecting the memories of Animal and Fire Guardian in a Memoria Arbor.

Either way Lila figured out the truth, and she chuckled, "Terrence . . . your nature betrays you . . . you did know, didn't you?"

Again I didn't answer, and she lifted her head seemingly calm and happy, yet still stern when she demanded, "I think it's time you told me the truth about us . . . for starters, you can tell me about this necklace . . ."

She then pulled my clenched hand up and tapped on my knuckles, hoping I would loosen my grasp on the white oak tree pendant inside—the one I refused to let anyone else touch while she was in surgery.

I glance up in a bit of shock at how she knew and her smile got wider, "...I know you broke into my home and left it for me. And I know it means something special to you because you keep staring at it. . . You also made sure no one else held it except for you, when I was in the surgery room."

Yeah — I think I'm busted. She really does know how to ask the direct questions now, doesn't she? And again, I just sat there, becoming frustrated at the very pointed questions that Lila continued to ask me, knowing that I was forbidden to answer any of them and answered,

"It's classified."

"Well, can you at least tell me what the General was talking about? What happened 20 years ago?" she asked again.

"That's also classified."

"Well un-classify it," she loudly demanded, pulling away from me, "Terrence I've had enough with the lying and the half-truths you give me. You said we used to be friends. So, tell me what happened to us?"

I needed a moment to contemplate my options of either ticking off The Board and revealing my past or losing Lila's trust and the friendship that she had offered me.

Very quickly I realised which option I wanted, and helped Lila to stand to lead her to a portal that I created, leading into one of my memories.

It was a memory from a long time ago. I held onto Lila as she leaned on me for support, and we stood in a wide-open field surrounded by trees and long grass.

This time, instead of being able to explore the memory, we were merely spectators as we watched our younger selves run past us, frolicking amongst the grass, playing tiggy.

We were celebrating Lila's 6 birthday and I had just turned 7 a month before. And we were running up towards a picnic that had been set up by our parents — My mother had died before I turned three, but my father Collin Vertelle was one of Richards work colleagues and spent quite some time with Richard and Hanna. There were also two other boys there, Ben who had only just turned 9 and John who never let Ben forget that he was older by 2 years and 11 months — They never got along — ever.

Lila watched her younger self laughing and playing with the younger me. She even smiled when she saw us sharing our lunches together. And when the younger Terrence had finished his lunch, he held on to young Lila's hand as they ran off to play again, exploring the trees.

I helped Lila to follow our younger selves, watching us getting into all sorts of mischief, climbing the trees and getting very dirty rolling around in the fallen leaves.

Little Lila shouted, "Come on, Terry . . . keep up!"

I loved that nickname and Lila was the only one who was ever allowed to call me that — I suppose I do miss hearing that from her.

Anyway — it was clear that my younger self was not as confident with the whole climbing trees thing, and dirt, and knowingly getting into trouble as he raced to keep up with little Lila.

I was the one who cringed at the sight of blood when the younger Lila slipped and grazed her hand, but young Lila just stood up and brushed it off.

They eventually ran far enough into the woods, that neither of our parents could see — us. And they had both stopped and stared in amazement at a gigantic, old tree that was black and burnt with no leaves growing from it. And it was surrounded by all of the healthy trees, so this one really stood out like a sore thumb.

The younger Lila, being the curious girl she was, tried to climb up to touch the tree, with my younger self silently freaking as he shrieked "Be careful."

But little Lila was determined and didn't listen as she replied, "But it's crying, Terry. Can't you hear it?"

We watched as younger me cautiously approached the tree and placed his hand next to hers. Then little Lila hugged the tree and rubbed her injured hand along the bark, whispering, "Cheer up, tree. It'll be okay."

As she said that, the charcoal on the tree began to slowly fall away, revealing strong healthy bark beneath it and the leaves and flowers started to blossom at the top of the tree.

Young Lila and Terrence were both so terrified and they screamed trying to run away, but little Lila's foot got caught and she slipped and hit her head on a rock, and her necklace snapped, falling to the ground beside her.

That seemed to be the best part of the memory for me to pull our older selves out, stepping back through the portal, and appearing back in Lila's dreamland, standing in front of the tree seat again.

Lila remained very quiet, still leaning on me as I helped her to sit back down while I explained, "Richard was so mad when I told him what happened and he thought I was the one who made the tree better. . . He then convinced my father to move me here to the village, and after that, I never saw or spoke to him again. . . It wasn't until I was about 14 or 16 when I discovered that my real father Collin, had essentially sold me to the highest bidder in exchange for his life and tidy sum."

"This is all my fault," Lila sighed staring at the ground, "You were only brought here because of me . . . if I hadn't of led you out there . . ."

I stopped her thought, resting my hand against her cheek, turning her to look at me, so I could clarify, "Lila . . . No . . . we both were to blame. Remember nothing happened until we were both touching the tree."

"And the necklace. . ." She excitedly gasped, "I was wearing it then, what happened to it?"

I smiled staring down at the pendent as I answered, "You wore this necklace every day. It was your favourite . . . I picked it up when you fell and I never got the chance to give it back"

Lila went a little quiet, and I peered up to see her smiling, as she commented, "I like the name Terry . . . it very much suits you."

Yeah — I had to smile, I tried not to but I did. I then turned a little to face her, readying myself to interrogate her. "Okay, now I have a question for you."

And now with a cheeky grin, she turned to face me, and it kind of looked like she was readying herself to be interrogated, waiting for me to ask, "After our shower the other day . . . when you ran out on me. You had the opportunity to leave and escape. . . Why didn't you?"

Lila pouted and seemed almost puzzled that I would ask such a question and replied, "Because I made a deal with you. And like I said, I've never broken a promise before. I'm not about to start now . . . Besides you're my friend. I'm not going to leave you here alone."

Wow — now I'm really overwhelmed with guilt, because if she really knew me and what I've done, she definitely wouldn't want to be friends with me.

After all, it was me who tried to kill her.

# Journal entry insert by General Richard Willows

There was no sign of that coward of a wannabe doctor, who was responsible for saving my Pumpkin. And one of the soldiers reported to me that Agent John had arrived, waiting for me on the ward. So I made my way back to Lila's room, only to see John waiting inside the room staring curiously and begrudgingly at Terrence who had fallen asleep on the bed, holding Lila's hand.

John turned to me and smirked, "Evening Father, how goes the experiment?"

I huffed and held back my rage, angry at the fact that Lila was still unconscious, replying, "Don't make me shoot you," as I stormed back out of the room.

He followed me, smugly boasting, "But then I won't get to share the good news." He then handed me my passport and flight details, saying, "You have your daughter's funeral to attend. And mother sends you her best. She is very anxious to see you again."

I glanced back into Lila's room and huffed again as I glared at John and demanded, "Take care of your sister."

But John angrily refuted, "She's not my sister. She's a nature freak that came from the bad seed."

"Fine then," I grimaced, walking towards the elevator, and instead ordering, "Take care of the target, or I'll shoot you for your incompetence." I then turned back to John and felt a bit smug, questioning, "Is that better for you?"

And as the elevator door closed, I heard him respond, "Not really."

He always was the jealous type and hated it when Lila came to live with us, and he was sent to military school -- for his protection of course.

But he always did do better with a little competition around.

# CHAPTER 8

# MY GALLANT HERO...S

*Journal entry by Lila Winters*

I had finally woken up from that coma, and my wounds were healing nicely but the stitches had yet to be removed. The doctor said, it may leave a nasty scar, to match the many other scars on me, but I was all set to go home – by that he meant return to the island.

Nonetheless, I was out of that hospital bed so that was something to be happy about.

Terrence was fretting over me though, as we walked back into the green house. I refused to let him carry me, and that really got him mad as he watched me hold my stomach and hunch as I walked. I will admit, I was playing it up a little, to make sure he felt really guilty and extra protective of me, now that the A-hole John had arrived on the island.

Urgh, he makes me so – incredibly furious – That lying, two-faced sack of – we're getting off track here – Let's try to focus.

Anyway, I was walking into the cottage looking around for my bracelet and walked back out into the green house having a minor freak out to ask Terrence where it was.

But he also didn't know. And I was irked because was really hoping to make a blue rose tonic to heal faster, but without the seed, I was stuck feeling like a wolf had just attacked me, which I also had no plans on letting Terrence forget about, any time soon. – I really like that his natural instinct is to protect me, he's going to be a really good friend.

I got a little worried looking for my bracelet, scanning the ground outside the cottage when Terrence grabbed hold of me. "Hey, hold still for a minute."

He then scuffled his hand into the hood of my jacket and pulled out a very feisty little gecko that squirmed around in Terrence's hand, trying to bite him. And in a frightened state Terrence threw the little guy into the nearby bush and hurried me inside.

"He must have been stuck in there for a while," he commented then worryingly asked me if I was Okay.

Before I could answer him though, he heard the sound of the A-hole John along with "Thing 1" and "Thing 2" walking into the smaller greenhouse where the memory tree was.

I tried to hide my grin as Terrence pulled a sour face. "What does he want now?" he irked then he stormed out of the cottage. – And I'm really glad he's my friend.

I stayed in the cottage and sat down on the stretcher bed, trying to relax a little, and didn't even notice that the small gecko had crawled through one of the cracks in the wall and made its way up to rest on the stretcher bed beside me.

In a fright I screamed, grabbing hold of the thing then throwing it across the room and hitting a wall. And as it landed to the ground, it morphed into a naked male human.

He sat up and grunted, "Ow. . . could you please stop throwing me!"

Oh, my gosh – I gasped under my breath in excitement. It was Alex – Alex was here – He found me. And now filled with joy, I raced at full speed into his arms and hugged him so tightly, causing him to lose his balance a little.

"Alex . . . it's you, it's really you . . . you're here."

I felt his arms holding me and hugging me back even tighter, whispering, "It's me. I'm here."

The downside was he was hugging me so tightly that I had to mask the pain, coming from my abdomen. But he's an animal guardian and when he eventually found the bandages, he stopped hugging me to inspect the damage, lifting my shirt.

I could tell he was angry and wanted to know what happened, but I didn't want to tell him. I thought it would be too much for him to understand. So, I played it down.

"It's nothing. It's just a few scratches. It'll heal."

It didn't help when he noticed some of the blood soaking through the dressing, and frustratingly huffed, "It's not nothing. . . You were in that hospital for a reason. Now tell me who did this to you?"

"You were with me in the hospital?" I deflected with a cheeky grin.

Yet he persisted, raising his voice as he tried to pull the bandages off my wrist and grunted, "Lila! Tell me, who did this to you?"

He then gasped in shock as he pulled back my sleeve and discovered more of the other scars. The worry filled him and he stood me to my feet, trying to pull off my jacket but I didn't want him to see, so held onto the jacket.

But when he said, "Lila please" I let go and let him take the jacket off, with me now standing in front of him in just a singlet and pants. I wasn't removing them though – those scars are a lot worse.

He moved closer to survey the damage and was left speechless. I think he was going to be sick. But before he could react or see any more of the damage, Terrence knocked on the door and walked inside, mumbling something about John and the tree, asking if I was still okay.

Luckily, he was distracted, still looking outside to keep an eye on John. Remaining oblivious to Alex as he quickly turned back into a gecko on the floor. Moving quickly, I pulled my jacket back on and casually stepped in front of the gecko to hide him, nervously replying, "Yeah, I'm great."

Terrence then went on to explain that The Board had given us a deadline and that if we didn't show any results within the next 24 hours, there would be severe consequences.

And we both knew what that meant, so I nodded, "Okay, I'll be right out,"

I waited for Terrence to leave before quickly grabbing the gecko and gently placing him back into the hoodie of my jacket and pleadingly whispered, "Alex, whatever you do, don't move."

I raced out of the cottage, ignoring the pain, to find Terrence and John waiting for me in the smaller greenhouse, along with the two lab techs, "Thing 1 and 2," both busy attaching their probes to the tree, and eagerly looking at their computer screens.

I glared at John and snickered "Hello John . . . did Richard send his errand boy to do his dirty work this time?"

To which John smugly replied, "No, he had to go to a funeral."

I could feel Alex shifting around in my hoodie, hissing at that comment or the sound of John's voice. So, I tilted my head, scuffling nervously to avoid anyone noticing.

But I suspect Terrence did, so I just avoided eye contact with him and commented,

"Oh, that's a shame . . . Was it anyone special?"

John looked at me oddly and creepily grinned at me when he replied, "Not really."

And since I didn't have much of a choice or any time to waste, I took a deep breath, grabbing hold of Terrence's hand and scowled back at John, "Well then . . . let's get this over with," then placed Terrence and my hand onto the tree, pulling us both into the dreamland.

When Terrence arrived in the dreamland, he stood in what looked a large tropical rainforest, alone, with me nowhere to be seen. Mainly because I was hiding behind one of the trees with Alex standing next to me, still naked. It was actually quite funny, and I had to ask the trees to make him some pants from the leaves and ferns.

"Lila! Where'd you go?" Terrence shouted, beginning to wander around calling my name.

I didn't want to keep him too long, and quickly demanded Alex to stay hidden before I raced out to greet Terrence, playing the ignorant act. "I'm here. What took you so long?"

He stared at me confused, probably sensing that I was hiding something as he answered, "Lila I was only a few seconds behind you."

Still, I continued the act and insisted, "Well, you're here now, so let's get started."

But it didn't fool him and he grabbed my non-injured arm at full speed and commanded, "Stop!"

He loosened his grip a little, carefully pulling me back towards him and questioned, "What's going on with you? You're acting very strange?"

I stayed quiet, still trying to avoid eye contact with him. But he placed his hand under my chin, lifting my face up to look into my eyes. "Lila, you're hiding something from me. I can tell!"

Well, two can play at this game, so I pulled away from him to bark back, "And so are you!" I stared at him as I grumbled, "What does Richard really want with this tree?"

I was obviously trying to deflect but I also wanted to know the answer and continued to glare at him as he rolled his eyes, and lied to me again, "I already told you this . . ."

"No, you told me a half-truth . . . and now I want all of it . . . Terrence, tell me the truth or our deal is off!"

I could sense that I was getting to him, watching his body roll in frustration. He then held his hands up and I watched as they tensed into little claws and he irked, "Why do you have to be so stubborn?"

He then started muttering to himself before he pulled me towards him, moving his hand to the back of my neck as he kissed me on the lips, very passionately. -- And Frac he's a good kisser and I know he shouldn't – but he tastes good too.

Oh, Frac and fruit cakes – I could feel my defences dropping, relaxing into the kiss when suddenly both our eyes glowed a deep purple as he shared with me his memories.

- The first was of Terrence and Ben in what looked like a very gory battle, surrounded by dead soldiers.

- The next was of Ben in Richard's office arguing with him, shouting, "Hundreds of innocent people are dying fighting your war!"

Richard stood up in huff and commanded to Ben, "Then find a way to keep them alive."

- The third memory was of Terrence sitting in his cottage looking through dozens of old journals. I recognised some of them, they were the ones John left with Matt when I was trapped in the Dreamland. But Terrence had stopped on a page that talked about 'Immortality' with a picture of the Bristle-cone pine tree.

- The last memory was of Terrence being berated by Richard as he yelled, "This isn't a game, son. This is war. Do you really want the deaths of your fellow guardians on your hands? If not, I suggest you find that wonder drug, you're so confident about . . ."

The memory abruptly ended when Alex ran out from his hiding place in a fury and tackled Terrence to the ground, beating him repeatedly in the face. With Protective anger emanating from him.

"Alex, stop!" I shouted, raising my hands to the trees and asked for assistance.

One of the tree branches obliged, quickly reaching down, wrapping around Alex to pull him away from Terrence, and held him there until he calmed down.

But I think that made him angrier as he yelled "What are you doing? Put me down!"

I however was just as mad at him and shrieked back, "Alex, you were supposed to stay hidden! Why don't ever listen to me?"

"Put me down now!" he demanded again.

Terrence stood up nursing his face, watching me lower Alex back down to the ground, and griped "This is what you were hiding! What is he doing here?"

Alex then stood protectively in front of me, glaring at Terrence, demanding "You stay away from her!"

And as predicted Terrence just ignored him and addressed his questions directly to me, asking "What the hell is he doing here?"

Yet I didn't get the chance to answer, because Alex kindly answered, "I'm here to save her."

"She doesn't need saving!" Terrence shouted back.

I tried to get their attention, but my voice seemed to be a distant background echo as they both bickered about who was stepping on whose territory – it all became very tiresome, very quickly.

I rapidly reached the final straw when Alex shouted, "Clearly she does need saving and she's obviously under some kind of spell or drug or whatever it is you use to make girls fall in love with you."

Yep I lost it.

"HEY!! Both of you sit down . . . NOW!" I screamed – and it was loud enough to scare the trees.

They both stared at me in a nervous shock and sat down on the nearby rocks, listening to me. "Thank-you . . . now . . . we are all missing a lot of information here, so let's all take it turns to ask the questions. Alex . . ." I was regretting this already, when I said, "...you can go first."

I stood in front of both of them, trying to control my temper when I felt the surge of pain from my torso, and had to nurse my stomach. Causing both of them to move, wanting to help me, but I demanded them to sit back down. And they <u>wisely</u> followed my request.

I then stared at Alex, waiting for him to ask his first question, "Okay, why were you kissing him?"

Great that's his first question – was he fraccing serious.

And I think Terrence was in a mood as he snidely answered, "It wasn't a kiss . . . I was sharing my memories about the tree . . ."

"Did your lips touch?" Alex interruptingly rebutted.

But before Terrence could answer that or do anything else stupid, I interrupted their bickering again. "Terrence, do you have a question, or would you rather keep fighting with each other over my lips?"

Frac -- I just had to say that didn't I. And I could see both of them trying to hide a smirk as I again regretted my words.

Terrence then unclenched his hands and asked again, "What is he doing here? And better yet how did he get here?"

I also wanted to know that answer and unwittingly sided with Terrence, which did not go down too well for Alex who defensively explained, "I came to bring you home and prove to everyone, including your kids that you're still alive . . . everyone thinks you're dead."

Everyone thinks I'm DEAD . . . WHAT!

I began to feel a wave of dread and panic over take me as Alex continued to describe how John had somehow managed to convince everyone that I was <u>DEAD</u>, and he grunted,

"They even had a burned corpse that had all your belongs on it, even your bracelet."

"My bracelet," I interrupted, then moved quickly, tackling Terrence to the ground with my hand around his throat, squeezing tightly. "Tell me you didn't know about this . . . tell me you didn't steal it from the locker room after our shower . . ."

"Wait, you showered together?" Alex questioned territorially.

"NOT NOW, ALEX!" I shouted, still squeezing Terrence's throat tightly.

Terrence tried to get the words out but couldn't, instead he reached up and held my cheek to share another memory as his eyes glowed purple. He shared the memory of the first time we almost kissed in the locker room. I had just run out on him at full speed, and it caused him to lose his temper, kicking the bench that had my old clothes and bracelet on it sending them flying across the room before he ran out at full speed looking for me.

Trying to break free of his memory, I shook my head and loosened my grip around his throat, standing back up to my feet, and instead started to pace, trying very hard not to lose – My FRAC and FRUIT CAKES!

I was lost for words, not knowing what to do and mumbling "I have to go back . . . I can't . . . I can't . . . I don't know if I . . ."

I suddenly had an idea and I asked, "Terrence, that memory transfer thing you just did with me . . . will it work on Alex?"

He seemed a little out of sorts, standing to his feet. I could sense he wanted to help me but I think he was nervous of what I might be thinking when he replied, "Well yeah, it'll work on any guardian . . . as long they are willing, but it can be more revealing then you expected . . ."

Alex started backing away and tried to shut down the idea saying that I may not like some of his memories. But I begged and pleaded with him, "Alex, we're running out of time and I have too many questions for you . . . Please do this for me."

He was reluctant at first but eventually nodded his head and looked at Terrence as he explained exactly what we needed to do. "You need to open up to her, share your emotions with her, and find the connection you both have between each other. Then try to remember in detail, every memory you want to share with Lila."

Terrence then turned to me and stated, "Lila, when you're ready, place your hands on his cheek and concentrate on his thoughts, as if you were pulling him into the dreamland."

I confirmingly nodded and stared at Alex as he stared back at me, trying to focus, and for some reason he was holding his breath. Still I continued and held my hand against his cheek, causing him to shudder as our eyes glowed purple. And I was really grateful that he was doing this for me.

He shared every memory and emotion that he had of the last few months – from the moment I was shot and disappeared behind a wall of flames – up until the moment I threw him against the wall and he transformed back into a human.

I pulled my hand away, breaking the memory link and started to feel overwhelmingly dizzy at the amount of information I got.

That is definitely an interesting ability – that I didn't know we could do.

I stumbled backwards, and Terrence moved to hold me and keep me up-right, but Alex became confused and questioned, "That's it? . . . Then why did you kiss her?"

Terrence shrugged his shoulder and just casually replied, "It was the only way to channel her emotions of sexual desires and find a connection between us."

Ah, sexual connection – I suppose it had been a while – and he is very attractive.

Alex definitely didn't take that one well, readying to punch Terrence again until I stood between them, protecting Terrence and shouted, "Alex, stop it! We still need him . . . He's going to help us escape."

To which they both confusingly questioned at the same time, with Alex grunting "He is?" and Terrence gasping "I am?"

And I know it wasn't complete in the whole unison crap but it still ticked me off, causing me to huff before I deviously grinned declaring to Terrence. "You are . . . Because we both promised to be friends and stick together . . . and I'm certainly not leaving you here."

I was a little worried right now, because I think Terrence sensed my protective nature of him and I caught him smile a little. – And I was really struggling not to smile back and accidentally tick Alex off.

"Alright," Terrence nodded with huge smile, but it disappeared when he stated, "But we can't leave the tree here. They'll destroy it."

"Which is why we're taking it with us . . ." I declared again. Which inevitably ended up with both of them saying in complete unison this time, "What?"

And I really hate it when guys do that – It's just weird.

Either way, I had to focus and grunted at them. "Look I have an idea . . . but we'll have to work together. As a team." – Which hopefully is not short lived.

It took them a while but we all ended up shaking hands and coming to some kind of agreement – Which we would definitely need to work on at a later date.

But for now, we were ready to kick some pretentious Guardian and Human arses –especially John's.

# CHAPTER 9

# FIGHT OR FLIGHT SYNDROME

*Journal entry by Alex Woods*

Urgh!! -- I can-not believe it. I came all this way to rescue Lila and now I have to work with the man who put her here. And I am seriously having a long conversation with Lila, if we survive this.

I was the first to be pulled out of the meditation, still hiding as a gecko in the hood of Lila's jacket. I pulled my head up slightly and stayed hidden beneath Lila's hair, curious to see what was happening, only to see Lila and Terrence still meditating and holding hands, touching the tree.

I looked over to see John getting very impatient. He looked like he was starting to sweat and his impatience turned to dread, when he looked back at the old tree in fear as it began to tremble and shake the ground beneath him.

He glared back at the other scientists and yelled, "What happening?" waiting for one of the scientists looking at his computer at the time shout back, "I don't know, Sir something's happening to them. Their heart rates have nearly doubled and their brain waves are going mental."

"Well stop them!" John shouted then pulled out his gun readying to fire, but before he could fire a shot, the branches of the trees surrounding the building had grown uncontrollable and smashed through the glass windows of the greenhouse, quickly and furiously destroying the building.

Now in a panic, John yelled into his radio, "All units to the greenhouse. I repeat all units to the greenhouse!" then gawked in amazement as the large old tree began to shrink back down into a large stone-like seed that glowed green.

Which in all honesty, looked freaky, amazing and terrifying all at the same time.

Lila stumbled and I freaked a little, sensing the amount of pain she was in, as both she and Terrence woke from the meditation in a hurry. Lila quickly picked up the rock-seed thingy and commented on how cool it was that it worked.

The down side was they were both distracted, watching and possibly panicking as dozens of agents swarmed into the greenhouse, all heavily armed, causing neither of them to notice that John had snuck up behind Terrence to hit him with the butt of his gun.

I'll admit – I did hesitate a little, but I leapt to his rescue, jumping out of Lila's hoodie and transforming back into my awesome – butt-naked – me again, right in front of John and punched him in the face. Celebrating and enjoying that long-awaited and glorious moment.

"Yes! . . . I have been wanting to do that for weeks!"

Terrence stared back at me, shocked at the fact that I actually did save him and kept up my part of the deal.

Lila also looked back at me, saying, "We don't have much time," but quickly averted her eyes and gasped, "Right, I forgot you were naked in this land."

They kindly gave me a few seconds, shielding us with tree roots and branches from the showering of bullets in order for me to steal John's pants at full speed.

Then, the second I had pants on, we all ran at full speed fighting as many of the guards and Guardians as we could, dodging fireballs and ice crystals, mud traps, and flying rocks.

There were even sparks of electricity being sent flying and hand-sized metal shards being propelled out of one of the guardian's hand. – And that was terrifyingly cool.

Everything was happening so extremely fast, and if this were a movie, I'd be on the edge of my seat right now. – The best part of it all, was not only were we working as a team, but we had all the trees and plants fighting with us as well.

That is until we reached one of the indoor corridors, that was – at this current time deprived of all plant life.

We were stopped by five guards who were clearly Guardians given their lack of weaponry and their overconfidence – They were waiting to ambush us in the corridor.

I was high on territorial and protective adrenaline, and thankfully, Lila turned to me and whispered, "Alex, you're up."

YES – I definitely enjoyed this – as I shoulder tackled two of the guards into a wall then threw two of them up in the air, smashing them into the roof, and punched the last one.

They're clearly not adequately trained – Thank you Lila, your training really has paid off.

I looked back at Lila and grinned as the five guards fell to the ground, either unconscious or writhing in pain. But my victory dance was cut short when three more guards ran into the hallway behind Lila and Terrence, this time fully armed.

Terrence looked like he was going to get the opportunity to show Lila what he learnt from all the training she gave him – which I will also be talking to Lila about.

But instead Lila stopped him and asked if she could do it this time.

From the look on her face, I got the not-so-subtle impression that she was mad and possibly recognised these particular guards.

As she ran at full speed dodging the bullets and slid down the hallway, kicking one of them in their privates.

She then rapidly pushed up from the ground to stand between the other two guards, grabbing both of the guards extended arms and simultaneously twisting them around, causing them to drop their guns.

Then while still focusing on them Lila kicked the guns backwards towards us and used one of the guards as a support pole as she started walking up and along the wall at half speed, swinging around and kicking the second guard in the face as she spun the support pole guy into the wall and kicked him in his privates as well.

And as Lila landed to the ground again, she glared at the men on the floor and bellowed, "That was for your stupid initiation phase, ya arseholes."

Both Terrence and I watched, cringing in slightly non-empathetic pain as the guards received an uncomfortable beating then Terrence commented, "Yeah they definitely deserved that."

We started moving again, weaving in and out of corridors trying to find a safe passage that had not been destroyed by trees or swarming with guards, yet we were not finding any luck.

Lila screeched, "This is taking too long . . . We need a distraction."

And Terrence then thought of an idea, yelling back to us, "Follow me."

The only problem was, his idea led us further into the building. Deeper into enemy territory as he led us down into the windowless basement corridor and into the island's holding cells, where we met four guardian elders being held prisoner.

Leeroy – an animal guardian, Samuel – a water guardian, Leah – a fire guardian and Broch – land guardian – you know rocks and dirt and stuff.

Lila stood with me as we watched Terrence use his security key card to open the holding cell doors and Leah – the fire guardian moved at full speed to hug Terrence.

Weird I know – and they asked who his friends were. But I wouldn't really call me a friend.

He then explained, "This is the guardian I was talking about," obviously referring to Lila as he opened the last cell door.

Samuel took one look at Lila's bandages and the blood seeping through her shirt and scoffed, "Seriously, this pretty little girl. This is the one."

And I was surprised that an African-American was so quick to judge someone based on their looks. But Lila took that demeaning comment well as she remained quiet, listening to Terrence ask, "We need your help getting off the island."

Surprisingly all the guardians immediately jumped to his aid, agreeing to help, asking, "What do you need?"

"A distraction," Lila said then shouted, "Get down!" as she knelt to the ground still remaining very calm. All while a large tree root broke through the walls of one of the basement cells, then grew through to the other side wall, snapping the cell bars as it went.

"What was that?" Leah queried looking around at the fallen debris.

Lila still stayed calm, but I could also sense her pain as she stood to her feet, helping some of the elders to stand, casually mentioning, "We're also destroying the island . . . so I suggest you move quickly . . . Elders, I recommend you work together and plot an escape path to the opposite side of the island to split the heard. You have roughly 30 minutes before this building is overrun."

She then ran back up into the basement corridor, waiting for Terrence and me. And Samuel chuckled, looking up at the tree roots still destroying the roof of his cell and said to Terrence, "I like this one," before he ran at full speed with the other elders out of the basement.

# Journal entry insert by Matt Winters

*Tomorrow is the dreaded day. Tomorrow is the day that I bury my wife, the mother of my two beautiful children. And I will tell you now I am still not handling it well.*

*Because tonight I'm sitting at the hotel bar drowning my sorrows with a heavy amount of alcohol.*

*I did mix it up with a glass of water and a bag of overpriced bar chips occasionally.*

*And Adela was kind enough to join me, sitting down on the barstool next to me, to make sure I was okay. — She was good that way. She's been so supportive ever since Lila —— you know.*

*She kindly reminded me, probably (in her own way) attempting to help my situation that Alex — the man who also loved my wife and Lila's best friend, had gone A.W.O.L and hasn't been seen in days and will also most likely not be in attendance tomorrow.*

*I mumbled something into my drink like, "It doesn't matter," or something along those lines. And when Adela asked if I was okay, and no I wasn't okay, I went on to educate her. "No . . . because exactly ten years ago was the day I met Lila. . . at my brother's stupid end of year school party. And now, exactly ten years and one day later, I'm going to say goodbye . . . And you're asking me if I'm okay."*

*I may have slurred a little and grunted at her — not a proud moment for me.*

*But Adela stayed quiet after that and just sat with me and ordered another drink.*

# Original journal entry continued by Alex Woods

We had finally made it out of the building, running towards the tree line at full speed still dodging bullets, fireballs and ice shards that were hurtling towards us by several guardians attempting to stop our escape.

We were doing pretty well until I got hit by a fireball in the leg. Luckily it only burned a hole in Johns pants, but it did cause me to lose focus and fall to a crashing halt, feeling a bit woozy in the head.

Lila and Terrence stopped running and rushed back to protect me. And I watched in amazement as Lila raised her hands up and a thin long tree branch came flying out from the tree line into her hand. She then stood protectively in front of me fighting off the guards as Terrence helped me to my feet and kept me upright as we rushed at a semi-half speed towards the edge of the island.

Lila stayed close behind, still fighting off the ever-persistent guards, when suddenly we heard her scream. One of the guards had managed to grab a hold of her, and she was struggling to break free.

Terrence glanced back and quickly let go of me, racing to help her, but by the time he got to her, she had already received assistance from the nearby trees. The branch had reached down, wrapping around the guard's legs and pulled him up into the air, unfortunately pulling Lila up in the air along with him.

When he finally did let go of Lila, she somersaulted back down to the ground, landing on her feet but again holding her stomach trying to bear the pain. And we all noticed the blood stains on her shirt were getting worse. But Lila ignored the pain and kept on running through the trees to the edge of the island.

I stared back to see the island plants taking over the building and trapping anyone who attacked it or dared to chase us.

Slightly puffed, we all stood on the beach wondering what to do next, and Terrence looked over to the pier, shouting disappointedly, "All the boats are gone." Stating the very obvious, which is usually my job in this part of the mission.

Terrence and I then curiously stared at Lila who was meditating at the edge of the water with her hands outstretched towards the trees as her eyes glowed a really bright green.

A few second later a large group of leaves came flying out of the tree line, spinning around us and creating a platform beneath our feet. Then it lifted us high into the air, flying us over the ocean and away from the island.

I won't lie – It was freaking amazing and scary at the same time.

## Journal entry insert by Matt Winters

I admit I had a lot to drink throughout the night as Adela so kindly escorted me back up to my apartment. — More like carried me.

We quietly stumbled through the apartment, being very careful not to wake anyone, tip toeing through the lounge room and snuck into my room. Where Adela sat me down on the bed as I continued to wallow in my own self-pity and mumbled, holding back my tears, "She's never coming back, is she?"

Adela stayed quiet and started readying me for bed, pulling off my shoes then she stopped, and sat down on the bed next to me then hugged me as I cried, for a very long time.

And when I finally started to feel a little bit better, I looked up at Adela to thank her and stared into her eyes, her very beautiful and empathetic green eyes, for what felt like a very long time then suddenly — I lost control of my urges, and will power, and obviously forgetting my morals when I kissed her.

But in the moment, I didn't care. I wanted to not feel pain. I wanted to feel something else — anything else. I wanted to lose myself in every other emotion that wasn't pain.

What surprised me though, was that she kissed me back. She held on to me as I pulled her further onto the bed then she ran her hands down my back, as I continued to kiss her wonderfully tasting lips, and chin, and neck, and chest.

We were both lost in the moment and between our groans of excitement, she pulled off my shirt and I hers and things got very physical — very, very quickly.

## Original journal entry continued by Alex Woods

We had been flying over the ocean for hours, and darkness surrounded us with nothing but the moon to guide us, and still with no evidence of land in sight.

Yet Lila was determined and also still in a meditative state, as she pulled us higher above the ocean to try and get a better view, but it seemed futile.

We were all beginning to get very cold, ice-cold actually – with me still topless and all. But I was starting to get very worried about Lila because she had been in a half-meditative state this entire time with her normally blue eyes glowing a bright green with a silvery blue tinge – You've just got to love that night vision.

My fear rapidly increased when we suddenly started to descend in our height and the leaves were beginning to slowly fall away. I looked over at Lila to see her nose dripping with blood, and her stomach bandages and clothes were now soaked with more blood.

I tapped on Terrence's shoulder to get his attention, "Something's wrong. She's losing to much blood."

He too noticed the blood dripping from her nose and lifted her shirt, beginning to freak out as well when he realised she had lost way too much blood. He then started to shake Lila's arm to break her from the trance, pleading, "Lila . . . Lila, look at me!"

When she finally did break out of her meditative state. She looked at both of us in fear before she passed out. And with that, all the leaves stopped and began to fall, bring us down along with them.

I grabbed hold of Lila as we rapidly plummeted towards the cold dark waters of the ocean. And while I held tight to Lila trying to wake her up, I screamed to Terrence asking him to do something.

Unfortunately, he was also filled with fear and worry, probably distracted by Lila's current condition, but he snapped out of it quick then reached out his hand towards the thousands of leaves plummeting down alongside us. And as his eyes glowed green, he held onto me and Lila, pulling the leaves closer to us, surrounding us and creating an extremely thick-pointed shield that hit the water first, making a slightly softer landing for us.

And Crap Damns – it was cold.

Terrence and I swam up to the surface of the water gasping for air, but when Lila was nowhere to be seen we freaked out more. We screamed her name, franticly looking around then took a breath to dive back under.

# CHAPTER 10

# A BITTER-SWEET FAREWELL

## *Journal entry by Adela Eden*

I woke up in terror after having a horrible nightmare of Lila's dead body floating in the dark water, and it scared me to no end. To make matters worse, I also woke up in the wrong bed. I was in Lila's apartment, next to Lila's husband and I quickly realised the worst of me.

So, now very much regretting my actions, I quietly grabbed my clothes and ran at full speed out the door. Then when I actually did get to my apartment, I decided to have a very long and reflective shower to think about what I had done.

While I sat in the shower, I closed my eyes for a split second and had another nightmare. It was of Lila's body floating in the water with skin pale as a ghost and hair floating around like Medusa. Only this time a dark figure appeared, grabbing hold of her and pulling her away.

I opened my eyes in a fright, to realise I was still in my bathroom, safe. But every time I closed my eyes, I saw her again.

I tried to convince myself it was just a nightmare, a bad dream and not Lila's ghost coming back to haunt me for the horrible thing I had done. I even tried taking calming breaths, but then it happened again. Only this time my eyes were wide open.

I had a vision of Lila's body floating in the water, and a dark shadow grabbing hold of her and pulling her up to the surface. I eventually saw the shadows face to reveal that it was Alex, floating in the cold night's water, gasping for air and holding Lila's body in his arms.

I shook my head, breaking free from the vision and coming to the damning realisation, "Oh, sweet mother of mercy . . . she's still alive."

## Journal entry insert by Terrence Connors

My heart had almost stopped and I was frozen in fear, wading in the icy water, looking for any sign of Alex or Lila. And when Alex finally emerged holding Lila, I was overjoyed, racing to help keep them afloat.

I realised as I pulled Lila's head out of the water to rest it on Alex's shoulder that she was still unconscious and had stopped breathing. Then at a half-speed, Alex handed her to me and demanded I start compressing her chest.

So as I held her in front of me with her head resting on my shoulder, I wrapped my arms around her, resting one hand on her back and one on her chest then started compressions. Repeating the movement as Alex breathed the cold night's air into her lungs.

Both of us refused to give up and we continued our makeshift CPR, wading in the waters trying to stay afloat until eventually Lila started coughing up water, and began to breath on her own. She was breathing her sweet and amazing breath—Thank the stars.

Yet as Lila started to come to, she stared around at the water and began to panic, gasping for more air. Alex then held onto her hands with his eyes glowing gold, trying to calm her down, "It's okay. We've got you."

But we also discovered her nose starting to bleed again, and she quickly lost consciousness again. And yeah ——I was really starting to worry because I also didn't know what to do.

All I could think to do was pull her close, lifting her head back onto my shoulder, trying to keep her afloat. The good thing was she was still breathing and that's what mattered.

"We need to get her out of the water!" Alex shouted, stating the obvious.

Well no, der — I looked around, still in a panic and yelled, "Do you have any ideas!"

"One . . ." he replied, "... but it's a long shot!"

He then dived back under the water, and stayed underwater for a long time, causing me to freak out more—shouting Alex's name until he re-emerged, panting for air and leading a pod of dolphins behind him.

Well would you look at that, he is useful for something.

As the dolphins circled us, Alex grabbed hold of Lila's hand, pulling it around his neck and demanded I do the same, to share the load. Two of the dolphins then surfaced beside us and we held on to their fins as they slowly pulled us away — hopefully towards land.

# Original journal entry
## continued by Adela Eden

Today of all days I had to have my doubts about Lila's death.

I was in the hotel's large function room arranging flowers for Lila's funeral, getting absurdly distracted by the very thought of Lila's funeral. And I was really struggling to come to terms with what had happened last night, still trying to convince myself that I was hallucinating and that I was just guilt-ridden, filling myself with false hope.

But a small part of me had that wonder. I knew Alex never gave up on me when I had been taken. Even after all the things I had said and done to him. So why then should I have doubted his abilities to find Lila?

But what about the body, what about all the evidence that pointed to Lila being dead?

My train of thought was derailed there by the sound of Matt snapping his fingers in front of my face, trying to get my attention and shouting my name. – Oh Fruits it's him.

"Hey, what happened to you this morning? I woke up and you were gone?" he asked.

I stammered and stuttered, not sure what to say and rigidly avoided looking at him, "I err . . . had errands to run."

Matt frowned at me, furrowing his brow and griped, "Screw the errands! We need to talk about this."

But No – I really didn't want to talk. So, I casually lead Matt out of the function room, away from the judgemental ears of Lila's loyal security team and whispered, "Matt, do you really want to talk about what we did. . . the day of your wife's funeral?"

But that only caused more agitation in Matt as he looked at the photo board of Lila surrounded by flowers and stormed away in a huff.

Looks like I wasn't the only one who was overcome with guilt last night.

## Journal entry insert by Matt Winters

My conversation with Adela did not go as I had hoped, and I stormed back up into the apartment in a fuming mess and slouched down onto the couch. My memory of last night was fuzzy, and it was no surprise why. Given the painful hangover I woke up with and the state of my bed, it was reasonable to assume that what little memory I did have of last night was correct and not a dream. Which meant I had done something stupid, and based on Adela's reaction to me – she agreed to that thought.

I picked up the photo of Lila and me on our wedding day, and fuelled with self-rage I threw it against the wall, shattering the glass. But when I realised what I had done, I was frantic, rushing to try and pick out the photo amongst the glass.

Suddenly there was a loud continuous knock at the door that echoed throughout the apartment. And the hangover was not helping me at all, as I rushed to open the door to see Wyala the Wood nymph Lila met last year in China.

She wore jeans and a hoodie to cover her wood-like skin, probably in the hopes to look like a random teenager wondering the halls.

She peered up at me excitedly smiling, "Hi Matt . . . do you remember me? I'm Wyala. We met in China after you were rescued from the dragon."

– Wow, could she say that any louder.

I grabbed the wood nymph's arm and pulled her inside, closing the door and telling her to shush then asked, "What the hell are you doing out in the open like this?"

"I was careful," she rebuked, "besides I came to give you information about Lila".

*Oh, dear. — I tried to break the news about Lila's death gently but she interjected, "No . . . she didn't die. My brothers have been watching over her in the dreamland. . . And she escaped from the island last night. . . And when Mother received the good news, she sent me here to tell you . . . I thought you'd be pleased."*

*What on God's green earth was she talking about?*

*I couldn't believe or understand what the Wood nymph was trying to say, and was obviously taking too long to process it as she repeated slowly, "Your wife Lila is still alive."*

*Right — I think I was in shock when I walked out of the apartment and led the Wood nymph up into Max's office and told her to tell Max the whole story.*

*Max just sat there nodding with his brows pinched together as Wyala told the story of Lila's courageous escape and how she had destroyed an entire island, rescuing and freeing who she could. Wyala then stated, "Mother is searching the neighbouring lands, but she believes something has gone wrong, and we are now here to ask for your help, and to make sure you do not go through with the goodbye ritual."*

*I still didn't believe the story, but somehow it piqued Max's interest, and when Adela walked into the office, things definitely got awkward. She too was puzzled and asked, "Wyala, what are you doing here?" greeting her with a hug.*

*Wyala then explained again and also added to Adela, "Mother said Lila's presence was found in the Mal'e islands. And it has since disappeared over the water which is where we ask for your help."*

*Max pulled up the Google maps on his computer as Adela asked the nymph for specifics. But I really had to interrupt there, yelling to gain the attention of the room, "Sorry . . . Sorry. Are you telling* me, you both believe this story? My wife's body is downstairs. Her funeral is being held today . . . How is this happening? How are you believing this?"

I was obviously still quite sceptical, and still with many questions, mainly at Adela.

Adela sighed and broke her news in a not so gentle way, "I think I may have had a vision of Lila last night. She was pale and unconscious, sinking to the bottom of the ocean . . . At first, I thought it was just a nightmare, so I brushed it off. But then it happened again and I saw Alex pulling her up from the water."

ALEX!! —— You've got to be kidding me.

I was still struggling to come to terms with everything and quietly mumbled, "Is that why you left this morning?"

"One of the reasons," she replied, glaring at me and then over to her father, who confusingly asked, "Have I missed something here?"

And we both answered simultaneously "No", before Chase walked into the office to inform us that the guest had arrived for Lila's funeral.

Great isn't this just perfect timing.

I turned to Max, hoping not to sound panicked when I asked, "What are we supposed to do now? We can't hold the funeral for Lila if she's still alive."

Adela then moved to stand in front of me to suggest, "Actually I think that's exactly what we should do . . . Someone went to a lot of trouble to make us believe Lila was dead. We still need to keep up that act, so no one suspects that we're still looking for her."

As Adela readied herself to leave, she wrote down the islands she could see on Google maps then on her way out of the office, she explained, "I need to make a quick run down to the park with Wyala. You boys should go and get ready for the funeral . . . And whatever you do, don't tell anyone about what we've discovered."

And like anyone would believe me.

Both Adela and Wyala disappeared, running at full speed out of the office, leaving Chase standing there confused as to what was happening.

I still felt confused myself needing to take a moment to compose myself before I walked out of the office and sarcastically grinned, "Let the show begin, then."

Quickly racing down to the apartment, I changed into my suit but before I left, I hesitated, glancing back at the wedding photo that was now scratched and crimpled by the broken glass and shoved it into my pocket along with my eulogy.

When I got down into the reception room, Adela had already returned and was waiting with Danny and Ruby for me at the front. The room was filled with random family and friends of Lila's parents, and quite a few from Hanna's church had attended. With two full rows of just the hotel security guards and retail staff. And to my surprise, Lila's old work colleagues Emma and Ali were sitting with the man Lila had nicknamed Big Mike—who seemed to be in a blubbery mess.

As I stood up to the podium to greet all the guest, I glimpsed over to see Richard sitting and comforting Hanna as she sat crying. And for some reason I got this dreadful gut-churning feeling in the pit of my stomach again as I cleared my throat. "Thank you all for coming to honour and remember my wife Lila Winters . . ."

## Journal entry insert by Terrence Connors

We had been in the water for hours. The sun was finally beginning to rise again and the warm glow was refreshing, but we were struggling. Alex and I were both growing very tired with our arms growing weaker by the minute from pulling Lila's body against the current as the dolphins dragged us along.

I peered across to see if Lila was okay, but she had pale blue lips and ice-cold skin. And I just felt powerless to help her. — I'd only just managed to get her back into my life, obviously not under the best of circumstance. But still, I have no plans on ever giving her up.

I was planning to say something to Alex, questioning what the plan was, but before I could, he quickly let go of the dolphins and shooed them away as he pointed to a small American Navy rescue boat heading our way. So, instead I helped to keep Lila afloat until the marines had pulled her from the water, and escorted all of us back to a US air carrier waiting in the distance.

But for a brief second when I stared into the water, I thought I saw two bright balls of light following us at a depth, but I just shook it off — claiming fatigue.

We were rushed down into the sickbay of the aircraft carrier with Lila their main priority, as the doctors frantically tried to stabilise, and stop the bleeding from her stomach wound — again. All while the others assisted us with a change of clothes and a hot drink.

The hours passed and Lila's heartbeat had slowly become stronger and stable, but she remained unconscious with pale white skin. She was hooked up to yet another blood bag to try and replenish what she had lost. But all I focused on was her heart beating and kept whispering to myself, "She can't die. . . she promised me that she wouldn't."

When the doctor finished taking Lila's blood pressure, he looked over to see Alex asleep resting against the wall next to me. I think the doctor may have noticed that we were taking it in shifts to watch Lila, and were not all that comfortable with their MPs standing guard.

"Your friend's starting to get her colour back," the doctor whispered, "It's a good thing we found you when we did. . . She looks exhausted. How long has she been in the water like that?"

"All night," I sighed trying to mask my yawn.

The doctor then quietly walked around the bed and placed a blanket over Alex as he whispered, "Well, she's lucky to be alive. You did a good job holding onto her for so long."

Yeah well —— No offence to anyone — but I'd hold onto Lila for an eternity if that's what it took.

# Original journal entry
## continued by Adela Eden

Chase and I stood close to Matt, Danny and Ruby as they said their farewells to the guests after the reception. Many of the guests commented on the heartfelt eulogy and that Lila was such a kind and gentle soul. But I could tell something was getting to Matt, then as Hanna and Richard came up to say their goodbyes, Matt's entire body tensed up.

"Matt . . . beautiful service . . . Your eulogy was very touching," Richard commented with what looked like a practised smile and a tear in his eye. But he quickly had to excuse himself when his phone began to vibrate.

As he stepped away, Hanna commented dotingly, "Always work with that man . . . he's been back all of 12 hours and has been glued to that phone since he landed. He hasn't even had time to grieve . . . Lila was everything to Richard . . . it was even his idea for her to come and live with us when her parents passed."

Matt nodded, pretending to understand, and asked if Richard was staying for dinner. But Hanna declined for him, and her response definitely gained my interest when she explained, "From what I've heard from his phone calls, one of his base camps has been ambushed and the entire site has been destroyed. Richard's been called back to work his PR magic to keep certain interested parties at bay."

Hhmm – An entire base camp destroyed, what was it that Wyala said—something like, "Lila destroyed an Island." Which is actually really impressive but clearly not impossible for Lila.

That information definitely intrigued me, so I decided to eavesdrop on Richard's phone conversation, but it sounded scrambled with a high-pitched hum. It's a sound that I've heard before – Mission control uses it to speak to their field agents, preventing other guardians from listening in.

The puzzle pieces all started to fit into perfect place – a military man who trained Lila since she was a baby. His actions were sketchy, and he showed no grief or remorse over Lila's death, which meant he must have known she wasn't dead – or didn't care.

"He's one of them," I whispered.

Chase must have heard me though and confusingly asked, "What are you talking about?"

But when he turned to face me, I had already disappeared.

I decided to cash in a few favours, to try and delay the General from leaving town for a few days. And I very eagerly waited at the Hotel's reception desk to watch my triumph as Detective George Nell stopped Richard in the lobby and requested that he be escorted back to the station for questioning, after he was found to be carrying illegal drugs and an unregistered firearm.

My grin was so wide when I quietly boasted, "That should hold him for a few days," then I continued to watch as Richard was unwillingly escorted into a waiting police car.

Oh, if only Lila could see him now.

# CHAPTER 11

# UNKNOWN ALLIES

*Journal entry by Lila Winters*

It was the middle of the night when I finally woke up. My vision was blurry and I looked around to realise that I was in some kind of medical room with Alex and Terrence asleep either side of me, holding my hands. They both looked very tired and very worried.

I didn't know what was going on and I really hoped that we were safe, but for some reason amongst the silence of the night, I could hear this loud whispering in my head.

I scanned the room to find where it was coming from, and when I looked at the small window across the room, I could have sworn I saw a man – or a fish – or a fish-man. But when the doctor came over to check my vitals, the fish-man disappeared into a blue light.

Weird?

The doctor moved quietly around me, trying not to wake Alex or Terrence, whispering "Hey, it's good to see you're awake."

It was interesting, he reminded me of the medical staff from one of the Australian Army bases that I had visited when I was younger. That is until I looked at the uniform he wore. Underneath his doctor's coat, I saw the horrid colours and realised why he looked like a military man — because he was.

Oh, Fracitty Frac, Frac.

He explained to me where I was — and it was no surprise that it did not comfort me.

As he spoke to me though, the whispering in my head became louder, and I became agitated as I heard the whispering voice say, "Run Lila . . . Run."

So I did — I pulled my hands away from the boys in a rush, trying to pull out the tubes and cords that were attached to me. The doctor tried to stop me before I could pull out the blood bag and urged me to calm down, still I was determined. But in the scuffle I woke Alex and Terrence, who began to help the doctor try to restrain me and calm me down.

What the—?

The whispering got louder and I was freaking out, struggling to understand why Alex and Terrence were helping them. — Oh Frac, what if they've been turned?

I heard Alex say to the doctor something about my nose bleeding, and it was also when my vision became blurry again. But the whispers in my head had turned into a loud screeching sound as well, and I held my ears in pain, realising that they too had begun to bleed. Only causing Alex and Terrence to freak out even more.

My fear had reached the breaking point, so I used all the force I could muster to push Alex and Terrence away then ran at a semi-half speed, still disoriented and in a weakened state pushing the MPs standing guard to the sidewall as I passed them. —— Obviously not that weak.

The ship was brought to high alert as the crew all worked to try and track me, but I was too quick for them, dodging in and out of corridors, and hiding amongst bulkheads and storage cabins. It was a good thing I had been on a carrier ship before, I easily recognised the layout.

Eventually, I managed to borrow one of the female crew's fitness uniforms and changed out of the hospital thing they had me in. But my vision began to blur again as I heard this loud piercing noise in my head causing me to scream. The scream was so loud it echoed throughout the ship. – And that definitely doesn't help when you're trying to hide.

I waited until the corridor was clear, taking a deep breath in before I used all the energy I had to run at full speed through the passageways and out onto the flight deck.

With the night air biting my skin, I just kept running as fast as I could along the airstrip towards the ocean. But when I reached the side of the airstrip, I froze in fear, looking around at where I was. – Surrounded by water – with no land in sight. – And this was a very bad idea.

Naturally I started to panic, and the fear only rose in me as I heard the screeching noise in my head, when suddenly I saw this ball of blue light burst up from the water heading straight towards me.

## Journal entry insert by Alex Woods

After Lila's sudden display of strength and physical agility, the MPs were on high alert and no longer trusted us. Holding us at gunpoint in the sickbay while their crew searched for Lila.

We were originally happy to comply and stay put even after we had offered to help. But when Terrence and I heard Lila's scream, we both knew what we had to do. So, moving at full speed, all four MPs were unconscious on the floor as both of us disappeared.

I used my tracking senses to find her, and it led us up out on to the top deck, where we found Lila standing at the very end of the ship, not far from the edge. She was acting chaotic, holding her head in pain and I raced to pull her to safety. I saw her eyes glowing a glorious green blue as she tried to pull away from me in a panic.

So, in the hopes to calm her, my eyes glowed slightly gold, "Lila stop! It's me! It's Alex!"

But she broke though the charm I was using, then held her head in pain again as her nose began to bleed. "Argh!! Stop please stop. It Hurts!".

It gutted me seeing her in pain and not knowing what to do. Still I held on to her and pleadingly asked, "Lila tell me what's wrong . . .What hurts?"

Then using all of her strength, she pulled free of the hold I had on her and stared back at us with eyes glowing a brighter blue – like headlights in the night. And it wasn't long before we were surrounded by marines all yelling at us to get down on the ground.

Terrence shouted back at them, begging them to give me a minute to calm Lila down. But the marines didn't respond well when they saw Lila's eyes glowing, as well as her nose and ears beginning to bleed more, and she held her stomach as she coughed up blood.

Eventually the coughing stopped and she stared back at me before she fell unconscious.

I managed to catch her before she went over the edge and pulled her back to safety as I laid her down on the ground, complying with the marine's orders. It was then I heard Terrence whisper to get my attention and discreetly pointed to the blood Lila had coughed up where a small shiny red stone was hidden. When I realised what it was, I looked up to inspect Lila's neck to see that her tribal marking had disappeared.

In shock, I discreetly peered over to Terrence and asked, "What the hell's happening to her?"

But he shrugged his shoulder, looking just as ignorant as I was, concerningly staring at Lila.

We then both freaked a little when Lila opened her eyes and stared at me. I was confused, and watched as her glowing blue eyes reduced to a faint light glow around the rim of her iris.

She then stood up and spoke – clear as day to the marines holding us at gunpoint and said, "They're here . . .," then pointed across the water to the three warships approaching us at a rapid speed, in the dead of night.

Judging by the reactions of the marines, I guessed correctly when I assumed, they were not expected and they were not friendly. We were also very quickly ushered back off the airstrip and isolated. With Lila escorted back to the sickbay, and Terrence and I locked in the brig with the captain's orders of "If they move – shoot them."

# Original journal entry continued by Lila Winters

Well, I'm back in the med-bay again, and they've now restrained me to the bed with handcuffs as a precaution.

I was pretending to be asleep while I watched who I think to be the Commander, rummage through my old bloodied clothes looking for something, and he became puzzled when he found the large tree stone wrapped in cloth and hidden in a zipped pocket.

That worried me, but what worried me more – was what was going on inside me. – I mean I felt like me but didn't – there was someone else controlling my actions and my emotions. And honestly, I just felt like a passenger. It was very similar to the time when I had to fight Adela to rescue my family – but again different. I mean I definitely wasn't in the dreamland this time. At least I don't think I am.

The Commander had grown impatient at the doctor's inability to give the right answers after she had run a dozen test and scans on me. It was interesting and very telling to see the first doctor, the male doctor who was originally treating my injuries was all of a sudden very distant and very quiet.

But he occasionally glanced at me as this other female doctor tried to explain to the Commander, stating "Sir, I don't know what she is . . . She has no markings or implants in her, and there's no way to tell if she's the one they're looking for, but her blood work did come back positive. So it's possible."

The Commander looked out the porthole at the three warships and groaned, "If this girl really is the one they're after, then she's strong enough to destroy an island in less than a day . . . I'm not just going to hand over such a valuable asset willingly."

He then stormed out of the sickbay, taking the tree stone with him as one of the MPs walked back into the sickbay to check my restraints. I don't know why but I felt compelled to open my eyes fully to look at him. He was slyly smiling at me and seemed very calm around me, which was more than I could say for his cowardly friends in the hall.

But when I looked at him closer, I noticed his eyes had a faint blue glow around the rim of his iris. And when he looked into my eyes, I could hear the whispering again, I couldn't understand it but it was there. Then when the doctor walked past the bed again, I quickly closed my eyes and the MP stood back against the wall.

Looks like now, all I had to do was wait. For what? – I had no idea.

## Journal entry insert by Alex Woods

We've been locked in the brig for hours now. I sat down leaning against the bars, eyeing off Terrence as he paced around the cell and occasionally peeked out the porthole, trying to get a better view of the warships.

Eventually I grew tired of waiting and questioned, "What do you think they're waiting for?"

But his answer didn't feel me with much confidence as he replied, "They're most likely negotiating . . . John's probably made up some lie about us being wanted fugitives and demanded our return to his custody to face criminal charges . . . and all that bull."

"You seem to have quite the knowledge of this process," I snickered, "Tell me, how does it feel to be the one being hunted for a change?"

I don't think he took that question too well and grimaced at me. So, I asked again, "What was it that really made you switch sides?"

But again, I got no answer, he just kept staring out the porthole, and I just kept glaring at him and stated, "Well, it seems fairly obvious that you haven't been cured of the Neuritamine, seeing how you have all your memories . . ."

"I was never under the influence of Neuritamine," he snapped briefly glaring back at me, "and neither was Lila. That drug doesn't affect Nature guardians."

I leaned forward and kept staring at him in my own judgemental way, and he could definitely tell I blamed him for this entire mess. So he stopped pacing and stood in front of me, trying to defend his actions, "Alex, you have no idea who I am, and you can't even begin to imagine the reasons why I did everything you currently think I'm responsible for . . . I'm sure you already know why my kind are so rare . . . and I was a child when I was taken to that island . . . I did what I had to do, to survive."

I got up and towered over him – slightly glad I was taller by just a little bit, and judged Terrence intimidatingly, then I broke the silence. "Look man, sob story or not, I just don't like you . . . or trust you . . . but surprisingly I have been in your position before."

He looked at me in disbelief as if I had gone mad, but I continued my spiel, explaining how Lila and I first met and how Matt didn't trust me at first, then I stated, "The only reason why Matt put up with me was because he trusted Lila . . . so in case you're wondering, the only reason why I haven't pummelled your arse into next year is because for some reason Lila trusts you . . . but the moment you cross her . . . it will be open season for your self-righteous and arrogant face."

He wisely nodded, accepting my not-so-subtle threat then went back to pacing, and as he did, I noticed there was no tribal markings on his neck and was reminded of Lila's suddenly disappearing.

When I questioned Terrence about it, he seemed cagey as if he knew something about the ruby stone and what link it had to Lila's tribal mark disappearing. So, I pressed him further, "What happened to Lila's tribal mark and why don't you have one?"

My constant questioning caused him to get upset and he griped, "Let me guess, you learnt to ask the pointed questions from Lila?"

I nodded seeing how it was true, she is quite stubborn when it comes to finding the truth and everything else. But I still kept staring at him until Terrence caved, clearly realising that I had no plans in dropping the subject.

"The tribal mark, as you say, is not a birthmark like everyone is told. It's a branding created by The Board and distributed amongst its collection agencies. . . The mark you have on your neck was adopted by The Board from the old Viking tactics . . . They too were the collectors of their day . . . Your marking means 'fate' and the rope used to encompass the symbol means sealed."

I was almost in disbelief of his explanation, but considering I had already been lied to by Mission control, it didn't seem that farfetched. So I stayed quiet and listened to Terence continue. "The Marking-stones and it's branding make it easier for The Boards hunters. . . like myself, to discern who has already been collected and who they're owned by . . . I never received one because I was collected as a child and was deemed the property of one of the CEO's private collection, Mr and Mrs Connors. . . And instead of being given the Marking-stone, I was branded with their name . . . just like Lila was."

He stopped his speech and glanced back at me to make sure I was following along then sarcastically asked, "You happy . . . or are you still confused."

I was kind of following along, but I still had to ask, "Wait, if Lila was branded with a name then why did she get a Marking-stone?"

He smiled back and told me my questions were surprisingly not that dumb, as he went on to explain, "While Lila was in a similar circumstance to me, having already been collected by General Richard. The man did encounter certain difficulties in maintaining his legitimate claim to her, given that he was not yet a CEO when she was acquired. . . Instead he married into the family and took on the Willows family name in order to maintain blood right . . . if a guardian is born into the family of an already existing Board member or organisation, the child is deemed off limits to all other interested parties and collectors. . . Lila is obviously quite stubborn . . . and once she changed her name Richard lost his claim."

I took a moment to properly absorb all of what Terrence had explained, and I felt sick to my stomach, realising the horrible truth but I again had to ask, "One more question. . . if mission control is part of The Board's network, then why did they pin us against you?"

It was clear that I had asked yet another pointed question, because I heard him sigh under his breath, "Lila taught you well." He then stared out the window and answered, "Your organisation. . . Mission control was only recently acquired by The Board, and in order to reduce the risk of other political parties immediately shutting down the program, they placed agents to work from within the organisation and slowly gain control of its agenda."

"Agent John," I snickered, wanting confirmation.

Terrence nodded to confirm but wanted to add one more horrifying piece of information, and turned to me, grinning as he asked, "Do you know what Agent John's last name is?"

"Yeah, it's some German name like Jaeger. . . Agent John Jaeger."

He nodded again to confirm then chuckled, "The General's real last name is Jaeger. . . General Richard Jaeger . . . And while you believe you were sent to Lila's house to protect her. You were merely a pawn used by the Jaegers and Mission control to trick Lila into coming back, and willingly work for the General again. . . To them you were just another hunter. Tasked to collect her before she was collected by any of the other Board members. . . like my master . . . Only Richard's plan backfired on him because he wasn't expecting Lila to have an amazingly strong moral compass. . . She's also not easily fooled . . . unlike us."

I very much wanted to be sick and struggled to come to terms with everything he had said, realising that I had been a fool this whole time, and that I was a Hunter like him.

Clearly, I was blinded to the truth – Was everything I stood for a lie?

## Original journal entry continued by Lila Winters

I was beginning to grow impatient of waiting for – something – anything to happen. I mean I'm not the kind of person to sit around and wait for the war to come to me. I wanted to go home – I wanted to see my kids and my husband – I wanted to tell them I was sorry.

When the Commander finally walked back into the sickbay, he was staring at some files and looked surprisingly perplexed as he stood at the end of my bed and arrogantly spoke, "So here's the deal. I'm going to ask some questions and you're going to answer them. . . If you answer them truthfully, I'll take you to see your friends."

Alright – that was hilarious it's as if he was expecting me to just do as I'm told.

What an idiot.

"Counter-offer," I replied trying to hold back my laugh. "You ask a question and I answer . . . Then I ask a question and you answer, sound fair?"

The Commander needed to take a moment, probably sizing up how stubborn I am – and the answer is <u>VERY</u>. He then crossed his arms and caved as he sighed, "Fair . . . let's start with who you are."

I sat up in the bed and smirked wryly answering, "My name is Lila Winters and my 2 friends are Alex Woods and Terrence Connors. But you already knew that . . ."

The Commander nodded and agreed, "Yes, I know all about your friends. We have files filled with information about them. . . But when I went looking for your file, nothing came up, absolutely nothing. . . It's as if you were deleted from our system. . . So I ask you again who are you?"

Frac – files and systems, I've heard those words before, and I'm pretty sure he wasn't talking about the Department of Human Services or medical records or anything remotely along those nice lines.

Play it cool, Lila. – Play it cool.

"You know who I am . . . just like I know who you are," I answered, and that was a total bluff but I'm not letting him know that, and I smilingly questioned, "So why isn't your crew playing nicely with the other warships?"

It was beginning to be very telling that The Board obviously didn't play nice with each other when it came to valuable objects or apparently assets like myself. – Great they're fighting over a girl – What's new in the world of war.

The Commander could definitely tell I was playing hardball when he huffed, "Because they're warships and they're not mine . . . why do your eyes have that blue glow?"

He was starting to grow suspicious of my calm demeanour, and it didn't help when I answered, "I don't know . . . I can't really see them at the moment."

As suspected, he didn't like vagueness and scowled at me, trying to figure out if I had a tell, but so far, I hadn't lied – so there was nothing to tell. He then whispered, "You're lying."

And with a chuckle and replied ever so calmly, "Am I?"

– That's actually one thing that Richard had going for him, when I was growing up – and I know it's sad but I learnt how to lie – by not lying. – I also learnt how to deal with arrogant Jarheads as well.

The Commander pulled the tree stone out from his pocket, holding it in front of me. It was so large it filled his hand and he demanded "Tell me about this."

"It's a seed," I replied. – It didn't help that when he moved it closer to me it started glowing a bright-green hue, like it was a freaking Nature guardian detector.

Still he kept staring at me in the hopes that I would tell him more, but instead I replied again, "It's just a seed."

Yes, well he clearly wasn't liking how I played his games, and he grinned before replying, "Well, if that's the case, you won't mind me giving this seed back to the warships, who claim you stole it after destroying their training camp."

He then stared at me to see my reaction as I watched him place it back in his pocket.

Now, keeping in mind, that I'm still not in full control of my body. I'm still a passenger, as I watched myself break free of the handcuff and move at full speed to stand in front of the Commander, seething, "Sorry Commander, but I can't let you do that."

The two MPs standing in the hallway heard the commotion and rushed in with guns drawn, aiming at me and waiting for their orders, but the third MP, the one standing guard next to my bed – he hesitated and for a brief moment he looked scared.

"Hand over the seed or I'll destroy your ship," I threatened.

But the Commander looked around at all the guns aimed at me and decided to call my bluff, shaking his head as he said, "No,"

I stood calmly, eyeing off the Commander as my eyes glowed a bright blue and the sweat on my skin turned to ice. The ice began to grow along the floor and walls of the ship toward the Commander and the others. But again, I stayed calm, only causing their fear rise.

"No . . . That's not possible," the Commander gasped, fearfully watching the ice grow up and around his legs. He stared outside the porthole window to see a large wave barrelling towards the ship and knocking it sideways, causing the boat to rock ferociously.

The ship's crew were then thrown around like dolls as the waves kept on coming, and it was hilarious to watch such an arrogant man fearfully try to keep his balance, and break free from the ice that had him trapped where he stood.

My eyes glowed brighter, and suddenly the boat started to spin and rise up from the water as a water tornado grew from beneath the boat.

The Commander eventually bellowed, "Don't just stand there. Shoot her" at the MPs, but when they opened fire, the bullets were embedded into the protective ice layer on my skin.

*Okay – so that's Fraccing Cool.*

I watched as the MP who guarded my bed rush to aid the Commander and help him break free from the ice. I was smiling as I surveyed the chaos, but for a brief moment, my mind was distracted as I thought about the safety of Alex and Terrence.

And in the moments before I blacked out, I saw the female doctor hurtling towards me with her fist covered in a steel plating, punching my face.

I then heard the Commander scream, "Throw her in the brig with the others."

Well eventually he said it – after the ship had plunged back down into the water, spinning uncontrollably to a stop.

*Cool – I didn't know I could do that.*

## Journal entry insert by Alex Woods

I'm not going to lie. After the roller coaster of whatever the hell that was, had finished, I was seasick, and it was really bad.

"What the hell was that!" I grumbled to Terrence in between hurls.

But he looked worse than me, curled up in the corner nursing his head as he threw up as well.

Our attitudes quickly changed though, and we stood defensively as we watched Lila being carried in unconscious on a stretcher bed, sporting a new bruise across her face.

One of the MPs carrying her complained about getting a cramp in his hand, letting go of Lila's stretcher bed. And as she fell towards the ground, the MP moved at full speed, shooting ice from his hands and burying the other guards under a mound of snow then caught Lila before she hit the ground.

Why the hell was he touching my Lila – I mean – touching Lila?

The MP pulled her close to him and studied her to see if she was okay. He ran his finger around the bruise on her face, which for some reason worried the guy a lot.

I admit I was a little overwhelmed with protective jealousy as I demanded him to get away from her. But he just stood up in a huff and unlocked the cell doors, then picked Lila back up and cradled her in his arms as he ordered us to follow him.

We all ran at full speed – including the MP, through the corridors of the ship, and as we ran, I noticed the crew members were all distracted, fixing and patching the ship.

The MP led us to where the emergency rescue boats were held in the lower hangar. And when we entered, we all hid amongst one of the side beams while Terrence and I confusingly watched as the MP gently rested Lila up against the wall. It was almost as if he cared for her.

There were two marines working in the room to check over the boats and make sure they were secure. So staying quiet, the MP stood up getting ready to sneak away, but turned back and told us to be quiet and to look after Lila. -- And like I have to be told that.

We stayed hidden and kept watch as the MP casually walked up to the marines to talk. And it became harder and harder for us to determine if this guy was on our side or not – until he clocked one of the marines over the head, and threw the other against the wall where we were hiding.

"Who the hell is this guy?" I whispered back to Terrence as I moved to pick Lila up and carried her onto the boats.

Once we were safely in the rescue-boat the MP quietly lowered it down into the water then jumped from the hangar onto the boat without a care. His eyes glowed a bright blue, similar to Lila's back on the flight deck, then suddenly the water current started pulling us gently and silently away from the ship.

When we had gotten far enough away from the air-carrier, the MP started up the engines of the rescue boat and asked Terrence to steer, because apparently this MP doesn't know how the boat works. – Seriously? – He's a marine.

Either way Terrence knew what to do, so the MP instructed him to travel in the direction of the two brightest stars overhead until sunrise – because that really comforted me – NOT.

Yet again, we were being taken to an unknown location by a weird military guy, who seemed to have a thing for my Lila – I mean for Lila. – I really have to fix that.

But still – How is any of this okay?

I sat at the front of the boat holding Lila, trying to keep her warm and became very protective of her when the MP knelt down next to us. He didn't say a word to me and didn't even look at me. He just stared at Lila with worry and fear in his eyes.

I told him not to touch her but he didn't listen. Instead he held both of Lila's hands against his and closed his eyes, chanting in some weird foreign language. It sounded Greek but very old Greek. And as he did Lila's body started to glow a bright blue, and I watched in confused amazement as she opened her eyes and looked up at the MP smiling.

What weirded me out even more was that they both hugged each other and both spoke to each other in that same weird old Greek language. – What the HELL.

And then I snapped and yelled, "What the hell is going on here?!"

– Not surprisingly I seem pretty good at speaking my mind these days. Although I think one day soon it will bite me in the arse.

I waited for any kind of response from them, until Lila just gazed at me and smiled, replying, "Alex, please stay calm. We are nearly at the mainland. You will have all of your answers there." But when she spoke it was echoey and it didn't sound like her.

I wanted to argue back – I wanted to ask more questions – and I was beginning to fear that we had willingly walked into a trap, and that Lila had actually been mind-wiped and turned into a minion of whatever the hell this guy was.

But I didn't argue or question, because I kept sensing this vibe from Lila as if she was trying to tell me that everything was going to be okay. So instead I stormed off and sat at the back of the boat and watched as Lila was hugged by this other guy.

When we finally reached land – India according to the MP, the sun was just rising on the horizon. The boat pulled up to the empty beach, and Terrence and I jumped out into the water to hold the boat steady while the MP helped Lila out of the boat. But before he did, he pulled Lila close and gave her a passionate over-the-top kiss goodbye.

And that definitely did not sit well with me or Terrence, as we looked at each other in sheer confusion. I mean come-on – Was Lila actually willing to seduce a man into helping us escape?

.

As the boat began to make its way back out to sea, Lila watched from the sandbank then turned to us and said, "Hurry, we need to hide," but again it was with the echoey voice as she started walking up towards the trees. Until Terrence demanded, "STOP!!!" raising his hand towards Lila. And as he did roots grew from the ground in front of Lila to block her.

She stopped and slowly turned to look at Terrence as he forcefully yelled, "Where's Lila!" Well he obviously wasn't fooled either, and waited for Lila to answer, but she remained quiet just staring at us. So, he repeated again in a more threatening tone, "We know you're not Lila, so I will ask again . . . where is she?"

"She is here," Lila replied with the echoing voice, "Please, Terry . . . We are only trying to help."

Something that Lila said in her reply, caused Terrence to waver, and he grew short of breath not knowing what to do. So, I stepped forward and demanded, "If you want to help then show yourself."

I briefly glanced back at Terrence and asked if he was alright, and he nodded, but we both then gawked in complete surprise as a glowing blue water began to seep out of Lila's skin, wrapping around her body. The glowing water then pulled away from Lila, forming a new female shaped body of water, leaving Lila breathless and confused.

The fear in Lila caused her to tremble as she looked at Terrence and then to me, and struggled to say my name before she fainted.

I rushed to help her and yelled at the water thing, "What did you do to her?"

And the water thing replied, only this time her voice sounded like an echo of many voices all at once, "We did nothing to her . . . We simply wanted to help her."

Terrence, just as confused and panicked as I was, asked, "And who are we?"

"We are the spirits of the sea . . . the life force that drives the ocean. We felt Lila's fear when she fell into our waters, but by the time we had arrived to help you, the humans had already rescued you. . . .We went aboard their vessel to ensure her safety. We were about to leave when we discovered who Lila really was . . . It was then we had no choice but to save her."

Who Lila really was – what was that supposed to mean.

I was failing to wake Lila as I listened to the water thing and asked, "What's wrong with her now?"

The water thing slowly leaned down, placing her hand on Lila's forehead and replied, "Lila's fear is paralysing her. . .When we first tried to help her, she was confounded by something unknown to us. I took over her body and pushed her mind into a meditative state so she would be calm. . . I am unsure as to why she is not waking up."

Right – I glanced around to see the obvious environment that was fuelling Lila's fear, and I quickly scooped her up into my arms, muttering, "We have to get her off the beach," as I hurried her towards the tree line.

As suspected Terrence just looked at me confused and asked, "Why?"

But I didn't answer him. I just listened to the water thing explain, "There is a small hut at the end of the path where one of your Elders dwells. She will help you get home."

Then before Terrence followed me off the beach, he thanked the Water thing as it returned back into the ocean.

# CHAPTER 12

# I'LL BE HOME FOR . . .

*Journal entry by Lila Winters*

I woke up again in yet another strange bed with Alex and Terrence asleep on either side of me, holding my hands. This was beginning to feel like déjà vu, only this time I was not in a boat or a hospital – which was a wonderful relief.

I quietly and very carefully got up from the bed, as to not wake Terrence or Alex, and wandered around what seemed like an island hut with the walls held up by bamboo and a leafy roof. But I was quickly filled with dread when my eyes stared at the object in the middle of the hut. It was a small Christmas tree, surrounded by presents. And a tear rolled down my cheek as I watched the lights flicker.

My sniffles must have woken Alex because he quickly appeared next to me, holding my hands in his as he asked, "Lila, are you alright?"

"I didn't realise it was Christmas . . ." I whispered. But before I could say anything more, John interrupted, standing at the door of the hut, stating, "It's Christmas eve actually."

Terrence awoke from the sound of John's egotistical voice and stood defensively next to me and Alex, glaring at John as he smiled back at me and pompously commented, "That was a neat trick you pulled there, cousin. Sneaking off in the dead of night . . . Father would be very proud. . . It was also very convenient for me, seeing how my ships were watching you at the time."

John's arrogancy radiated from him as he completely disregarded Alex and Terrence's protective demeanour of me. It only caused him more joy to be challenged and he continued to talk directly to me. "I am actually very curious, as to who was really responsible for that brilliant water display . . . because for some reason the Commander swears that his boat was almost destroyed by a small, insignificant, and very annoying nature freak . . . and we all know that's not possible."

His grating voice was annoying, but I couldn't get over the fact that he called me cousin. I mean I knew he reminded me of Richard – and that's probably why I never trusted him or liked him. But to hear him call me family only made me want to hate more, for what he did.

I didn't answer him, and John grew tired of waiting for one of us to respond, but we were all a little busy analysing the best possible escape plan.

I think he picked up on it though, and he chuckled as he sneered, "No . . . alright then, I guess I'll get my answers the hard way . . . come on then, Lila. Let's not keep Father waiting," he then held his hand out towards me expecting me to do as I'm told.

But Terrence stood in front of me, still glaring at John as he seethed, "She's not going anywhere with you."

I like the fact that even after my terrible escape plan went horribly wrong Terrence was still willing to stand up and fight – I think he was determined to get me home again.

John however, revelled in the challenge and pulled out a gun, threatening Terrence with it. I wanted to help Terrence but Alex held me back. So, all I could do was listen to John mockingly boast, "Now isn't this a sweet sight . . . your mother will be so proud of you, Terrence . . . Falling in love with your assignment, and if the rumours are true, you slept with her as well . . .Hmm. . . I hope she was worth it?"

Again, he got no response. Not even Alex reacted, although I did feel him tense a little while holding my hand. But I was sure he knew better of me – I would never break the promise I made to Matt.

Either way, the silence said everything for John, knowing he wasn't going to get to me with Terrence in the way, and he mockingly tittered. "Well, at least I can take comfort in the fact that I was the one who finally got to kill the golden boy. .

. but don't worry I'll make sure your mother knows where your loyalties really lay."

It was like John was trying to goad Terrence into moving, but when he didn't, John fired his weapon. He missed though because Alex had moved at full speed at the last minute, pulling Terrence out of the way. We then all stood in a huddle, with Terrence and Alex covering me as we cautiously waited for the next gunshot.

But instead we heard the gun drop to the floor, and we all looked up to see John standing there in shock, staring down at a large branch that had been driven through his chest by one of the outside trees. Blood started gushing from his mouth as he fell to the ground, drawing his last breath with his eyes staring up at me.

FLYING FRUIT CAKES AND HONEY BADGERS—that seriously just happened.

Terrence knelt down to check his pulse. "He's dead . . .," he gasped then looked back at me and asked, "did you?"

But it looked like he was in shock at the thought that I would ever intentionally kill a person. – I mean sure, John was a real prick of a human being – but I'm no killer.

I shook my head answering Terrence's question, and I too was in shock staring at him, mainly because I thought it was Terrence who did it.

But there was a wave of relief when we saw an old female wood nymph appear at the door and claim, "I did." – Oh, Thank God.

I ran to hug her so tightly as I took a joyful breath. "Agetha . . .," I then looked at her with tear-filled eyes, excited to see her not in the dream land, "I am so happy to see you and . . ."

I was about to ask her how she found us until I looked outside to see an old woman – who I now know to be Lisa – guarding 16 unconscious Board agents swinging upside down in the trees. I couldn't help but chuckle. Agetha certainly did have style.

She held my hands and her lips pulled into a gentle smile as she said the words that I so desperately wanted to hear, "I think it's time for you to go home."

Yep – the perfect words – go home.

Agetha then led Terrence, Alex and myself through the jungle to find a very old and large twisted tree. She placed her hand on the trunk of the tree and closed her eyes, waiting for a white-glowing portal to appear in the middle of the tree where the trunk had twisted.

It startled Alex and he stood back, fearfully asking, "What the hell is that?"

She turned and answered with a smile, "This is a portal that is connected through its root system to the many different trees throughout the world. . . Wyala is waiting on the other side of one of the Melbourne trees for you . . . Now quickly, the portal will not stay open for long . . . Oh, and Merry Christmas."

My smile was so wide, and I was incredibly thankful to Agetha, hugging her before I held out my hands to Alex and Terrence, and waited for them to hesitantly take it. Then we walked through the portal together.

The journey through the portal was fast, and it felt like we were in a spiralling roller coaster, going up and down and sideways. And when we emerged on the other side, I was greeted with a very tight hug by an over-excited Wyala knocking me to the ground.

The pain was excruciating as I gasped, "Ow, bruised . . . Ow still sore . . . stitches . . . stitches!"

I needed Alex to intervene and pull her away. – Obviously, I was still not strong enough for those kinds of hugs.

Wyala stepped back apologising and explaining how worried she was about me, while Alex and Terrence both kindly helped me to my feet, as I replied, "It's okay, Wyala. I'm glad to see you too."

I peered around at the dark field we were standing in, slowly realising where we were, and that we had just stepped out of a portal from a large old willow tree.

"Is this . . . the Willow Farm?" Alex muttered.

And I excitedly nodded, because we were home. – Well almost because this was not my home. But we're a hell of a lot closer now.

"We did it," I whispered with an excited squeal.

I then tried to run at full speed up to the house but I couldn't. I wasn't sure why, maybe it was because of my injuries. Instead, Alex helped me to walk up to the house. Then as I walked through the house, I called out for Hanna but there was no one there.

I also noticed Alex and Terrence were still on high alert, looking around, and given that this was General's house, I wasn't surprised.

"Do you think anyone's home?" Alex asked.

"They shouldn't be" I replied, "Every year my family attends the Christmas carols in the city. If Matt was smart, he would have invited Hanna. . . you know to keep her from worrying"

My eyes scanned around the house and I then smiled rebelliously at the boys. "I have an idea . . ." I grinned, cheekily biting my bottom lip. – I like this plan – I like it a lot.

And I very happily half-skipped bearing though the pain, to make my way outside to the garage door, lifting it to reveal a very nice and shiny red 1965 classic Ford Mustang, hidden beneath its car cover. – This was Richard's baby – his pride and joy and I was looking forward to leaving it in one of the worst crime-ridden suburbs of Melbourne as part of my revenge.

I think Alex could tell I had something deviously horrible planned for this car as he sat in the passenger side, staring me, and almost regretting staying quiet. He really did like his cars. Terrence and Wyala then jumped in the back seats and buckled up before I sped down the driveway onto the road. Not caring if I kicked up rocks or accidently scratched something.

## Journal entry insert by Matt Winters

We had just arrived back at the hotel after finishing at the Carols by Candlelight. It was an amazing night and the music and singers were fantastic, especially the fireworks display at the end. But this year it just felt different – it felt – empty.

I walked through the lobby of the hotel holding Danny and Ruby's tired little hands as Max and the team followed in behind. Max thought the carols would be a good distraction for the team, but he was wrong. He looked around to see Adela and Jess's sad long faces, with Chase following behind them struggling to keep it together. – Lila and Chase were a really good team when it came to looking after the hotel – he really respected Lila.

As we walked through the lobby, we heard the chime of the Melbourne church bells ring, telling the world that it was Christmas. But no one wanted to celebrate this year.

I was trying to keep it together, be the strong one for my kids, and hide the tears from them, needing to turn away sometimes. But when I heard the elevators open Danny and Ruby let go of my hands, and started running as they saw Lila step out of the elevator and wave to them with Alex and Wyala standing behind her.

The team heard the cries of Danny and Ruby shouting the word "MUMMY!" and we looked up to see them wrapping their arms around her. Then in joyful shock we all of us rushed to greet her with a group hug.

Hanna looked up from the hug and saw Alex standing with Wyala looking tired and dishevelled. It was clear to Hanna that they were responsible for saving her baby girl, so she reached her hand out and pulled them in to join the group hug.

Surprisingly she didn't react to the way Wyala's wood-like skin appeared. Maybe she was distracted by Joy.

But there was someone else standing behind them, watching the group all hugging Lila and looking very guilty – feeling like this was all his fault – which it was.

He looked like he was just about to leave when Lila broke free from the group and grabbed his hand to stop him, whispering, "Terrence."

What on earth was she doing?

It was weird. She just stood there and smiled at him, holding his hand. "Please stay . . . It's a tradition in my family to celebrate with pancakes for breakfast . . . and I'd really love it if you could join us."

She did not just do that? –– What on earth is wrong with her?

He tentatively glanced back at the group, and I was pretty sure he picked up on the tension around him, but when Lila said "Please" he nodded, following her back into the elevator.

Huh – I guess a lot had happened while she was gone.

Nonetheless, we were all happy to have Lila back, safe and sound. But I'm not sure how I'm supposed to feel, because while we were all in the apartment I watched as Lila, Alex and Terrence made stacks of Pancakes for everyone.

Lila had the biggest smile on her, while she listened to all the stories Danny and Ruby had to share. And when the pancakes were ready, we all sat around the table and lounge area having a midnight breakfast, listening to Lila tell the story of her journey home after being 'lost in the woods'.

Obviously, it wasn't the full truth — remembering to keep it PG for the kids and for Hanna. But I'm sure when she gets the opportunity, she'll tell us the rest of the story.

For now, I suppose we're all just glad to have her home.

## Original journal entry continued by Lila Winters

Christmas morning – one of my favourite times of the year. And it was hard to believe that I was actually home and that this wasn't just a dream.

After Max and his family had left for the night, Danny and Ruby had this brilliant idea of watching the recording of the Carols by Candlelight. But as I suspected they couldn't make it all the way through. Danny fell asleep on the floor snuggled up in his sleeping bag, and Ruby fell asleep snuggled up in Alex's arms. – And that was a cute sight to see.

Matt had fallen asleep with my head resting on his chest, while my legs rested on Terrence's lap, sharing my blanket with him. And everyone was asleep except for me – I think I was too excited to be home. Instead I stayed awake watching the TV, enjoying every moment of this.

I closed my eyes for a second, and then felt Terrence gently lifting my legs and sneaking away. He was clearly waiting for me to go to sleep, so I kept my eyes closed – partially. I was still able to see Alex rush to put Ruby down, and stop Terrence from leaving.

I didn't move I just listened to them talk as Terrence whispered, "What are you doing?"

To which Alex quietly replied, "I could ask you the same thing," as he glanced back at me – still supposedly sleeping.

"Look I don't belong here and you know it," Terrence whispered, opening the apartment door then added, "It's not safe for her."

He was just about to leave when Alex stopped him again, "And you think it'll be safer when you're gone? The girl you say you're trying to protect just risked her life trying to save yours. And I'm not sure if you've noticed, but since that water thing left her body, she hasn't been as fast or as strong as either of us."

That was a hard bit of info to process for me – I didn't think anyone else noticed my lack of superpowers.

Still, Terrence was determined to leave. I knew he could tell no one wanted him here. And the only reason why no one had asked him to leave was because of me. I mean who's going to argue with a woman who's just come back from hell.

Alex grabbed Terrence's arm trying one more time to stop him and whispered, "Look, I know you're not telling me the whole story about you and Lila, and I don't want to know. But before you turn your back on her, think about how she destroyed an island, stole an ancient tree, and ticked off the US Navy with you . . . Do you honestly think they're just going to let this go? And trust me when I tell you . . . and I hate saying this . . . but you are the only person who knows how to help her . . . She needs you."

I wanted to say something. I wanted to ask Terrence not to leave, and tell him that he would always be my friend – no matter what he had done. But I also knew that he'd feel guilty saying no to me, and I wanted Terrence to make the choice to stay on his own.

It looked like he was contemplating it though, as Terrence stared back at me. But he pulled his arm away from Alex and with the look of sadness all over him, he whispered, "I'm sorry," before he left.

Alex didn't know what to do and I could tell he was scared when he silently stormed out on to the balcony to vent and stared out across the city. So, very quietly, I walked out to stand next to him, watching the sunrise with him and explained, "Fear is a powerful emotion . . . some people can be blinded by it . . . some can be crippled by it . . . and others can be ruled by it."

I could tell he was listening to me, but he kept staring out across the city, refusing to look at me. So I took the hint, and walked back inside, but as I did, I muttered, "You can't force people to be brave, Alex. That strength has to be found on their own."

## Journal entry insert by Terrence Connors

It was such a surreal Christmas morning. One I had dreamed of for years, waking up next to someone who didn't want to hurt me, who wasn't afraid of me and stupidly I walked out on her.

I ended up walking to the Melbourne botanic gardens not knowing where to go now, and sat down on a park bench, trying to remember the last Christmas I had ever felt happy.

I think it was when I was six, the year before I was taken. I remember waking up excited to hear my front doorbell ring, and ran down the stairs of my ridiculously oversized mansion to see one of the maids greeting Sergeant Richard and his wife Mrs Willows. But my heart sank because my best friend was nowhere to be seen.

I had such a sad face when I walked into the sitting room to greet my father — Collin. But that's where I found her. I found Lila sitting by the Christmas tree, staring at the twinkling lights and holding a Christmas present that she had made just for me.

I rushed to sit next to her and rummaged through all the Christmas presents sitting under the tree to find the tiny box that I had wrapped just for Lila.

Her smile was amazing when she opened her present and gazed at the white oak tree necklace inside. It was a family heirloom that my real mother had given me just before she died.

My mother made me promise to give it to the girl of my dreams — that best friend, who would stand by me no matter what. — And I know I was six — but I knew it was Lila. — Its always been Lila.

I remember helping her to put it on and she stared at the ruby stone in the center, then hugged me with an amazing smile, "Thank you, Terry. I'll love it forever."

I tearfully shook out of that memory and sat on that park bench, looking down at the white oak tree necklace that I had not yet given back to Lila, and honestly, I felt like letting go of the tears and crying it out.

I wanted to go back, give her the necklace, and tell her how sorry I was for causing all of her pain. But I was also terrified that she would blame me and hate me — What if she was only being nice to me just to get home? And even if she wasn't, how would her friends ever accept who I am or what I've done? — I can't even accept myself.

I got lost in that thought and didn't realise I had company, until I heard a voice say, "I see you made it home safely."

I turned around to see Agetha standing there wearing nothing to disguise what she was. And I was silently freaking out, but she clearly wasn't. She just sat down next to me and enjoyed the early-morning air. "What a beautiful Christmas morning . . . So peaceful . . . . It might be more beautiful if you were with your friends."

With a regretful sigh, I shook my head, putting the necklace back in my pocket, causing Agetha to chuckle at me, "Do you remember when you were little? . . . You and Lila used to climb the trees near your old house. . . The youngest guardians of the flora, getting into trouble for climbing trees."

"Yeah" I replied with a slight grin, "That is until Lila fell out of one of them. . . I can still see the scar next to her eye."

Agetha laughed even harder than, "Oh, that little girl constantly found trouble where ever she went. . . but there was always one who was there to help her out of it." She peered across to me then handed me the ancient green tree stone from the island, as she explained, "This was recovered by your new water friends. I'm sure you know what to do with it."

I gazed at the tree stone then glanced up in a happy shock to say thank you, but Agetha had already disappeared.

# CHAPTER 13

# MERRY CHRISTMAS, PUMPKIN

*Journal entry by Lila Winters*

When the family had all woken up to the joys of Christmas morning, I sat next to Alex and watched as the children unwrapped their presents. It was understandable that I had no presents of my own to open, and I didn't care, just being here was enough for me.

But throughout the morning I noticed Matt felt a little uncomfortable around me, probably unsure how to feel now that the reality had set in.

And I obviously didn't look too good with the cuts and bruises on my face and a bandaged arm. I wore a long sleeve, turtle neck skivvy – that I grabbed from my old wardrobe at the Willow farm, and changed into it before we had arrived at the hotel last night. So that he couldn't see the rest of the damage.

Mainly because I didn't want to scare anyone with the state of my body, with all its scars and the still healing injuries – I especially didn't want to scare my children.

I think it's for the best this way – and I'm happy to hide.

While Matt and Hanna were preparing more pancakes for a second breakfast, I was attempting to set the table with Alex's help. It was a struggle and I occasionally held my abdomen in pain, desperately trying to hide it from Matt and the children.

At one-point though Alex had to disappear at half speed into my room and returned with a jumper. I stared at him confused, because I didn't feel cold. He then discreetly glanced down at the fresh blood seeping through my skivvy and whispered, "Your wound needs redressing . . . it might be easier if we did that in my apartment."

But considering I had not yet told Alex the circumstances behind the wounds or even showed him the full extent, I quickly snapped back, "No . . . I'll be fine."

He definitely didn't like that response. And I know he was only trying help and that he worried about me, so I didn't get cross at him when pushed the issue, quickly making up some excuse for us to leave, saying that he had a present back in his apartment for me.

But as Alex opened the door to leave, we found Max standing on the other side holding a stack of presents for everyone.

"Good morning," he said, walking into the apartment, "I can't stay for long I just came to deliver some presents."

Max cheerfully roamed around the lounge and dining area, handing out the presents to everyone, including Alex. Then when he got to me, he was all teary-eyed and proud, as he whimpered, "And this one's for you," and handed me the last present.

"Me?" I gasped in disbelief. – I was really confused because not more the 8 hours ago he thought I was dead.

With a nervous grin, I opened the box to see a beautiful beaded Christmas ballgown. And I know I am not a dress person, but wow this one looked amazing. It looked like it was designed just for me – with the beads sewn in the shape of leafy floral vines, spanning up and around the bodice of the dress.

"It's a dress for tonight's Christmas ball," Max boasted, and proudly explained, "You've now been made the honoured guest of the evening."

I shook my head, humbled by the offer. "Max, that's not necessary."

But Max interrupted with an insistent stare, "Oh yes. . . it definitely is. All the hotel staff want to celebrate your homecoming, Lila . . . we all thought you were . . . huh . . . this is a chance for us to celebrate such a wonderful miracle. So, yes, it is necessary."

I didn't know what to say, I knew all of my work colleagues would want the chance to see me. I mean Chase was sending out text messages of my — return, to all of the security team at 1am this morning. So, they're obviously excited.

And because I don't want to let the team down, I smiled and nodded. "Max . . . I think that's a wonderful idea . . . I'll see tonight."

At that he was over the moon and happily left to be with his family. Then as the door closed, my family all sat down to eat breakfast, and Alex and I joined them but it was no surprise that Alex stayed very close to me, helping me with everything. — He also grumbled a little not getting his chance to change the bandages.

We were both concerned that my stitches may have reopened, so we waited patiently for the first opportunity for us to leave the table. And once the kids finished breakfast, running off to play with their new toys, Alex and I tried to excuse ourselves as well.

But Hanna just had to ask, "So Lila, where have you really been for the past few weeks? And don't give me that half-baked story of being lost in the woods after the fire because we both know it's not like you to get lost in the woods."

Matt nearly choked on his food after hearing that question. And I needed a moment pondering what to say. I didn't want to lie to anyone, but I also didn't know how much she knew of Richard's true business activities or if she was playing both sides.

So, I replied, "I'm sorry but my memory's a bit fuzzy. . . I remember waking up in a medical room with Alex sitting next to me. And the first opportunity we had . . . we left to come back home."

I don't think she was convinced with my answer, but I wasn't going to stick around to argue, so I made up an excuse and left.

Alex hurried me over to his apartment, and he suggested I have a shower, while he gathered up the supplies he needed to change my wound dressings.

I won't lie, I very much needed this shower, but while I was washing the dried blood off me, my thoughts began to race. The sound of the water landing on the ground became so loud, and the memory of me falling into the ocean and sinking into its icy darkness overwhelmed me with fear.

My breathing was difficult and I began to panic, pushing my way out of the shower only to see Alex appear in front of me, wrapping a towel around me and holding me tightly.

He placed his hand on my chest, and held my hand on his, as he whispered, "I'm here, Lila . . . it's alright . . . just listen to my heart, okay."

I nodded, trying to focus on feeling his heart beating through my hand, as I began to calm down and breathe slower. I was still crying but I felt so thankful he was there and that he was doing this for me.

But while holding me close to him, Alex noticed that I still had soap and shampoo all over me. So he very slowly walked me back into the shower. He had to remove the towel from me to clean off the soap, but his eyes stayed focus on my teary blue ones while his hands gently cleaned off all the soap and shampoo.

I kept my hand on his chest feeling his heart beat, and just continued to breathe, watching the water start to soak through his clothes.

There was a moment when the fear started to come back to me, and I heard Alex whisper "I've got you, Lila . . . I'm not going anywhere."

When I heard Alex say those words the fear melted away, and I moved in closer to him, clutching his wet shirt in my hand as I rested my head on his chest and cried.

He wrapped his arms around me, holding me tight and close to him. It felt like he was never ever going to let me go again. And for me just being in his arms made me feel like I was finally safe, and that everything was going to be okay.

But things got really awkward when we had finished in the shower because just before my panic attack, Alex had texted Matt asking him to bring over some fresh clothes. And when he did, he found me wrapped in just a towel being carried out of the bathroom by Alex in his dripping wet clothes.

I was still an emotional wreck when Alex placed me down on the bed, and he casually glanced back up to Matt, and stated, "Matt, now's not the time to feel territorial . . . come over here and help your wife get dressed." Then disappeared into his walk-in robe to change into dry clothes.

I know I shouldn't have, but while Matt was helping me with my bra, I felt a little exposed, especially when I had to lower the towel a little and he noticed the large bloodstained, wet bandages wrapped around the length of my stomach.

My breath was short with my body feeling incredibly tense, as Matt's eyes studied and stared at the scars on my neck and shoulders. Then when I felt him touch one of the scars on my shoulder blade, I flinched and I heard him frustratingly grunt a little under his breath.

He clearly noticed I was holding the towel close to me not letting him see all the damage, and he asked "Lila, what happened to you?"

I tried to play it down and smiled a bit, "Nothing much. It's just a few cuts and a few bruises . . . That's all."

I know it was a half-truth, but it was only in the hopes of protecting him. – Not only that, if you take one look at the bandaged wounds, you would instantly realise it was an animal attack. And knowing Matt, he would definitely jump to the wrong conclusion and act rashly.

Still, Matt persisted and demanded I let him see everything, reminding me that he was my husband. And I don't know what came over me but I fearfully snapped back, "No!"

Before Matt could argue further, Alex walked back into the room carrying fresh bandages, "Alright, Lila, let's change your dressings."

Matt quickly flew into a jealous temper, shouting at me, "So he can see the damage they did to you, but I can't. He's allowed to know what happened to you, but I can't. He's allowed to know where you've been, but I can't . . . Lila, you've been missing for over 2 months. They made me believe you were dead. I had to tell my children that their mother was never coming home . . . Only to have you return with your captor and ask him to stay for breakfast. . ."

I'm not a fan of people yelling at me, especially after a panic attack and I'd had enough. – I also knew that the half-truths were pointless for both of them. So, before Matt could continue his rant, I quickly grabbed the scissors off Alex, dropping the towel to cut away the bandages, showing Matt the truth.

Then standing in front of them in just my bra and undies, I turned to show them everything. And when Matt looked down to see the mangled mess of stitches and bruising, it rendered him speechless.

Alex already knew there was damage, because while his eyes stayed on mine when we were in the shower, I felt his hands track most of the scars.

The ones he wasn't able to track though were the those hidden by the bandages. – The three very deep and large slashes on my stomach, all poorly stitched and coming away, and just barely clotted. They stretched from just below the left side of my bra, all the way down to the tip of my right hip bone, and surrounding that was the remnants of the many, many tests and experiments those people did to me. There was so many scars and they spanned all over my body from my wrists, neck and face and down to my toes.

I stood in front of Matt and Alex, staying very quiet, but I felt extremely vulnerable as Matt stared – and the closer he looked at the scars – the more my story was told in the silence.

I became tired of Matt staring, so nodded to Alex before I sat back down on the bed for him to clean and dress the wound again. Alex didn't say anything he just knelt down next to the bed and started to clean the wound, but when he cleaned all the blood away, he realised what the injury was from, and whispered, "This is a wolf's..."

"I know," I interrupted with a timid breath. And before Alex got a chance to ask who, I pre-emptively answered, "It was an accident and he wasn't in control of his actions."

I watched the rage fill in Alex's eyes, briefly glancing back at the still dumbstruck Matt then turned back to me, calmly helping me to stand so he could wrap the new bandage around my torso, and questioned, "Lila, why would Terrence be channelling a wolf? How is that even possible?"

I was very surprised that Alex was handling this so well. – But Matt, he didn't handle it well, and he shouted, "Terrence!.. . You invite that monster into our home after he did this to you."

He then grabbed hold of my freshly bandaged hand in anger, completely disregarding the pain I felt, and shamed me, pointing to all the cuts and bruises he could see, and screamed, "That monster did this to you and yet you treat him like a friend . . . Why? What happened to you on that island?"

The pain was almost unbearable to the point where I struggled with the tears, and as I heard him shouting the horrid memories started to rush through my head again, making it difficult for me to control my fear with my heart racing.

What made it worse, was that Matt's yelling had become so loud that it had gained the attention of Danny and Ruby who ran across the hall to see if we were okay. But when they rushed into the apartment, the door slammed loudly behind them, triggering the painful memory of Ben getting shot and bleeding out in front of me.

I couldn't hold it any longer and was overcome with fear, trembling as Matt held my arm. Alex could sense my fear rising again and rushed to help me, pushing Matt away as he growled, "Matt, that's enough . . . you're scaring her!"

He glared at Matt before he turned to me trying to calm me down again, placing my hand back onto his chest, asking me to listen and breathe.

As Matt scanned the room, he realised what he had done, in losing his temper, and apologised to me. I nodded but I was still scared clearly making Matt feel more guilt, and stormed out of the apartment.

Danny and Ruby stayed behind though, still worried about me and climbed up onto the bed to give me a hug, whispering, "It's okay, Mummy."

I felt their arms wrapping around me and my fears quickly disappeared as I hugged them back. When Ruby finished her hug, she smiled handing me one of her floral headbands that she had received for Christmas and added, "Nana's invited us all to her church today . . . and I brought you this to wear . . . just like me."

She placed her other headband on her head and beamed with joy as I nodded, "Sure, hon, we'll head out in a minute."

I was still in my undies so I needed to get dressed. But I started to feel slightly better about myself because when Danny and Ruby looked at me, there was no fear – all they saw was their Mum.

They both excitedly ran back over to my apartment, all while Alex stood there waiting, holding my shirt and jeans for me. He kindly helped me to get dressed again but stayed silent.

I could tell he was looking at the scars, and the look on his face told me everything.

"Please don't look at me like that," I whimpered, wiping the tears from my cheeks, "I know I look horrid . . . but none of this is your fault . . . and it's not Terrence's either. He tried to stop this the first chance he got."

I had to turn away from him, feeling so ashamed of the mangled mess my body had become. But Alex, he stood in front of me and gently held one of my hands, using his other hand to catch the tears from my cheek, then slowly lifted my chin, so I would look at him as he stared into my teary eyes, whispering, "Lila, you have the heart and body of a warrior. And you should never be ashamed of that . . . All of these scars. . . they're just marks of the battles you've overcome. And I want you to know that no matter what. . . you will always look beautiful to me."

That was something I really needed to hear, and I smiled as he pulled me close, embracing me with the best hug he's ever given me. And I loved this hug — because I felt like I was melting in his arms feeling so incredibly safe, and loved, and respected by him.

# Journal entry insert by Alex Woods

This was a terrible idea. I know it's Christmas, and at first glance, this family-church outing was a great idea. But I just know Lila's nervous as hell, not only because she was tired but she was also still healing. And I worried about her, mentally and physically, and considering how slowly her wounds are healing I fear she may have lost her powers completely.

We walked through the car park towards the church, and as Lila held on to my arm for support, she glanced at me briefly, taking one look at my face before she said, "I know what you're thinking, but I can do this . . . just stay close to me, okay."

There was no way I was going to let her go, so I confidently replied, "Always."

Lila and I followed Matt, Danny, Ruby and Hanna into the church. And the tension in the church was very high as people stared at Lila in shock, whispering amongst themselves.

The silence was deafening until the minister shouted, "It's a Christmas miracle, Thank the Lord for the return of this precious child." His proclamation gained the attention of everyone as he stopped in front of Lila and commented, "You gave us quite a fright, my dear. Everyone here thought you were dead. . . What happened to you, my child?"

An awkward silence filled the room, as all the church-goers listened in, and the minister stared at Lila waiting for the answer. Thankfully, no one noticed the heavily applied foundation on her to hide all the bruises and scars. But the silence was becoming more tense until we heard a familiar voice break through the crowd, "So many questions, Father Thomas. Give the girl a chance to breathe."

As Richard stepped out from the crowd, I felt Lila's arm tighten around mine, pulling me closer to her. I could feel her terrifying fear but she was smart enough not to let it show as she grinned, "Hello Richard . . . Merry Christmas."

It was gut churning watching Richard beam with pride as he kissed Lila on the cheek, replying, "And merry Christmas to you, Pumpkin."

I really, really wanted to hurt him – unfortunately we were in a church, and I'm not sure how God feels about violence in holy places.

Thankfully, Christmas music began to play in the auditorium and the minister shouted, "Well that's our cue. Everyone, please come in and find a seat."

So, we all walked into the auditorium, but still I kept Lila very close to me.

Matt could clearly tell something was up when he noticed Richard offering Lila a seat and sitting right next to her the entire service. I could also sense Matt's jealousy as he watched Lila hold on to my arm, refusing to let it go throughout the entire service as well.

Add to the fact, and honestly, I hope Lila can't hear them, but all through the service, people whispered amongst themselves, gossiping about her, whispering, "She's just attention seeker."

Another commented, "She faked her death for the insurance money."

But the worst one of all was, "She faked her own death to get out of a loveless marriage . . . and now she's parading her new lover in front of everyone."

The nerve of these people. If only they knew how much Lila's been through and how much she's sacrificed all to help a stranger.

When the minister finally concluded the service, I was extremely relieved and tried to gently hurry Lila out into the foyer. I could see the daylight as I walked next to Lila, holding her hand. We were so close and had made it halfway through the foyer, smiling and wishing people a Merry Christmas when suddenly a group of female voices excitedly squealed Lila's name and five women, all around Lila's age, came rushing up to give her a hug, completely oblivious to the pain she was in.

One of the women stood in front of Lila, waving her hands around in front of her as she very nasally said, "Oh my gosh Lila, do you remember me . . . it's Megan, your Sunday school BFF. I'm so glad you're alive. But seriously . . . you look like you've been through a war or something. What happened to you?"

As she asked that not so wonderful question, the foyer came to a dead silence as people again, stopped and listened in for the answer. I noticed Lila briefly glance over to Richard who was scowling at her, and discreetly shaking his head as he dotingly held his wife's hand.

And yep – I was still really wanting to hurt that man. I also wanted to race Lila out of the church at full speed and not look back – but that's not going to happen.

Instead I just stood there, sensing all of the horrible and judgemental emotions from the strangers surrounding us, all directed at Lila. But to my surprise, Lila responded by laughing, gently holding her stitched stomach as she stared at Megan's now baffled expression.

"That's your question. No one here wants to know how I am or if I'm healthy. You all just want to know what happened to me? Is that it?"

She peered around at the room and disappointingly shook her head. "Well, alright then . . . I was kidnapped by a crazy, deranged psychopath who thought I could talk to trees."

That response obviously left everyone flabbergasted as Megan jokingly questioned, "Err, are you serious?"

So Lila putt on a fake smile, replying, "Yeah, I'm as serious as the bruises on my face and the bloodied wound on my stomach . . ." then while using the sleeve of her skivvy, Lila gently rubbed the foundation off her face to reveal the large purple bruise and some of her scars. And listened to silence of the room as people stared at her, before very sweetly and seriously stating, "Oh, but you don't need to worry. . . the crazy psycho can't hurt me anymore . . . because he's dead . . . he was killed by a tree."

Yep – I was struggling not to smile, and I proudly watched as Lila glared back at Richard and grinned – clearly knowing the relationship of John and Richard.

Then as we began to walk out of the church, Lila looked back at Megan and very sarcastically added, "But seriously, Megan, thank you so much for your concern . . . it really does mean a lot to me."

Right – I don't think we'll be invited back to this church any time soon.

Lila was on a slight high as we made our way out to the car and I loved seeing her smile, but by the time we had gotten out to the car, Hanna had rushed out of the church in a furious rage, directed at Lila.

She grabbed Lila's arm and pulled her away from me, causing Lila to tense from the pain and hold her stomach again. And I know my actions didn't help, but I moved at full speed to grab Lila's hand away from Hanna and stood protectively next to her.

Hanna's confusion of my movements only lasted a brief second before her anger returned and she shouted at Lila, "How dare you make a mockery in my church . . . Lying to everyone like that. You made them all feel very uncomfortable . . . with all this talk of death and kidnapping!"

"They asked me a question, Hanna. And I answered it truthfully," Lila replied, now with her smile completely gone.

And I became saddened as I listened to Hanna's reply back, "Do you honestly think people believed that story! You embarrassed me today and you embarrassed your father." She then pointed back to Richard who was just watching from a distance.

It became very clear to me what Lila's childhood was really like, with a mother as ignorant as this – clearly ignoring Lila's visible bruise and scars.

Still, Lila held her own and used her calm yet scary voice to reply, "So what do you want me to tell them? What do you want to hear, Mother? That I skipped town for a few weeks to spend time with my secret lover . . . Tell me, what kind of lie will make you feel better?"

– Damn, she did hear the gossip.

"Make me feel better?" Hanna sneered glaring at Lila's challenging defiance. "How could you think that a lie about you being kidnapped by an insane psychopath would make me feel better? You've made a mockery of this family."

In anger Hanna raised her hand to strike Lila across the face. And I was not going to let anyone hurt Lila, so I moved at full speed again, pulling Lila towards me, pressing her tightly against my chest while covering my arms around her as we watched Hanna miss her strike, and stumbled a little.

Lila then peered over my arm to scowl at Richard, but happily stayed within the safety of my arms as she replied to Hanna's question, "You're right. This obviously means a great deal to you. And I really don't want to lie to you."

Hanna huffed triumphantly, smiling back at Richard, feeling like she had finely convinced Lila to tell her the truth. But when she turned back to listen to this new amazing truth, Lila had disappeared. Because I ran at full speed carrying Lila in my arms with Ruby clinging to my back to the nearest train station. It must have confused Hanna to no end as she looked around for Lila only to see me reappear next to Matt and Danny then disappear with them too.

And as we sat down on the train heading back home, Lila laughed so hard that it hurt. But to be honest, that was the best sound I could have heard in months. And I swear my heart skipped a beat when I saw the biggest smile appear across her face – you could just tell the pain was worth it for her as she snickered, "Let's see Richard talk his way out of that one."

## Original journal entry continued by Lila Winters

We arrived back at the hotel just in time for the Christmas festivities. And I, the guest of honour, did my best to put on a happy smile as I walked around the room greeting everyone and wishing them a Merry Christmas.

The ballgown looked beautiful on me but it didn't cover my shoulders, so when Alex helped me to get dressed, he also helped to cover the visible scars for me. He found me a pretty cardigan and has become quite talented with the foundation and blush.

I'm not used to wearing this much make-up. But I wasn't complaining if it helped me to appear normal. And honestly, it wasn't that hard to appear happy either, seeing all of my friends and co-workers again all laughing and enjoying themselves. It was a definite turnaround from these last few months. But every now and then, the sadness crept in and it was hard to shake.

I wandered up onto the rooftop garden to get some air, and when I heard the footsteps behind me, I whispered, "It's okay, Alex. I just needed some air."

But it wasn't Alex. It was Richard, standing behind me admiring my ballgown, "You look like a princess, Pumpkin."

"Richard?" I shrieked, obviously in a failed attempt to compose myself as I turned to face him.

He slowly paced across the balcony, keeping a safe distance from me and commented, "You know there was a time, when you would call me dad."

I scoffed, glaring at him in sheer annoyance, "And there was I time, where you wouldn't have faked my death or imprisoned me, or murdered my friends in front of me."

Richard then stared down to the ground all pouty faced, casually inching his way closer to me while he replied, "Alright, you got me. I'm not a very good dad . . . I never was, not even to my own son."

He stood in front of me in silence, sizing me up until he finally got to the point, "Alright, I think we've both had enough fun and games for one day. So let's get down to the brass tacks . . . You stole something from the island, and I'm here to get it back."

"Then I'm sorry you wasted your time . . . Because what you're looking for is in the middle of the Indian Ocean in the hands of the American Navy and most likely being used as a paperweight."

I chuckled at him trying to hide my fear, but also hoped that at any moment Alex would walk out on to the balcony and save the day like before. But I wasn't having much luck and Richard ever so casually stood next to me, leaning on the balcony railing and tsk-ed, "Well, that is a shame," then he pushed me over the balcony railing.

FRAC – I grabbed hold of the bannister and hung off the edge of the building, holding on for dear life and desperately convincing myself not to look down. I screamed for help, but it seemed futile over the noise of the Christmas music.

And as Richard leaned his head over the side he said in a cocky tone, "Well Pumpkin, it looks like you've really made a mess of things now. And . . .I know The Board ordered me here to retrieve you and the tree, but you know . . . you destroyed my newly obtained island, killed my only son, and stained my reputation . . . and well . . . that makes me mad, and I just can't risk you getting in the way again . . . sorry about this, Pumpkin."

FRAC! – LILA – WHATEVER YOU DO – DON'T LOOK DOWN!

# Journal entry insert by Terrence Connors

After an entire day of trying to work up the courage and failing to find any. I decided to take my chances and return to Lila and beg her for forgiveness. I know that her friends and family would probably hate me and would most likely never trust me. But Lila had such faith in me on the Island, even Alex trusted me and tried to stop me from leaving. So, maybe there's hope for me.

I nervously walked into the Eden Hotel ballroom, looking around for Lila but instead I was greeted by Alex, sounding like he had way too much Christmas punch as he slurred, "Terrence . . . It's so good to see you . . ."

I asked if he was okay, questioning how much he had to drink, and his answer didn't settle me as he mumbled, "Oh, I haven't had anything to drink. I have to stay alert . . . ready to fight for . . . Lila."

Yeah, that's not going to happen — not in his condition. Add to that Lila was nowhere to be found. I did however notice that all of the party guests seemed to be intoxicated even the children.

"Something's wrong . . ." I whispered, then acted fast, running at full speed out of the hotel and returning with hundreds of white lilies.

I handed a lily to each guest and stood in the centre of the room, closing my eyes so no one would notice the green glow then reached my arms out towards all of the lilies. And as they began to glow and wilt in their hands the room fell silent, and the guests began to look around feeling a bit woozy and forgetful.

I then rushed back over to Alex, who was now frantically looking around for Lila, and started asking all of Lila's friend until one of them told him, "I think she was headed up to the garden."

With a horrible feeling in the pit of my stomach, we both raced at full speed through the hotel out onto the roof-top garden. Only to see Richard standing at the balcony railings with Lila hanging over the side.

Alex ran to pull Richard away, throwing him backwards into the wall. But that didn't seem to affect him. I suspect Richard may have been using some sort of ability enhancer as he ran back to tackle Alex to the ground, striking him repeatedly.

I raced to help Alex, pushing Richard into the garden, angering him as he stood up and pulled out his gun, firing at Alex.

At super speed, I moved to protect Alex and closed my eyes, hearing Lila shouting Alex's name in terror, expecting it to be the last time I ever heard her voice. But instead I heard the sound of Richard's body falling to the ground, and I turned back to see him lying there with a tree branch impaled into his chest. — It looks like Agetha was still looking out for us.

But my fear returned as I heard Lila's scream and saw the last of her fingers let go of the railing. Alex and I both moved at an incredible speed, jumping over the railings as she fell.

I then caught Alex's legs as he grabbed hold of Lila's hand and we all came to an instant jolting stop causing Lila to scream as the jolt tore away at her wounds. And you could see the pain all over her face as we hung mid-air off the side of the hotel building while the tree branches from the rooftop garden tightly wrapped around my legs, slowly pulling us back up to safety.

As we helped Lila to climb over the railings she was trembling, and Alex tried to calm her as she cried into the crook of his neck, shuddering from the pain and the fear.

I heard her mumble Ben's name as she started to breathe slower and eventually realise she was safe. She then peered up from Alex's hug to see me nervously standing next to them, and she smiled at me then raced to hug me, squeezing me tightly as she whispered, "You came back?"

I felt a wave of relief as I held her in my arms, but then she pulled away from me and asked, "Why."

So, I took a deep breath and started my very nervous speech, "I came back because I made a promise to someone very special to me. . . and I know I haven't been very good at keeping that promise . . . but I was hoping . . . if I apologised and renewed my promise. . . she would give me another chance to prove myself."

Then while still feeling extremely nervous, I handed Lila's necklace back to her, along with the green tree stone and held my breath as I waited for her response.

I thought she'd be angry. I thought she would blame me for everything that happened to her. Instead she hugged me again and breathed, "You will always be my friend, Terrence . . . always."

Yeah — I loved hearing that, and I started to relax, taking a calming breath as I wrapped my arms back around her, loving that she still calls me her friend.

I had my friend back — I had Lila back.

Eventually I had to let Lila out of my hug, but she leaned on me for a little support. And although she looked stunning in that beautiful gown, she did have a little blood seeping through from her abdomen.

She looked down at the blood and irked, "Great. . . I can't go back to the party like this."

My brows pinched together as I tried to think of an idea, and the best I could think of was to button up her cardigan. She watched me, and bit her bottom lip, smiling as I finished the last button then I asked, "How's that?"

She beamed with a smile glancing back at Alex and replied "It's perfect, thank you, Terrence."

Now happy again, Alex and I started to help Lila walk back into the hotel, but she stopped and knelt down next to Richard, who was just barely breathing, and sighed, "Merry Christmas Richard."

She started to walk inside again, leaning on Alex and myself for support, but as we got into the corridor, a sudden gust of wind streamed around the hotel building with a thick hazy cloud smothering Richard's body. And when the cloud disappeared so too did Richard.

# Journal entry insert by Matt Winters

When I saw that monster — Terrence standing in the middle of the ballroom and all the guest holding dead lilies, I knew something had gone wrong. Not only that, I knew it had to be his fault, but before I could go over and confront him, both he and Alex disappeared.

I hate it when they do that!

It took me a while, but I finally caught up to them. I saw him standing on the balcony hugging <u>my</u> wife and I grew enraged and suspicious. So, I hid in the corridor and watched from the window as Terrence handed Lila a necklace along with some kind of rock.

The worst part of all of it, was watching Lila cuddle him.

I can't do this anymore. This morning I was happy just to have her home again. But now, seeing her like this — Something is just not right. So, I raced up to Max's office to look for the blood test results he had asked for, upon Lila's miraculous return. And I scanned through all three of their test results, only becoming more frustrated because none of them had traces of Neuritamine in them, which meant she wasn't under any drug or spell when she was on that island or even when she asked him to stay.

I slumped down into the desk chair with my heart sinking further and further, letting my suspicions became more and more real. That's when Adela rushed into the office.

"Hey, I just heard about what happened are you okay?" she asked.

I nodded as she apologised for not being there to help, explaining that the food had been laced with something. And that she had been called away to help out a hotel guest when the frenzy broke out. She held my hands trying to comfort me as she watched my face grow gloomier then asked, "What's wrong?"

"It's Lila," I angrily breathed, "and Alex . . . and Terrence . . . and Chase . . . and all of them surrounding her . . . protecting her. . . I have no idea what she's been through, and I don't think I'll ever know because she can't tell me, or she won't tell me . . . But she'll tell him . . . her so-called protector Alex . . . and now there's two of them. How can I ever compete with that?"

Adela knelt down in front of me, still holding my hands in hers, and sighed, "You don't have to compete. You're strong, smart, kind and brave, and I know you can protect Lila, just like you protect all of your family." She stared up into my eyes, trying to reassure me, whispering, "Just give her some time."

Adela then wrapped her arms around me to give me a reassuring hug, and I tried so hard not to let my anger or territorial urges get the best of me. But I didn't care. Adela was the only one who stood by me, looked after me and my kids while Lila was off – who knows where, doing whatever it was she was doing.

I quickly realised my emotions had actually gotten the best of me as I pulled Adela up onto the office desk and kissed her fervently. And as I did my rage was subdued by the tender touch of her lips on mine.

# CHAPTER 14

# A NEW YEAR – A NEW DAY

Journal entry by Alex Woods

I know we've all been through a lot this past year – and as I lay on the couch in Lila's apartment watching the sun rise, I spent time reflecting over this year and everything that's happened. And to be honest – I'm very eager to start the new year on a much happier note.

I knew that Lila wasn't up for attending the festivities Max had planned throughout the hotel, so I was going to suggest an alternative. I was thinking about a pizza party instead with just her family – and Terrence – seeing how he has nowhere else to go and is staying in the spare room of my apartment.

We're both taking it in shifts protecting Lila because she still hasn't regained her strength or abilities since the boat, and I have a very strong suspicion it has something to do with that ruby stone.

My thoughts were interrupted by the sound of a slight thud on the apartment door, and I quietly walked over to look through the peek hole. I was speechless and shocked when I saw Matt leaning on the adjacent wall, lip-locked with Adela.

I didn't know what to do – I knew this would absolutely crush Lila's heart if she ever found out. But they seemed to be making quite a ruckus in the hallway. Any louder and they might have woken Lila up.

And I certainly didn't want to catch them in the act—that would have been way too awkward. Considering the amount of times Matt's found Lila in my arms, it was enough for me to stay out of it. Instead I decided to race back to the couch and turn the on the TV with the sound on loud enough for them to hear out in the hallway – well at least loud enough for Adela to hear.

My plan worked out well, because a few seconds later, Matt walked in acting all casual, saying good morning to me, and explaining how he had just gone out for a morning stroll in the park to watch the sunrise.

Yep – would you like some syrup with that stack of lies – Maybe even a side order of truth.

I didn't say anything, I just nodded and pretended to believe the lie, watching as he wandered off towards the bedroom. But I thought I'd give him the heads up before he got to Lila's room and whispered, "She's still sleeping."

And that seemed to stop him in his tracks as he stood, staring at the bedroom door then slowly walked back out of the apartment, grinning at me. "You know what, I just remembered we need to pick up some more milk for breakfast . . . I'm just gonna . . . I'll be back."

Yep – not enough lies on his stack – he's going back for seconds.

I tried not to snicker when he left again then quietly snuck into Lila's room to see if she was okay. Sure enough, she was sound asleep, and it was a beautiful sight to see.

I know I shouldn't think this way, and I know she's married – and she never ever breaks her promises. But that A-hole of a man doesn't deserve her, and she doesn't deserve any of this. She's too amazing and precious to have gone through everything she has this year.

I stood there at the end of her bed, watching her sleep – slightly creepy I know. But the peaceful moment was interrupted by the sound of my phone receiving a text message.

I raced out of the room to silence it, hoping I didn't wake her up, and just as I finished reading it, there was a knock at the door. – Now this was getting creepy.

I went to open the door and found Chase standing out in the hallway with Terrence, explaining that Max wanted to see both Lila and myself in his office today – but Max was also hoping to speak to me first.

Um okay – Max wants to speak to Me – Can this morning get any weirder?

## Journal entry insert by Lila Winters

I woke up to an empty bed again, and I was unfortunately starting to feel the distance between Matt and I.

He said he was just needing some time to process everything and that he was still in shock, which is understandable, but it seems like the only time we see each other is during family mealtime.

I had planned to confront him today, wanting to try and find some way to rekindle our relationship. But instead, when I went out into the kitchen, it was Terrence standing at the bench making breakfast for Danny and Ruby – which I liked but it was very odd, considering nobody but me trusted Terrence, and yet they were all happy to leave him alone with me and my children.

Terrence sat and ate breakfast me and we both waited for Matt to return. But when he did, he didn't seem all that interested to talk to me. Instead all he wanted to do was sit and play on the gaming station with Danny. – Maybe he still needs more time.

Picking up on my disappointment, Terrence quietly let me know that Max wanted to see me in his office. Giving me the perfect excuse to leave, so we went up to see Max in his office as requested. And I was very much hoping he wasn't planning on inviting me to any more surprise parties for the New Year's Eve celebrations because that would be a big No.

When I walked into the office, I found Alex already in a meeting with Max and another woman. I stammered a little unsure what to do, "Oh, I'm sorry I thought you wanted to see me . . ."

I turned to leave with Terrence when Max stood, inviting me in, "Yes, I did, Lila. Please have a seat."

It was curious though – Max didn't seem to be very happy. So very cautiously, Terrence and I walked towards the desk, viewing a large stack of manila folders piled on his bureau with dark red lines marked on the side of them. And sitting on the very top of the folders was Bluey – that ever so famous and not-so-loyal bluebird who landed on my door and lied to me, claiming to be my ally. – I should have used the frying pan when I had the chance.

The woman stood up to greet me and introduce herself, "Good morning Lila. My name is Agent Kerry from mission control. I was hoping to have a moment of your time. If that's alright?"

Uh-huh – I took one look at Agent Kerry and responded with the quick words of, "No . . . no, no, and no," as I rushed to leave.

But Alex raced to stand in front of me and begged, "No Lila, stop."

He grabbed hold of my still healing arm which caused Terrence to leap to my defence, and pull me away, very suspicious of Alex's motives. They stood at a mutual distance staring at each other with Terrence holding me behind him. – Well, this was a twist.

"Alex, let me pass," I demanded.

Yet Alex persisted, "Please Lila, it's not what you think. She's not one of them, or at least she claims she's not. Max was hoping that you or Terrence would be able to sense if she was telling the truth, and then maybe hear what she has to say."

Terrence looked back at me to get an indication as to what he should do, knowing full well that it was his powers that were needed here. Given that mine were M.I.A.

I nodded, and he tentatively walked closer to Agent Kerry while still holding me closely behind him as he took a few moments to concentrate. He held on to her arm then relaxed his hold on me.

"She's fine," he sighed in relief, then sternly threatened, "But if you try anything, I will kill you."

"Now that I believe . . ." Kerry sneered, taking the threat quite well. She then turned to address me with a smile. "Firstly, Lila. I would just like to say to you that we are deeply sorry for everything that you have been through."

"Apology not accepted," I snapped back, crossing my arms, "You and I both know that the government is never really sorry when they're deep dark secrets are compromised. You merely work harder to cover them up . . . or dispose of them."

She didn't respond to that – probably because she knew it was true. So I figured I'd cut straight to the point and jeered,

"Now, you can either tell me why really came here . . . or you can let Terrence show you the door. It's your choice."

I was beginning to think I wasn't in the right mood to deal with the government but then again – I don't think I'll ever be.

Kerry looked at me and then glanced at Terrence still standing very close to me, and realised there was no way of explaining away their actions and no way of gaining my favour.

So she sat back down and looked over at Bluey, who for a bluebird looked like he deeply regretted his actions, as he explained, "It's true . . . Mission control has been compromised, and there is still no way of knowing how far the deception runs, which is why the government has decided to shut down the agency."

Well what a shocker – of course, the agencies being shut down, they would do just about anything to save face. Especially knowing that a very wealthy and well-known family –the Eden's –have now been made aware of what the government has been doing on the side. And considering my 'death' and 'miraculous reappearance' was so very public, they would probably want to distance themselves from any of the guilty parties.

Figures – Huh.

Surprisingly, Kerry found her voice again and added to Bluey's statement – I think she was assuming that Bluey would have softened me up at bit – "That's why we're here. We were hoping you would still help us."

She then placed her hand on the stack of files Bluey was sitting on, explaining, "These folders contain the information on all the agents that have gone missing since the agency began. And since you have already managed to find 4 plus an extra . . .," She sighed briefly glancing at Terrence before she continued, "We . . . I mean, I . . . hoped that you would continue to find the rest of them."

Kerry stared back at me hoping to get some sign or indication that I was willing to help as Bluey went on to explain, "We no longer have the resources to look for them."

"But we also don't want to give up on them," Kerry interrupted, looking down at her wristwatch, seeming somewhat agitated, "None the less, I believe you have the best chance of finding them . . . I've seen you in action and read Bluey's reports. You're good at what you do . . . probably the best. And right now, you hold all the cards . . . Especially because one of those cards is responsible for their disappearances . . . and is now standing here, protecting you."

Wow – Can she be anymore – Subtle.

Terrence definitely took offence to her statement and glared at Kerry in a huff, interpreting her words as a threat to him, which in a veiled way they were.

So instead, I stood in front of Terrence defensively, and snarled, "Terrence is not a card to be played . . . and as for your request, I cannot help you . . . I have not yet fully recovered from my last mission, and escaping from that island has taken its toll."

I could tell at that revelation Max was disappointed, and I glanced back at Bluey, who still looked incredibly guilty. I assumed as I looked at Bluey's sad demeanour, that he was deceived and used along with the rest of them. "I'm very sorry Blue. But I can't help you this time round."

Bluey flew up into the palm of my hand and looked up at me to respond, "It is I that must apologise. . . Please know, Lila, even though I have betrayed you and your team, I still hold great admiration for you. And I am honoured to have served with you."

For a little bird, he seemed to have a big heart and he looked incredibly sad. So I gently stroked the feathers on his back to comfort him and replied, "You too, Bluey."

As he heard Kerry loudly clear her throat, Bluey flew over to her hand ready to leave with her, and with a sigh of disappointment, she left, leaving her stack of confidential files on the desk. – Possibly in the hopes that we'd change our minds. – Again subtle.

# Original journal entry continued by Alex Woods

The meeting with Max surprised me. And after Lila had left, Max asked Terrence and me to stay back and discuss an important issue – more like interrogate.

Max accused Terrence of being here under false pretences, and was hoping I would back him up on it. He strongly believed that Adela and Matt's recent disloyalties were because of Terrence and that he must have drugged them or brainwashed them into acting so carelessly.

I was stunned that Max was aware of the affair but even more shocked to see just how many times Matt and Adela were caught on camera. I mean Adela knows where all of the security cameras are – it was almost as if she wanted someone to see them.

Terrence insisted to Max that he had nothing to do with it, to the point where I actually defended him. That's right – I defended Terrence – the man that up until this point I was only using for his knowledge and abilities. I was shocked. Even Max was surprised at my actions.

He was also surprised when Terrence confessed to having never been under the influence of the Neuritamine drug. In the attempt to explain that because the substance was mostly plant-based, it has very little to no effect on Nature guardians, which is why both he and Lila are unaffected.

It took a while, but Max eventually came to an understanding with Terrence, similar to the one we have. And we were now all on a mission to uncover the truth.

If Adela and Matt were under the influence of the Neuritamine, then Terrence would neutralise the drug. However, if they both came into this scandal on their own, then we would all need to protect Lila.

The plan was simple – all we had to do was trust each other. Yep, Trust – that's a big ask.

As Terrence and I walked into the elevator to find Lila, I was still curious and I had to ask, "So why did you really change sides?"

I know I had asked that question to him before, but he hadn't actually answered it, and if I was planning on trusting him. I needed to know.

"I did it for Lila," he replied, "She showed kindness to me when I didn't deserve it."

I looked back at him suspiciously, knowing that there was more to it than Lila's random acts of kindness. I mean considering the things he had done, one kind act shouldn't have easily swayed him.

He must have sensed my suspicions of him still, and frustratingly groaned before he explained, "Lila had the opportunity to let me die back on that island, several times . . . The first time was when I was dragged into the cottage after being punished for my failures. I was covered with blood and bruises, with a lot broken bones, and I struggled to breathe or keep my eyes open."

I gasped in confusion and asked why he was beaten. And he became sad and almost teary-eyed as he answered, "My master doubted my loyalties . . . when I convinced her to stop the experiments they were doing . . . to Lila. . . I was ordered to receive a reminder of who I served, and the other guardians took great pleasure in giving me that reminder . . . Lila had the choice to watch me die. After all it was my fault she was there. Instead, she saved my life and all she asked for in return was my friendship . . . The nature of Lila's heart is something I have not seen or felt in a long time . . . She gives me hope and reason to fight."

I was beginning to understand why Terrence was so loyal to Lila, realising that if Terrence was truly taken at such a young age, The Board's agenda was probably all he knew of the world, and that Lila most likely gave him the opportunity to see the world differently when she showed him her kindness. She has an amazing talent of inspiring people to do good. – That's why I love her.

It must have been perfect timing because just as he had finished his explanation, the doors opened onto the lobby floor with Lila standing there looking amused at both of us.

Her eyes darted from Terrence and then to me as she chuckled, "Don't tell me you guys are actually getting along now. . ."

I stepped out of the elevator feeling a bit uneasy. Because I had promised Lila I would never lie to her again, so this plan of ours felt a bit difficult for me.

Luckily, Terrence must have sensed that, and quickly jumped in to fill the void of awkward silence, asking Lila if she would like to go for a walk with him, pleading, "I thought maybe you could show me the sites around the city . . . Because . . .um . . . the last time I was in Melbourne . . . I was a little preoccupied."

– Well I suppose hunting someone does distract you from the attractions.

Lila glanced at me, suspicious of why I hadn't objected to his request, so I added, "Look you don't have to go if you don't want to. I just think it would be good if the new guy doesn't run off on his own and get lost or shot . . . unless you want him to get shot?"

I smiled at that last bit to give Lila the impression I still didn't like him. And it seemed to work because the next thing I knew, Lila and Terrence were walking out the door, giving Max and me enough time to find out more about this 'problem' and if there was anything else involved.

I still wasn't overly confident with the plan and as I walked back into the elevator I mumbled, "Something tells me this year is going to end badly."

## Journal entry insert by Terrence Connors

Lila and I wandered around the city for hours, walking through its amazing parklands.

We both loved and marvelled at the wonders of nature and I sat down on one of the large roots of a very old tree and awed, "Amazing, aren't they?"

She sat down next to me and agreed but still seemed distracted and sad as if her heart were slowly breaking. It did have me wondering, if maybe she already knew what was going on and was simply turning a blind eye to Matt's affair. But Honestly, I was too afraid to ask.

Instead, I went around the issue, "So, Nature girl . . . what's the deal with your powers? They should have recovered by now."

I stared at Lila waiting for her to respond when suddenly she ran at super speed to sit on a tree at the opposite end of the park. I raced to follow her and smiled gleefully, but she didn't seem to share my joy, as I grinned "Well, you don't have a problem with speed. Maybe there's still a chance."

"No, there isn't" she sighed, looking incredibly sad, "Yes, I have my speed back and I can hear a bird chirping from a mile away. But my strength has barely recovered, and my healing has slowed to that of a human and . . ." Lila paused, staring up at the trees whimpering, "I can't feel them anymore, Terrence. The trees, the plants, the flowers, I can't feel any of it . . . it all feels different."

Wanting so desperately to make her happy, I sat down next to her, pulling her close to me, and she hugged me so tightly as she cried, "I don't want to play the hero any more . . . and the trees know that."

Oh gosh, what was I supposed to say to that? — I was very slowly starting to understand Lila and her relationship with her abilities. But I think I know how to cheer her, so while holding her just as tight I explained, "Lila, when I was growing up as one of the collected, one of the other guardians took me under his wing and tried to teach me everything he knew about nature and my abilities. . . When I felt lonely and started to miss home, he would sneak me his old comic books . . . I read all there is to know about heroes and how they would give up everything to save humanity. And yes, I grew up wanting to be a superhero . . . and instead I played the villain . . . But the trees never gave up on me, and I don't think they're going to give up on you now . . . You just need to give yourself time to find that bond again, that emotion that links you to nature."

I heard her sniffles and she kind of curled up a little, resting her head on my chest. So, I tightened my embrace and let her cry — loving the fact that she trusted me like this.

But our heartfelt moment was hilariously interrupted by the sound of my new phone ringing and vibrating in my pocket, causing Lila to laugh, "Since when did you get a new phone?"

She kept laughing, all while I fumbled around, quickly glancing at the message, desperately trying to stop Lila from seeing — and yes, I was being very cagey about it which didn't help the trust thing we had going for us — but it was for her own good.

Still a bit evasive, I stood up and put the phone away, explaining that it was Alex's idea, and then mumbled, "That was also Alex, he's was just checking in, making sure you were still okay, which I know is his subtle way of telling me not to do anything stupid."

Yeah — alright, I lied.

And very nervously I glanced back at Lila and smiled, hoping she would buy the story. The last thing I wanted her to know was the truth. But she wasn't buying it and I had to think of something quick.

"You know what . . ." I grinned, pulling Lila to her feet, still being very cagey — but trying to hide it. I then held my stomach and pouted, "I am starving . . . so tell me, Ms Tour Guide, where's a good place to have a late lunch?"

For some reason, Lila believed me or at least she gave up on the phone issue, and agreed to take me out for lunch. So we caught a tram through Melbourne and Lila led me into a small dumpling restaurant down one of the alleyways of China town.

Okay, I admit I wasn't expecting her to lead me to China town. And as we sat and ate, I commented, "Huh, so this is an interesting Melbourne tourist attraction."

"Oh yeah, you haven't experienced Melbourne until you've had our Chinese food," she boasted with such confidence, almost inhaling the vegetarian dumplings. I really couldn't help but smile. And Well — when you're in Rome — I suppose.

When we finished our lunch, almost dinner, we started heading back to the hotel. And we had just walked in through the lobby doors when Max accidentally bumped into Lila.

"Ah Lila, perfect timing as always," he said not so discreetly, putting his phone away.

And considering Lila's hearing was just fine, she would have definitely heard the vibrations of the many phone calls I had received during lunch.

"What's up, Max?" Lila asked, veiling her suspicions and grinning at me.

Yeah — I was so busted.

And Max looked nervous as well, but he eventually replied, "I . . . err . . . need a woman's opinion on a gift for my wife, um . . . but my daughters seem to be busy . . . too busy to help their poor old father. Err. . . Terrence, would you mind if I steal her away for an hour or two?"

I instinctually nodded and wished Lila good luck, telling her that shopping really wasn't my thing. "I'll meet you back at the apartment."

Max then led Lila somewhat reluctantly into the shopping complex that was swarming with partygoers celebrating the New Year's Eve festivities.

# Original journal entry continued by Alex Woods

I was waiting in the hallway just outside Lila's apartment when Terrence appeared next to me, holding two white lilies and looking just as nervous as I was. And when we knocked on the door and heard Adela's voice, both our nervousness increased.

I took great comfort in knowing that Danny and Ruby were downstairs with Jennifer and Henry, enjoying the celebrations. It meant that I had no qualms about knocking Adela out cold as soon as she opened the door.

I quickly dragged Adela inside as Terrence closed the door, asking, "Was that really necessary?"

And I glared at him, "Do you honestly think she would do this willingly?"

He quickly conceded to my actions, placing the white lily on Adela's head. The flower started to glow for a few seconds then slowly withered and I assumed that was a sign of confirmation that she really had been drugged, feeling slightly calmer. That is until Terrence reminded me that the flower removes any toxins from the body, and that for all we knew she had just been drinking.

But then Matt ran out of his bedroom, shouting, "What's going on? What are you doing to her?"

At half-speed Terrence moved, pulling Matt into a headlock, and held the lily to his forehead. Matt struggled and tried to break free, as the lily started to glow and when the flower withered, Terrence let go of him and waited for Matt to regain his balance.

"What the hell did you just do to me?" Matt question, scowling at Terrence, "And what have you done to her?" He then rushed to help Adela and see if she was okay, "Alex, why did you punch her?"

Oh crap – I stood back as I realised the horrible truth and disappointingly sighed, "You shouldn't be able to remember that."

But then Adela started to wake up, and took one look at Terrence before she moved a full speed to tackle him to the ground, punching him repeatedly.

"Where's Lila!" she shouted, "What have you done to her!"

I rushed – kind of, to pull her off him and may have briefly smiled at the very black eye Terrence had just received, and then tried to tell Adela that Lila was safe and that Terrence was on our side now. But her reaction and sudden memory loss only confused Matt further as he stared at me wanting an explanation.

Still I had to focus on Adela and asked, "Adela, what's the last thing you remember?"

Needing to take a moment she eventually replied, "I don't know . . . we just finished Lila's funeral, and I got asked to check out some homeless guy in the alleyway who was causing a scene."

Double crap.

"Wait . . ." Matt gasped, starting to put the puzzle pieces together. "You don't remember anything else? . . . You don't remember us or anything from this last week."

"Week?" Adela shrieked in shock, "Us? Matt, we didn't . . . oh not again"

She then crouched down, pulling her hands through her hair, realising what she'd unwittingly done.

Terrence and I briefly glanced at each other, and neither of us looked happy with the results, because Adela accidently indicated that she knew about at least one of their misdeeds.

Matt had stayed quiet watching as Adela curled down into ball, rocking back in forth on her feet mumbling to herself. But that only made him more confused and agitated, turning to me as he shook his head, "No, I don't understand . . . what does this mean?"

But I think he did understand – I think he just didn't want to admit it. So without displaying any of the anger I held towards him – I explained, "It means you knowingly cheated on your wife . . . and Adela was . . . for the most part was used as a mindless weapon against you."

Suddenly the sound of glass shattering just outside the apartment door had us all on edge.

Awe – Crap.

Terrence stared at the door in a panic. "Damn it. . . no Lila, wait!" he pleaded, racing to open the door.

We all rushed out into the hallway to see a smashed bottle of champagne flowing out onto the carpet and the sound of the elevator doors opening, and Lila trying to hold back the tears.

Matt chased after Lila, shouting her name, but the elevator doors closed before he could get to her. The last thing he saw was Lila's teary-eyes staring up at him, disappointed and heartbroken.

Awe – Double Crap.

## Journal entry insert by Lila Winters

FRAC – That hurt – that really did hurt. And I don't know what to do. I had to get away from my home – If I could even call it that now. So I ran as fast I could through the streets, past the crowds of drunkard rowdy people, who were excited and partying to welcome in the New Year.

I just kept running until I felt something grab hold of my arm. I thought it was Alex chasing after me. And right now, I didn't want to see or speak to anyone. So I pulled away from him and ran even faster, trying to lose him.

I stopped in a tunnel under a road bridge, leading towards some kind of suburban park, and I fell to the ground and wailed, letting out my screams and it felt like my heart was being ripped from my chest.

I stood up and paced the tunnel entrance, back and forth until I got so enraged that I slammed my fist into the side of the tunnel wall, creating a rather larger crack. – Oops.

Starting to pace again, I tried to compose myself and breathe through the pain, but I was failing because my heart was hurting too much. That is until three guardians appeared in front of me and I had no choice, because rule 2 – demands you to not let it show.

I glared back at them, furious that they interrupted my moment. But while I stared, I studied their faces and remembered them from the island—Zera, Jordan, and Tora; they were all from an African tribe that prided themselves on being the chosen from their tribe. They even boasted about being the best hunters and taunted Terrence for failing his last assignment – Which was me.

To be honest, part of me was glad they were here. Because I was in the mood for a fight, and this time I didn't have to hold back. So while seething in rage, I scowled at them and snickered, "I destroyed an island and they respond by sending only three . . . well, now they've really hurt my feelings."

With an evil grin across her lips, Zera grunted, and created a fireball, throwing it into the dark end of the tunnel to reveal a tiger, two grey wolves, and a black panther.

I then looked back at Tora as she morphed into a large polar bear and snarled at me with an all-mighty roar. While Jordan's eyes glowed blue as it started to rain. He then pulled the water that fell toward him, creating a frozen weapon in the shape of a very big axe.

Well frac – I was clearly outnumbered and knew the odds weren't entirely in my favour, given my diminished capacity with the trees and still healing. Which only meant, there was a very strong chance that I might lose this fight. – But they didn't know that and I was still hankering for a fight. So I pulled my fist up and sneered, "Bring it!!!"

Then at full speed I moved, dodging fireballs and flying ice axes, somersaulting over animals as they barrelled towards me. I eventually caught control of the ice axe, smashing it against the wall above Jordan's head then grabbed hold of the panther's neck, spinning it around and throwing it towards Jordan, screaming, "CATCH!"

Zera tried to sneak up behind me, and as she punched, I ducked, spinning behind her and kicking her in the back. But the polar bear and tiger took a lot more effort – they were too strong, and I was clearly out of my element as the polar bear charged towards me and threw me out onto the wet grassy fields, tackling me to the ground and pinning me under her paw with claws digging into my chest – Ouch!!!

## Original journal entry continued by Alex Woods

I ran around the streets of Melbourne frantically looking for Lila with Terrence right behind me getting just as agitated.

Why did Lila have to take off – Why did she have to be there – at the worst possible moment – Why?!

I was really struggling not to freak out, all I want is to find Lila and tell her I'm sorry, and that this was not the outcome I was hoping for today. – She doesn't deserve this.

To make things worse, Terrence and I were struggling to run at full speed, frantically trying to dodge the many people in the streets celebrating and cheering. All of them distracted, watching the clock countdown and the loud musical displays.

And I know it's not the best time, but right now I was really regretting not opting for a damn pizza night. But it only gets worse, because there's only 10 minutes till midnight, and Terrence and I both knew that the streets were going to get more and more crowded.

There was already too many people, and with the smell of the food carts and the many alcoholic beverages, and other odours in the air that are just gross. I kept losing Lila's scent because of it – And it was infuriating me – because all I wanted to do was find her and hold her and tell her it was going to be okay.

## Journal entry insert by Lila Winters

I struggled to break free from the polar bears clawing foot, and I screamed in pain as her claws pierced my skin. But eventually I mustered up the strength in my legs to kick the bear upwards, sending her into the air and running for my fraccing life as she landed.

But with a wave of his hand, Jordan created a giant hand of water from the garden-sprinklers that had automatically turned on. It grabbed hold of me, picking me up and throwing me into the side of the playground swing set. And again — Ouch.

The pain overwhelmed me, and I struggled to stand, nursing my ribs. And I very much knew that this fight was not going to end well for my stitches.

Clearly noticing my struggle to even stand, Zera walked towards me and jokingly asked her crew, "Are you sure this is the same girl who destroyed the island? She's not putting up much of a fight."

I tried to run, but they all circled me as Jordan pushed me to the ground, with the water on the ground around me beginning to freeze — trapping my hands and feet. They then all grinned at each other as Zera made a phone call, reporting their success.

And as the fireworks explode in the night sky, announcing the arrival of the new year, my heart ached realising now that

I had lost – I had lost my husband – my family – my friends – and my life, and it was all because of them – the greedy, murderous, cold-blooded people that call themselves The Board.

I felt so much pain before but now all I feel is a swell of gut-wrenching emotions stirring inside me. I wanted to kill them all, destroy everything they loved – like they've done to me. When suddenly my eyes glowed a dark ray of colours, and my hair faded into a pale white. I felt a burning fire of rage inside me and watched as my body started to glow red hot, melting the ice that trapped me.

The leaves from the nearby trees flew towards me, rapidly circling me and helping to cut the ice that held me down, but also forced the hunters to step back needing to shield themselves. Then as the leaves dropped to the ground, Zera stood back in fear and sheer confusion, uttering, "That's . . . that's not possible."

They were all in awe and terror, staring at me, a very angry, very large white wolf. – I felt empowered and angry as I raised my head, and towered over them, staring at them with fire in my eyes. And the ice shards that once trapped me before, had now reformed and hovered around me ready to attack them at my will.

Well this was new – and I was not going to waste a second of it.

## Original journal entry continued by Alex Woods

I finally picked up Lila's scent and could now sense her fear, and anger, and something else. So, I waved to Terrence letting him know, and he followed me running as fast as we could out of the city and into an old park. We stopped at the edge of the grass fields, that was for some reason on fire with a stream of water sprinklers dousing the flames and putting them out.

We cautiously canvased the area, noticing evidence of a very messy struggle. And when I found the bloody ice shards on the grass, I feared the worst.

I screamed Lila's name, but all I heard was the sound of a wolf howling. So we followed the howl and found a very large white, sitting at the end of an under-pass tunnel, covered in blood from the many wounds it endured and caused.

We approached the wolf cautiously as it watched over all the unconscious and very injured bodies, that were tied up in vines and roots from the nearby trees.

"Hunters," Terrence grunted, inspecting the face of the unconscious bodies.

I stayed focused on the wolf though, and could feel Lila's pain inside of it as I reached out my hand slowly and began to pat her gently behind the ears. She whimpered then rested her head on my lap then slowly morphed back into the Lila I recognise – almost.

My hand gently stroked her fore head as I looked over her. She was covered in fresh, mangled cuts, and bruises and what looked like a large animal bite on her leg. The stitches on her stomach were thankfully still being held together and had started to heal a lot faster. But her poor heart was aching as she let out a little whimper and her tears fell.

I admit I was in a bit of shock, but quickly took my shirt off, and gently wrapped it around her to cover her naked body, then as

I picked her up and held her in my arms, I looked back at Terrence in the hopes of getting some kind of reasoning or answer as we both stared at Lila's now very long pale-white hair and pointy elf-like ears.

She stayed quiet as I held her and didn't look at either of us, shielding her face in the crook of my neck to muffle her whimpers – yet the only time she whimpered was when I accidentally touched one of her injuries. But there was nowhere on her body that I could place my hands that didn't have any wounds. So, all I could do was just keep apologising to her as I ran her home at full speed.

When we arrived back at the hotel Matt was waiting in the hall outside his apartment wallowing in his own misery. And when he noticed Lila being carried into my apartment in such an unbearable state, he raced toward us to see her writhing in pain in my arms.

He followed us into my apartment and stood at the door, gasping at the state of her as I placed her down on the couch. She was so still and quiet and didn't look at anyone as Terrence tried to clean her wounds with whatever he could find from my first aid cupboard.

So, while Terrence was looking after Lila, I stood back up and turned to Matt to say something but before I could, he put his hand up to stop me then shook his head as he skulked back out of the apartment. And I wasn't going to stop him.

Instead I knelt back down and tried to hold Lila's hand, but it felt warm – too warm for a normal Nature guardian.

Crap – What the hell is happening to her?

# CHAPTER 15

# CHOICES

*Journal entry by Lila Winters*

*Well, it looks like the New Year was welcomed in, on what would be a very memorable event. – Not that I would tell anyone exactly what happened – and I don't think Alex or Terrence knew exactly what they saw when they found me.*

*Honestly, I don't even know what I saw.*

*Alex was happy to let me lay on his couch resting and attempting to sleep, and I was being extremely careful not to move while the many wounds started to heal.*

*At least on the bright side – now that my abilities were back at full strength, so was my healing. But while I rested, I could hear Alex and Terrence sitting at the dining table behind me whispering away, being left with so many unanswered questions.*

*Frac – what exactly did they see?*

*I stayed quiet and listened as Alex asked, "What's with the pointy ears and the white hair?"*

But Terrence didn't answer. Probably because he had seen my hair change colour like this before, instead he was more concerned about my abilities – the many different abilities.

My eyes were closed but I could sense him move and stood behind the couch, watching me as he whispered, "When we found her, she had turned into a wolf . . . and I could have sworn she was controlling that fire . . . Nature guardians aren't able to do that."

I sensed his worry when he spoke then he quietly walked toward the door as he added, "I think I might know someone who can help with . . . this."

But as Terrence opened the door, Matt, who was asleep on the other side of it, fell to the floor and woke up.

"Matt, what are you doing out here?" Alex whispered, rushing to help Matt to stand, and again I didn't move or open my eyes – I just listened.

"I have to see her. I need to explain," Matt answered, but when he looked at me, I could feel his heart aching and the confusion racing through his mind as he gasped "What the hell happened to her . . . why does she look like an elf from the Lord of the Rings?"

An Elf – is that what I look like, I hadn't actually seen myself yet.

Matt became more agitated the longer he looked at me and started demanding answers. But Alex shushed him, pushing

Matt back out into the hallway in the hopes I wouldn't wake up. – Too late.

I could tell Matt was getting more upset and confused as Alex tried to explain what he knew. But while I listened, I felt Terrence's hand hold mine and he kneeled down next to me to whisper, "I'll be back Lila, I'm just going to get some answers."

He moved closer to the point where I could feel his breath on my cheek and spoke very quietly. "I'm so sorry about yesterday . . . but I just want you to know that I really liked spending the day with you . . . and I really hope that you're not mad at me."

I really liked spending the day with him too, and I wasn't mad at him. All he did was try to help. So, I tightened my grasp of the hand he was holding to let him know I heard him and he took that as a good sign, pulling the blankets up to cover me before he left.

Alex however was not having much luck with Matt, in his vague and uncertain explanation of what had happened to me. And Matt seemed determined to see me and begged Alex to let him pass and to let him talk to me. But Alex wisely refused his request and explained, "Matt, she's just been through one hell of a fight, taking on several guardians on her own . . . her emotions are all over the place. The last thing we want is for her to wake up in a panic or in a rage and unintentionally kill you . . . Just let us get her back to normal and then you can talk to her."

Oh – does Alex really think I'm capable of killing? – Come to think of it, I don't really know what I'm capable of anymore. And for once Alex's logic made sense to me.

Matt begrudgingly accepted Alex's demands and walked away, with a request, "Okay, just tell her I love her."

But I really didn't want to hear that at the moment and to be honest I didn't believe him – not fully anyway.

When Alex came back into the room, he took deep breath out to relax then knelt down to adjust the blankets over me as I pretended to sleep.

I felt his gentle touch as he wiped the tears off my cheeks, and whispered, "I know you don't want to talk to me right now . . . and I get why you're pretending to be asleep . . . but just know I'm here for you."

He then kissed me on the forehead and lingered a little. But when he started to get up, I quickly grabbed hold of his hand and didn't want to let it go. So instead, he sat on the floor next to me and turned on the television with the volume low.

## Journal entry insert by Matt Winters

How could I have been so stupid – How could I have fallen for such a horrible act?

Adela had tricked me into loving her. She took advantage of my grief and anger towards Lila for leaving me – for dying.

And now I don't know what or how to feel anymore. At first, I was angry at Lila for taking a job she knew would risk her life. And I know she discussed it with me at first, but I don't think I fully comprehended the dangers she would be facing on almost a daily basis.

But what was worse was when she miraculously came back from the dead after months of searching and worrying, she returned with the monster who took her away from me, the man responsible for all of this.

I wallowed and muttered to myself as I walked into my apartment, feeling nothing but self-pity and loathing. I hated myself and I hated the world.

Unfortunately, Adela was waiting for me in my apartment. She wanted to apologise and see if Lila and I were okay. She clearly hadn't been taking it well either because she had drunk the entire bottle of champagne that I had planned to open with her as we watched the New Year's Eve fireworks together.

She then tried to explain what we had done away, and cried, "I know we both regretted our actions the first time, but they used us. We didn't know what we were doing." She stood in front of me trying to get me to look at her as she continued to argue, "This is just The Board's sick and twisted way of hurting Lila and tearing your family apart . . . Lila will understand. I know she will . . ."

I couldn't take it anymore and I was incredibly angry at the world, so I yelled at her — I told her to shut up — and told her that there were no excuses for what we had done because there was none. Then filled with hate, I glared at her watching her cry as I stated, "I had no Neuritamine in my system . . . I was only distraught and blinded by my anger . . . and you took advantage of that . . . I was a willing pawn in this sick and twisted game."

I tried to remain with some level of self-control, but I was barely holding on as my voice trembled, "You may be regretting your actions now, but just a few days ago, you had convinced me that my actions and my feeling towards you were justified . . . You told me that my wife had already betrayed me with the monster she had returned with. And that it would be better for both of us if we just moved on . . . you tricked me, and you pretended to love me, again and again!"

I became very bitter, fuming in my rage and I took it out on her — eventually I stood back, still struggling to control my anger as I opened the door for her. She apologised again to me and begged for forgiveness, but I couldn't even look at her. I just jeered the words "Get out" as I held the door open.

## Journal entry insert by Terrence Connors

It was ridiculously early in the morning when I left the hotel — well before the sun had risen. And yeah — I looked like a man who was up to no good, lurking around the Melbourne botanic gardens trying to avoid stepping in the many piles of rubbish and stuff littered everywhere.

I was trying to gain the attention of the trees or at least those who lived in them, but naturally they didn't come out so I shouted, "I know you're here. Please I need your help! It's about Lila!"

As soon as I said Lila's name Wyala revealed herself, looking down from one of the branches not far from me, and excitedly beamed as she jumped from the tree she was perched in. —— I will admit I was a little disappointed.

"I was hoping for your mother," I frowned slightly dismayed.

She stared back at me and smirked, "Everything the parent knows, the child only learns faster. But if you want me to go . . ."

She then started to climb back up the tree with a scowl across her face. And it quickly became apparent to me that I wasn't her favourite nature guardian and that the only reason she appeared was because I mentioned Lila. — I think Lila has an admirer — or two.

But I was desperate, so I asked for her help anyway, explaining what I knew.

# Journal entry insert by Alex Woods

I was abruptly awoken by the sound of a very loud and overexcited morning show host shouting, "Good Morning, Australia and welcome to the start of another fantastic year . . ."

Fantastic – my giddy aunt it's not.

It only got worse, when I rubbed the sleep from my eyes to realise Lila was gone and the door had been left open.

"Damn it – Lila," I shouted, running out into the corridor looking for her.

I think I lost my breath as I reached the elevator, and when the doors opened, I found my breath because I found her. – Lila was in the elevator wearing my oversized gym clothes—which looked incredibly sexy on her, with one of my baseball caps on to shield her face and her still very long, snowy-white hair draped down to cover her ears.

She seemed a little distracted, eating an oversized veggie burger combined with a bag of hot chips and chocolates. Her combination of food choices did seem a bit – odd to me.

Still I felt so happy to see her, rushing to hug her and spin her around. And the fact that she was still healing, completely slipped my mind as she dropped the chips and chocolates to hold the burger steady, "Ow . . . Alex . . . Ow."

I quickly put Lila down, apologising and helped her to pick up the hot chips, "I'm sorry, I thought—."

"I know . . ." she interrupted, "but don't worry, this is all Chase's cooking. He found me in the lobby trying to order take out, but apparently no one wants to deliver at this ridiculous hour on New Year's Day."

I explained to her that I could have made her something, but she rebutted, "You were sleeping so peacefully and I was starving. Plus,

I don't think you would've had enough food . . . I have no idea why, but this is my fourth burger and I am still hungry."

Wow – Lila really knows how to eat.

"Well, that explains the junk food," I commented, trying very hard not to laugh as I carried the bag of chocolates, following Lila back into my apartment.

She grabbed the chocolates off me and grizzled, "Hey, you can't judge. You eat like this every day . . . besides it's like you said. . . I'm an emotional wreck at the moment. Chocolates are good for me. . . Oh... and there's just one more thing that might help with my emotions."

I sat down at the table next to her, half expecting her to ask for a large bottle of caffeine or a good sparring session on the mat. Instead, I got a right hook to the jaw as she shouted, "That's for breaking your promise to me and not telling me the truth about Matt."

Ouch – she punched me so hard that I fell to the floor needing to hold my face in pain, then I watched her kneel down next to me to kiss my other cheek.

"And that's for coming to find me," She explained while giving me a hug.

Well, I can't argue with that one.

She sat back down at the table as I tried to clarify, "I'm sorry I didn't tell you. We just needed more information."

"But you were planning to tell me, weren't you?" she questioned, staring at me as she started wolfing down the chips.

My hesitation was a clear enough answer for her, and I certainly wasn't going to lie and risk getting clocked again. She then gave a greasy and huffed, "Alex, I trusted you to be honest with me. You're supposed to be my friend . . . not my protector."

I could see her point as I sat up to the table, rubbing my cheek, "Yeah well, now I'm a friend with a very confused face."

And with my pouty face I made her laugh. She then kindly shared some of her chips with me. – Not the best breakfast I had in mind for her, but she seemed happy.

We kind of sat in an awkward silence for a while, until I broke with, "So . . . Do you want to tell me what happened to you?" then casually pointed out her hair and her pointy ears.

But she couldn't really answer my question. What she could remember was scatty of a somewhat horrific fight scene along with the feelings of so much anger raging through her, and a lot of blood and a lot of pain.

I tried to follow along as best I could, then noted, "Lila, when we found you . . . you had turned into a wolf . . . I didn't know nature guardians could do that . . ."

That's when Terrence and Wyala walked into the room and interrupted.

"They can't or at least you're not supposed to," Wyala explained

I also noticed Terrence become puzzled observing the amount of food wrappers and junk food on the table as Lila rushed to greet Wyala with a hug.

Wyala marvelled at Lila's long white hair, "I am loving your hair right now . . . You know the Guardian Elders swore that your kind weren't possible and that there were steps taken to prevent this. But our elder Chief's saw through that lie."

Lila did not take that statement well and I think she felt slightly threatened, as she questioned, "What do you mean my kind? . . . Nature guardians are your allies, why would you want steps taken to prevent us?"

"Woah . . . calm down there, Lila," Wyala gasped, taking a few steps back and staring in I think awe as Lila's eyes turned black with what looked like flames in the centre of them.

Eventually Wyala found the courage to explain, "I'm sorry Lila, it's just my family has been watching you since you were a baby . . . and now I finally understand why. I believe that you might be an Origo hybrid . . . which actually explains a lot of things."

I don't think Lila or I understood any of that and we looked at Wyala dumbfounded, hoping for more of an explanation. So Wyala took a breath and explained again, "Okay, this is simple science really. If a Nature guardian breeds with an Animal guardian, the child becomes a carrier for both genes."

I interrupted in disbelief, refusing to believe it even though the evidence was literally in front of me. "That's impossible . . . that practice has been forbidden for thousands of years."

I had obviously struck a chord with Lila, who must have noticed that I had moved away from her. But honestly, it was a completely subconscious and learned response, and I swear it was not at all intentional.

Still she turned to me and grunted, "Why is my kind forbidden and why is it all of a sudden you are afraid of me?"

She then looked at me directly, waiting for my answer – but I didn't have one.

Then in seconds Terrence was in front of her and held her hands to reassure her, "Lila, we're not afraid of you. We are afraid of the stories . . . The last person who created an Origo hybrid was a German scientist during the First World War. . . He used the hybrid as a weapon, killing hundreds of German enemies. But when both wars had ended, the hybrid went crazy from post-traumatic stress, and he let his emotions and abilities consume him, turning against his people and destroying everything in his path."

"Are you saying I was created by someone, like some kind of sick experiment?" Lila whimpered with tears welling in her eyes. She became so distressed and tried to pull away from Terrence, but he pulled her closer and held her in his arms, shaking his head, "No Lila, that can't be true . . . you're not an experiment."

Then Wyala interrupted, "Well . . . that's probably true to an extent, mainly because an experiment wouldn't have the strength and control you have over your abilities. Someone like you would need to have a long line of guardian ancestors . . . Like an Origo hybrid pure blood . . . which explains why your abilities are so strong, and why you have a connection to more than one element."

"More than one," Lila shrieked, "How many abilities do you think I have?"

Well, she did almost destroy a naval air carrier, after completely destroying an island.

Wyala shrugged her shoulders at Lila, "That one. . . I don't know, but the sea spirits did explain to my mother that your connection to them was strong, stronger than any other Water guardian. So it may be more than you think. But you would have to ask your parents about that one."

That answer did not help Lila's mood, as she let out a groan of frustration and slouched back onto the chair in a sulk, stuffing her face full of chocolates and burgers again, and griped, "Great, so my parents were rebels, that weren't supposed to have me."

I glanced over at Terrence, who almost seemed like he knew more about Lila's parents and their forbidden affairs than he wanted to let on, and he definitely looked like he was contemplating something in his mind. But before he said anything, Lila sat up and frustratingly shouted, "Can someone at least explain to me why I look like an elf?"

She then pulled her white hair back and started tugging on her pointy ears as she pouted, causing Wyala to chuckle at her as she glanced out the window to see the sun rising and replied, "Well seeing how I'm not an Animal guardian . . . I'll leave that one in Alex's capable hands."

Um – my what now – Ah, right – I think Wyala is giving too much credit here. And I was going to say something but she and Terrence had already darted out the door in the hopes to return Wyala to the gardens before too many people were wandering the street. Leaving me to somehow figure out how to help Lila – who was now very sad and confused and angry at the parents she's never met.

Crap – seems like a dismal word at this point.

## Journal entry insert by Terrence Connors

I had just managed to get Wyala back into the park in time, before the locals had emerged to start their daily exercise routines. But when I raced back to the hotel, I got this horrible feeling that something was off. I mean I knew I was being followed, but I couldn't figure out why they hadn't taken any action yet. What were they waiting for?

It didn't matter anyway, I had to focus on Lila. And when I got back up to Alex's apartment, I was greeted by the sound of Lila throwing up in the bathroom with Alex sitting on the bed listening to her.

"I'm gone for 10 minutes and already you've made her sick?" I bickered.

Without a care, Alex rolled his eyes, "Um No . . . she did this one to herself . . . I have yet to meet anyone who can eat like that and not end up hurling."

Yeah — well he was completely lacking in sympathy.

I knocked on the bathroom door and asked, "Lila, are you okay?" Only to hear the sound of her throwing up further.

Eventually she opened the door after gargling a lot of mouthwash, looking very pale and complained, "No, I feel Terrible."

"You look Terrible." Alex chortled back, which clearly did not help, and I scowled at him, shaking my head. But Lila agreed and pouted, "He's right. I'm covered in dirt and blood and bruised from head to toe again, and I really want a shower but all of my stuff is in . . . his apartment . . . and Danny and Ruby can't see me like this or they'll freak out and . . ."

To my surprise, Alex's attitude quickly changed when Lila started to freak out, and he moved at super speed off the bed to grab her hands and tried to calm her down, "Breathe, Lila . . . remember to breathe."

And yeah — It was really cute watching Lila crinkle her nose and scowl at Alex, trying to breathe and calm herself.

When she had gotten to the point where she wasn't completely freaking out, Alex then calmly said "Alright, now let's sort this out one step at a time. Terrence will go and get some of your clothes from Matt's apartment, while you go and enjoy a calming and relaxing shower."

She begrudgingly huffed at Alex before disappearing back into the bathroom, still taking slow breaths all while I headed over to her apartment to knock on Matt's door.

He didn't seem too happy to see me, which is understandable but he was putting on the happy act in front of his children. But in the process of me asking for Lila's clothes, Mrs Willows walked up the outside hallway, to stand next to me, surprising both Matt and myself. "Hanna . . . what are you doing here?" Matt asked guardedly. Which was a really good question. It's like 7.30 in the morning — who rocks up unannounced at this hour?

And though I'd never met Lila's mother before, something about her made me feel nervous and uncomfortable — it might have just been because she was Richard's wife. — But it still felt off. Not only that she didn't even look at me as she replied, "Hi Matthew, is this a bad time . . . I just got this horrible feeling last night that something was wrong, and I thought I'd come visit to see if everything was okay?"

Matt nodded and invited both of us in but quickly excused himself into the bedroom to bring back a change of clothes for Lila while Mrs Willows was excitedly embraced by her grandchildren.

And I got this really bad feeling that Ms Willows presence here will not go well for Lila.

So, as soon as I got Lila's clothes, I didn't waste any time and returned to Alex's apartment, but as I did I got that same horrible feeling again — like someone was watching me. Still I had to focus. In the apartment, Alex had just finished a phone call with Henry, and before he was able to knock on the bathroom door to tell Lila some good news, I rushed to stop him. And whispered so incredibly quiet, "Lila's mother is here," in the hopes that Lila wouldn't hear. But she did and screamed, "What!" from the shower.

Damn.

Lila then appeared out of the bathroom in a half-speed panic, mumbling about her mother, and how she always arrives at the worst of times. Both Alex and I turned away to give her some privacy as she rushed to get dressed at a frantic speed. But when we noticed Lila's voice start to change, we turned to see her accidentally rip her top with her now claw-like nails. And she looked at us with her dark-black eyes, then in frustration, threw her top on the floor as she continued to get dressed in a noticeable mood.

While she was dressing, Alex whispered to me, "So Henry thinks that Lila's animal side is being fuelled by a strong emotion that she can't let go of. And in order to get her back to her normal self, she needs to change how she feels."

I looked back to him to clarify, "So what, we just need to give her a new emotion to focus on?"

Yeah well, that actually sounded easy — and when Alex nodded, I thought of an idea that might just work then ran to intercept Lila, holding her in my arms as I gave her a very passionate kiss, and as I did my eyes glowed purple.

Now this trick is usually only used to exchange memories, but I had used it once before to share my emotions with someone. And my emotions right now were really liking this kiss, and having Lila in my arms made me feel extremely happy as I remembered our friendship and loved that it's been rekindled.

I could feel the link working on Lila as her eyes turned back to her normal blue with a tinge of purple in them, and her body started to relax in my arms almost as if she was melting. But naturally Alex didn't see it that way and as soon as he got the chance, he pulled Lila away from me.

To be fair, passion is one of the strongest human emotions, which usually overrules anger, and the quickest way to express that emotion is through a kiss. My logic was sound — but Alex probably didn't take it well because Lila was only wearing jeans and a bra at the time.

Still, I stayed focused on Lila, hoping the kiss didn't have any adverse effect as she became drowsy and confused. Her hair colour had almost returned to normal, with a few white streaks remaining. But it stayed the same long length with the tips ending halfway down her back. But her elf ears disappeared — so that was good.

The problem now was, Alex was too busy glaring at me to notice Lila and yelled "Would you stop kissing her!"

"You wanted her to calm down, didn't you?" I snapped back, pointing out Lila's recovery. Finally, Alex actually looked back at Lila to see that my kiss worked. But she also looked like she going to fall down with Alex needing to hold her up as he barked, "Well, I could have done that!"

"Yeah, I doubt that." I snickered in disbelief crossing my arms.

Our arguing then continued and grew louder as we bickered about who was Lila's real friend and who was allowed to touch Lila — which was really stupid — it's not like he has claim to her.

Eventually Lila regained her bearings and yelled at both of us, "Would you two both grow up and stop fighting . . ." She then glared at me and snapped, "And you stop kissing me. It's clearly not helping the situation."

With my lips peaked at one side, I turned Lila to face the mirror, so she could realise what had actually happened, causing her to become ecstatic, looking at her now normal ears, tugging at them as she grinned. "Hey, it worked . . . let's do it again."

She darted back toward me and tried to kiss me again in the hopes of fixing her hair properly. — And I wasn't going to argue. — But Alex did, and as Lila's lips just barely brushed across mine, she was pulled away again while Alex sternly grumbled, "No! Let's not do that again."

He then stood between us, handing Lila one of his skivvy's and waited for her to put it on. She did as she was told with a crinkled nose — and again it was cute, it was almost like she was upset that she couldn't kiss me.

But as Lila finished dressing, she started sniffing the air and looked back at the front door of the apartment and whispered "Shane . . ." before racing at full speed out of the apartment.

## Original journal entry continued by Lila Winters

I could smell him, as I ran down the stairwell at full speed into the lobby. I stopped to scan the room, and there he was standing at the concierge desk pleading with Jessica.

"No, you don't understand. I'm here to see Matt Winters. He's expecting me," he urged.

Jessica, shook her head and kindly replied, "I'm sorry but Ms Willows was very firm when she said Mr Winters was not to be disturbed today."

But before Shane could argue any further, I raced towards him and excitedly pounced on him, pinning him to the ground and demandingly shouting, "Shane Winters, why didn't you tell me you were coming to town!"

He looked up at me in a shock and replied, "Nice to see you too, big Sis, considering your dead and all."

Ah, Right I forgot they had a funeral for me.

I wriggled back so Shane could sit up and greet me properly, and I noticed him briefly glance at the still healing injuries on my neck, face and hands. And right now, I'm actually very thankful that I was wearing one of Alex's long-sleeved skivvies, and decided to play it down. So I chuckled a bit as I jokingly replied, "Yeah, so being dead . . . it's not all that it's cracked up to be . . . it gets really boring, really fast."

His face puzzled a bit, and then relaxed, happily hugging me and explaining how he had missed my funeral and was slowly biking it back down to visit Matt and keep him company.

While I was listening to his explanation though, Alex and Terrence had run out of the stairwell looking for me, and didn't take too kindly to me straddling what looked like a stranger's lap. – And I'm not sure but I think I might have gotten a power boost last night, because I could sense Alex and Terrence's frustration and worry, as well as their protective nature for me. – Cool.

"Great, who the hell's that guy," Terrence grunted under his breath. And he knew full well I could hear him. He was probably sizing Shane up as well – judging his dishevelled bikie-gang-like appearance. And Shane's hairstyle – well let's just say he's had better days, with shaved sides and short brown tips at the top – that were now flattened from the motorbike helmet.

I helped Shane to stand, as Jessica ran out from behind the concierge desk apologising and trying to pick up Shane's duffle bag for him.

"I'm so sorry, Lila. I didn't know you were expecting anyone," she explained, "Your mother insisted that you were not to be disturbed."

Shane scoffed at her words, as he held up my partially white hair, and chortled "Looks to me like she's already disturbed . . . What's up with your hair, Sissy?"

Alex then ever so politely interjected, standing next me, casually pulling my hair away from Shane's hands as he introduced himself. "Hi, I'm Alex."

I know Alex meant well, being all protective of me, considering last night's saga. So I cheekily shook my head, and interruptingly smiled, "Oh, where are my manners . . . Alex, this is Matt's little brother Shane. Shane this is Alex, Jessica and over there is Terrence – and yes, Shane calls me Sissy to get on my nerves, but only he would ever get away with it . . . so don't you dare try it Alex."

I glared at Alex, knowing he was sizing up that dare, then briefly glanced back at Terrence, who for some reason seemed to be keeping his distance, standing in front of the elevator. But – I'm sure I'll figure out that reason later.

Greeting everyone with a wave, Shane looked around then asked, "So, Sissy, where's Matt?"

Ah – Well I suppose I had to bite the bullet at some stage today. So with a grin I rolled my eyes and grabbed Shane's duffle bag off Jessica, who looked like she was really struggling to hold it.

– I wasn't surprised, it was pretty heavy – Not for me though I just pulled it up into the crook of my arm, guiding Shane to the elevator and answered, "He's upstairs. Come on, I'll take you,"

Alex however didn't like that idea, and stood in front of me as we waited for the elevator, whispering, "Lila, are you sure that's a good idea?"

"Why wouldn't it be?" Shane griped, getting very suspicious of his actions.

To keep the peace, I just kept grinning at both of them and answered, "It's okay, Alex. You can come too." Then grabbed hold of Alex's hand, pulling him into the elevator with Terrence standing beside him.

Alex, Terrence and Shane all followed me, and we stood outside the door of apartment 147. But I wasn't overly sure what to do, I mean it felt a bit awkward just walking into my own apartment. So instead I decided to knock – which also didn't feel right.

"What's with the formalities, Sissy?" Shane asked as he laughed, "Are you afraid he might be naked or something?"

Actually, the fear was of seeing him naked with someone else – And getting that image out of my head is going to take all fraccing day.

I heard Matt quickly scrambling to the door and opened it with a brief smile that instantly disappeared when he saw his little brother. I think a small part of him was remembering that time when he couldn't argue his way out of 'the favour' of letting Alex stay in our guest bedroom. And now after all that's happened, I suspect he blames his younger brother for it.

I won't deny I was laughing internally – just a little.

Matt invited us all in for a hot drink, and we listened to Shane ramble on about his adventures around the world. – Shane was one of the cadet dropouts from my training days and it was no surprise that he didn't last long in my unit. Mainly, because he didn't have the discipline to make it in the military. But that's also how Matt and I met – I was sent to Shane house to break the news softly to him. Instead I walked out with a date.

As I sat and drank my hot-chocolate I scanned around the apartment half expecting Danny and Ruby to come and greet us. But with no sight of them, I turned back to Matt and questioned, "Hey, Terrence said that my mother was here?"

When Shane heard that question, he jumped so high out of his chair in a freak panic, "Woah Sissy, don't tell me that the Gen's here coz I am not prepared for all that . . ."

I laughed so hard at him that it hurt my injuries, and I know I shouldn't have – but he was being such a scaredy cat.

"Calm down, Shane," Matt sighed, standing up to reassure him, "Hanna is here, alone. And she's taken the kids downstairs to the café to get a real coffee and hot chocolate."

Huh – well that suck. She could have just ordered room services. I really did want to see my kids – while I wasn't a freaky elf or growing fangs.

Suddenly, the room started to get dark, as heavy storm clouds appeared rolling in over Melbourne with a thick curtain of rain crashing against the windows, making it almost impossible to see the city.

Shane gazed out the windows and revelled, "Wow, you always know you're in Melbourne when the weather changes like this."

But this wasn't Melbourne's weather, and I got a horrible feeling in the pit of stomach as I stared back at Terrence and Alex before whispering, "Something's wrong."

I then darted out of the apartment at full speed as the lightning struck the building with Alex and Terrence following behind me. And we ran as fast as we could up to Adela's apartment, pounding on the door, yelling, "Adela! Adela, open up!"

But when we got no response, Alex kicked the door in and found Adela unconscious on her couch with several empty bottles of champagne on the coffee table.

Frac — She was intoxicated and wallowing in her regrets.

The storm got worse when Adela heard me call her name to wake her up, and a burst of lightning struck the side of her balcony with a strong gust of wind shattering the window, forcing the rain inside.

This wasn't good — if she doesn't wake up, she's going to destroy the entire city. I had to think of something and fast.

Then with an idea, I turned to Alex and shouted, "Alex, go find Max. Tell him what's happening!" He nodded back to me and disappeared from the apartment, as I turned and screamed, hoping to be heard over the thunder, "Terrence! Help me get her to the roof top gardens!" Instantly, Terrence pulled Adela up into his arms but took one look outside and shouted, "Are you sure?"

With confidence, I nodded to him, and also asked for him to trust me. I know it was a big ask, but he didn't hesitate when he replied back, "I trust you."

He then followed me at full speed through the hotel, up onto the rooftop gardens, but we struggled to see as we were pelted with large heavy raindrops. Still Terrence was right beside me and as soon as we placed Adela down in the centre of the garden, he followed my lead and we worked together, swiftly grabbing a water lily from the fish pond and placing it under Adela.

We held our hands over Adela, and as our eyes glowed green, the water lily blossomed and grew large enough to encase her inside of it. It took a lot of effort and concentration to start the healing reaction because the amount of alcohol Adela had consumed, and it was starting to take its toll on the water lily, unfortunately stunting its healing abilities.

I became distracted for a brief second as I got another horrible feeling in the pit of my stomach, hearing the sound of my children screaming in fear.

Terrence noticed it and shouted "What's wrong!" as he continued growing the water lily. But I couldn't continue and I pulled my hands away, feeling torn as the blossom began to shrink, and I fearfully answered, "It's Danny and Ruby . . . I think they're in trouble!"

I suspect Terrence knew that he wasn't strong enough to create the water lily healing pod on his own, but he knew I would be. So ran off to find my children, leaving me to continue.

It took more effort from me but I eventually pulled the water lily up into its full growth and closed it over Adela like a cocoon, instantly causing the storm to stop and the rain began to calm until it was just a gentle shower over the city.

I felt pretty pleased with myself and did a celebratory dance in the rain, splashing around in the puddles. And when I heard the footsteps behind me, I turned excitedly, thinking it was Terrence coming back up to tell me my kids were all okay – instead I felt the sharp pains of a long cold ice shard, piercing into my stomach.

I was in a bit of shock but eventually I looked up to see Hanna standing there, smiling at me as she dug the shard in further, twisting it and tearing the skin around the wound open further, causing more excruciating pain.

Horrified at what she had done, I stared at her as she pulled me closer and whispered, "Your father sends his regards."

She then tossed me to the ground like I was a rag doll and scoffed as she walked casually back into the hotel, wiping my blood off her hands with a café napkin.

I tried to move – I tried to scream for help – but every time I did, the melting ice shard moved, causing more blood to spill out onto the grass.

# CHAPTER 16

# IF ONLY I HAD MORE TIME

*Journal entry by Lila Winters*

I could feel my heart getting weaker as the rain slowly melted the ice shard away. I really didn't want to give up, but I was beginning to feel like a had no other choice — I would die failing to protect the ones I loved.

I cried as lay on the ground, staring up at the sky and watching the rain fall, while I slowly waited for the end — until it didn't — I gazed around at the rain droplets to see that they had stopped — the raindrops just — stopped, suspended in mid-air.

Now I know I'm fast, but I definitely wasn't fast enough to make rain stop like that. And I honestly thought I had died, and this was my afterlife.

Had I really been that bad that I'd be forced to spend eternity stuck in the most excruciating moment of pain, betrayal, and death imaginable? – Whose fraccing idea was that?

A strange man then appeared standing over me. He looked at me peculiarly and I looked back at him peculiarly, he was a little young to be wearing the 80's-style old-man look with the business suit pants and shirt, covered over by a green knitted sweater. And his curly blond hair was combed to one side, creating a very high quiff that made him look—well, let's just say it wasn't a style I was used to.

I got a little nervous though, when he pulled out a photo of me from his pocket, and held it above me to compare and check if it was really me.

"Am I dead?" I asked him.

He knelt down next to me and pulled what was left of the ice shard out and replied, with a hint of an American accent, "Not yet."

He then rested his hand on my bloodied stomach, causing me immense pain as his eyes glowed silver, and when he stopped, he smirked, showing me his handiwork. I lifted my head slightly, looking down at my stomach to see that the bleeding had stopped with the wound now closed up and starting to scab.

But I wasn't overly sure how to feel or what to ask or even what to say. So many questions were racing through my mind like – Who are you? What did you just do? Are you a guardian?

Why isn't the rain falling? Are you a good guy or are you here to kill me as well? —things like that. That last one I struggled with a bit considering he just save my life — but hey, people do crazy things these days.

I was guessing based on my lack of speech and the confused look I was giving him, that he could tell I was needing more from him than — 'not yet'. So, he helped me to my feet and introduced himself.

"My name Tyme . . . and I'm sure at this point you could guess that I am a Guardian of Time."

I tried very hard not to laugh at the irony of his name as he explained that his parents had a twisted sense of humour and his dad especially was obsessed with plants and herbs.

But still very confused, I started to inspect the freshly scabbed wound again. "What did you do to me?"

I don't think he was expecting that question and he replied with a slight chuckle "I sped up the natural healing processes of your body."

Uh huh — because that was obvious — Not.

My next question was why, which is exactly what I asked him — still very, very suspicious of him — And seriously, I don't know why, maybe I'm just not used to strangers being nice to me anymore.

"Why not?" he replied flabbergasted at my question, "Look, if you didn't want to be healed, I can stab you again." He then pulled out his pocketknife and sarcastically smiled at me.

I quickly moved back, clearly in no mood to be stabbed again, responding "That's not what I meant . . . I am grateful for the assistance . . . I was just wondering why you're helping me . . . I'm sorry, but most of the Guardians I meet, want to hunt me not help me."

He almost looked concerned at my statement and asked, "So does this happen a lot?"

Right – exactly how much do you reveal of yourself to a person you've just met, even if he's saved your life. I mean, I could sense that he meant me no harm, but I could also sense an area of deceit in him, like he had an agenda. But he did save my life – so I thought I'd be nice and responded – truthfully, "Yes."

Again, I don't think he liked that answer and he grew more concerned as he moved closer to me, staring at the scars that he could see. He was just about to touch one of the scars on my neck when I stepped away from him and scowled, pulling my hair forward to cover them.

He quickly picked up on my dislike of people gawping at me and apologised before he explained, "I have been summoned here by my father . . . although I can't seem to find him at the moment. And I also wanted to ensure you make the right decision."

Huh, I was right he did have an ulterior motive.

"And what decision would that be?" I asked, crossing my arms feeling a little smug. And he replied "To fight or not to fight . . ."

But as he said that one of the tree branches unfroze, grabbing hold of my wrist and giving me a vision of a moment frozen in time that was unfolding out the front of the hotel.

-- In the vision Danny and Ruby were sitting in a car, crying. And Hanna was closing the car door looking panicked at the driver – Jordan, who was being tied up with tree vines by Terrence – who was standing in front of the car with his hand outstretched towards them, all while Zera stood behind the car, pulling the trigger of a gun aimed at Terrence.

Oh, Frac and Fruit Cakes this isn't good.

"Lila, are you alright?" Tyme asked trying to pull the branch off my wrist.

It was curious, I never told him my name and he also has photo of me. Something was definitely up with this guy. Unfortunately, I had no time to deal with him and I noticed him gawping at me again, when my elf ears reappeared and my hair streaked fully white with my eyes turning black. Then to answer his question I growled "No . . . but I will be."

I then ran at full speed jumping over the railings of the rooftop garden falling rapidly toward the ground. Thankfully the rooftop garden was not actually on the roof, it was only 16 floors up – 22 floors might have been a bit much for me.

Either way I was confident and determined as I rapidly approached the ground, and I called to one of the lower trees to give me a hand. The tree kindly obliged for me, stretching out its branch so I could catch it and slow my fall, but it also hurt all over my body when I did that — especially where the most recent stab wound was. It caused me to cringe — just a little as I landed safely on the ground and darted to the front of the hotel.

I stood on the foot path and examined what looked like a horrible nightmare still frozen in time. Then moved to stand behind Hanna, analysing the scene again. And I noticed that time was no longer frozen but moving extremely slowly as I watched the bullet travelling at a snail's pace towards Terrence.

My body tensed in a furious anger, and I really tried to control my new animal instincts and whatever else I had going for me, as I glared at the tribal mark of the collected Guardians tattooed on the back of Hanna's neck — realising that I had been a fool.

Luckily for me, I was able to use this anger to my advantage, knowing exactly what to do now. So at full speed, I grabbed hold of Hanna and threw her in front of Terrence, knocking them both to the ground, and pushing Terrence to safety.

But as I did, time unfroze with Tyme appearing next to me again, staring at my evil elf-like appearance and yelling "I can't believe you just jumped off a building. . . and survived."

He looked like he was in shock — but I really didn't care. I had to deal with some annoying Guardians first.

So I ignored him and I ran at full speed around to Zera, pinning her to the side of car she was cowering behind and crushed her hand, causing her to drop the gun as she screamed pain.

She stared into my very angry black eyes as I growled, "Taking my kids was a bad move." And while she was squirming to break free, I grew one of the seeds from my bracelet into the Amorphophallus konjac flower — also known as the Voodoo lily.

Zera clearly knew what that flower did to guardians, as she screamed, "NO . . . Please NO!"

But again, I still didn't care as I drove the stem of the flower into her shoulder, forcing her body into the awake-sleep— where you can see and feel everything around you but are paralysed to do anything.

And yes, that is what they tried to use on me during my many experiments and tortures, but apparently, I'm stubborn, and it didn't work for very long.

## Journal entry insert by Maxwell Eden

I was in a meeting with Jenny and Henry when our daughters Jessica and Katie rushed into the room to show us some damning new security fiasco that was unfolding as we spoke.

But before I could react to one problem, Alex appeared in front of my desk in a panic to inform me of my other daughter's condition.

He did seem a bit out of sorts and reluctant to say anything in front of the others as he demanded I come with him to the garden where Lila was trying to help her.

But Jessica interrupted him in a temper, shouting, "Um NO, she's not! Lila's gone all crazy ninja on us and is currently outside the lobby, tearing the street apart, looking all evil and bad arse!" She then stormed out of the office, handing the iPad to Alex to show him the live security footage of the hotel entrance.

I'm going to assume he didn't like what he saw, because he shouted "Damn it, Lila!" then disappeared from my office as well, clearly ignoring my rule of no running at super speed in the hotel.

Katie soon followed him, but before she disappeared, she ecstatically shouted, "This is going to be epic!"

Once all three had gone, I took a moment to fully grapple with what had just happed in my office in the space of two minutes. Then when I was ready, I adjusted my suit and smiled back at Henry and Jennifer, as I sighed, "There's never a dull moment in this hotel."

And I very calmly walked out my office ready to work my PR magic. Once the problem had been resolved of course.

## Journal entry insert by Alex Woods

I raced down the stairs of the hotel and out the lobby doors to see Mrs Willows unconscious, pinning Terrence down underneath her, all while Lila forced her way into a locked car by ripping the car door off its hinges. She then threw the door into the street to get to her children, who were trapped inside, screaming in distress.

I heard Lila shouting to Terrence, asking him to come and help her, but he was a bit preoccupied. So, instead I rushed to help Lila, demanding to know what she was doing, but as she pulled Danny out of the car to hand to me, I gasped at the sight of her bloodstained shirt and pants – again.

"Lila, I was gone for less than five minutes . . ." I commented, trying to survey the damage and find where the blood was coming from.

But Lila wouldn't let me see where the damage was, she was too focused on getting Ruby out of the car and placing her in my other arm, trying to calm her.

Both of the children were screaming in terror looking around at everything that was happening and at the state of Lila's bloodied elf like appearance, so I used a calming charm on them to help them to settle as they stared at my glowing gold eyes.

Lila thanked me for my assistance, but it was with a growling voice, "Thank you, Alex... Take them inside and don't trust anyone."

I didn't understand what she meant by that until I ran past Mrs Willows again and noticed the tribal tattoo on her neck.

"That's not Hanna" I whispered to myself, running into the hotel past Jessica and her team of security guards.

Thankfully, Matt and his brother stepped out of the elevator at just the right time. But I couldn't just hand Lila's kids over to Matt. What if he wasn't Matt and what if his 'brother' wasn't really his brother and Matt had been tricked again.

Awe – Crap.

I had to find a test that would definitely prove it was him, so I quizzed him, "Matt, the first time we met, what did you think I was trying to do to your wife?"

The random question puzzled Matt and he gawked at me, reluctant to answer it until I shouted, "I need you to answer . . . Quickly!"

"I thought you were trying to recruit her back into the General's army. . . Now what the hell is going on?"

Matt then tried to move towards me and take Ruby from my arms, but I pulled back and grunted, "There's no time to explain. Just quickly ask your brother something only you would know."

Again, he didn't like what I was doing and took an extremely long second to think before turning to Shane and asked, "Why did you hate me back in high school?"

Shane also didn't like what I was doing and glared at me, as he answered the question, "Because you fell in love with my best friend and stole her away from me."

– I'm assuming he meant Lila with that answer.

I waited for Matt to confirm it was the right answer and he nodded to me, hoping that answer would satisfy me and that I would answer his question. But he was only partially correct, as I placed Danny and Ruby in their arms then pushed them back into the elevator, pressing the apartment floor and rushing back out of the elevator, mumbling, "I'll explain later . . . just keep them safe and don't trust anyone . . . not even your brother."

Once the elevator doors were closed, I turned around to see Terrence and our security guards carrying two unconscious people, who I now realise to be Jordan and Zera – the Guardians who attacked Lila at the park last night. They were also carrying the Hanna imposter with them towards the service elevators down the other end of the lobby.

I rushed out onto the street again to see Lila running toward Katie, shouting, "Katie, we need a cover story . . . burn it and do it fast!"

The fear increased in Lila as she listened to the rapidly approaching sirens of police cars. Katie then jumped in excitement as she moved at full speed, throwing fireballs into the car, setting it ablaze – Which admittedly, her excitement is a fleeting concern for me.

While the car was being engulfed in flames, Lila rushed to pull the hotel's fire hose outside ready to douse the fire. But she paused, waiting a few more moments for the flames to grow large enough to destroy any evidence that may have linked back to her. Then just as the police and fire engines pulled up to the hotel, Lila started hosing the car down with the water as the firefighters rushed over to help put out the flames from the other side.

The only problem was the fire seemed to have a mind of its own refusing to be quenched. And it wasn't hard to guess why, when I heard Lila whisper to Katie, "That's enough."

I watched on in absolute confusion as Terrence appeared next to me, also watching the flames disappear, and staring at Lila trying to figure out what the hell just happened.

Once the fire was out Max rushed from the hotel to greet the police officers and praise the firefighters for a job well done.

Still, I was in a frantic state, wanting answers and scowled at Terrence, "What the hell just happened! . . . I leave you and Lila alone and I come back to this!"

He turned and looked at me, just as stunned and confused as I was. He shrugged his shoulders, becoming short of breath as he looked around for Lila, only to realise she had disappeared amongst all of the commotion.

What the Hell just happened?

# CHAPTER 17

# ONE PROBLEM AT A TIME

## Journal entry by Lila Winters

I was in a fury and I looked scary as hell — with blood all over my and still looking like an elf, as I stormed up into Maxwell's office where I demanded the security guards to take our new guests Jordan, Zera and the fake Hanna.

But I was also followed into the office by an overexcited Katie, who I'm guessing doesn't get to see much of this side of the guardian life. And when I got into the office Henry and Jennifer were trying to tend to Hanna.

"Lila . . . she needs an ambulance," Henry stated, then gasped, looking at the state of me and added, "You need an ambulance . . ."

And like hell I was going to let that happen.

I smiled back and snickered, "We don't need an ambulance," as I pulled them away from Hanna for safety, and demanded everyone in the room to get out.

Chase and the other security guards on our team, were wise enough and always trusted my judgement on these matters, and left without arguing.

But Jennifer was stunned and griped, "Lila . . . this is your mother . . . she's barely conscious."

And right now, I was barely holding control of my temper, and growled, "My mother just tried to kill me . . . Now GET OUT!"

My black eyes glowed green as I raised my hand towards the door, and the office plants reached in from the hallway wrapping around Jennifer and Henry, pulling them out of the room and closing the door behind them.

In the background, Katie was sitting in Max's office chair quietly watching. I didn't look at her but I warned, "If you stay, you stay at your own risk."

She didn't say a word she just got comfortable and smiled at me, waiting for me to do whatever it is I was going to do.

The downside was – I was going to look a crazy-elf-nut to her. But I didn't care I just started looking around the room, still struggling to hold my temper and barked, "Tyme! I know your still here you coward! If you want my help . . . if you want me to fight, then get your arse in here, Now!"

I tried to take a few calming breaths waiting for him and I knew he was here. I don't know how – but I just did.

And as suspected Katie gawked at me, slightly concerned and asked, "Who are you talk—"

But she froze mid-sentence as Tyme appeared behind her. – And for a man who's just met me and witnessed everything that I just did in the last 15 minutes. I was actually impressed that he was still determined to stick around.

Why? Is a good question, but not the one I wanted answered now. Instead I pointed down to Jordan, Zera and Fake Hanna, who were now frozen in time as well, then demanded, "Start talking. Who is she and what does she want with my kids?"

Tyme casually sat down on Max's desk and answered, "They're hunters sent by The Board to kill or collect. But you knew that part already, because you met them on the island."

How the hell does he know about the island? Who the hell is this guy?

Frac – I really didn't have time for these questions. What I needed was to find out what the fake Hanna wanted with my kids, and then it dawned on me.

"So, what? The Board thinks that killing me and collecting my kids is the better option for them." I sneered, struggling desperately not to turn into a wolf.

He didn't answer and unfortunately my interrogation was interrupted by Alex and Terrence banging on the office door, shouting my name and trying to force the door open, which at this point was being held shut by the office plants.

"I thought you froze time," I snapped back at Tyme. Causing him to stammer and tense a little, trying to explain, "Err. . . n . . . not quite. . . You see freezing time more than once in 24 hours can push the all of time off balance . . . so, instead I created a time bubble and—"

Suddenly the doors flung open as Alex kicked it in and looked around the room in confusion. But for some reason, he couldn't see me. From his perspective the room was empty, except for Katie who was frozen in the chair.

I tried to tell Alex not to freak out and that I could explain everything, but he walked right through me – as if I were a ghost. He stood in front of Katie to see if she was okay, with Terrence standing at the door also having the same issue of not being able to see me as he asked, "What's wrong with her?"

Tyme then moved out of Alex's way to finish his explanation, "As I was trying to explain, I didn't exactly freeze time. I . . . sort of . . . took you out of it."

Okay – Frac was just not the right word here, but honestly, I can't figure out a better word.

I cradled my head in my hands just barely understanding what he meant and mumbled, "I swear Steven Hawking would have had a fraccing field day if he ever met us . . . this whole thing is just insane."

Tyme tried to comfort me, hesitantly walking towards me and apologising, explaining how he was only trying to give us more time. And I snarled at him, holding back my rage, "More time! You haven't given me more time. You've taken time away from me! Now please just stop this!"

Then with just my luck to make things really Frac-tastic, Matt ran into the room demanding to know where I was, sparking a horrible turf war between Alex and Matt – again.

This is really getting old – really fast.

Alex glared at Matt in a confused anger and grunted, "What do you mean where is she . . . where are the kids . . . And don't tell me you left them with your supposed brother!"

Naturally, Matt got very defensive at that remark and shouted back, "And what's wrong with my supposed brother. He passed your stupid test and both Lila and I trust him with our children."

The bickering got worse from there, as both of them blamed the other for everything that's happened to me, and it ended with Alex shouting, "At least I'd never betray her like you did . . . and I'd never give up on her . . . like you did."

Those words only led to Matt punching Alex repeatedly, and Alex tackling Matt to the floor.

I shouted at them begging them to stop, futilely trying to pull them away from each other, and failing as my hands brushed straight through them and into Terrence.

I'll admit, it was a little creepy seeing my hand stop inside Terrence's body, but somehow, he felt it too, stepping backwards in a fright.

He looked around suspiciously then tried to get Alex and Matt's attention by shouting their names. But when that failed, he raised his hands up and his eyes glowed, calling the office plants to grow around both Alex and Matt separating them. Terrence then scanned around the room again and called out my name.

"Lila, was that you?"

I was absolutely devastated at the words Alex and Matt had said. Barely holding back the tears as I nodded to Tyme, pleading with him to make things right.

"I'm sorry Lila," he sighed then with a wave of Tyme's hand, I appeared, standing in the middle of the office looking teary-eyed at Matt, with Tyme standing next to Jordan, Hanna and Zera. And Katie finally unfroze and finished her sentence.

She then peered over to Tyme and asked, "Who the hell are you?"

But she didn't get the answer, because everyone was a little distracted watching, as Hanna shuddered and started to wake, transforming back into Tora.

With the tears falling and the rage barely being kept at bay, I darted towards Tora and greeted her in kind, stabbing a Voodoo lily into her stomach in the exact same location of the wound she gave me. – It's only fair, don't you think.

As Tora went into the awake-sleep I stood back up and scanned the office to see all of them staring back at me – Katie, Matt, Alex and Terrence – I could feel all of their emotions of concern, worry and anger. And I was tired of being angry at the world, so I left.

I rushed back out onto the rooftop garden, wanting to scream but couldn't because I still had a someone, who needed my help.

Matt didn't help the situation though, stupidly following me out into the garden, begging me to let him explain. I however didn't want him to explain. I knew I wasn't in the right frame of mind for this kind of conversation. So while holding back my tears I turned to him and shrieked, "I don't want you to explain! . . . I don't want to know the answers to the many questions I have . . ."

"But I want to," he insisted and started to explain anyway, "Lila, I thought you were dead."

I started feeling the tears pool in my eyes again, and it was clear he wanted to have this conversation, so I let him have it and refuted his statement. "And how long did you wait?"

I don't think he was expecting me to ask such a direct question because he stayed silent, so I asked again, "How long was I dead before you chose to move on? . . . Had you even buried me yet?"

Clearing his throat, Matt tried to excuse his actions by claiming that he had been tricked, but we both knew he wasn't under the influence of Neuritamine. He moved closer to me and tried to hold my hand, asking me to sense his nature and feel the love he still had for me.

But I pulled away from him in fear for his life, knowing that I was still enraged and being flooded with a whole lot of emotions, and I didn't want him to get hurt.

I desperately tried to keep my distance from him and in tears I whimpered, "Don't . . . just don't. . . Matt, I can understand if it was just a case of you thought I was dead. But then how did Alex and Terrence find out if they arrived home the same time I did?"

I didn't need him to answer that question, because we both already knew that answer. But it still hurt just as much, watching him stare at the ground, not knowing what to say.

"And there's your problem," I sniffled shaking my head in disappointment, "The more you try to explain, the more questions I ask . . . that you can't answer."

I gave him a moment and I stayed quiet, slightly hoping that he would say something but when he didn't, I begged him to go.

The pain in my heart was becoming unbearable again, but still waited and watched as Matt looked at the ground trying to think of his response, and it was only then that he spotted the pool of my blood. He peered up at the bloodstained clothes I was wearing and the freshly scabbed wound, and eventually he conceded to my request, walking back inside all pouty faced and angry.

I took a deep breath in and out, before I knelt down next to the large water lily, trying to dry my eyes before I raised my hand over the flower to open the petals, hopelessly whispering to myself, "Every time one problem is fixed, another always takes its place."

I then waited for Adela to wake-up and it didn't take long for her. She opened her eyes, fearfully looking around at the shrinking petal and then up at me. Instantly I sensed all of her guilt and confusion, – and I won't lie, I'm definitely over the whole animal guardian ability of being able to sense emotions, – especially crappy ones.

Yet in wanting to be nice, I put on the best smile I could find and whispered "It's okay, just relax. You're safe."

But judging by the look she gave back to me, I don't think she was convinced.

"What happened?" she asked, looking down at the surrounding blood and then at the state of me and my obvious tired and fake smile.

I really didn't want to answer the question she wanted answered, so instead pulled the focus back onto her, "Well, from my observation, you tried to drink yourself to death."

She was stunned, and needed a moment to process before she asked, "But why would you save me . . . I've done so many horrible things to you."

I was beginning to understand why Tyme was frustrated at me when he saved my life – I mean, being questioned for doing a good deed, does not always happen.

But based on the guilt exuding from Adela, I thought it best to explain, "There are a lot of reasons why I could have let you die . . . but there are so many more reasons to let you live . . . for starters you're more useful to me alive . . . I don't know many water guardians round here that don't want to kill me."

I tried giggling a little to lighten the mood, but it didn't work. She just stared at me, still baffled, clearly needing more than that, so I continued, "Adela . . . just because you've done something bad, does not always mean that you can never do anything good or make it right —that choice is yours remember."

## Journal entry insert by Terrence Connors

Yeah — I'm still trying to wrap my head around everything. Today has been to the point of extremely fast paced, and honestly, I cannot possibly fathom how Lila is still standing and has not gone all crazy-animal-girl on us again.

After Lila left the office, Alex was roped into giving a statement to the police, and Jessica had called an emergency meeting of the team to ensure they all give the 'right statement' of what happened. But because I'm not part of their team, I got pushed out of the room and told to go find Lila.

Naturally I decided to go to the last place I left her, which was on the rooftop garden, and I was really hoping to get some answers from her about — how in the space of 10 minutes she ended up causing this much chaos. But as the elevator doors opened, I accidentally bumped into Matt, who seemed somewhat heated from what I'm guessing was another failed attempt to talk to Lila.

I knew he didn't like me and he scowled at me as soon as he saw me, but I really wanted to be that person Lila believed I could be — you know the nice guy and all — Not that I wasn't a nice guy — I just didn't have much of a choice in the matter.

Still, Lila believes that I can change the opinion of how people see me, by letting them see who I really am. So I ignored his scowls and smiled back, "Hey, I'm guessing you found Lila?"

He grunted as he nodded, but Matt still looked really sad, so I commented, "I'm also going to guess that you didn't get a chance to explain your piece."

Matt cleared his throat and straightened his demeanour before he replied, "No, I said my piece and she's right, I think I just need to give her some . . . you know time."

He then took a breath and mustered up a fake smile as he switched places with me in the elevator. But as Matt held the elevator doors open, he briefly glanced at the doors that led to the rooftop garden and then to me, looking very puzzled.

"Terrence, right?" he asked confirmingly, and I nodded, turning back to him to listen as he asked, "Look this might be out of line here . . . but I just gotta know . . . when you guys were on the island, did you two ever . . . you know?"

Yeah — I'm going to assume that was a natural leap for him given the situation. But at the same time, I knew he was looking for some kind of justification for what he did.

So, I replied, "Matt, as tempting as it was, nothing happened. Every time we were alone, she . . . well, she thought of home."

That response only made Matt sadder as hung his head and let the elevator doors close.

— And I wasn't overly sure if I was being nice at that point.

I also needed to take a moment because I was a little angry at Matt for hurting Lila. Once I was calm again, I walked out onto the rooftop garden to see Lila releasing Adela from the flower pod and helping her to stand. I thought it would be best to give them some space, so I waited in the doorway and listened.

It was unbelievable that Adela even had to ask why Lila had saved her. I mean if Lila's willing to save the man who hunted her and was responsible for her kidnapping and imprisonment, I don't think adultery is where she's going to draw the line.

While they were talking though, I realised that Lila wasn't alone in the garden, and I caught a glimpse of a man hiding in one of the side gardens. Not only that I could sense him, and I would recognise the nature of that man anywhere.

So I waited in the hallway and walked with Lila and Adela to the elevator, letting Lila know that I was going to stay back and do a little clean up, discreetly hinting to the bloodstains all over her and trying not to act suspicious. Then as soon as the elevator doors closed, I ran at full speed to catch the intruder by surprise, standing in front of him.

"Well, isn't this a shock . . . first the island and now the hotel, you know some people may find this little suspicious."

The intruder's name was William Knight, the one who acted like the fake groundskeeper back on the island, but really, he's just the terrible father who handed his baby girl to General Crush-Your-Soul Willows and called it love.

"Hello, Terrence," he greeted, crossing his arms, "I see you're playing the role of the protective lover quite well, or is that Alex's job . . . I'm starting to lose track here."

I didn't answer that, I just stood and watched him slowly inch away from me, roaming around the garden as he disappointingly shook his head. "You know, I was absolutely shocked when I watched my baby girl take you with her off that island . . . I really thought she knew better than that."

It didn't take me long before I accused him of sending those hunters to kill Lila. But he flat out denied it.

"No . . . unlike you, I came to protect her," he snickered then pointed down to the pool of Lila's blood seeping into the grass. "Your mother is the one responsible for this mess."

Yeah — I really don't like this guy. And I think I may have let my protective nature of Lila get the best of me, because I was not proud of what I'm going to do. But I also wasn't going to risk Lila discovering this kind of truth, and trust me, she's been through enough harsh revelations to last a lifetime.

So let's just say — I made the problem go away — and we'll leave it at that.

It took about an hour to fix the 'problem', and I was on my way back to Alex's apartment walking up from the stairs when I bumped into Alex just stepping out of the elevator.

"Hey, where's Lila?" I asked, slightly concerned.

He shrugged his shoulders, "I thought she was with you."

And with that we both started to panic a little and picked up the pace, rushing into the apartment looking around for Lila.

I wasn't sure how to feel when I found Lila's bloodied clothes on the bedroom floor and her sitting in the shower. She was curled up in ball in just her bra and undies, crying and watching the old blood trickle down towards the drain.

I was really struggling to breath, and felt so sad for her. — I wanted to just pick her up and run as fast as I could away from here and hide her from all of the bad stuff.

This was supposed to be her home — she's supposed to feel and be safe here — but she not.

My heart ached for her, as I watched Alex carefully open the shower door and sat down next to Lila, trying to comfort her. And I felt so helpless as I listened to Lila whimper, "This is never going to end . . . They're not going to stop coming for us."

She peered up to look at me with her teary eyes. "I'm going after them Terrence, and I'm going to destroy them . . . their entire organisation will be burnt to ash by the time I'm finished with them," she then wiped the tears from her eyes and asked, "Will you help me?"

I was shocked at Lila's sudden change in attitude towards the fight against The Board, but it was understandable given her reasoning. And I kind of needed a second to think.

On one hand — I know The Board, they're not going to go down easily, and they certainly have what it takes to bring us to our knees.

On the other hand — if my mother truly was the one who sent those hunters, then 1 — she's an idiot who just made a really bad enemy, and 2 — it means they're desperate and threatened by Lila's abilities. Which also meant that Lila was right—it was never going to end.

Still staring up at me Lila tearfully waited for my answer, and as soon as I looked into Lila's eyes, I knew exactly what I wanted to say. And that was yes.

So, I nodded to Lila and agreed to help her in whatever she needed, then sat down in the shower on the other side of her. And as the water drenched my clothes, I held Lila's hand with her resting her head my shoulder. I then heard the best word come from her mouth when she breathed, "Thank you, Terry."

# CHAPTER 18

# SECRETS

## Journal entry by Alex Wood

It was time to face the aftermath of the New Year's Day incident – and the day wasn't even over yet. The burnt-out car had finally been towed away after Detective George Nell and his team had done their sweep for any evidence. And the media were as usual trying to stick their nose where it doesn't belong, taking photos of everything.

The last statement the police needed was Lila's, and George had been waiting for hours to see her. But she kind of needed a little longer in the shower to process everything. – That and I needed to track down some clothes for her. So while she was getting ready, Max was down in the lobby trying to delay – I mean talk with George and his partners.

When Lila finally did step out the elevator, she looked very different. She had worked really hard to make sure there were no obvious or visible signs of injuries, by using make-up and my large zipped-up black jacket – and we'd also managed to stop her looking like an elf, so yay.

Still, something was bugging me because Lila hadn't yet explained to us what happened to her. I mean when Terrence left her on the roof, she had no new injuries, and then 5 minutes later we see her covered in blood with an old stab wound—that was not there before, while tearing the street apart – going all elf ninja on us. And I saw the amount of blood she'd lost. It covered her, and there's no way she could have healed that fast.

I sat in the lobby lounge and listened in to Lila's conversation to Max and George, knowing full well it would not be revealing the whole truth. The problem was because this isn't the first incident Detective George was assigned to investigate, I was beginning to suspect that it wasn't a coincidence either.

Add to that – I don't think George believed Lila when he questioned, "So you're saying the car just burst into flames? . . . What happened to the passengers?"

Lila cleared her throat as she replied, "As far as I know, they were sent to the hospital. We just followed up to check how they were, but the nurse said they refused treatment and left."

George stared at Lila, taking a moment, waiting for his partner to document the statement. And I'm guessing Max could sense the tension as well because he wrapped the interview up fairly quickly and started walking the detectives out of the lobby, until George stopped and loudly asked one more question, probably hoping to catch Lila off guard.

"Oh, I nearly forgot. . . we found a bullet casing underneath the car. You wouldn't know anything about that would you?"

Luckily it didn't catch her, instead Lila stayed calm and with a chuckle replied, "George it was a car fire, not a shooting." He nodded his head, accepting Lila's answer, then Lila smiled back and added, "It was nice to see you again, George"

The last comment George said really got me on edge. And it became clear to Lila and myself, that he wasn't just going to drop the investigation when he said, "It's nice to see you alive Lila."

Max quickly escorted George out of the hotel and ran back to catch both Lila and myself waiting for the elevator. He was a little out of sorts and his voice was shaky as if he were holding back tears, when he sighed, "Lila, I just wanted to say thank you for helping Adela today. She never actually explained what her reasons were for drinking so heavily, but I have a fairly good idea."

Lila grew a little uncomfortable realising that Adela and Matt's secret wasn't so secret, but I'm guessing she wasn't overly surprised given that it was Max. Still she stayed quiet and walked with me into the elevator, listening to Max as he added, "If you need anything at all, please just ask . . . even if it's just to talk."

With an obvious fake smile, Lila thanked Max then waited until the elevator had started to move before she let out a massive breath of relief and nursed her stomach.

That poor, poor abdomen was copping a beating.

"So are you going to talk to me yet?" I demanded quite frustratingly.

But Lila just brushed me off, saying, "Not now, Alex."

And that was it. I had had it. So I stood in front of her and demanded, 'Yes now . . . Look, I get that it's been a long day and night for you. But you need to unload on somebody, now let me have it."

"Why?" she snapped, "Why should it be you, and what about Terrence? Do I have to tell him as well or Adela or better yet why don't I just pour my heart out to my cheating husband . . . Why is it whenever I've had a rough day, you're the one who's there wanting to help?"

I moved closer to her and held her hands so she would sense my intentions as I explained, 'Because you are my best friend, and I care about you very much . . . And no matter how many times you push me away or how many moods you throw at me, I will never give up caring for you."

She then looked up into my eyes and groaned with a slight grin, "You're an arse you know that." And I chuckled back, "Yes, but I'm a very sweet arse."

I could sense her mood become slightly happier, while we were gazing into each other's eyes, but as the elevator door opened again, we were interrupted by Terrence standing there waiting for the elevator as well and holding a bag of Chinese takeout for all of us.

He grinned at us, clearing his throat, "Should I . . . um . . . wait for the next one?"

I quickly stepped away from Lila, replying, "No . . . I was just proving a point to Lila," then held the door open for Terrence to step into the elevator and stand next to us.

He had a huge grin on his face as he nodded "Ah huh . . ." but remained quiet and judgemental after that.

## Journal entry insert by Lila Winters

Terrence bought me food – and I know food doesn't usually taste this good, but after the day I've had, that slightly too oily vegetarian stir-fry was the best in the world. Yep – I like food.

After dinner, I needed to put on yet another brave face to head over to my – I mean – Matt's apartment in the hopes of checking in on Danny and Ruby while I wasn't a crazy elf. So, while I walked down the hallway I focused on staying calm, and I took slow deep breaths, taking comfort in knowing that Alex and Terrence were just a few steps behind me.

I know I'm internalising my emotions from the day and yesterday, and it's a definite struggle to see Matt's face and not let some of those emotions seep out, but I was doing this for my kids.

I stood outside Matt's apartment door and again, I didn't know if I should knock or just use the key, but before I could do either, Matt had opened the door. He must have heard me or something.

"Hi . . ." I said with a nervous grin.

Matt helloed me back with a smile, and the emotions started stirring inside me and I struggled to find the words and eventually I blurted out, "I just wanted to say hello to the kids and see if they're okay."

I then took a very big breath out and waited for Matt's response. He seemed slightly disappointed as he looked behind me to see both Terrence and Alex standing guard and asked, "Do you mind if I talk to Lila alone?"

They didn't answer him, instead they both looked at me for a sign, and I was a bit nervous but I nodded my head. Then Alex replied, "We'll be right here if you need us . . ."

Matt obviously didn't take that response very well as he walked me into the lounge room to sit and rambled to himself. He then sat on the coffee table in front of me and nervously spoke, "Look I know I'm not your favourite person at the moment . . . but. . . I just want you to know that I'm here for you if you need to talk."

Oh frac, not him too – I tried very hard not to roll my eyes, tying to be calm and let him continue, "Lila, there was a time when we could tell each other anything."

Um pot, this is kettle – Time to start fessing up.

It became very clear to me that my emotions were not helping me through this conversation. – I was just glad my hair hadn't turned white again.

But it was a real struggle when he held my hands and pleaded, "Look what I'm trying to say is . . . I love you . . . and I'm sorry . . . and I want you to come home even if that means I have to sleep on the couch."

He even looked at me with the puppy-dog eyes. But to my non-surprise, the puppy-dog eyes didn't work this time. And I weakly smiled as I stood up, pulling my hands away from him to say, "Thank you."

But unfortunately, neither of us realised that our conversation was being overheard by a nosey little brother — who clearly didn't like my response as Shane burst out from the guest room. "That's it . . . the man tries to apologise and begs you to come home, and all you say is thanks. . . come on, Sissy, give it a little effort here."

Matt tried to jump to my defence, telling Shane that it was more complicated than that and that he didn't understand. But Shane just walked past him to tower over me.

"No," he huffed glaring at me, "I think I do understand and I think that this whole situation just needs to be hugged out."

Oh Frac No – that was a very, very bad idea. In fact, it's the worst idea he's ever had.

Still, Shane was determined and stupidly grabbed me by the arms, clearly not knowing that I could pummel his oversized, egotistical brain in a second. And worse, he was pushing me towards Matt, trying to stretch my arms out to hug Matt, all while I was trying to object and hold back the emotion of rage and heartbreak, as I fearfully warned, "Shane, I don't think hugging will help right now."

I tried to break away from him without hurting anyone, but he wouldn't listen and urged "You won't know unless you try it . . ."

FRAC NO, FRAC NO, FRAC NO

As I suspected I could feel a lot of bad things inside me and when my hand brushed up against Matt's arm, instantly my hair turned white and my eyes turned black.

I had to get away, so using all of my strength, I pushed Shane backwards away from Matt, grabbing his arm and flipping him onto his back with an almighty thud, screaming in a growling voice, "I said NO!"

Frac – what did I do.

Shane stared up at me, shocked at my sudden hair colour change then looked back at Matt, realising he had some explaining to do. With Alex and Terrence quickly appearing in the room, standing between me and Shane, trying to keep me from hurting them, while telling me to calm down.

I know their intentions were in the right place. But seeing my friends standing there protecting my family from – Me. Well that just hurt even more than any of the pain I had felt before. My chest really hurt when Alex asked, "Lila, are you okay?"

But I wasn't and he knew I wasn't as I growled, "No . . . I'm not okay . . .," then disappeared.

## Original journal entry continued by Alex Woods

I'm beginning to agree with Lila when she says her family always rocks up at the worst possible time. I mean if Shane had arrived maybe even a week later, we might have had a better handle on all – this.

As I helped Shane to his feet, I tried to ignore the many questions he was asking like – Who the hell are you? Why is Lila acting this way? How did her hair change colour like that? – and the best one was – Did anyone see her eyes change colour?

Yep – that would have been a wonderful story for Matt to explain if he knew anything about it – but he didn't. So instead I sat Shane down at the bench, patted him on the shoulder, and sarcastically said, "I think your eyes are playing tricks on you mate," then casually rushed out of the apartment.

I hurried back into my apartment where Terrence was kneeling down on the floor trying to coax the large white wolf out from underneath my dining table and I grumbled, "Well, that went well."

Eventually Terrence convinced wolf-Lila to crawl out from underneath the table, and she rested her head on Terrence's shoulder as he tried to calm her.

I however wasn't calm and grunted, "I knew that Shane guy was going to be trouble."

Which was replied to by Lila growling at me. I just glared at her and snapped, "Well you can't talk. He brought out the animal in you."

And just to push our luck, Matt knocked at the door holding a stack of Lila's clothes as a helpful, apologetic gesture. But that only caused wolf-Lila more frustration, causing her to growl at him then pounced up onto Matt, knocking him to the floor and leering into his eyes.

We rushed to help – Matt as he stared back at the wolf and shrieked, "What the hell is that?"

And once we finally managed to pull Lila away, Terrence stood to his feet and snidely replied, "That would be your wife . . . she was just barely holding it in while she was listening to your apology speech. I'm surprised she lasted as long as she did."

Matt became enraged when he realised both of us were listening in on his conversation to her and took a swing at Terrence. But Lila quickly broke free of my hold on her and rushed to protect Terrence, pushing him down onto the couch and standing protectively over him, snarling at Matt. It didn't take long for Matt to get the hint and wisely put his hands out in surrender, backing out of the apartment slowly.

This time I remembered to close the apartment door then I heard Lila start to whimper, looking back at Terrence as she realised she had accidentally made him bleed. I personally didn't care about it, but she obviously did, licking his cheek to apologise.

I might have gotten slightly jealous. But when I sat down on the couch, it showed Terrence who Lila trusted more as she rested her head down on my knee and not his.

"Good Girl" I grinned, scratching her behind the ears as I turned on the TV and began the long waiting game of Lila turning back into her human self.

## Journal entry insert by Lila Winters

Well that was a frac-tastic meeting – I didn't even get to see my kids. Instead I watched TV for most of the night, while Alex and Terrence ever so patiently waited for me to turn back to my human self. They were very nice though and placed a blanket over me, knowing that when I transformed back, I would need some sort of covering.

But still, it was taking a while for me and the boys eventually fell asleep. I looked up at them and felt this warm fuzzy feeling in my chest as I started to remember all the times they were there for me, looking out for me, keeping me safe. And that feeling transformed me back into my human self.

Feeling ecstatic about being myself again, I celebrated – but on the inside as to not wake the sleepyheads. Besides I had somewhere I needed to be, and this time the boys weren't invited, so I very quietly moved at full speed to dress and run out the door.

I covertly made my way down to the indoor swimming pool, which was strategically closed for renovations then knocked the secret code.

When Adela opened the door, she looked at me in shock, gawking at my hair. I guess I was still holding on to some residual anger because my honey-blonde hair was streaked with white again.

"What the hell happened to you?" she gasped.

Then with an eye roll and grunt of annoyance, I pulled my hair up into a ponytail, and retorted, "Family dramas" as I walked into the poolroom, locking the door behind us.

I followed Adela around the pool, while she filled me in on what had been happening while I was pre-occupied as a wolf. – I had asked her earlier today while we were in the elevator if she could do a favour for me – and she was actually quite helpful.

The pool water has been partially frozen over – by her, and resting on the top of the ice were three large pink water lilies, each containing one of our not-so-nice guests from earlier today.

I waved my hand over one of the lilies to open it just a little to reveal Jordan, sleeping so peacefully. But one of the lilies was empty, because Zera was being suspended in a column of water while Adela interrogated her for information.

I briefly glanced at Zera who was still fully conscious – just trapped, and I ignored her scowls as I closed Jordan's water lily back up.

"So how's our patients doing?" I asked, but I didn't get the answer I wanted.

Adela just shook her head in disappointment, "Your treatment theory didn't work . . . the blood work definitely showed the presence of Neuritamine in all of them, but using the water lily pods to cure them was a bust."

Well Damn Fracs – I was just as disappointed. – I really need to find some way of curing them without causing the memory loss. So, I twiddled with my fingers, biting my bottom lip as I thought, and it didn't help that Zera was grunting and glaring at me.

She snarled, "You are your wasting your time . . . We will never tell you anything . . . we will serve The Board until death."

–Oh, how cliché

I continued to ignore her as I picked up the voodoo lily from a nearby table and threw it into the column of water, embedding it into her thigh. And as she grew limp and stopped struggling to escape, I pushed the water lily into the column to catch her as she fell then closed it back up – but not before I pulled the voodoo lily back out and handed it to Adela.

"I need more time," I said, puzzled with thought while pulling the water lilies together and mumbling to myself, "I need to do some more research and find the right tonic . . . I can't keep rescuing them without some way of curing them . . . I mean some of these people have been under the influence of Neuritamine for years. They could lose an entire lifetime of memories . . . families . . . and friends."

Adela interrupted my mumbling, adding her own thoughts, rambling, "Not to mention all the information they could have about The Board and the organisation . . . you know who's in charge . . . where are they hiding . . ." She kept on rambling while inspecting the voodoo lily then stopped her ramble to ask, "What the hell is this?"

"An *Amorphophallus konjac* flower . . ." I replied, quickly pulling the flower from her hand before she could do anything stupid like kill herself, then explained, "It was used in the village to cause total paralysis to the prisoner during interrogation and experiments. It can even cause death . . . if used improperly."

Gently placing it back on the table, I looked back at Adela who seemed somewhat grateful I took it away from her when I did.

"So what are we going to do now?" she asked, trying to divert the subject, "We can't keep the pool closed for renovations too long without Max and others finding out . . . And on that note . . . can you tell me again why you made everyone believe they had been sent to hospital, fully cured of Neuritamine?"

I was still a little lost in my thought when she asked her question, busy twiddling with my fingers and walking around the lily pods as they rested on the ice. But eventually, I answered, "Because I didn't want people to lie for me . . . I know the detective assigned to this case. He's an old friend from school. . . and he's damn good at his job. If he suspects more than one person in a lie, he'll smell a cover-up. And one lie is enough for the team to handle . . . the only reason you know is because you were heavily intoxicated at the time, and you can use that as an excuse not to give a statement."

I think she was happy with my answer and impressed that I was able to give it that much thought with everything else going on around me today.

She then helped me to pull the water lily pods up onto the edge of the pool. But as we moved the last lily, I started to feel weak, and the pain in my stomach intensified. I still don't understand what happened to me when Tyme did whatever he did to me, but I was a little happy with him because most of the wounds from the New Year's Eve fight had healed, even the wolf lacerations. But this new wound was deep and caused a lot more damage than anyone realised.

Adela noticed me struggling a little and asked if I was okay, as I sat down to take a breather. And I knew I wasn't okay because I was starting to sweat, but didn't want Adela to worry, considering we were currently standing in an ice room. So I just nodded and diverted the subject, explaining that I had an idea on how to hide the pods. All I needed to do was call him a not-so-nice name to get his attention.

I'm not sure why, but I think Tyme likes me because I could still sense his intriguing nature hanging around me – just not quite in our time – and I was positive he followed me into the pool room and had been watching me. So, I walked around the room, trying to track where abouts he would be and smiled staring at nothing, "Alright Tyme . . . I have favour I need to ask of you . . . So here's the deal, you can either show yourself and listen to my request . . . or can stop following me and get the hell out of my hotel . . . it's your choice."

I waited and ignored Adela's weird stares at me thinking I was a nut, and sure enough, I was right, Tyme appeared standing in front of me, extremely puzzled.

"How the hell did you know where I was?" he asked.

I grinned back at him with a chuckle, "It's a trade-secret. . . I'll tell you mine if you tell me yours."

I think my talents intrigued him, but he also intrigued me with his kindness as he helped me to sit down on one of the pool chairs before he explained how his abilities work. I then kept up my end of the deal and explained what I knew of mine, before I asked a favour of him.

He agreed to help me on the proviso that I would set aside some time to talk with him about something that was apparently extremely important. I suspect it's most likely something about him needing my help to save his family from The Board, and if that was the case, he'd have to get in line. So I agreed to look at my calendar and find some time.

## Original journal entry continued by Alex Woods

Well it looks like watching TV and a good night sleep had worked to help Lila turn back into her human self, because Terrence and I both woke up to see Lila asleep on my bed.

I stood at the end of the bed smiling at her and whispered "She's so peaceful when she sleeps."

Terrence stood next to me holding a plate of pancakes and juice for her and in shock he asked, "Is that more blood?" He then moved at full speed, placing her breakfast on dresser and pulled the bed covers down to reveal her blood-soaked singlet – again.

For some unknown reason to us the mysterious wound had reopened and infected, and when I knelt down to inspect it, I could feel her body radiating too much heat with her skin covered in sweat.

We both tried to wake her up but she was out cold. And the fear built up in me as I turned to Terrence, asking if he knew how to make that blue rose thing. But he shook his head in a panic then stated, "We need to call an ambulance."

I knew he was right, but I also knew Lila would absolutely hate waking up in a hospital, and I was torn but I wasn't just going to sit here and watch her die, so we called the ambulance.

When the paramedics arrived, they took one look at her and rushed her down through the lobby and into the ambulance van. While they were loading her in, Adela ran up, asking what was going on. But when I explained Lila's condition, she was confused, "I don't understand. She was fine when she left the pool room last night—"

"Wait... what do you mean the pool room last night?" I said interrupting her.

She became illusive and seemed like she was trying to find a good lie to spin me, but before she could say anything, Terrence interrupted, "Hey, they've agreed for one of us to ride in the ambulance with her."

Well that must have taken a lot of convincing for him – considering we weren't family and all, but neither of us were planning on letting Lila out of our sights after the day we had yesterday.

Again, I was a little torn about what to do, but in the end, I replied "You go . . . I'll run down"

Terrence seemed grateful for that as he climbed into the front passenger seat. And as I watched the ambulance drive away, Adela grinned at me instantly, knowing how to change the subject when she asked, "Since when have you two become such good friends . . . I thought he was still the Dark man to you . . . or has he grown on you as well?"

Obviously that last pun was intended as she hinted to him being a Nature guardian, but I was not amused and grunted at her before I disappeared down the street.

When I arrived at the hospital, Terrence was sitting in the ER waiting room where he had been asked to wait when they discovered he wasn't family, which was where I ended up waiting until Matt arrived with Shane in tow.

Great – if this goes badly, the entire world is going to know they have a shape-shifting wolf girl loose in Melbourne City. And to make things worse, less than an hour later, Detective George Nell walked in looking for Lila.

Matt stood up to greet him and asked what he was doing here, and the detective reluctantly replied, "The doctors are required to report any suspicious injuries to the police. So here I am."

Yep – this was going to go badly.

Matt looked at him, befuddled and asked, "What do you mean suspicious injuries?"

And in a definite mood, the detective opened his notebook and read aloud, "We have a report of a stab wound approximately 3 cm in diameter in the middle top left of her abdomen . . . The doctors have also noted three old laceration scars stretching across the abdomen from top to bottom consistent to an animal attack as well as bite marks on her upper thigh and arm, also consistent to an animal attack. . . Although the doctor believes they're from several different animals, all at different times."

He stopped reading his notes and peered up at Matt with a begrudging sigh trying to indicate his frustration of being lied to, before he continued, "They also suspect that Lila may have been or is still the victim of abuse, and have reported over a dozen laceration scars, with clear signs of trauma . . . and apparently they still have more to add to the report."

Well, Matt already knew about most of the wounds, but not necessarily the circumstances behind them, so he honestly replied that – he didn't know anything.

He did also remind the detective – that Lila had disappeared in the woods and hadn't told him anything about what happened, in the hopes that that explanation would satisfy the detective.

But it didn't the detective just had more questions and he glanced back at Terrence and myself being very quiet and listening as he huffed, "Does anyone want to tell me what hells going on yet . . . or am I going to have to find that out myself?"

He then glared at Matt waiting for a response, but when he got none, he grew more agitated and irked, "Well, why don't we look back over the puzzle pieces and see if it jogs any of your memory's. . . Your wife went missing more than 2 months ago in a suspicious bush fire and was reported dead . . . then out of the blue, she rises from the dead and returns on Christmas eve with no explanation as to where she's been. And yesterday we had a suspicious car fire outside the hotel Lila works in, with the passengers of that car fire yet to be found . . . And now Lila is in the hospital with what looks like an infected knife wound . . . and a lot of unexplained scars . . . Does anyone want to start talking yet?"

Yep – this was bad. What made it worse was when Matt started getting angry looks from his brother as the puzzle pieces started looking more and more suspicious. Then Shane asked the worst question, at the worst time, "What the hell kind of trouble has Lila got herself into this time?"

Awe – Crap

The detective quickly picked up on that commented and snickered "This time . . .? And here I thought Lila was one of the good ones."

And yep – it got worse, because his interrogation was quickly interrupted by the loud commotion coming from the ER ward with the nurses rushing to assist.

Terrence and I got a really bad feeling that it had something to do with Lila and rushed into the ward, not caring if any human noticed us, forcing the security doors open.

We were easily able to find Lila as we heard her voice scream, "No! Get away from me!!!" She was standing next to the hospital bed surrounded by medical staff and security, looking like she was ready for a fight.

"Stay away!" she shouted as one of the security guards tried to grab her arm and restrain her, but in the end failed, being pushed to the ground along with his colleague.

I think the commotion was causing her to have another panic attack, as her heart rate spiked and her breathing became short – and I could definitely sense the fear in her.

While Lila was trying to breathe through her fear, Shane stupidly stepped in, helping the detective try and grab hold of her. And again, Lila pulled away then somersaulted over them, landing in the hall behind them.

Both Terence and I noticed Lila holding her stomach as she landed then stood glaring at us because she knew this was our idea. But when she saw Matt the anger rose in her as her eyes turned black and she disappeared, running at full speed out of the hospital. And without hesitation, Terrence and I disappeared at full speed in pursuit of her.

We chased Lila through the streets and caught up with her, with both of us grabbing her by the arms and pulling her into a nearby alley, pinning her against the wall.

She didn't struggle, she just glared at us and shouted, "What were you guys thinking! . . . Why would you take me to a hospital?"

So I shouted back in the same tone, "You had a fever, you were bleeding, and you wouldn't wake up. What were we supposed to do?"

Shrugging it off, she tried to and play it down, claiming, "It was just a flesh wound."

But I wasn't buying it and sarcastically asked, "And how did you get this flesh wound?"

Unfortunately, Lila didn't want to answer that question, instead she started playing with her fingers and biting her bottom lip – which I knew was her trying to think. And that only ticked me off more – there shouldn't be much thinking needed when it comes to telling the truth.

"Lila…" I grunted incredibly frustrated and worried, "We left you safe and in one piece and then minutes later find you covered in blood . . . and you expect us not to ask questions."

She stopped biting her lip, but she couldn't look at me either and she was still reluctant to answer – holding back tears. Until I urged, "Tell me, Lila!!"

"I was stabbed . . ." she cried, with tears streaming down he face, "And I nearly died . . . the very minute I was left alone . . . and I didn't want to tell you because I didn't want you to feel like you do now."

As Lila whimpered, she looked down at mine and Terrence's face and saw the disappointed failure-look that we both felt like, both knowing that the only reason they got this close to her was because we weren't there. I couldn't breathe properly because I was so mad, even Terrence was short of breath.

Lila then held her hands to our cheeks and whispered, "I don't want either of you to feel like this is your fault . . . because it's not . . . all of us did what we could, when we could, to save our friend and my kids . . . And I would do all of it again in a heartbeat . . . um. . . But right now, I would like to let you know that there is an elderly couple staring at us and the old man is calling the police."

I slowly turned my head, following Lila's gazes to see an old man and woman standing at the end of the alleyway staring at us in shock, possibly fearing for Lila life as two men pin her against the wall – not the best look.

Thankfully, Lila's a lot smarter than me in these situations and waved to them with a smile, loudly stating, "This isn't what it looks like . . . we're . . . um . . . just playing an intense game of tag . . ."

Lila kept smiling and told both of us to smile as well until the elderly couple had moved on then she looked back at us and explained, "Look I'm sorry about not telling you . . . but I'm sure you've both noticed that a lot of fraccing crap has happened in last 48-hours. . . and I'm still trying to process it . . . the worst part for me is that right now I don't know who to trust. . . I mean . . . they used my mother."

I was beginning to see her point and I felt like I could finally breathe properly as I loosened my grip, slightly lowering her to the ground, then Terrence let go as I cradled Lila in my arms. But she looked at us suspiciously when she noticed us both working together and in agreement with each other.

"What," I grinned.

"You didn't think we were going to let you walk home?" Terrence added with a snickering smile.

Lila bit her bottom lip again as she relaxed into my arms and chuckled, "You know it's creepy how well you two are getting along . . ."

"Hey," I barked, trying to correct her, ". . . let's just say we have a mutual understanding and leave it at that . . . okay."

She giggled at me as she wrapped her arm around my neck and braced herself as we ran home at full speed. Then once we got her safely back to the apartment, Lila worked with Terrence to teach him how to make the blue-rose tonic. And as Terrence poured the tonic on to Lila's wound, it started to heal – properly this time.

## Journal entry insert by Matt Winters

After Alex called and told me he had found Lila and that they were safe at the hotel, I made my way back home from the hospital with Shane who remained particularly quiet on the ride back. He was silently fuming to himself because I refused to answer the many questions that had arisen since the moment he arrived.

So, when we got back to the apartment, he stormed off into the guest room while I was greeted by Maxwell, who was eagerly awaiting an update and watching the kids for me.

"Hey, how did it go?" he asked quietly.

I slumped down at the dinner table next to him and replied, "Terribly . . . Lila woke up in a panic. And now we've got George and the ER staff asking questions about everything, and I don't have any answers about anything."

Maxwell looked at me and started to make a coffee for me as he asked, "So why do I get the feeling that that's not why you're upset?"

He was beginning to know me far too well as I held my head in my hands, and groaned, "I saw Lila's face today . . . there was anger in her eyes. I don't think she'll ever forgive me."

Maxwell sighed as he handed me the cup of coffee, "Matt, she's only had a day to process . . . this. Just give her a chance to cool off . . . she will forgive you."

I know he was trying to be encouraging, but it wasn't working. And I stood up in frustration, knocking the chair over and glared out the window, trying desperately not to cry.

"But how can I compete with Alex and Terrence?" I grumbled, "They're guardians. They have more in common with her than I ever will . . ."

Max remained seated at the table and picked up the chair that I knocked over as he calmly reminded me, "It's not a competition, Matt . . . Yes, they are guardians and yes, they share something in common with your wife. But Lila loves you. . . and you both have more in common than you think."

He then stood up and readied himself to leave, but left me with one final piece of advice, "Matt . . . I've been married quite a few times, and trust me, I know . . . that when it comes to betrayal . . . it always hurts more when you truly love the person . . . and in my experience, that true love plays a big role in the forgiveness process . . . so just give it some time."

Before he left, he patted me on the back and said good night as he walked out the door, leaving me to wallow a little while longer.

# CHAPTER 19

# BOYS WILL BE BOYS

*Journal entry by Terrence Connors*

It's official, although Mr Eden was reluctant, he's agreed to Lila for me stay at the hotel and work for her as part of her security team — I'm finally part of the team — sort of.

Today was the first team training session, and I was having a lot of fun. And as usual, it was Lila's favourite — Shoulder tag. I was up against Lila, while Alex was paired up with Adela. And the human security man — Chase, he was there along with two of his colleagues.

I think was doing pretty well in the session, however, I did struggle with the rule of not using my abilities. And by the end of it — Lila won.

But I really think she took advantage of my nice guy attitude — because while we were training, I'd accidentally knocked her in the chest, and when she took a few steps back, I saw the pain on her face and hesitated. She then ended the fight with a high spin, kicking me to the ground, and smiling as she tagged my shoulder and helped me up.

I heard Adela chuckling under her breath as she listened to Lila call it for the day.

"We'll meet back in the conference room at 10, 'kay?" Lila said grinning back at me as she gained a general consensus from the room.

Adela seemed to be in a hurry though as she grabbed her bag and walked out of the gym, waving back at Lila. All while Alex stood next to me also somewhat baffled by Adela's quick exit and commented, "She's in a hurry."

But he also had to highlight that maybe she just doesn't like me because of what I did to her, which does not help my confidence for my first day on the team.

Alex and I waited for Lila to finish talking with Chase and his team, but as she slowly made her way back to her gym bag, I noticed she was discreetly nursing her stomach as she walked, and I just knew I had made her injury worse. So I raced to walk alongside her wanting to help and sighed, "I really did hurt you, didn't I?"

"It's fine," she breathed with a smile.

But it wasn't fine. It's almost been two weeks now and the wound still hasn't completely healed.

She must have picked up on my disbelief as I loitered closely around her, so to help prove her point, she rolled up her top to show me the wound, "See no blood . . . just bruises and scars."

And yeah, it was a relief to see no blood on the outside of her body, but the bruising and the swelling did not comfort me, especially because she had a blue rose crushed in the water of her drink bottle, and it doesn't seem to be helping her.

I thought it was supposed to be a healing tonic but something's gone wrong or maybe I made it wrong and Lila's just not telling me.

Either way I had to say, "Lila, it's been weeks now. Don't you think we should take you back to the—"

"Say that word and I will knock on your arse again . . ." she snapped glaring at me.

She definitely knew what I was going to say, but I'm smart enough not to argue. Instead I smoothly changed the subject to her current hunger predicament and suggested we go out for breakfast, and that idea was greeted with a very wide smile from her — I'm just guessing here, but I think she really likes food.

Since Lila was still in a competitive mood, she raced me and Alex to the elevator and started listing suggestion of where we could go for breakfast. She was actually pretty excited while we waited for the doors to open, but as they did, we saw Matt standing in the elevator ready to leave for work, and Lila's excitement quickly disappeared.

"Hi" Lila said awkwardly.

"Hi," Matt replied just as awkwardly, he held the door open for us as he asked, "Are you going down?"

There was a brief moment of silence until Alex chimed in and said, "Yes we are, thank you," as he gently nudged Lila into the elevator.

While we stood in the awkwardly silent elevator, I noticed strands of Lila's blonde hair turning white. The tension was very thin and when the elevator doors finally opened on the ground floor, Lila smiled at Matt and said, "Have a good day at work Matt."

Matt then looked back and waved saying "You too" as we went our separate ways.

And yeah — this was awkward, and in a way, very telling.

# Journal entry insert by Adela Eden

As much as I loved seeing Terrence being thrown to the floor, I have to admit the best part of my morning is walking into the swimming pool room carrying two bowls of fruit salad, and seeing two hotel guest swimming laps, completely unaware of what was really going on.

I casually walked into the women's changing room and then back out to see a slightly different perspective – with the water lilies that Lila was using to contain our guests Zera, Tora and Jordan suspended by vines hanging from the roof above the pool.

The two hotel guests were completely oblivious to me as I walked to the other end of the pool room where Lila's new friend Tyme was sitting on the deck chair relaxing in the sun that was shining through the window. He seemed to be in a sour mood as I walked towards him and he griped, "You know . . . I only agreed to help Lila on the proviso that I'd get a chance to talk to her . . . but it's been two weeks now."

"I know," I replied handing him a bowl of fruit and a fork, "But she's had a rough couple of weeks recovering."

He didn't seem too convinced with that, making the brief comment, "Yeah, training in the gym really sounds like recovering."

He then started eating his breakfast all mopey and sad. I think he suspected Lila was avoiding him, so I thought up a compromise, "I know, why don't I talk to her for you?"

But he didn't go for it, shaking his head as he played with his food.

"Oh, come on," I pleaded, "I can help. . . I might even be able to persuade Lila into talking to you. . . But I can only do that if you give me a hint as to what the topics about."

I eagerly waited for Tyme as he took a moment to think. The offer clearly intrigued him, and eventually he replied, "It's about her brother."

And that was where he completely threw me – What the fruits!

My jaw dropped as I gasped, "Brother?" and I stared at Tyme, shaking my head in confusion trying to think what he meant by that. "Lila doesn't have a brother."

Still he sat there continuing to eat his fruit as he casually explained, "No, I'm her brother."

WHAT THE FRUITS WITH EGG ALL OVER.

Alright – I wasn't expecting that one and naturally, I was surprised by this new information and choked on my breakfast, spitting one of the fruit pieces out and caused it to land in the pool.

"You're her brother?" I wheezed, with my head filling with so many questions. The only one I could think to say was, "Why haven't you told her yet?"

He looked over at me weirdly, and still in a grumbling mood replied, "It's not something you can just blurt out to someone . . . I mean when Lila and I first met, it wasn't really the best of circumstances . . . and what was I supposed to say . . . oh hi Lila, I see your busy dying and jumping off buildings to save lives and all. But I just wanted to mention that I'm your half-brother and that your real father William Knight sent me to come find you —"

"Wait . . . Lila's real father is alive" I shrieked interrupting Tyme's little tangent to early and I stood up shouting, "How could you keep something like this from her . . . We have to go and tell her."

I was about to demand that he put me back into the normal time, but before I could he stood up to meet my eyes and made me swear not to say anything.

"No Adela," he urged, "I need to be the one to tell her this, and I need to do this right or she'll never trust me.

. . I have waited so long to be able to meet my sister. . . and I don't want to stuff this up. . . Promise me you won't tell her."

Alright, well, he seemed pretty desperate to want Lila to be a part of his life and I really wanted to help him with this, so I promised I wouldn't tell her. But I also knew that it would be a struggle for me, considering I was just about to have a meeting with her.

# Original journal entry continued by Terrence Connors

Lila, Alex and I decided to go to a café in Melbourne Central for breakfast and we had a lot of fun and laughs just talking with each other. And yeah, I was right, Lila does like her food, and I was impressed because she had 3 tomato and cheese toasties to herself and a muffin.

But I was still a little distracted by my curiosity, so while we were slowly walking back to the hotel enjoying the summer air, I thought I'd confront Lila about the randomly appearing white streaks in her hair. I mean it had started off with just one appearing in the elevator, but a lot more appeared while we were eating, and if I was right in my theory, it meant that something was still bugging her.

The only problem was, I couldn't really find the best way to ask the question and I was afraid she might just shut me down, but I did it anyway, hoping for the best.

"So, Lila, when are you going to work on the thing between you and Matt?"

Surprisingly, it wasn't Lila who tried shut me down — it was Alex

"Knock it off, Terrence."

Yet, I persisted and argued, "Alex, she has to deal with it at some point, because she can't keep turning into a wolf every time she sees him."

"She was fine this morning," he irked, stopping our walk to argue with me.

So stopped to argue back, "Are you seriously telling me you haven't noticed her hair slowly turning white. She's definitely not fine."

We began to bicker with each other, completely oblivious to any attempt Lila had made to get our attention until she stood between us and shouted, "HAY! <u>She</u> is right here and <u>She</u> is just fine. However, <u>She</u> is very concerned about the fight that <u>He</u> and <u>He</u> are having in the middle of the damn street . . . And why do I feel like I've had this argument before."

She grunted at both of us, before she cradled her head in her hands, trying to breathe and calm herself. Which only helped my case and Alex eventually agreed with me as he commented, "He's right you know. There is an awkward tension between you and . . . him."

YES — he said I was Right.

I was internalising my joy at this moment and Alex definitely noticed it but before he could say anything Lila quickly and discreetly silenced us as she noticed the unmarked police car not far from us with Detective Nell sitting in the driver's seat, drinking coffee.

She then spoke at a whisper to reply, "Look, I am planning on talking with him. I just need more time . . . now can we please change the subject?"

Alex pulled a wry grin and suggested, "We can always talk about how Terrence got beaten by a girl this morning."

To that Lila just rolled her eyes and reminded Alex about the first time they met and how he also got beaten by the same girl.

And Yeah — I couldn't stop smiling after that, and I happily walked next to Lila as we made our way back to the hotel in time for her first security meeting of the year.

When we got up to the conference room, half of Lila's team were already waiting, except for Adela who ran in just after us, seeming somewhat befuddled.

Lila confidently stood at the end of the large conference table and greeted everyone by name as they all took their seat and she started the meeting.

I will admit, I was a little excited to see Lila in action. Not only that — to finally be on this side of the door and a part of her team and not hiding in the shadows was very much a proud moment for me.

The downside was — I got so caught up in my proud moment that I almost missed all of Lila's speech and only heard her say, ". . . Now to business, at the end of last year, Max was approached by a woman named Kerry. Some of you know her from mission control."

"Kerry, what did she want?" Adela interrupted territorially.

Maxwell also interrupted and answered for Lila, explaining, "She requested that since Mission control has been shut down and because we have the manpower and skills, we might be willing to complete the search for the missing guardians."

The room instantly went quiet as I felt the dagger-piercing stares from Lila's fellow teammates. — Not exactly the best 'welcome to the team' moment for me.

Thankfully Lila brought the attention back on to her, by clearing her throat loudly and stated, "I have taken on the mission . . . but I can't do it alone. Now, I'm sure you all understand from what happened last year . . . that this is a very difficult and dangerous request, and I view all of you as very dear friends. So I put this request to you all, and I ask that you please do not accept this mission unless you are 100% committed to finding the missing guardians."

The group took a moment to think about her request, as they whispered and grumbled amongst themselves. But while they did, I noticed Lila look over to me and Alex and nervously smiled at us, knowing that we had already committed to her cause. Still the tension in the room grew as no one else had yet put their hands up.

Until Adela and Chase both stood and said, "We're with you Lila."

After that, the rest of the team stood in agreement with the last person being Maxwell as he stated, "Well Lila, it looks like you've got a full house now . . . Just let us know what you need."

Lila then peered around the room at her willing and eager team and grinned, "Then let's get started."

The first thing Lila addressed as everyone was taking their seats, was me.

"Terrence, can you join me please."

Okay, I was beginning to feel like I was in trouble but I did as I was told, and stood next to Lila at the end of the conference table. And as I did, I felt the dagger piercing stares again. Not from Lila though she smiled at me, before turning to address the group, "Now, some of you may know this man as The Darkman. . . which I still think that's a silly name. . . But now I would like to introduce him properly to you . . ."

She then hooked her arm around mine and proudly added, "This is Terrence Connors . . . and he is actually one of my oldest friends. . . we just lost touch for a while . . . and he has also proven himself to be a very good friend to me. . . and I'd really appreciate it if you all treated him a little better and quit with the judgemental stares. . . unless you all need a gentle reminder of what you regret and are responsible for."

I noticed a lot of Lila's team start to shift around in their chairs, feeling a bit uncomfortable, probably under the assumption that Lila's last statement was directed at them. But what surprised me, was that it was quite a few of them.

Chase eventually piped up and said "Welcome to the team Terrence."

And yeah — I got my proud moment back, then nodded thanking Chase, as Lila pulled up a chair for me to sit next to her, and asked if I could help her with the rest of the meeting.

I was more than happy to do that, and Lila and I then spent hours getting everyone up to speed with all the information we had so far.

Quite a lot of the team were surprised that I was so forthcoming with such sensitive and classified information that I had learned over the years. So, by the end of the meeting, everyone knew about The Board, and its organisation's structure, along with certain influential people they had in play. I also told them about some of the many organisations that The Board were using as a front. And to be honest, I had only just scratched the surface.

But there was a moment when Lila was asked about what happened on the island, and she stuttered, struggling to get the words out.

I could tell she was trying to hide her fears and push-back certain memories as she started pulling at the sleeves of her turtle-neck skivvy.

Luckily, Maxwell picked up on it as well and intervened, "Well, I think my brain's currently on information overload, and I could definitely use a break for the day. So, I suggest we meet back here tomorrow and form some strategies."

As the group all started to leave, Henry caught Lila's arm and wanted to talk to Lila and thank her for rescuing him and his daughter Katie, adding, "I know the only reason you agreed to meet Terrence in that park was to find any information that would lead back to us . . . so thank you."

He was a little shaky in his voice and held back his tears as he hugged Lila. But Lila then replied to him with something I was not expecting as she grinned, "The person you should really be thanking here is Terrence . . . he knew we were looking for you. And he was the one who pulled the strings to have both of you assigned as his backup."

I was in a slight shock as Henry pivoted on his feet to look back at me and smiled, shaking my hand and thanking me. I grinned back at him, accepting his thanks, but I was still really confused, trying to figure out how the hell Lila knew that piece of information — because I was pretty sure I never told her that.

Once Henry had walked out with his family, Alex and I stood in front of Lila and asked, "So what do we want for lunch?"

But before Lila could answer, Adela stood behind us and replied, "I'm afraid you two puppies are going to have to find your own meal."

She then grabbed Lila's hand and walked with her towards the door, while Lila explained, "Adela has requested I join her on a therapy and girl bonding exercise."

Yeah — well both me and Alex were very confused and concerned by what Lila meant by that, and at how she said it because she didn't seem very happy when she said — therapy.

It also caused Adela to huff in a slight annoyance and looked back at us to clarify, "She means shopping. . . Come on — the girls are waiting."

She then started pulling on Lila's arm again, but Lila quickly broke free of her and turned to hug us goodbye.

"If I'm not back before dinner, please come rescue me." She whispered very nervously.

"I heard that," Adela grumbled, as she grabbed Lila's arm again and pulled her out of the room.

And now it made sense to me — I didn't think Lila was the shopping type.

In the end it was just Alex and me left in the conference room, still a little concerned for Lila, and Alex turned to me and asked, "Should we follow them?"

But he also felt the need to remind me about Lila's last shopping adventure with Adela not going very well — which again was my fault.

I however had a different plan in mind for today, one I wanted Lila to have no part in. So, as I walked out of the room, I replied, "Actually, I have a more dangerous mission to go on."

The problem was I wasn't expecting Alex to follow me, but he did, almost intrigued at what I was going to do as he joked, "What's more dangerous than shopping?"

# Journal entry insert by Katie Hooper

Look, I know the only reason I was allowed to tag along on this shopping field trip was the safety and numbers thing, that and because Jessica invited me. But either Lila forgot I could hear them or they're just being snobs talkin' in code and all.

So like, we get to this shopping centre, that's way out of the city, you know to divert from the usual points – shake up the routine and all, and Jess and I were walking just ahead of Adela and Lila when I overheard them whispering.

"Hey, how'd you go with our guests this morning?" Lila mumbled.

"So far everything's good, but I really think you should talk to . . . him," Adela replied covertly. – Not.

It wasn't hard to guess who they were talkin' about. I mean we all heard the rumours about Lila's husband cheating on her with Adela. But seriously it's just weird how chummy they are with each other considering that fact.

"I suppose I did promise him," Lila replied, "I'll go see him after training tomorrow."

Huh – I mean seriously, it's like watching a soap opera going horribly and weirdly wrong.

When we finally did start shopping in an actual store, we all started scouting the clothing racks for some good outfits, except for Lila – she just sat back and watched as we tried on different outfits. It was very obvious to us that this was so not her scene, but that attitude was totes an easy fix.

"So tell me again why shopping was prescribed as my therapy?" Lila asked, looking at the store catalogue.

"Because it gets you out of the hotel," Adela replied, assuming that would be a good enough reason.

But it wasn't, Lila just scoffed back, "I've been out of the hotel several times . . . I even had breakfast with Alex and Terrence this morning."

That's when Jessica added her reasoning, that most definitely shows her flair and passion for shopping as she explained, "Yes, but this is way better than breakfasts with the boys. . . This offers you the excitement of trying something new, expressing yourself in new and daring ways, and generally having fun with just us girls. You know doing something just for you. When was the last time you bought new clothes just for the fun of it?"

Lila put the catalogue down and sarcastically glared at Jessica and answered, "Last year on your father's birthday, not that it's worth remembering. Your father asked me to look after you while you went shopping . . . turned out to be just a ploy for you and Adela to hand me over to Terrence and his men."

Seriously, how is this girl still friends with these people?

Adela stood in front of Lila and replied with a smile, "Well, that just means that we have to give you the full experience, this time with no bad guys." She then handed Lila a pile of clothes and demanded her to try them on, snapping, "Come on, we need to see what we're working with here . . ."

Inspecting the pile of clothes she was given, Lila held up a rather tiny red dress and questioned, "You seriously want me to try this on?"

And Adela responded by staring at Lila in a huff until she caved and walked into the change room.

## Journal entry insert by Alex Woods

It definitely felt a bit awkward, being just Terrence and me, and I admit I had that uneasy feeling about letting Lila go out on her own – but I had to trust in the team, and trust that Lila knew how to keep everyone safe.

I was planning on following the girls, just to keep an eye on them but knowing that Lila also had animal guardian instincts going for her now, I wasn't sure how she'd react to me following them, and it probably wouldn't be showing the best of trust.

Besides for some reason, Terrence had decided to go on his own mission.

And I did not trust this man at all to stay out of trouble – even though he said it was to help the team.

I stood at the kitchen bench of my apartment, watching Terrence fiddle with the computer tablet that Max gave Lila for Christmas. And for some reason, he was looking at a map of Victoria.

"There . . ." he said, pointing to an island just off the coast of Queenscliff.

I looked at the map closely and asked, "Are you trying to tell me that Swan Island, the island that is supposedly occupied by the Department of Defence is where you hid all of your incriminating evidence. . . and you want us to just sneak in there and take it?"

Well – it was a bold idea – Stupid – but bold.

Terrence smiled cockily and said, "Yep," as he put on his jacket and shoes.

I raced to put on my shoes and added "You know Lila will kill us if she finds out."

And as Terrence walked out of the apartment, waiting for me in the hallway, he replied, "The island is an hour away by boat and if we hurry, we will be there and back before Lila gets home . . . Now are you coming or not?"

That uneasy feeling came back again as I reluctantly followed him down the hallway, agreeing to his madness. – I really think this is a bad idea.

But I also think that Lila's going to be mad at me anyway – if I let the idiot go off on his own.

# Journal entry insert by Katie Hooper

So, the shopping adventure continued, and we have been to so many shops and I bought a lot of new clothes for myself, especially some really nice sparkly shoes.

However, the most entertainment I had today was watching Lila argue about trying on yet another dress with Adela. My guess is she was not a dress person either.

And as she stood in the dressing room trying on the dress, she yelled out to us, "I don't think this dress is really my style . . . it has barely anything to it."

That's when her phone received a text message, and she shouted over the changeroom door, asking one of us to check it. Jess and I got a sneaky suspicion she was hoping it was Alex coming to rescue her because of some made-up emergency.

Sure enough, it was, but he wasn't rescuing her.

The message read: "Hope you're enjoying your therapy. Remember to stay out of trouble."

I thought at this point, it would be the perfect opportunity to get some answers about Lila's relationship dynamics. I mean she was on that island for months. You know — things happen. And now she's not even living at home. So I asked, "What is this guy, your boyfriend or your babysitter?"

But then I got the stern looks from Adela to stop talking — you know — like I was pushing a nerve or something. But that's exactly what I wanted to do.

"What . . ." I grumbled, "I'm just saying she's got a lot of options at the moment. I'm just wondering which one she's going to choose."

As I finished saying that Lila walked out of the dressing room, wearing a rather-tight dress that left nothing to the imagination and replied, "Katie, it's not like that. They're my friends. It's just slightly different to the friendship we have . . . it's more like . . ."

She really struggled to find an accurate description for her relationship with Alex or the Dark man – I mean Terrence. That is until Jessica piped in, "More like your brothers?" in the attempts to help . . . I suppose.

But I still didn't agree. Those boys were totes wanting more than just a friendly ship with her and I grinned as I commented, "I don't know. Alex definitely looks at you a lot differently than a brother would."

I watched Lila fiddled with the dress, trying to get it to sit right and grunted back at me, "Well, I don't have a brother, so I wouldn't know."

But as Lila finished her comment, we all turned to Adela, very concerned – as she started choking on her iced tea. – Seriously, who chokes on tea.

Lila rushed to help her, asking, "Are okay?"

And Adela gasped for air and tried to shrug it off, explaining that it just went down the wrong way. – Coz that happens

Either way, I started getting suspicious, and it even caught Jessica's interest as we formulated a rather devious plan. We waited for Adela to compose herself, then before Lila went to change, we shouted at her to smile to take a photo on her phone.

The photo couldn't have looked any better — It was a back-dress over-the-shoulder smile that made her look totes hot. Well until the sales assistant came over to see if we needed any assistance and gaped, staring at the scars on Lila's back and arms and chest and legs and pretty much everywhere you can see.

Seriously every shop we went to, it was the same thing. And you could just tell Lila really struggled with her body confidence each time — it explains why she always wears the skivvy's and jumpers in the middle of summer. I'm mean it's like boiling degrees outside.

I guess it was hard for us to relate to her in moments like these because none of us had that kind of experience or even remembered what it was like. I mean both Adela and I had scars, but they were minor and barely noticeable.

Plus, Lila hasn't told us what happened to her, and to be honest I don't think I want to know.

But I definitely knew how I could totes make this situation better for her — right now. So, I asked to take over the styling project and picked out way more suitable attire — ones that suited Lila and covered all the — stuff.

And Adela, Jessica and I all agreed that no matter what Lila wore, she looked hot, and with each outfit, I took another photo.

# Original journal entry continued by Terrence Connors

We made it to the island in good time, and I pulled the boat up to the docks just below the connecting bridge to the mainland then explained to Alex, "The warehouse is 1 km inland, not far from the base perimeter . . . We'll need to move at full speed and approach from the waterfront."

Alex then jumped out of the boat and replied, "Right, I'll circle the perimeter and meet you there," and ran off at full speed.

But before I got a chance to do anything, I received a text message and started to dread.

I honestly thought I was busted and that Alex was just playing along with my plan — only to rat me out to Lila and prove to her that I really couldn't be trusted. But I swear I'm doing this for her, because I want to make her happy and prove to her that I can be a valuable asset to the team.

I held my breath, when I realised the text was from Lila. But she wasn't mad, instead, it was a couple of pictures of her in some of the outfits she was trying on. Her smile was so sweet and the confidence on her face was amazing. I especially liked the two-piece, dark-green bathing suit with the little strings that hugged her hips. She looked really nice in that one. — after all green is naturally my favourite colour.

The message read — "Having a blast, see you tonight."

Relieved, I took a breath and smile as I ran at full speed up to the warehouse, only to be greeted by Alex, who was leaning on the warehouse wall, smiling as well. I asked why he was so happy, but he just deflected and instead asked why I was happy.

I certainly wasn't going to share my joy, especially knowing what kind of relationship Alex and Lila had, so I replied, "Just really enjoying the fresh air."

I picked the lock of the warehouse and led Alex inside to show him my home away from home. Which come to think of it, is rather depressing. And yeah — It was another greenhouse, only a little smaller and not as many side windows or any guards.

Alex followed me through to the back end of the warehouse where my second little cottage sat. He took one look inside the cottage to see one bed and table, and instantly commented, "Well, this feels a lot like déjà vu."

I ignored his remark as I ran my hand along the woodwork of the cabin wall and pushed a secret panel that triggered the bed to lift up and reveal a hidden passage to my underground hideout, then boasted, "I work better with nature around me."

I grinned back at him before I walked down into the basement along a short corridor covered in tree roots, leading to a small room lit by one small light and a computer station hooked up to several different screens.

"Well, this isn't creepy at all. I can see why you like it here . . . it's definitely you," Alex mockingly commented.

Yeah Well — I could understand why he would think that, but I soon showed him as I ran my fingers over the wall of tree roots causing them to illuminate, giving off a soft brown glow. So instead of it looking like a dark dingy basement, it looked like a secret underground treehouse that as a young teen, I used to play in — a lot.

Now feeling a lot more confident about myself, I sat down at the computer station and turned on the computer to transfer the files across to a USB. But then Alex got upset and demanded, "What are you doing? Just grab the computer and let's go."

"I can't . . ." I explained, "the computer has a failsafe device, so that if the monitor is ever disconnected from the tower in any way, both devices will return to factory setting and all the memory is wiped."

It was an ingenious plan when I thought of it — but I don't think my teenage-self expected that he was really just self-destructing his own escape.

Either way I had to use the USB. But while I was busy Alex grunted at me and stood at the end of the corridor, looking slightly nervous, "How long is this going to take?"

"About 10 minutes — why?" I replied.

He then stood with his back up against the wall, hidden from the light of the corridor and answered with a whisper, "Because we've got company."

Moving quickly, I set up the files to transfer then joined Alex standing up against the wall, hidden. And we listened as four agents entered the corridor with their weapons drawn.

I signalled Alex to let me handle it and I waited until the last man had entered the corridor before I waved my hands over the tree roots embedded in walls. Then with that we heard the screams and scuffles as the agents shot at the tree roots trying to attack them.

The tree roots eventually trapped the agents, unconscious against the walls and roof of the corridor.

The downside was, I had missed the fifth agent who had not yet entered the corridor. He played it smart and ran at full speed, dodging all the tree roots. But his efforts were thwarted by Alex, who tackled him to the ground as he entered the room then threw him back into the corridor to be caught and trapped amongst the tree roots with the rest of his friends.

Finally, the file transfer had completed. So, I quickly grabbed the USB and tossed it to Alex for safekeeping as I disconnected all the monitors from the computer to force a factory reset.

We then ran up the stairs at full speed, only to be greeted by several more agents just waiting to catch us by surprise. But Alex and I weren't surprised and worked as a team, fighting our way through the warehouse to the outside. It was actually quite fun for me because I recognised some of these agents, and they were real jerks. So I had no qualms about throwing into the side beams of the warehouse or trapping them amongst the many trees.

Alex was actually putting up a good fight as well. But as we exited the building and saw the daylight, we were abruptly stopped by two very large, flaming circles surrounding us and trapping us where we stood.

— Damn.

I looked over the flames to see my brother Keith standing there with his arms stretched out and his eyes glowing a fiery red. He was also collected at a young age and raised to be an obedient son, but he was very much the opposite of me.

He always sought the approval of The Board and especially mother, but never got it because I was the favourite and the rare collectable. Still, he never understood how to play the game —he wore jeans and a shirt, and I wore business pants and sweaters. He had unkempt shaggy brown hair and mine was always neat and tidy. I always did my best to look the part, but he never understood why. — He just never understood how to play the game.

"Keith!" I shouted to him with a pleading tone, hoping he would lower the flames. But he didn't. And as Alex tried to escape, the flames around him grew hotter.

That is until we heard the soft voice of an old English lady say, "That's enough, dear . . ." causing the flames to die down to a soft flicker around our feet.

And now filled with dread again, I looked up, only to be greeted by the woman I swore to Lila I would help defeat and sighed, "Hello, Mother."

# CHAPTER 20

# PARENTAL LOVE

## Journal entry by Lila Winters

Okay, so yesterday's shopping field trip was not as bad as I originally feared it would be. Considering the last several field trips to shopping centres ended with me either destroying the building, jumping off balconies, or fighting for my life, this trip was rather uneventful.

The only weird part was this sudden gust of wind that greeted us at the door of the hotel at the end of the night. It carried with it hundreds of leaves and flower petals that covered Adela's sports car, and because she had the top down, her car now needs a serious cleanout.

It was very weird though. This morning I woke up to an empty apartment. I called out to Alex but got no response. So, I assumed he was off getting breakfast from one of the cafes downstairs and instead I started looking around the apartment for Terrence, but he too was missing – and that was very weird.

I wasn't sure what to do, I mean do I call them and check if their okay – or would that send the wrong message to them – of you know being control freak.

And what if they're just both having breakfast and being friendly, trying to get to know each other – yeah that was probably not happening.

My train of thought was derailed when my phone rang, and I originally thought it was Alex or Terrence, but it was Adela and she sounded really serious.

"Hi, Del, what's up?" I answered, "Yeah, I'll meet you downstairs in 20."

Turns out Adela had arranged for our guest, Tyme and I to have a breakfast meeting downstairs, and she was just calling to make sure I was actually going to show up.

And yes, I know I made a deal to make some time to actually talk to him and that Adela was just helping me to uphold my end of the agreement, but wow, was she getting pushy.

I thought maybe I could win a few brownie points with Adela if I wore one of the outfits she and Katie picked out for me yesterday. So to find the best one, I emptied out all of the many shopping bags I brought home onto Alex's bed. It was then I noticed a handful of the leaves had made their way into the bags.

The leaves smelt beautiful, like a gentle sea breeze had washed over them, but when I picked them up to clear them away, I received a vision of Alex surrounded by fire and dropped the leaves in shock. I didn't know what the vision meant, but I knew somebody who could help me, so I dressed at full speed and gathered the leaves back up into a shopping bag before I ran out of the apartment.

I raced down into the lobby, struggling greatly not to break Maxwell's rule about our super speed. But before I left the hotel, I quickly stopped at the reception desk to leave a note for Adela in the hopes that she wouldn't be too mad about me standing her and our guest up yet again

# Journal entry insert by Terrence Connors

This was bad, very, very bad. The last thing I remember from last night was being hit in the back of the head while watching Alex being thrown into the boot of Odele's car.

And today I woke up, back in my childhood bed at Mother's holiday mansion in the Yarra Ranges — the one we went to every Christmas.

I was escorted down into the dining room and forced to sit at a very large table where breakfast had already been served and waiting for me. And while still filled with dread, I looked over to see Alex, chained to a chair at the end of the table. He looked like he had been beaten very badly with a collar locked around his neck and a small silver box attached to it.

Keith was sitting on the other side of the table from me, tossing around a fireball in his hands as if it were a toy.

Suddenly all the servants and guards stood to attention as Odele walked into the room and greeted us, "Good morning, my sons, I trust you both slept well."

Keith smiled and replied, "Good morning, Mother,"

But I didn't, instead I just scowled rebelliously at the cooked breakfast in front of me, refusing to acknowledge her. And as expected, Odele got upset and stood next to me, adjusting her dismal grey pantsuit and repeated, "I said good morning, Terrence," then waited again for me to respond.

She sighed when I gave her no response and sneered, "Terrence Connors, you may not like me at this very moment . . . but I did not raise you to be so disrespectful to your family. Now you will still treat me with the proper respect . . . is that understood?"

She then glared at me and waited for an answer but again received nothing from me, until she directed one of the guards to hurt Alex and insisted it be painful.

I tried not to give in to her controlling tactics but as I heard Alex hold back his yelps, I shouted, "STOP!" then stood to acknowledge Odele and said, "Good morning, Mother."

I peered back at Alex apologetically, hoping he would know how sorry I was. — I swear never meant for any of this to happen.

Once Odele was satisfied with my response she sat down at the table and grinned, "See . . . now that wasn't so hard, was it, dear?"

She then demanded we eat and not let the food get cold. So, I sat back down feeling incredibly sorry about all of this, and in not wanting anything else to go wrong, I glanced over to Alex, who had also been served a meal and nodded my head in the hopes that he would trust me and follow the instructions.

He did, and as we ate, Odele looked at me then said condescendingly, "Good boy."

## Original journal entry continued by Lila Winters

I was actually really proud of myself – and I know it's sad, but I was able to make it in and out of the hotel alone, without any incidents or running into any bad guys. Which is a big surprise for me and a huge breakthrough, considering the threat that was out there.

I raced through the hotel and up to the conference room, and left the door open as I waited. And it wasn't long before Wyala appeared in front of me in a flurry and gave me her usual greeting of a hug. She then stared at me in a panic and asked, "Lila, what's wrong?"

I didn't want to waste any time, so I tipped out all the leaves I had gathered on to the conference room table – I even rounded up all the leaves that had landed in Adela's sports car as well.

I then turned to Wyala and explained what happened to me when I picked up the leaves, and she looked almost amazed and stunned as she studied the leaves, "Huh, it looks like each leaf contains a small snippet of a memory."

Okay, that helps me – I think.

Err, No, it really doesn't help me, – I was still confused and I had to ask "From who?"

But Wyala looked just as puzzled as I was as she shrugged her shoulders. "I don't know. No guardian has the knowledge to imprint their memory into nature like this . . . it requires a living specimen to keep the memory alive, like a memory tree . . . but these leaves here, they've been artificially preserved in order to hold the memory . . . It's possible that one of our Elder wood nymphs could do it, but it would be at great risk to themselves. I mean these leaves would have been literally shed from the actual wood nymph with the memories attached."

Okay – I'm not sure if that's supposed to be yuck or not.

Even if it was, I was still confused and stared at her, hoping for more answers as I irked, "Um. . . alright, would you know which one? So I can ask them what happened?"

She shook her head at me, frustrated because I didn't understand, "No, Lila, these are the nymphs' actual memory's . . . in other words . . . even if I knew who the nymph was, they wouldn't remember sending them."

Okay, that still doesn't help. And I wasn't really sure what to do here, especially now that I know that a wood nymph shed its own leaves and memory and sent them to me.

– And yes, that was slightly gross and creepy. But they clearly sent them for a reason and judging from what little information I had received so far, it was obviously important that I figure it out.

Scrubbing my fingers through my hair, I stared at the leaves and grunted, "Well what am I supposed to do with them . . . they're all snippets of a . . . picture."

I continued to stare at them trying to will some kind of answer to just pop into my brain. Then Wyala stood next to me and hesitantly suggested, "I might be able to put them in order for you."

YES! – that's a good start and an excellent suggestion. And I really like this nymph.

So still not wanting to waste time, I eagerly nodded to her, pulling all the leaves together on the table in the hopes that she would start immediately.

## Journal entry insert by Terrence Connors

After we had finished our breakfast, we were forced to take a stroll through the garden around the mansion with Keith and I walking alongside Odele and her assistant Alice just a few steps behind. All while Alex was kept under heavy guard walking just a few metres behind us to remind me to behave, and not do anything stupid.

Odele seemed very calm while walking next to me, and she smiled marvelling at the finely manicured landscape, almost as if she were enjoying a nice stroll through the gardens with her sons. So I played along and asked, "So, Mother, what brings you to Australia?"

"Is it a crime for a mother to visit her son?" she replied, playing up her British accent to make her sound innocent and regal.

But I wasn't buying into it and sighed, "It is when you hold his friend at gunpoint . . ."

She grimaced at me for a second then composed herself. "Oh hush dear . . . your new friend is in perfectly safe hands back there . . . Now tell me, what . . . or should I say who is so important . . . that you had to literally pack up and disappear just days before Christmas?"

And here we go, we've finally come to Odele's specialty—the guilt trip veiled by the subtle tones of a mother's worry for her son.

"Mother, skip the act and just tell me what you want?" I barked, in the hopes to get to the point a lot faster.

And it worked, as Odele gasped and stopped her little stroll, glaring at me as she sneered, "Fine . . . I want you to invite your new girlfriend over for a visit . . . I think it's about time I met her in an official capacity. . . The last time I saw her she was in bloody pieces on the floor, the poor girl. . . It wasn't until you started showing your lovey-dovey side to her that I started paying attention."

Odele then snatched the computer tablet from her assistant's hand and showed me a picture of Lila and I walking in China town, looking at the sights as Lila held on to my arm.

And yeah, I was right there were spying on me — But I shook my head, "She's not my girlfriend."

"Don't play games with me, Terrence," Odele snapped pulling the computer tablet away, "I haven't the time . . . nor the patience. This girl destroyed an island for you, and you were willing to drown in the ocean for her. She's clearly more than just an asset."

It wasn't a surprise that it was Odele that was spying on me, I kind of guessed as much. But this picture revealed the fact that Lila and I were alone, and yet we returned to the hotel unharmed, which meant Odele was playing another angle and has probably been planning this for a while.

She walked over to one of the rose bushes and pulled a rose from its stem, as she explained, "I will be hosting a charity ball in the city tonight, raising money for some illness research or whatever it is. I want you to invite her to the ball and given that it's last minute . . . you will need to call her now . . . for her to be ready in time."

She calmly handed me back my mobile phone and waited for me to dial the number, but instead, I delayed. There was no way I would ever willingly lead Lila into trap again. So, I replied, "No, I won't play this game with you, Mother. You'll have to jump through your own hoop this time."

I glared back at Odele as she studied the petals of the rose and remained creepily calm as she said, "If you insist. . ."

She then glanced back at her assistant, whose hazel eyes had formed a brighter yellow tinge around the iris. And as Alice snapped her fingers, Alex fell to the ground with his body charged with an electrical current, streaming from the silver box strapped to his neck.

I watched Alex writhe in pain, and I feared for his life as Odele turned back to address me, "Now about your plans for tonight . . . are you sure you don't want to reconsider?"

I stood my ground, taking calming breath as I replied, "I'm sure," then I tossed the phone at her feet before I added, "I'm also positive that Alex would rather endure this pain a thousand times over than have Lila fall victim to your selfish and vindictive misery."

I turned back to see Alex, hoping he wouldn't hate me for any of this, then Odele moved closer to me and spoke softly, "Oh, Terrence, you can't imagine how much that hurts me, but I'm growing very impatient . . ."

The fear rose in me as Odele held her hand up to the guards and with that Alice snapped her fingers again, causing the electrical charge to cease in order for the guards to pull Alex up onto his knees. One of the guards then drew his gun, readying to shoot Alex at Odele's command and waited.

I wanted to do something but Keith grabbed hold of my arm with his fiery hands, burning through the sleeve of my shirt and onto my skin. The pain of the heat was hard to endure until Odele said Keith's name in a whisper, and the heat disappeared, leaving the blistering burn marks of his hand around my arm.

While trying to hide the pain I felt, I stayed standing and watched as Odele pick up the phone again, holding it in front of me, shaking her head, "Now son, I'm not sure you're thinking this through clearly . . . I agree that your friend Alex would rather die than hurt the woman he loves . . . as would you. But do honestly think Lila would agree with you . . ."

Again, she placed the phone back in my hand then asked, "Shouldn't you at least give her the courtesy to choose if her friend lives or dies?"

## Original journal entry continued by Lila Winters

It took a while for Wyala to sort through the many leaves, but eventually the puzzle was complete and the leaves rested on the table in a spiralling pattern.

Wyala then stood next to me and told me what to do step by step, and as I raised my hands above the leaves, a white mist appeared, rising up and streaming in and around my hand.

It was freaky as – when my eyes turned white and hazy but then I started to receive the fragmented visions.

I remained completely oblivious as my team started to arrive in the conference room ready for the daily meeting. Maxwell and Chase were especially surprised as I described the details of what I saw, "Alex . . . Terrence . . . a greenhouse and fire . . .. and a fight . . . they're on an island, but I still see the city . . . and there's a woman . . . Hello Mother?"

Suddenly, the vision stopped as the conference room doors burst wide open, and Adela stormed through in a huff, causing the leaves to be blown off the table. And by the looks of it, she didn't get the note I left for her either.

"What the hell, Lila, you were supposed to meet me hours ago," Adela screeched.

To which I tried to explain, "I'm sorry, something came up . . . I did leave a note for you."

"Well, you could have at least told him that," she screeched again, "He would have understood."

I tried to defend myself, arguing with Adela as we completely disregarded everyone else in the room, and eventually I asked, "Why is it so important that I talk to him?"

For some reason, that question seemed to shut down the argument as Adela struggled to find a response, stammering, "It . . . It's . . . err . . . It just is."

– Yeah, because that's the best way to win an argument.

Finally, someone else interjected bringing the focus back to where it should be, as Max asked, "Wait, what happened to Alex and Terrence?"

"Alex and Terrence have gone missing," Wyala snarked, "We were in the process of getting more information until miss hot-head here burst through the doors and ruined hours of my work."

There seemed to be a stand-off between me and Adela as she still struggled to find the words but also seemed slightly apologetic. So instead I huffed, "Look it doesn't matter now . . . I got the basics of what was going on . . . Adela, I will talk to him . . . when I have a chance like I agreed, but for now we need to find Alex and Terrence."

"Who were you guys talking about?" Jennifer asked curiously.

"No one," Adela and I replied in unison.

And I still hate it when people speak in unison — even when I do it.

The team were all in agreement to help me find Alex and Terrence, so I broke the group up into three teams and searched the hotel for any clues, including pulling both their phone records in the hopes that if they'd received any communication, that the nearest cell tower would give us a clue to their location.

After about an hour of searching Max pulled me aside and handed me a folder with some infuriating information on it. And I really tried to stay calm as I asked Jessica and Katie to join me outside the conference room.

They could both tell I was angry when my hair began to turn white, as I stated, "You know, I thought yesterday's little shopping adventure was supposed to be about having fun and building friendships."

To that Katie and Jessica both looked at each other nervously and replied, "It was. We had great fun."

And I think my eyes flickered black for second as I handed them the printed-out version of the text message and pictures they had sent to both Alex and Terrence, and snapped, "I know you had fun, and now you need to explain your fun."

Katie looked at the pictures and shrugged her shoulders, trying to laugh it off, "Look Lila, it was just a harmless joke. We wanted to see which one of them you were sleeping with."

Wow, that there just crossed so many boundaries that I struggled so badly to hold my temper in check as my eyes definitely flickered black this time.

I needed take some calming breathes trying to keep my composure as I explained, "Katie, I am married and I honour my vows."

But Katie didn't accept that answer, and rebuked "Oh, like Matt did when he slept with Adela."

Oh frac – she's really asking for it – isn't she.

Jessica tried to stop Katie from making this worse, clearly picking up on my struggling temper, but Katie insisted on speaking.

"No . . . if you're so loyal to your husband . . . then why are you giving him the cold shoulder, and you're best buddies with the home wrecker?"

She then pointed back to Adela, who was sitting at the conference room table clearly listening in – as was everyone else.

And my hair had turned completely white now, with my eyes staying black as I calmly explained, "Did you ever stop to think why Adela was chosen to be the homewrecker, or why my husband was chosen as the target? . . . The enemy tried to create a rift in the team . . . they tried to create a distraction. Because they know that in this hotel, we work best as a team . . . if there is even the slightest issue of trust, this team falls apart . . . they took advantage of that weakness once, and it almost destroyed us . . ."

I stopped my speech when I noticed Katie backing down, and started to understand my point of view as she looked back into the conference room to see everyone working as a team. I then thought now would be the best time to offer Katie a chance to choose again, but I also wanted to discover if she was truly here to help and be a part of the team or if she was just in it for the fun.

So as I stood at the door of the conference room I turned back to them and said "Jessica and Katie . . . if you chose to follow me back into that conference room, I will give you my full trust as will everyone else in that room because that's how this team works. But I will also expect you to do the same . . . along with respecting everyone's right to privacy, is that understood?"

Jessica didn't hesitate and nodded as she apologised for her part, but before Katie could respond, we were interrupted by Maxwell's receptionist. And with her timid Irish voice she spoke, "Excuse me, Ms Winters, you have a call waiting on line 2. . . She says her name is Mrs Connors and she claims to be Terrence's mother."

Oh Frac – well at least that explain the "Hello, Mother" part of the memory.

And right now I'm really starting to miss Alex, because I've got so many emotions racing through me at the moment, and I was really scared that at any minute I'm going to turn into a wolf again. – And that's not going to help anyone.

All I could think of to do was breath, and think of that one emotion that had helped me turn back to a human the last time – and that was the warm fuzzy feeling I got when I was with Alex and Terrence. So, I held onto that emotion as I thanked the receptionist and walked back into the room, and to my surprise, Katie followed me in but said nothing.

I hurriedly picked up the phone and put it on loudspeaker for everyone to hear and greeted, "This is Ms Winters speaking."

The woman on the phone introduced herself as Odele. "My darling, I'm calling on behalf of my son Terrence. He's attending a charity ball tonight but doesn't have a date . . . and he may have suggested that you might be willing to accompany him."

Peering up from the phone, I scanned the room, noticing the many shaking heads and the silent whispers of "It's a trap."

But I continued the ruse and replied with a very sweet voice, "Really, I was just speaking to Terrence yesterday . . . he never mentioned anything about a charity ball."

## Journal entry insert by Terrence Connors

Odele did it anyway. She called Lila, and it made me sick to my stomach to hear Odele asking so nicely on my behalf for Lila to waltz right into a trap. And all I could do was stand there, listening to Odele explain my reasons for not inviting my best friend to her potential death or imprisonment — again.

Pure evil that's what Odele is and yet she sounded so innocent as she spoke, "Darling, I'm sure you know how men work, always leaving things to the last minute. . . Besides it would be an absolute treat to finally get to meet the woman who stole my son's heart."

I was sure Lila picked up on that obvious double meaning — insinuating that it was Lila who stole my loyalty away from the family business. But still my whole body was tense as I listened to silence on the phone, waiting for a response, until Lila replied, "Your invitation does sound wonderful, Ms Connors . . . and I'm very thankful that you called me, but I am old fashioned when it comes to being asked out on a date. . . If your son really wanted me to attend, he should really ask me himself. No offence to you of course."

Seeming over-joyed by that response, Odele covered the speaker on the phone and whispered, "Oh, I like this one . . . she definitely knows how to play the game and the right words to say . . . she wants to know if you're still alive, clever girl." She then handed me the phone and ordered, "Well, go ahead dear. . . ask her."

I really, really didn't want to, and I rebelliously stared at the phone, discreetly glancing back at Alex, who looked like he was ready to die as he took a deep breath in and closed his eyes, all while the guards readied to open fire.

"Lila!" I choked reluctantly. Causing Alex to open his eyes in shock realising that he would live, and stared at me as I hated saying the next words.

"Lila . . .would you honour me. . . with your presence tonight?"

There was a long pause of silence from the phone as we all eagerly awaited Lila's response, all hoping for a different one, until her beautiful voice returned and replied,

"I would be delighted, Terrence . . . Have the details sent to the hotel reception, and I'll meet you there . . ."

The phone call ended abruptly as Lila hung up on Odele, which was a bold move, but Odele seemed to be proud as she grinned, "Oh . . . I really, really like this girl . . . she doesn't play the fool easily . . . I'm sure she would make a great adversary on the chessboard."

What is wrong with this woman — Why is this always a game to her?

I couldn't breathe and I couldn't believe what I just did. All I could do was watch as Odele handed my phone back to her assistant and smirked, "Come on boys . . . We have a party to ready for." Then with a waltz in her stride, she walked through the garden, back into the mansion.

## Original journal entry continued by Lila Winters

The conference room remained quiet as I hung up the phone and the team watched my eyes flickering black, and my ears begin to morph.

Thankfully, Henry – the only other animal guardian in the fraccing room, jumped to my rescue, holding onto my hand with his eyes glowing gold as he told me to breathe,

"Lila, you can't attend the ball as a wolf . . . we need you to be human . . ."

His calming charm was working, and I took some slow breaths and managed to stop the morphing process to the point of only having just the long white hair. – And that was obviously the best I could do.

Unfortunately, some of the team also noticed the scented candles on the side counter spontaneously light.

Fraccing Frac bucket – I really have to focus on that one.

As Katie moved to inspect the candles, she glanced back at me suspiciously then blew out the candles with the wave of her hand. – And I was really starting worry about how long I should keep my many hybrid-abilities secret – or how many abilities I actually had.

I mean this morning I had turned the apartment light on without using the switch — and again I didn't know I could do that.

Right now, all the team knew was that I was half animal and half nature. But I feared I was much more than that, and I worried what that would mean to the others.

Either way I'd have to work on that fire thing.

Once I was back in reasonable control of my emotions, I pulled my hand away from Henry and thanked him, but then I had to deal with the next problem — of the team being divided as to what we should do.

Katie was the first to object, "Lila, you can't be serious . . . this is clearly a trap . . . you can't possibly be thinking of attending."

Jessica then chimed in sarcastically, "I just knew Terrence was playing us from the start, but does anyone listen to me?"

But Jennifer defended Terrence, as she thought, "It doesn't make sense. Why would he choose a place so public? And why now? He's had so many opportunities before this."

Alright — that wasn't quite a defence, it was more a question of motives.

Chase and Max however were willing to give Terrence a chance, and argued "If Lila trust him then so should we."

And it seems that the room is divided by Terrence's actions. But I know Terrence and he wouldn't have betrayed me, and he would never willingly ask me to walk into a trap, not unless he had no other choice. So, at this point I'm going to trust him – even if no one else did.

The room was still arguing, even though I had made my decision but before I could bring the room to attention, Wyala stood in front of me and begged, "Lila, please tell me you're not really going to do this?"

Well she saved me the trouble of getting everyone's attention as room fell quiet, all waiting to hear my answer. I then spoke clearly and firmly, looking at the team and replied, "To save my friend, yes, I'm going to do this. But if I'm walking into a trap, I want to be prepared . . . Jess, find everything you can on Odele Connors, work with Henry and Jennifer. Katie, find me a dress, preferably one I can fight in . . . Adela and Chase, I want all the information you can find on this charity ball including staff, security, and blueprints of the building."

Everyone had their orders and started to scurry out of the room, but Adela caught me, marching into the stairwell, like I was a girl on a mission.

"And where are you going?" she shouted.

"To have a chat with our guest," I yelled back as I disappeared down the stairs.

I was really impressed of how the team instantly jumped into action and trusted my judgement. And though it took a few hours to formulate a plan – by 6.30pm, I was in the car driving towards the Melbourne Exhibition Centre where the charity ball was being held.

According to Katie, the theme of the charity ball was nature, so she managed to find me an emerald-green dress. And I can't knock her on practicality, the base of the dress was cut diagonally, and the slit stopped just above my thigh. This dress gave me the ability to fight and draw the attention of a crowd, and for this plan to work — attention was what I needed.

All Eyes On Me.

Jessica was placed in charge of my hair and make-up and she did a damn good job covering all the visible scars. My snow-white hair was tied up in a ponytail with curls flowing down around my neck, and I added the finishing touches of a Singapore lotus blossom tucked into my hair tie.

While I drove through the city, I looked down at the passenger seat at the second Singapore lotus blossom and started thinking back over the plan, remembering specifically the conversation I had with Tyme.

"Tell me what you know about Odele Connors," I demanded.

Surprisingly Tyme was very helpful as he answered, "She's one of The Board CEO's. And she's the kind of woman who will stop at nothing until she gets her way, her money, and her power. She was the woman who discovered the key to perfecting the Neuritamine formula . . . but her methods are brutal."

He went on to explain how in order to speed up the Neuritamine's effects, Odele would eliminate any reasons the subject had to fight or to live. But Tyme then grew very sad as he added, "She targets everything you ever held dear to your heart . . . your family . . . your friends and your home . . . and destroys it, ensuring that you witness the devastation."

"Is there any way of stopping her?" I asked.

When Tyme realised what I was about to do he seemed reluctant and even tried to talk me out of it. — It was very weird, he barely knew me, and I even stood him up at breakfast this morning, and yet he still showed a genuine concern for my wellbeing.

But for this mission to work I needed him to help me, so I explained, "Tyme . . . you may not know me . . . but I need you to trust me. I never give up on my friends or even a stranger if they asked for it . . . and right now I need your help."

It was interesting — when I said those words, I sensed in Tyme something very strange, but it also convinced him and he agreed to help, stating, "The one thing stronger than Odele's love of power and success is the love and pride she has for her collected children. . .Your friend Terrence is the key to stopping her. . . eliminate him, and she will crumble in your hands."

Right — well, all for one I suppose.

As I pulled up to the conference centre valet, Terrence was already at the door waiting for me. He looked very nervous as he straightened the jacket of his tuxedo, discreetly glancing back at his mother who was hovering closely behind him. And as I stepped out of the car, handing the keys to the valet, I looked up at Terrence and smiled, slightly amused by his reaction.

"Wow, she came." He gasped, staring back at me and struggling to hide a smile.

But Odele quickly ruined his moment of joy, whispering in his ear, reminding him of the deal they had made, and warned, "Don't screw this up again . . ."

She then gave him a gentle nudge towards me before she disappeared into the ballroom. But it only caused Terrence's nerves to return to him, and he walked towards me, reaching out his hands, stuttering, "You . . . look . . . amazing."

I calmly held on to his hand as he led me into the ballroom and commented, "Thank you . . . You scrub up pretty well too."

The ballroom was filled with well over 200 guests, all dressed in fancy floral formal wear, and decorations of flowers and foliage adorned the walls – all fake of course – and not at all useful to Terrence or myself.

While I walked with Terrence around the room, I casually noted all the security guards and anyone else who might have been armed. But with a live band on stage, it was hard to get a read on people's intentions and feelings.

However, I did notice Terrence become more and more anxious, the closer we got to his mother – Odele. She was standing just off the side of the dance floor, watching the guests dancing and talking, waiting for Terrence to formally introduce us.

When we eventually stood beside her Terrence was so nervous as he spoke, "Excuse me, Mother . . . I would like to introduce my . . . date . . . Lila Winters. Lila, this is my mother, Odele Connors."

Odele's grin grew wider as she looked me up and down and boasted, "It is so nice to finally meet the infamous Lila . . . you are quite the talking point at our business meetings. And I don't joke about that. Every single one of my business associates wants a piece of you . . . And honestly, just seeing you here . . . looking fabulous . . . it's simply divine."

Wow — did she sound evil. She sounded like a cat and I was the bird about to be slaughtered.

I won't lie, right now I'm glad my hair was already white because my temper was just barely being kept at bay. Instead I smiled with a slight titter, "It's a pleasure to meet you as well . . ."

But I really needed to ensure that her attention would be focused on me the entire night, and I had been practising this trick all day, so I asked, "Would you like to see something cool, Mrs Connors? . . . I'm sure your business associates would love to hear about it."

Yep — I was really going to do this.

She leaned in, watching intently as my eyes flickered black and with the snap of my fingers a small flame appeared in my hand. I then quickly closed my hand, quenching the flames. Secretly glad it worked – YES!

My eyes peered up at Odele, to see her almost licking her lips at the sight of me, as she smiled, "Well, that is a very . . . attractive development . . . you're right my business associates would love to hear about that. But I believe information equals power . . . so be a dear for me and not show that trick to anyone else . . . okay?"

Very cheekily, I nodded to Odele's request, then grinned at Terrence who now looked flabbergasted at what I could do – and so far this plan was working perfectly.

I then went back to holding of Terrence's hand, but I think he was getting confused as to why my fingers were twirling around his – I do tend to fidget a bit when I'm concentrating, and I didn't want to let go of his hand because I was trying to play-up the doe-eyed I'm in love with your son act. So he kind of had to put up with it.

But it was working out quite well for me because Odele noticed our fiddling hands and smiled so deviously at Terrene.

I thought this would be the perfect time for the next phase, and handed Odele the lotus blossom that was in my other hand with an eager smile and explained, "This is a Singapore lotus blossom . . . I created it myself, changing the molecular structure just slightly to add a unique fragrance."

She looked at me suspiciously and smiled as she tentatively smelled the fragrance of the blossom. "Mmm, strawberries and cream . . . delicious," she said, taking another sniff of the fragrance and unwittingly breathing in a very small amount of yellow powder.

"How did you know strawberries and creams were my favourite?" she questioned, handing me a glass of champagne.

I bit my bottom lip and grinned ever so slightly, "Terrence let it slip once when we were reminiscing about our childhood. It's hard to imagine how we ever lost contact with each other . . . Terrence has been such a wonderful friend to me."

I sensed Terrence's nerves calm a little as he sensed my confidence and sincerity in that statement. But I stayed focused on Odele as she held the flower close to her, still watching us holding hands as she grinned, "Be careful, dear . . . if you get any sweeter, I might need to convince my son to marry you."

Both Terrence and I chuckled at that comment, knowing full well that she wasn't kidding, which did not help keep Terrence's nerves at bay.

"How about we start with a dance . . . and see where it goes from there?" I said, winking at Terrence and then glancing back at Odele as my eyes flickered black again.

– I was getting really good at that.

Terrence led me out onto the dance floor, and I glanced back at Odele and smiled, but I was actually looking Adela and Tyme as they appear standing at the bar, listening in.

They watched Odele call a man over to her, who I think was Keith based on what little information we could get on the Connors family. And as Keith disappeared out of the crowded room, Tyme held on to Adela's hand before he disappeared, phasing out of time.

I could feel their presence as they brushed past me and to no surprise at all, so could Terrence and naturally he was freaking out.

I tried to ignore his freak out and jokingly commented, "Okay. . . so I warn you. I'm not a very good dancer. . . so I'm relying on you here to lead me."

Terrence stared at my smile, still in a confused shock as he held my hand and started to lead in me in a dance, and to my non-surprise he's a pretty good dancer. But he was still freaking out.

"How did you do that fire thing with your hands" he quietly questioned as he twirled me, "And why did you show my mother . . . you know she won't stop now until you're part of her collection."

I could tell he was scared and feared that I was in way over my head, and I wanted to let him know that everything was going to be okay, but I couldn't – not yet anyway.

And to be honest, conjuring flames was actually a really difficult thing for me to do, so I thought he would be a bit more amazed than this. — Oh well, I guess I just had stay focused on the mission.

"It's a bold move introducing me to your mother on the first date," I joshed, continuing the ruse, dancing along to the music. But it caused him to frown with such worry and sadness, twirling me around again. "I'm sorry . . . I never meant for any of this to happen . . ."

It was clear he was trying to keep me at arm's length, but I pulled in closer to him, pressing my chest up against his and whispered into his ear, "Let me guess . . . you thought you could help the team and earn everyone's trust by going off on your own . . . breaking into what is probably one of the many secret buildings you know of, and steal the information we needed to bring down The Board . . . stop me if I'm getting it wrong."

But he didn't and we continued to dance as he stayed silent, so I continued, "I'm guessing, you knew that it would be dangerous, but you weren't expecting Alex to follow you . . . let alone agree with your ambitious plan . . . Then when everything went wrong, you handed your mother the ammunition she needed to lure me away from the safety of my home."

Terrence's hand stiffened on my back as he looked away and sighed, knowing that I was right, and he worryingly asked, "Then why did you agree to come if you knew it was a trap."

I twirled back into his arms as he led me down to a dip and while staring into his eyes, I replied, "Because you asked me to . . . and because you're my friend . . . I know you would have never asked me to come unless you had no other choice. And I would never let you do this alone."

He slowly pulled me back up, gazing into my eyes and then twirled me again, looking around the room in the hopes of seeing any of my team standing in the crowd ready to back me up. But when he saw no one he pulled me closer to him and whispered, "Please tell me you have a plan?"

"I do . . ." I replied, pulling the lotus blossom from my hair tie and holding it between us. And as I gazed into his bluey-green eyes I asked, "Terrence . . . do you trust me?"

## Journal entry insert by Maxwell Eden

It was like clockwork, watching each scene unfold from a safe distance – of which I am not at liberty to disclose. But it was as if Lila knew exactly what Odele's target was.

At exactly 9pm, the power was cut from the hotel, and a swarm of men dressed in black armour stormed the building with guns drawn.

They broke down the door of apartment 147—Matt's apartment and searched the rooms to find nothing. And it was like watching a scene from a movie as Katie appeared in the centre of the room and fought the agents, knocking them out one by one while using their own tranquiliser darts against them.

A second team of men had broken into my office and started tearing it apart, looking for something and finding nothing. They listened to their radios and heard the other team screaming for back up and warning that it was a trap. But as the agents rushed to leave a wall of fire covered the doors, blocking all the exits.

When they realised Jennifer was standing on the other side of the fire, they raised their weapons to shoot her, but as they did Wyala and Henry jumped down from the air vents and knocked the agent out one by one.

## Original journal entry continued by Lila Winters

I stood there in Terrence's arms waiting for his answer as I asked again, "Do you trust me, Terry?"

I held his hand up to cup my cheek, so he could sense my true nature, and he smiled at me as he replied, "With all my heart . . ."

With that answer I kissed him and held him close to me, and as we kissed, our eyes glowed a deep purple with a tinge of green. My hands then moved from his, as one of them ran up through his dark brown hair to hold his head close to me, and the other rested on the back of his shoulder still holding the lotus blossom.

I knew this was going to hurt, so I held him close to me as his arms wrapped around me, and once the memory link was complete, I stabbed the stem of the lotus flower gently into the back of his neck at the very tip of his spinal column. His arms tensed while holding me as he felt the pain, yet endured through it as we continued to kiss, but he accidentally bit my lip as he flinched.

In the corner of my eye, I noticed what looked like Odele's secretary scurrying in a panic to whisper something to her, causing Odele to leap to her feet in a rage and rush to pull me away from Terrence, shouting, "Where is he?"

I held my lip in a little bit of pain and played ignorant, asking who and what she was talking about, which only enraged her more. She raised her hand up ready to slap me for my defiance, and as she did, Terrence let out a yelp in pain and his body collapsed to the floor, feeling the overwhelming surge radiating from his neck.

Odele rushed to Terrence's side in a fret, demanding someone to call an ambulance. And while all the attention was on Terrence, he just stared back at me as I disappeared before his eyes as Tyme phased me into his reality in order for us to make it back home safely without the risk of being followed.

I rushed Alex up into his apartment and sat with him throughout the night, making rose tonics and pastes to help him heal. He looked similar to the way I was after my first round of initiation treatment, and I would never wish that on anyone.

Peering up at me through his swollen black eyes, Alex wiped a tear from my cheek as I watched him fall asleep. And while he slept, I stared out the window, gazing up at the full moon, desperately hoping that Terrence would understand the decisions that I had to make.

# Journal entry insert by Terrence Connors

As I sat in a private hospital room of the Royal Melbourne, I listened to the sound of Odele berating the hospital staff and yelling at her security for being utterly incompetent.

I stared out the window looking up at the moon, remembering Lila's kiss and all the memories she had transferred to me in that brief moment. I pondered on one particular memory where Lila was talking to her new friend — the man who called himself Tyme.

I could hear the concern in her voice when she asked, "What will happen to Terrence if I do this? Will it hurt him?"

She looked so sad and worried as she listened to Tyme explain his part of the plan, "The yellow powder contains a series of nanobots programmed specifically to target the negative emotions Odele feels at any given time, anger . . . greed . . . her need for revenge. Each time that happens, an electrical current is released into your friend's nervous system, causing an immense amount of pain . . . so yes . . . it is going to hurt him . . . but it's your best chance of distracting the Connors long enough to take down their organisation."

My memory of Lila was interrupted, and I held back the tears as I felt the pain streaming through my body, all while listening to Odele go on a rampage through the hospital, shouting at everyone she sees.

It was a struggle to cope with the pain, but I drew strength from the note I clutched in my hand. The one that Lila gave to me seconds before she was ripped from my arms and disappeared.

It read: "I'll save you, Terry — I promise."

# CHAPTER 21

# HAPPY BIRTHDAY PRECIOUS

*Journal entry by Matt Winters*

I wasn't surprised when Maxwell offered me and the children, a spontaneous holiday to Sydney on the exact day Lila was seen without her bodyguard – Alex hovering over her.

That day I watched her racing through the hallways like a woman on a mission, and with stark white hair—it was obvious that something was wrong. So when Max told me to get on the plane with him, I didn't argue.

We've spent a week now in Sydney, staying at his Sydney Eden Hotel. And Max has paid for all of the sightseeing and activities for the children, which to me was a blatantly obvious distraction to the fact that we had over a dozen of his security guards escorting us to each activity.

But since all of the security guards are Mummy's friends, the children didn't seem to mind. However, every night when I go to bed, I fear what we were actually running from, and I fall asleep with the hopes that Lila would call and tell us everything is okay.

It's Ruby's birthday today, and I awoke to the sound I dreaded the most, hearing the noise of someone else in our hotel apartment. I quietly leapt from my bed and snuck out of my room, holding the yellow pages phone book up as a weapon. Then slowly made my way into the kitchen and dining area, only to see the table set with four place settings and a stack of pancakes in the middle of the table, along with a jug of juice.

Scanning around the room, I was confused seeing no one until Danny, Ruby and Lila leapt up from behind the couch and roared in the hopes of scaring me. And it worked, but my fear was quickly abated when I saw Lila laughing and smiling with the children.

I jumped in fright and shouted, "Oh no, it's the pancake munchkins," all while Danny and Ruby tackled me to the ground.

"Daddy, Daddy, it's my birthday today," Ruby shouted.

"Is it?" I grinned sarcastically, "Well then I should say happy birthday then, shouldn't I?" Ruby got even more excited when she pointed to Lila and exclaimed, "And look Daddy, look Mummy's here, and she made my pancakes."

Cheekily, I grinned and kept up the sarcastic surprise, "Are you sure coz I think I might still be dreaming."

And I was surprised when Lila grinned back at me as she sat down at the table with Danny and Ruby, and retorted with a cheeky giggle. "Well, if you're not happy, you can always wake up,"

Ah – No, I think I'd much prefer to keep this dream, so I decided to quickly sit down at the table with a slight smile, snickering, "And miss out on these dreamy pancakes . . . nah-uh."

*Lila tried to hold back a laugh and miserably failed, but once she composed herself, she turned to the children with excitement. "Eat up, guys. . . Mummy stole Uncle Max's plane, and I have a really big surprise waiting for you back home."*

*The thought of going home made my lips tighten into a bigger smile, but honestly, just seeing Lila sitting at the table next to me, eating breakfast as a family – that's already made my day.*

## Journal entry insert by Terrence Connors

I was beginning to feel like a prisoner again, being reminded of those hospital walls back at The Village. I know it has only been a week since I was admitted to the hospital, and I still take comfort in seeing the city of Melbourne, knowing Lila wasn't giving up on me.

I sat in the armchair staring out the window at the city, when Odele walked into the room.

She was holding my tray of hospital food and she stood near the door, looking unusually calm. I didn't look at her, I just kept staring out the window hoping for a better view soon.

"Hello Mother," I said breaking the silent tension we were in, but stayed staring out the window.

She placed the tray of food next to me and worryingly replied, "Hello dear . . . the doctor tells me you're not eating." She then inspected the contents of the food and pulled a grimacing face. "Well, I can see why . . . Not to worry, dear, you tell me what you want, and I'll have it sent up straight away."

She stood next to me, waiting for me to reply but I didn't. I just continued to stare out the window. And it only made her mad.

"Terrence, you know I don't like to be ignored," she barked, raising her voice and obviously failing to control her anger as she yelled, "Terrence!"

When she did, I felt the surge of pain course through my body again causing me to cringe and I grunted, holding the back of my neck.

Odele tried to comfort me, apologising and saying, "I'll fix this. Don't you worry, dear. I will fix this."

And she looked like she was in tears as she stormed out of the room, trying to compose herself. — Wow, does the ice-cold woman really have a functional heart?

I glanced back, watching Odele leave and I could see Keith and one of the doctors standing in the hallway waiting for her as she rolled up her sleeve to receive an injection into her arm, all while she seethed, "I swear if I ever see that little wench again, I'll . . ."
Suddenly all the pain I was feeling in my body disappeared, and I saw her sigh in relief as she began to calm down.
My brother watched Odele and smirked at her condescendingly, "Feel better?"
"Shouldn't you be doing something useful?" Odele snickered back. Instantly causing his grin to disappear as he walked down the hallway and rolled his eyes in a huff, glancing back into my hospital room again.

## Original journal entry continued by Matt Winters

*Finally, the Winters family were on our way back home and we were all very excited to be on the plane, with Max at the front of the cabin talking with Chase and the many security guards that had accompanied us. And Ruby and Danny were both distracted with the many birthday presents Ruby had received from Max and his wife – Sarah.*

*Lila was sitting opposite me, staring out the window at the clouds brushing over the wings of the plane. And I couldn't help but stare at her when I noticed a small strand of her white hair – the hair that she had been so desperately trying to hide from us all morning, by wearing a beanie and hoodie to cover it.*

*I know I probably shouldn't have acknowledged it, considering the last time her hair had turned white – it was because of me. But I eventually had to break the ice between us somehow, and thought I'd ask, "So . . . what do you want to talk about first, the sudden last-minute holiday plans or your hair?"*

*It probably wasn't the best ice-breaker, because it caused Lila to pull her hoodie further forward to cover the white hair and play ignorant, but it miserably failed.*

*Nonetheless, I needed some answers, so I leaned forward in my chair, ensuring I spoke soft enough that the children wouldn't hear.*

*"Lila . . . Max doesn't usually send people on random holidays with a handful of security guards unless there was a damn good reason . . . and everyone seems to be keeping me in the dark. Now I know we're not on the best of speaking terms at the moment, but I still think I should be told if we were or are still in danger."*

She briefly glanced down the cabin aisle to check on Danny and Ruby then leaned closer to me to quietly explain, "Alex and Terrence got into some trouble . . . and we formed a plan to rescue them, but I was afraid you and the kids might have been put in harm's way in the process."

I started to get a warm fuzzy feeling inside my chest, "Aww . . . So you do still care about me."

"Of course I care about you," Lila murmured, pulling our sour face, ". . . I wouldn't have married you if I didn't care about you."

Right — I didn't know how to respond to that one, given our current relationship limbo, so instead I tried to move on to the next topic regarding her very obvious white hair that she seemed to be hiding from everyone. But somehow, she knew what my question was going to be and stopped me before I could say a single syllable.

"If your next question has anything to do with my hair or my job, then you'll have to save it for tomorrow . . . Today is all about our daughter and her birthday . . . So just for today we are going to be or at least pretend to be a completely normal family."

A completely normal family? I needed to internalise my chuckles — just a little. Finding amusement at the thought of being a normal family, given our past year of adventures.

But once I had composed myself enough, I leaned forward again in the attempts to push my luck of rekindling just a little love from Lila, "Okay, but you do look amazingly sexy with the white hair."

I was right. It did push my luck and I curiously watched Lila's eyes turn black as she leaned back and stared out the window.

Well what do you know — my little brother actually did see Lila's eyes turn black, when he stupidly ticked her off. The question is why?

# Journal entry insert by Jessica Eden

Today was a pretty hectic day, and it seemed like everything was happening all at once.

I had spent the majority of the day organising a surprise for Matt and Lila at the request of my father. And Adela had been put in charge of organising the surprise party for Ruby that Lila had requested. It was a hard task – but not impossible as we worked together.

Adela and I had just finished the finishing touches of Maxwell's surprise and came down to the function hall to check on the preparation for the party. It was almost finished and it looked amazing, and we were both smiling as Katie raced past us, holding a handful of balloons and streamers.

She was just about to climb a ladder to hang them when we saw Matt's brother Shane march into the room in a fury, looking around and huffed, "Has anyone seen Matt or Lila or anyone I know?"

"They're in Sydney," Adela replied.

But he didn't seem too pleased with that response, and grunted back, "Well, can you please explain why Matt and Lila's living room looks like a war zone?"

Ah – right, I forgot he was staying at their place, but where has he been for the last week?

I smiled at him as I picked up a handful of balloons and pretended to be busy.

"Oh, that would be Katie's fault," I replied casually pointing to Katie standing on the ladder, feeling a little snobby. Let's see her explain her way at of this mess.

Not that I wanted to get her into trouble, but Katie and I were really starting to hit it off as friends, and she kind of threw us both in the deep end with her little phone stunt last week. So I was really eager for her to—you know—learn from her mistakes.

And I know she didn't plan to, but during the hotel's invasion saga last week, she might have accidentally — set Lila's apartment on fire, causing a lot of damage in the process.

Shane still in a furious huff and demanding answers, turned around ready to interrogate Katie and get some answers, but for a very obvious reason became lost for words as he –– let's just say –– studied the beauty of her body from behind.

"Um . . . does . . . anyone know when they'll be back?" he asked in a very different and calmer tone, watching Katie climb down the ladder.

Katie was a little oblivious to the audience she had as she replied, "Well, we're all hoping they'll be back in time for the party . . . why, is there a problem?"

As she turned to face Shane and address him properly, he started to stutter and Adela and I tried to stifle our laugh, still pretending to look busy blowing up the balloons.

But it was hilarious watching him as he tried to explain, "Well . . . um . . . no, not really. I was just hoping Lila could help with a tiny problem I seemed to have found myself in . . . but it's all just a complete misunderstanding you know . . ."

Ah – Problem.

I was pretty sure Katie could tell what he meant when he said 'problem', and she glanced over to Adela, getting a general consensus to offer our — assistance, all while Shane continued to mutter a completely bogus story of how he ended up in trouble.

He then stopped with an idea, "Hey . . . um . . . do you think your boss Max would let me borrow a few of his security guards, you know to give me a hand?"

Yeah ——That's not going to happen.

Katie finished putting the last of the decorations up and while packing up the ladder she answered, "I'm pretty sure his answer would be a no . . . but I might be able to help, maybe pull a few strings for you . . . and if anyone asks, we're chasing a lead for Lila."

Bugger — maybe she hasn't learned her lesson.

Shane nodded his head in agreement, assisting Katie to put the ladder away and eventually he clicked and questioned, "Wait, what do you mean a lead . . . a lead for what?"

Again — Bugger.

We all ignored his question, realising he had not been made aware of Lila's vocational endeavours, but he persisted and tried asking Katie again as they walked out of the conference room carrying the ladder.

And with one problem almost taken care of, it didn't take long for another to arrive as Alex appeared next to us, looking flustered and also looking for Lila. — What a surprise.

"Hey . . . have you guys seen Lila at all . . . she wasn't in her room when she woke up this morning?"

I know it was wrong of me, but I couldn't help but snort back, "You mean your room, right?"

Adela then kicked my leg, casually reminding me to be nice as she answered his question, "Lila's on her way back from Sydney and should be landing any minute now."

Naturally he jumped into the over-protective-not-quite-sure-where-the-line is friend mode and grunted "She's going to see Matt . . . is she mad? The last time she spoke to him, she turned into a wolf and nearly killed him."

Again, I snickered, "Yeah, well she's not doing too well around you either . . ."

And again I got kicked in the leg by my loving sister.

"What's that supposed to mean?" Alex barked back.

Unfortunately, Adela interrupted me before I could respond with my very judgemental response and instead, she calmly and nicely explained, "Think about it, Alex . . . You and Terrence aren't exactly in Lila's good books at the moment. I mean because of you, we were all put in danger. . . And ever since Lila heard that you had gone missing, her hair has been as white as a ghost, and her eyes look like mood rings on a roller coaster. . . If you ask me, Matt is probably the easier one of her choices to deal with."

Hooray! I'm not alone in my thoughts of judgement. Not that I'm usually a judgemental person – I just feel really bad for Lila.

I mean, Katie and I were the ones who helped her get ready for the ball last week, and I saw the extent of the damage done to her. She's been through so much – the last thing she needs is her friends crossing the line or taking off on her.

I stayed quiet and tried not to externalise my thoughts as Alex listened to Adela and you could just tell he agreed with us – a little. But then he tried to excuse it all, explaining how and why he got captured. Because obviously we cared or believed him.

"So it was all Terrence's idea?" I asked cynically.

"Yes," he nodded.

But this time instead of getting kicked by my wonderful sister, I just got glared at and I wisely stayed quiet for Adela to respond, "Don't you think it's a little odd that it was Terrence's idea to go to an island that only he knew about? Then suddenly out of the blue, his mother finds him and already has this elaborate plan in the works with a charity ball to use as her distraction. . . Alex, doesn't it make you question just a little bit if he was really on our side or if he was just playing us?"

Surprisingly Alex stood his ground and defended Terrence, which surprised the heck out of me. Especially when he handed Adela a USB and replied, "We went to get information and that's exactly what we got. . . Before Terrence was unwillingly dragged to that sad excuse for a charity ball and paraded around like a trophy, he risked everything to retrieve this USB that contains all the information we need to bring down The Board and their entire organisation. He also saved my life . . . so no I don't think he's playing us."

Right – well there's that.

I watched in a slight hesitancy as Adela gazed at the USB as if it were a piece of delicious candy and mumble, "Huh . . . I guess it wouldn't hurt to take a look . . . you know see if he was telling the truth and all . . ."

She then looked back at me with pleading eyes in the hopes that I would finish organising the surprise party <u>on my own</u> as she casually backed out of the room, waiting for me to begrudgingly agree. Like I had a choice.

I mean, she was holding the USB like it was the holy grail of her revenge. And I totally I knew what her plan was, and it wasn't fooling me.

But, because I'm a loving sister – I agreed.

I finished organising the party on my own, and I had perfect timing because Lila and the rest of her entourage of security and family had just arrived back at the hotel. And when I went in the lobby to greet them, my father raced ahead of the group, rushing to me and asked quietly if everything was ready, looking slightly nervous as I nodded.

It wasn't long before Lila appeared next to him with Danny and Ruby hand in hand. "What's everything?" Ruby asked.

It was hilarious seeing Max jump in fright, startled at the sight of a little girl. He then turned to her and whispered, "I have a surprise for you and your mummy . . . all we have to do is follow Jess . . ."

Now I know my father was nervous, but I was just as nervous, and I really hoped Lila was going to like it.

## Original journal entry continued by Matt Winters

*Alright, I'm going to admit it — The surprise Max and Jessica had organised had me slightly suspicious when they led us up to apartment 201, saying, "Welcome to your <u>new</u> home."*

*The apartment is on the top floor of the hotel, and as we walked through it looking around at all the rooms, we were amazed, including Lila.*

*Danny and Ruby both ran through the apartment in awe of the size of their newly decorated rooms of Princess's and Robot's, and I was also just as amazed. And I really think I was in state of shock as I listened to Jessica explain, "We combined two apartments to make one larger home for you with a study and guest bedroom . . ."*

*I turned back to see Lila hugging Max and thanking him, "Max, it's perfect and again I am very sorry about the other apartment."*

*Okay — I've clearly missed something about the other apartment, and I was going to ask but before I could Max shrugged it off.*

*"Oh, don't worry about it, Lila . . . The apartment needed a make-over anyway. . . I'll let you guys get settled in . . . oh and don't forget about the other surprise. It starts in an hour."*

*Lila then nodded back thanking both Max and Jessica again as they snuck out the door.*

*I leaned on the kitchen bench staring at Lila and mumbled, "Should I even ask about the other apartment?"*

*"Probably best not . . ." she replied, casually shaking her head as she strolled around the new apartment, looking at the amazing views.*

*The silence grew awkward between us again until I said, "Um . . . so . . . new apartment huh. This is huge . . ."*

*Yeah, good line opener, Matt.*

I cleared my throat and grew increasingly anxious, fearing Lila's response as I started to ask, "Lila, I have one more question and you don't have to answer it if you don't want to . . . but is there any chance of us getting back together or at least getting back on speaking terms for more than just today?"

*Please say yes – Please say yes – Please say yes.*

I stared at Lila, still very anxious as I watched her leaning on the back of the couch and awkwardly smirked back at me. I also noticed her eyes turn black for just a brief moment.

*Oh gosh, she's going to say no – Why did I even ask?*

Fearing I already knew the answer I cradled my head in my hands, listening to her reply,

"I was actually going to talk to you later tonight about that, but I was kind of hoping that the fourth bedroom could be for me. . . I mean I know we've hit a rough patch, and it is also my fault for a lot of the situation we're in, but I miss my kids and I . . . miss you . . . I mean, if it's okay with you."

*If it's okay with me—that was the best thing she could have ever said.*

I was shocked and overjoyed, and I may have held my thoughts and response back a little too long as she stared at me, waiting for a response.

"Are you kidding," I smiled, rushing to hug Lila, picking her up in my arms, and spinning her around, "This is great. It's wonderful. Of course, it's okay with me."

This day was just filled with amazing surprises one after the other, and I was overjoyed just looking around at this new apartment and smiling at Lila.

When we were all ready for the next surprise, we led Ruby downstairs to the function hall, where everyone was waiting and all yelled, "Happy Birthday" when Ruby entered the room.

She explored around the room admiring every pink and sparkly decoration, and waved to everyone, rushing to greet my mum and dad—Rob and Rebecca Winters ——and they were holding what looked like another new princess doll as a present for Ruby.

The room was covered with party decorations keeping Ruby very busy, and Danny naturally ran straight to the jumping castle that was set up in the corner of the room.

There were so many of Ruby's friends there, and she was entertained for hours opening presents and running around on a sugar high, chasing after Max's dog Prince.

Lila and I decided to divide and conquer – walking around the room to say hello to everyone. A few of my family were a little surprised to actually see Lila here, mainly because the last family gathering we had was for her funeral. So there were a few questions asked – that I struggled to answer. But thankfully Lila took or dodged the questions well.

And I know she shouldn't have to, but I was a little glad Lila made that extra effort to cover all the——scars, it did lead to less unusual questions being asked that again, I still can't answer.

The next awkward moment that I noticed was when Chase and almost everyone of Lila's guardian friends watched, very closely and anxiously as Lila went over to greet her mother Hanna – even Max hovered just a little.

And sadly, I also caught Lila as she leaned in to greet her mother with a hug, glance down to check the side of Hanna's neck for any sign of a tribal tattoo.

I can't even begin to imagine how hard it would be for Lila, not knowing who she can trust, and I was beginning to understand why she still had the white hair.

As the party continued, and it almost grew time for cake. Max stood up onto the stage and tapped on the microphone to interrupt everyone and gained the attention of the room.

"Good evening, everyone. . . I hope you're all having a wonderful time . . . I know I have had an absolute blast seeing the joy on little Ruby's face as she enjoys this fantastic party that Lila and her team have organised . . . but now we've finally come to a very serious issue . . . that was brought to my attention just this morning actually. . . Today I was informed of a beautiful tradition that Lila and her family have performed every year for their children's birthday . . . so I think with a little coaxing, Matt and Lila might be willing to share this tradition with all of us and sing us a little song."

The crowd began to applaud and cheer encouragements as both Lila and I were pulled up onto the stage, and Lila was handed her guitar – that I am assuming she had hidden in the back of our wardrobe for a reason, but I guess her secret had to come out eventually.

As Lila stood on the stage, she quickly glanced at me and then looked down at the front of the stage to see both Danny and Ruby standing there ready to hear the birthday song.

So she cleared her throat and spoke into the microphone, "Err . . . Hi . . . so we have a bit of a tradition in my family. It's a birthday song that I wrote when Danny was born and we sing it for each family member on their birthday, to remind them just how wonderful life is and can be for them."

*She then looked back at me, noticing that I had a massive smile across my face and as she strummed away on her guitar, we sang together our happy birthday song to Ruby — wishing her all the joys of life as the birthday cake was brought out, and she blew out the candles.*

# CHAPTER 22

# THE BEFORE AND AFTER PARTY

## Journal entry by Alex Woods

-2 hours before Ruby's birthday party-

I was really worried when I woke up this morning, unable to find Lila anywhere.

Every day this week while I was recovering, she would hang around me to ensure I was resting, and she made the blue-rose tonics for me. But she always stayed quiet and I just knew she was angry.

Now that I had fully recovered, I had hoped that we could sit down talk and maybe make things right with her. But when I found out she had left the state without me, I really didn't know what to feel or even if I was justified in my feelings.

It especially didn't help – feelings wise, when I was following Adela up to her apartment to look at the USB I had acquired, and she started filling me in on everything I had missed during my recovery process. From the – Invasion of the hotel, to the explosion of Matt's apartment that forced Lila's family to go into hiding. Adela even raved about the way Lila had organised every detail of the mission and pulled every string she had to rescue me and keep everyone else safe – as well as keep herself from turning into a wolf.

I quickly realised that I had no right to be mad at Lila. If anything, I should have been proud.

A bit mopey with myself, I stayed quiet, sitting next to Adela as she turned on her laptop and opened up the USB files. She scrolled across each thumbnail of the various blueprints, emails, business intake forms, and shipping receipt and eventually she clicked on a group photo of what looked like a gathering of CEOs and politicians.

To the untrained eye, it would just look like a random networking event until you looked closer to see certain people standing amongst the group – like Terrence's mother Odele Connors, General Richard Willows, and one other member, who I had already met before. He was the US Commander who rescued Lila, Terrence and me from the middle of the Indian Ocean, and when we searched the files, we found out his names was Commander Eric Peterson.

Unfortunately, Adela and I had become so engrossed in the picture, attempting to ID the others in the photo that neither of us noticed the USB flashing red and in time. Until some guy appeared standing behind us, shouting Adela's name and pushing us to the ground.

He moved at full speed and grabbed Adela's laptop, throwing it into the middle of the room as it disappeared into nothing, then he dived to the ground next to Adela to shield her as the room began to shake and a bright shimmering light surrounded us.

In seconds, the light disappeared, leaving scorch marks and glowing embers in its wake.

"What the hell was that?" I shouted, looking around the room to see no remaining traces of what looked like a very large explosion.

The guy stood to his feet, helping Adela to stand and explained, "That would be a micro time bomb – you activated it when you opened the files."

"I thought you said Terrence was on our side. . .Why would he try to blow us up?" Adela shrieked, angrily turning to me.

But before I could respond, the other guy jumped to Terrence's defence. – And that was new.

"I wouldn't pin that on Terrence just yet. What you just saw was the result of a micro pressure plate that's easily inserted into the shaft of the USB and mistaken for the groundings of the device. Anyone could have placed it there."

"What?" I gasped, completely confused at the entire situation.

But Adela seemed preoccupied, standing in the centre of the room looking panicked as she said in a very angry yet freaked tone, "Tyme, where'd the bomb go?"

Okay, so I'm not even going to hark on about the fact that this guy was named Tyme, but wow – that's a stupid name.

Anyway – Tyme replied back slightly defensive, "What was I supposed to do, let you die?"

Which led to Adela losing it, "Argh. . . Lila is going to kill us if we screwed this up!"

Clearly, I had missed yet another thing while in recovery and I demanded someone to fill in the missing pieces.

Eventually Adela stopped pacing and bickering with this guy – Tyme and said, "Okay Alex, we're going to need to show you something, but you need to swear not to freak out or tell anyone."

Huh, well this was suspicious, but I was intrigued so I nodded, "Okay, I swear."

Adela stared at me for a moment – probably to check if I was being genuine, then nodded to Tyme as he explained to me that I may feel some temporary discomfort and to keep still.

His eyes then glowed a dark silver and the room slowly changed in its colour and appearance to the point where the walls and furniture were almost disintegrated with scorch marks spreading from the middle of the room outwards. What was worse was that the wall leading into Adela's bedroom was completely missing and all of the windows were shattered.

As I stared at the chaos and mess in the apartment there was one thing that seemed to be almost completely unharmed, and were also not in the room just a few seconds ago, and they were the three giant pink water lily pods sitting on the side of the room, all slightly scorched with burn marks.

Adela started to inspect the tightly closed up pods and explained that each of the pods held one of the Guardians from the New Year's Day incident inside —Tora, Jordan, and Zera, who were also all unconscious.

I walked around the room still in bit of shock and found some very interesting items sitting on the kitchen bench, of what was left of security photos of the hotel and of Mrs Willows's house and of Matt and the children.

I was gobsmacked and lost for words, all I could muster was the word, "Okay."

Still needing answers, I turned back to Adela to see her studying the damage of the waters lilies and peeling back one of the petals to check the pulse of each of the guardians and sighed with relief, "Good. . . they're still alive . . . Honestly, these things that Lila designed are literally the perfect life pod."

And for some reason Tyme chuckled back and joked, "Maybe, we should start up a business with her."

And as if either of those comments led to any explanation as to what the hell was going on here – and to no surprise, that was exactly what I shouted. Only to get Adela glaring back at me and disappointingly shaking her head as she replied, "Alex, you swore not to freak out."

So I shouted back, "That was before I knew what type of freak show you were running here. Lila's going to flip when she sees this."

"Actually," Adela interrupted, "this is all Lila's idea. . . These are her pods. That was Lila's computer that just blew up and over in the kitchen is what's left of Lila's Neuritamine cure samples." She then pointed to the many vials and test tubes that had shattered in the explosion as she added, "Lila was trying to develop a way to cure the patients of the Neuritamine without harming any of their memories."

What the hell – I was gobsmacked and now slightly furious at all the secrets Lila was keeping from me. Why wouldn't she tell me any of this? – She made me promise to always be honest with her and here she is deceiving the world.

I glared back at Adela still in fury and snapped, "Why would anyone want to remember the atrocities they did under the influence of this drug. I thought you of all people would be glad you don't remember anything."

And yep – that was probably a low blow.

"That's not fair!" Adela shouted back at me, almost in tears, "You have no idea what it's like to be judged for something you have no memory of ever doing. I have lost months of my life and hurt so many of my friends and torn apart a family with no knowledge of how or why . . . Alex, we have no idea how long these people have been affected by this drug. We could be wiping away years of their memories. It could destroy their lives and their relationships . . ."

She handed me what was left of a photo of Lila and Hanna, and I just stared at the photo feeling like an absolute tool of an idiot as Adela continued, "Do you honestly think Lila's mother would be completely oblivious to what her husband was doing or where he was going?. . . Lila told me once while she was up here, that her childhood sucked and it was very painful for her. She didn't want go into specifics but what she did say, was that the only good thing that came from her child hood was the care and love she has for Hanna . . .and now Lila is desperately hoping that her entire life. . . her childhood wasn't all a lie."

Well damn – again I had no right to be mad.

I started to feel like a real jerk – judging and getting upset at Lila without even taking the time to think about how Lila would be feeling about all of this.

While Adela was busy lecturing me, Tyme had received an alert on his phone. And for some strange reason, he had very easy access to our hotel security cameras.

He very easily pulled up the footage of the basement car park of Katie following what looked like Matt's little brother Shane out of the hotel, along with three of our newest security guards.

I couldn't understand it – Adela seemed perfectly okay at the sight of one of our newest Guardian recruits travelling off with someone we know very little about. – It baffled me – but again this isn't the first thing that baffled me today.

Her mood quickly changed when I pointed out the undercover police car that was following Shane and Katie from a distance, and stated, "Isn't that the detective that's investigating us?"

"Oh crap," Adela sighed, frustratingly rolling her eyes and looking at the time.


-1 hour before Ruby's party-

We followed Katie and Shane through the streets of Melbourne and down into Flagstaff Station with our new security guards in tow. And we stayed in what Tyme explained to be a time dimensional rift – where no one could see us. Giving us the benefit of watching them from a safe distance. – Creepy I know.

Katie and her group followed Shane and walked to the far end of one of the platforms, which was empty of other patrons because of the weekend. However, at the end of the platform stood 6 hooded men who looked very much like they could be part of a gang or a drug cartel. Interesting – Now what's Matt's little brother doing with people like this?

But we had a more pressing concern that needed our attention, and I was very worried about what Detective George and the back-up he had called were planning on doing—if and when things went sideways.

Adela, Tyme and I watched as Shane handed a yellow envelope to one of the hooded men. And we freaked out a bit when we overheard George give the order to move in on his count while he was hiding on the other platform.

– To be honest I think the police could really use a lesson in stealth.

Adela quickly turned to me and demanded, "We have to get them out of here."

"What do you mean? Can't this guy just phase them into whatever the hell this is and be done with it?" I asked – pointing to Tyme.

But Tyme just shook his head, "No . . . Humans can't handle the time distortion like we can. I can only pull Katie into the rift."

The tension rose when we heard Detective George and his team of police officers start moving and shouting, "Freeze" and "Get on the ground."

Adela jumped into action and demanded Tyme to phase Katie into this rift thing and to phase me and her out of the rift thing to grab Shane and the others and run.

Her plan went off in seconds as she shouted go and we were both phased into the real-time and ran at full speed toward our team. I grabbed hold of Shane and one of our security team members, and Adela grabbed the other two.

I briefly glanced back in fear, as I watched Katie create a fireball in her hand about to throw it at one of the police officers just before she disappeared out of this time.

What the hell was she planning to do?

# Journal entry insert by Lila Winters

<u>-5 minutes before Ruby's party-</u>

Well I'm in my new home now and I have my family back – almost. And I'm really hoping that Matt and the kids feel and are safe here now. I still can't believe that they were put in so much danger like this – that I had to ask them to run and hide.

As I stood on the balcony of my new apartment, I stared out across the city off in my own little world of thought, playing with the vines of one of the balcony plants as it grew up and around my hand, blossoming tiny white flowers, when Matt interrupted my trance.

"I thought you were trying to be normal today," Matt commented.

Normal – What the frac does normal mean anymore?

I jumped in fright and apologised but didn't want to tell him what I was really up to. So, instead I told him I was day dreaming.

Apparently, Max had arrived early to check that we were all settled in and wanted to escort us down to the surprise.

"Okay," I said feeling slightly flustered. But Matt could clearly tell I was not acting like myself and walked closer to me to ask if I was okay.

Yet again, I have to question – What does <u>okay</u> mean?

*I didn't want to tell him how I really felt because honestly, I didn't even know. My head and my heart have been in this kind of limbo mode while I'm dealing with everything, and I'm waiting for the right time to process it. But still Matt wanted an answer.*

"I'm fine . . . I just need a minute to change," I replied as I moved to walk back inside.

Matt caught my hand to stop me and smiled, kissing my forehead.

"I didn't get to say thank you before . . . you know for protecting us from whatever happened last week. I don't even want to imagine what might have happened if we were in Melbourne when the apartment went up in flames."

I could feel my emotions stirring up inside me as my eyes turned black – hating myself for ever putting my family in danger, and I quickly turned and pulled away from him.

But it inevitably sent the wrong message as Matt stepped back and ached with regret.

I wanted to tell him that I wasn't trying to pull away, that I really did like the kiss, and that I was just trying to protect him. But I knew he wouldn't understand the lack of control I felt – not now – not after everything that's happened.

Instead I just let him walk back into the apartment, shaking his head in frustration.

## Journal entry insert by Terrence Connors

Again, I was stuck in this hospital room waiting as I looked out my window across the city, playing with the vines of a small pot plant that an 'anonymous friend' had sent me.

She had actually sent floral gift arrangement to every room on the ward including the nurse's stations. The ward was now filled with greenery and I loved it.

While I was playing with vines of my present, they started to grow up and around my hand sprouting little white flowers and it brought me comfort to know she had not forgotten about me.

I smiled through my tears, because I really missed her. Suddenly I hunched forward in pain, holding my neck as I heard the screeching sound of my mother's voice yelling at someone.

"I don't care how you get to her, just do it quickly and quietly."

I peered out the window down at the road where I could see Odele speaking on the phone to someone and rudely hang up as she approached her limo. And there waiting next to the limo was what looked like the Commander who had supposedly rescued us from the water, and a woman who I know to be a Kim — but she's really water nymph and a very skilled assassin.

"Good evening, Odele," the Commander gloated.

I could tell my mother was not expecting him but knew exactly who he was as she sneered, "Oh, please tell me you are not here to gloat, Peterson . . . it is a very unattractive quality for you."

"Not at all," the Commander replied, "I've come to help. . . The other Board members and I are simply . . . worried about you. We all heard the news about your son. It's such a shame.

It must make you so angry at that little . . . now what was it you called her again?"

"Wench," Kim interjected.

To which the Commander continued his boast, "Ah that's right, a wench. Fine words coming from a lady in your status."

Odele huffed before pushing the Commander aside to open her limo door, "You claim you've come to help, how? You had all three of them. . . including the tree in your custody for days. A ship full of armed men at your disposal and what . . . she just walked off the boat. How could you possibly help me?"

I got a very worrying feeling as I watched the Commander smile back at her and whispered, "By starting a war that no one can resist"

He then climbed into the limo with Odele and demanded the driver to take off.

# Original journal entry continued by Alex Woods

- 20 minutes before the end of Ruby's party-

I couldn't believe what I was doing, rescuing this idiot. And for what? I missed Ruby's party and she's not going to forgive me – that little girl holds a grudge better than her mother does.

I ran at full speed up into my apartment and threw Shane safely onto the couch after leaving the young security guard safe in the hotel lobby – I'm sure someone will fill him in as to what happened.

As soon as Shane landed on the couch he immediately stood back up to his feet, petrified at what just happened, looking around and asking all sorts of stupid questions.

That is until I lost my patience and gave him a gentle knock on the head to make him go to sleep. Well, it was at least gentle enough not to leave a large bruise – I think.

Either way, he's quiet now, falling unconscious back onto the couch. And I ever so nicely covered him with a blanket to make it look like he was sleeping.

But before I could take a moment to process and think through everything – including how to get back into Ruby's good books, I stood up and found Terrence standing at the door, waiting for me and slightly out of breath.

"Hello Alex," he rasped, but he didn't look happy. He almost looked scared as he started to feel an enormous amount of pain surge through his body. I raced to catch him as he collapsed from the pain and as I held onto him, he looked back up at me.

"Well I guess she found out I was gone."

I picked him up to rest him next to Shane on the couch and went down to the party to find help. The problem was I didn't know who to go to. It seemed as though everyone believed that Terrence was a traitor or a double agent.

The only person I knew who could tell if he had turned was Lila, and by the time I got to the birthday party, Ruby was just about to blow out her candles while Matt and Lila sang to her on stage.

Awe damn – she can play the guitar as well – Is there anything she can't do?

I stood and watched as Matt held Lila's hand and gave her a cuddle, but it was then I noticed her eyes flickering black and she desperately tried to hide them from the crowd.

I was going to go up and try to help her stay calm, but as soon as she looked over at me standing at the door her eyes went back to their normal blue, and her lips peeked at one side.

She rushed as fast as she humanly could to greet me with a very excited hug, "Alex, you had me so worried. I thought you'd be here earlier. . . Ruby is not going to let you forget this."

– Well don't I know it.

I could sense Matt's annoyance radiating towards me as he stood next Ruby sharing some of her birthday cake. He was watching Lila talk to me and I don't think he liked the fact that she was able to hug me without going all black eyes. And it obviously didn't help the situation between them when I took Lila away from the party either.

When Lila and I got back up to the apartment, it was as if it was one big happy reunion, and Lila jumped into Terrence arms and hugged him so tightly, thankful to see him.

Her snowy-white hair returned to a soft honey shade as she snuggled up next to Terrence and excitedly smiled, "It worked . . . the plan worked."

'The plan worked' – Right, yet another thing Lila had forgotten to mention to me.

We all clearly had a lot of catching up to do as Lila looked up to see Shane still unconscious on my couch, and Terrence and I looked back at Lila just as confused.

# CHAPTER 23

# THE ASSASSIN

## Journal entry by Kimberly Black

Mission report

The target's name was Lila Winters. It wasn't easy to access the accommodation of the target and ended up being rather expensive. The idea was to rent the room below hers, slip into the apartment through the air vent, and deliver the package.

I must say it does make it exceptionally easy for me as a nymph, having the ability to liquefy myself.

The only difficulty I encountered was carrying the package through the air vents with me without risk of contamination to myself.

As I entered the target's apartment, I regained my natural form, glancing around the dark room then crept quietly to the bed where the she slept, placing the package of five small silver beads into the target's hands. And watched as they dissolved and were absorbed into her skin.

Five beads are a significant amount for one guardian to handle, being five times the amount of the standard dosing, but Commander Peterson was convinced that this target in particular is anything but standard.

There was however a very minor hiccup as the foliage in her room grew to a large scale, attempting to apprehend me, but as it did, I returned to a liquid state and retreated back through the air vent.

Now all that is required of me, is to monitor the progress and if necessary, acquire more targets.

# CHAPTER 24

# HEATWAVE

*Journal entry by Lila Winters*

I was having a lot difficulty adjusting to the new apartment and its sleeping arrangement. I guess I'd gotten so used to the comfort Alex provided me when he was sleeping on the makeshift bed next to me — that and Terrence wasn't far away either, sleeping in his room. But now I'm several floors away from them, and if something goes wrong — I might accidentally hurt the wrong person.

I know it's going to be difficult, but I had to at least try to get used to the new apartment and the new relationship void with Matt — and that was hard.

I mean, Matt originally seemed thrilled that I had made the first step towards mending our relationship. But now it feels wrong to me — It feels distant.

I also no longer feel comfortable telling him about everything that happens, and has happened to me – personally it feels like I'm trying to protect him from the horrors.

He knows that I only ever give him the PG version of the events from the island, which in turn makes him become more distant. For example, a few days ago I rushed out to the laundry basket to grab some clean clothes, and on my way back, he caught a good look at me in just some bed-shorts and a bra. And before the island, I'd usually catch him with a cheeky grin – but now all he can see are the scars – and all I sense is his guilt.

It must have been really hot tonight as I tossed and turned, struggling to sleep. And I didn't understand what was happening when Alex crawled up from the end of my bed and started kissing me passionately along my arms, and the collar of my neck. The strange part was I really enjoyed it and I groaned in desire for more as we got carried away.

Eventually I broke away from Alex and leapt from the bed in a confused panic,

"Alex, stop. . . we can't do this."

But then Terrence appeared behind me, staring at me like I was his sweet delicious candy and groaned with desire, "No, but I can."

He wrapped his arms around me and caressed me, putting his hands and lips everywhere – and I loved every second of it.

My entire body felt like it wanted more, like it was longing for him to touch me more.

Then when Alex heard me moan in pleasure and stood up in a jealous rage trying to pull me away from Terrence, I woke up. – This time for real in my very empty bedroom in a panicked and very perplexed state with beads of sweat dripping off me.

I was short of breath and glanced back at the clock, realising it wasn't long before the sun would rise, so I started the day early at the unearthly hour of 4am and I tried very hard not to think about my – unusual night.

I tried doing a workout in the attempts to clear my head, but it was of little use. So I went up to the conference room and got stuck into planning the next team meeting.

I stood at the end of the table looking at some of the photos and files we had managed to recover from my blown-up laptop. Most of them were fragmented and hard to read, but they were able to give me a few ideas.

I was so caught up looking at the photos that I didn't even realise that Alex and Terrence had both walked into the conference room. And I jumped in a fluster, dropping the files on the floor – I think I was still a little freaked from this morning and I wasn't overly sure if they were really here or if I had fallen asleep again.

So with short calm breaths, I took a few steps back trying to regain my thoughts but then accidentally tripped over the office chair, falling to the floor. As I felt the pain, I realised that I definitely wasn't dreaming and embarrassingly sighed as I started to pick up the fallen papers.

They both knelt down to help me as Alex started to apologise, "I'm sorry, Lila, are you okay?"

– Uh huh, there's that question again – That ever so famous and over used question that also never gets answered truthfully.

I cleared my throat and tried to act all casual, but it was hard, "Yeah . . . I'm fine . . . why?"

Suddenly, I started feeling some very confusing emotions as I studied Alex's strong and well-defined muscles. And I subconsciously bit down on my bottom lip and groaned a little.

Come on Lila – keep it together.

I tried very hard not to feel anything specific, knowing Alex's abilities to sense certain things. But it caused Alex to look at me oddly, trying to figure me out as he puzzled,

"Um . . . Matt called, he sounded worried about you. Apparently, you just disappeared in the middle of the night. . . We went down to the gym assuming you would be there but instead, we found a punching bag shattered in pieces and a sparring stick snapped in two. . . And now we find you here, sweaty and a little rattled with your heart beating erratically."

He started looking at me suspiciously. "Lila are you sure you're okay?"

Clearly, he realised I was trying to mask my emotions and keep them jumbled with other thoughts – like rainbows and dancing unicorns and other glittery things that make people happy.

I stayed focused on picking up the last pieces of papers from the floor, and desperately tried to avoid eye contact with Alex, insisting that I was fine and that I was just having trouble sleeping.

I then very quickly and very carefully placed the files onto the conference table and tried to keep my distance from Alex, unwittingly backing into Terrence's amazingly strong arms.

TERRIBLE IDEA.

Oh frac – as Terrence's arms enveloped me, I felt so content and happy, and my heart jump a little inside. It was like I wanted to stay wrapped up in his arms forever, and his T-shirt smelled amazing, like the old oak trees after it rained. It was very, very nice.

SNAP OUT OF IT LILA

I shook my head trying block that thought from my mind and – Oh frac, Terrence could clearly tell what my desires were, and he noticed me biting my bottom lip.

"Lila, are you sure you're okay?" he asked with his lip pulled together so tightly with his striking blue-green eyes looking down at me, still holding on to me with his ––

NOPE – I really wasn't okay.

And I really struggled to shake away the memory of last night, so as soon as I could, I willed myself away from Terrence, very much unsure of how I felt towards him.

Then very cautiously, I started backing away from both of them, mumbling "Um . . . I, err . . . left something back in the apartment. I'm just going to . . . yeah . . . I really can't do this."

In a hurry I rushed out of the conference room, leaving absolutely no opportunity for anything else to go wrong.

THIS CAN NOT BE HAPPENING.

# Journal entry insert by Adela Eden

I was just giving Tyme an official tour of the hotel and of our operations when we bumped into Lila rushing out of the conference room in a flurry. I heard the words, "I think she hates me" coming from the conference room, and as I turned into the room, I saw both Alex and Terrence looking speechless at whatever just happened.

"Hey," I rejoiced, looking at Terrence and boasted, "I see Lila's escape plan worked out well for you. How are you feeling . . . any pains lately?"

He stared at me confusingly and queried, "What plan?'"

Oh Fruits – I wasn't sure if I had said too much, but since the cat was out of the bag, I explained, "Lila had been planning out your daring escape all week. . . She's very clever that woman . . . She believed that if she was able to keep Odele's focus solely on her by sending annoying messages and playing cat and mouse with her. . . that the distraction would provide the perfect cover for Agetha and Wyala to swoop in and rescue you. . . She also may have let it slip in one of the many messages she sent to your mother . . . that the nanobots roaming around in your bloodstream emit a small magnetic field when near another infected person, giving the nanobots a stronger effect on the subject . . . and that if your mother truly cared about you, she should keep her distance."

Pretty neat plan, huh – That chick's got style and brains.

Again, Terrence just looked at me confused and gobsmacked, and it became very clear to me that Lila wasn't planning on playing that hero card with him.

"She did that for me?" Terrence gasped completely puzzled, "Why didn't she say anything to me? Alex, did you know?" He turned to Alex to get an answer and realised he was completely oblivious to the conversation and asked, "Hey are you okay?"

But Alex was lost in his own thought, staring at the door, "Ah huh, sure. I'll. . . I'll be back in a minute." And he too looked very confused as he walked out of the room.

Well, that was weird – I was half expecting Alex to act all overprotective and upset at the fact that Lila literally dangled herself as live bait in front of The Board and didn't tell him.

I turned back to keep talking to Terrence and properly introduce him to Tyme, but when I did Terrence had disappeared, running out of the room at super speed.

Very, very odd.

## Journal entry insert by Alex Woods

Something just didn't feel right with Lila, so I went up to her new apartment to check on her. It didn't help that Shane had answered the door, sporting a rather large bruise on his head – I swear I only gave him a small knock, but wow does he bruise easily.

"Shane. . . hi. . . wow that looks really bad," I commented, pretending to be ignorant of how it happened.

He nodded and boasted, "Yeah, scored it in a fight down at the train station, although I don't remember ever being in the fight. . . weird huh."

Still holding back any derogatory comment of his idiotic behaviour, I grinned, "Yeah weird . . . Is Lila home?"

He opened the door a little further and I sensed a level of confusion as he replied, "Yeah, she just ran into her room. I think she was a bit upset. I'm guessing it was about Danny . . . It's his first day of school today. And he was really upset that she wasn't here to say goodbye."

And with that piece of information, I nodded my head, realising what was going on with Lila now, "Right, do you mind if I talk to her?"

He then escorted me through to Lila's room as I tentatively knocked on the door, and eventually after I got no response, I walked in and closed the door, gently trying to give Shane a subtle hint to go away.

This was actually the first time I had been in Lila's new apartment, and it was interesting to see that she had opted to sleep in a separate room to Matt.

It did, however, suit Lila's style a lot better than my apartment did, with green and purple bed sheets and a lot of plants and flower pots.

I wandered around Lila room and found her standing over the bathroom sink splashing cold water on her face when I interrupted, slowly moving closer to her.

"So, I heard about Danny's first day of school. . . I'm sorry you didn't get to say goodbye . . . it's still 8.30 . . . if we hurry, we can still make it in time to wish him good luck."

In a panic Lila stared up at me and screeched, "What? I missed Danny's first day of school. Oh god, he is never going to forget this."

She darted towards her bedroom door, brushing past me. And I, now realising she was upset for another reason, raced to block the door. "Wait if you didn't know about Danny, then what's going on, why are you upset?"

I noticed her fingers start to play and twirl around each other, and she was determined not to look at me. So I held my hand on her cheek to try and sense the answer when I realised she was running a high fever and was extremely sweaty with very confusing emotions racing through her.

"Lila, your burning up," I noted, with the worry increasing me, "and your heart and your emotions are all over the place . . . what the hell's going on?"

I waited for her answer but she didn't say anything, she just peeked up at me as I felt her forehead to get a better sense of her temperature. Her breathing became short as she pushed my hand aside, wrapping her arms around my neck and locked her lips with mine.

She was kissing me with so much passion in her, and I won't lie – she was amazing.

I heard Lila moan as she pushed me down on to the bed, holding me close to her and straddling my hips.

I struggled to understand what was happening, and got so lost in the moment as my hands wandered up her back. – And oh, just listening to the sound of her breathing with so much pleasure as I got to bite her bottom lip this time, and she loved it.

Her body rolled in my arms, grinding against mine and I sensed that she wanted a hell of a lot more than this from me – she wanted all of it.

But as Lila started removing my top, she stopped, pushing herself away from me and uttered, "No."

She then darted at full speed to stand on the other side of the bed and tried to regain her thoughts. She was out of sorts with her breath still short and laboured, staring back at me in a sense of confusion as she slowly backed towards the door and whispered in tears,

"I'm so sorry, Alex . . . I don't . . . I didn't . . . I."

But before Lila said anything else, she ran at full speed out of the apartment. Leaving me to just lay on the bed confused and in a sense of extreme frustration as I touched my lips and remembered how she tasted.

But I then sighed, quickly realising where Lila was going, because I knew she would need back up, and I may have grunted a little venting my frustrations before I ran at full speed, chasing after her.

Lila knew I was following her as we ran though the city, and she made it just in time to see Danny into the school. It was so sad – and I could feel Lila's heart break just a little when she saw Danny standing in front of his dad with tears on his cheeks.

But when he saw Lila appear standing behind Matt, his smile beamed from ear to ear as he dove into her arms and gave her the biggest cuddle.

I kept my distance, staying on the other side of the road, hoping not to ruin the tender family moment as Lila walked with Matt and Danny into the school to get him settled. She even waved goodbye to Matt as he left for work then crossed the road to walk back with me, and thanked me for coming along and being her back up.

But then we walked in silence the rest of the way home. I was hoping Lila would eventually clue me into what the hell was going on. But maybe she needed more time to work it out – she did seem very confused.

## Original journal entry continued by Lila Winters

Frac. Frac. Frac – alright today is starting to feel very weird for me. And I can't believe what I did to Alex, and the fact that I liked it, and that I wanted – um – it.

The worst part was Alex could definitely sense everything I was feeling then and now, and he was very, very worried about me.

And I couldn't blame. – I'm seriously struggling to make sense of all these feelings I have towards him, and it also doesn't help that I have a ridiculously high temperature and fast heart rate, which just causes Alex to worry more about me.

I did however notice while we were walking back to the hotel at a slight distance from each other, that I was able to keep my desires in check. So I strongly believe that I just might be able to make it through the day, if I stuck to the rule of:

DON'T TOUCH ALEX – It sounds simple enough – I think.

When we got back to the hotel, we walked back up into the conference room just as Adela and Max were starting the meeting, with Katie running in just behind us, feeling flustered, seeming to have a massive headache and surprisingly looked how I felt.

We got straight into the meeting as to not delay anything, but the tension in the room became quite obvious. And while Adela was busy talking about Neuritamine and the trauma, I drifted off into another daydream.

TERRIBLE IDEA.

In my daydream, Terrence had walked into the room, pulling me into his arms and caressing my shoulders and chest with his beautifully soft hands. Then pressed his lips against the sensitive part of my neck where my pulse thrummed.

I was slightly listening to the meeting when Adela presented her theory about the blue rose and lily tonic that I had created.

"Lila," she said, trying to pull me from my trance.

– and honestly, I didn't want to go.

"Lila!" she called again.

– No, I'm not going Terrence is just too pretty and really good with his tongue.

It wasn't until Alex grabbed my hand that I got pulled out of my – interesting daydream, only to realise everyone was waiting for me to have some kind of explanation as to how it would work and if it could be done.

Oh Holy Fruit Cakes.

All I could think to do was agree randomly, that yes it could be done. But as they moved on in the meeting, I realised that I hadn't even tried the new tonic yet and that it was still just a theory.

And Another Oh Holy Fruit Cakes.

I got so lost in thought, trying to figure out where my thoughts were damn well going and why, that I completely zoned out in the meeting. Then eventually, Max concluded the meeting, happily stating that we now had a way of healing the rescued guardians, and thanks to Henry's research, we knew where our first target was going to be.

"We'll reconvene tomorrow to discuss our next mission and the details of how we get to Canada. . . without arising suspicion," Max explained before he dismissed everyone.

That's right he said Canada – and because of my distracting feelings and thoughts, I now have no idea why we were going.

FRAC-DAMN.

# Journal entry insert by Adela Eden

We'd just finished the team meeting – and it was the first one that Tyme was invited to sit in on, after agreeing to help Lila and join her team in the fight against The Board.

But unfortunately, all through the meeting I was finding it difficult to concentrate. It was strange. I don't usually get headaches, but today it was a bad one and I started to run a fever.

It all started this morning when that barrister gave this horrible-tasting coffee. I wanted to spit it out and not drink the rest but she seemed so sweet, and nervous because it was her first day – and I might have been a little distracted by the absurd amount of foundation and make-up she wore.

I really do regret drinking the coffee, and I was starting to get side-tracked in my own thoughts as Tyme came over to help me pack up. He's so sweet and has been so patient and helpful around me, and I don't even fully understand why.

I know he's waiting for the perfect opportunity to tell Lila who he really is, and that him using his powers to help her was a smooth way of earning her trust. But there was something else that was mysterious about him, and yet so very calming.

Oh Fruits – I didn't even realise that I had completely zoned out while staring at Tyme or that Katie was trying to get my attention until she clapped her hands in front of my face.

She too seemed flustered and tense as she questioned why she hadn't been rostered on for any recon missions. I tried to break the news gently to her, but she still didn't take it well as she stormed towards the elevator to yell at Lila – who also did not look like she was up for a fight either as she held a cup of ice cubes up against her neck, trying to convince Alex and Max that she was fine.

"You're benching me!!!" Katie yelled.

"I'm sorry, what?" Lila asked shaking her head, trying to follow along.

Katie then tried to explain that her reasons for helping Shane were valid, and that her actions were justified and only in self-defence. And it seemed like Lila was struggling to concentrate as she muttered, slightly out of breath in response to what was actually my decision. "Katie. . . you need to learn how to fight before we can bring you back onto active duty."

But Katie took that as an insult, and grunted, "I know how to fight," as she threw a fireball towards her.

Somehow Lila deflected the fireball then ducked down, spinning under Katie's extended arm to stand up next to her and kicked the back of Katie's knees – knocking her to the ground. Then while stepping back a little, Lila waited for Katie to settle down and pick herself up off the floor before Lila very sternly spoke, "Katie, you're a hot head and until you learn how to win a fight without setting the building on fire, we can't use you . . . If you want, Alex can teach you how to fight . . . we were just about to head down to the gym for a sparring match. I suggest you take my place . . . maybe let off a bit of steam while you're there."

The room stayed quiet and tense as we all watched Lila take a few more steps back and decided to take the stairs instead as Katie stormed into the elevator.

I looked around to see where Tyme had disappeared to, and I found him intrigued with a now overgrown office plant that had grown large enough to catch the fireball before it hit the walls or anything else. It looked like he was fascinated, watching the small embers burn out and I heard him whisper, "That is so cool."

He then invited me back to his new apartment – the one Lila arranged for him because he was being so helpful, and is now one of the team perks.

I sat on the couch next to Tyme, eating lunch as he talked and I listened – slightly. I was getting a little carried away with my thoughts. And before I knew it, I was on top of him with my hands running through his sandy blonde hair, and my lips and tongue exploring his.

But now seeming slightly confused of my actions, Tyme pulled me away for a second, and stared at the smile on my lips.

"What's wrong?" I quizzed, desperately wanting more of him.

An amazing grin then appeared on him as he gazed into my eyes with his hands now resting on my hips and his finger gently tickling the skin beneath my shirt. Then finally he pulled me closer to him. And as soon as I had my lips on his again, I let out my groans of pure pleasure, removing his clothes at superspeed and he removing mine.

I was loving this, and eventually I was lying flat on the couch with Tyme leaning over me, getting lost in my arms, and legs, and body, and all things amazing.

## Journal entry by Maxwell Eden

The team seemed a bit distracted today as the tension between Katie and Lila became more apparent. Still, I understood and agreed with Adela's reasoning and request for Katie to be taken off the team until such time as she knew how to be discreet and less destructive. But the fact that Lila was willing to take the brunt of Katie's anger was very noble of her. – I applaud the current team camaraderie.

After the team meeting, I asked for Jenny and Henry to meet me in my office to arrange their pre-flight details to Canada. They had volunteered to go ahead of the team and scout the area before the team's arrival and even acquire a home base for us to work from.

I waited in my office with their itineraries and travel expense card, ready to go and grew quite impatient with their tardiness. That is until they burst through the door, very anxious and placed a small silver bead onto my desk.

"Maxwell, your security has been compromised," Henry bellowed.

I admit I was bit sceptical, and pointed to the silver bead, asking, "What is that?"

However, Henry looked reluctant to tell me then tried to explain in the simplest human way, "It's a highly potent and very dangerous sex drug. And we found it when we were in the elevator heading up to your office."

I didn't seem overly shocked at that news, given that it was not uncommon for certain travellers to use recreational drugs – although I am not at all condoning it, and it did alarm me slightly. "Okay, we'll need to turn it over to the police."

"No, you don't understand," Jennifer rebutted, clearly upset at my calm demeanour as she started to explain, "If a human takes this, all they'll get is a mild headache and really strong hangover, but Guardians react a lot differently to it, and I think we might already be too late. I'm sure you noticed both Lila and Adela struggling to concentrate this morning. And while my baby Katie is a hot head, she's never usually that quick to react."

Jennifer had now gained my full attention, "Exactly how dangerous is this drug?"

Unfortunately, Henry then gave me the long-winded answer, "This drug significantly enhances the production of dehydroepiandrosterone and testosterone. If the body is not able to use the hormones or break the hormones down naturally, it accumulates in the brain and eventually causes the brain to shut down."

I most definitely struggled to follow along with that explanation and just looked at him stunned until Jennifer kindly rephrased, "If they don't have sex, they'll die . . ."

Well, I understood that statement, and instantly I thought about my sweet Adela and what might happen to her.

"Right, well I think we need to call Lila," I replied, in the hopes that she may be able to whip up a healing tonic or three.

## Original journal entry continued by Lila Winters

I couldn't think straight, and the long hallway towards Alex's apartment felt like it was taking forever for me to eventually walk down. And I may have stumbled a few times, needing to use the wall to guide me because I desperately needed to talk to Terrence. I knew something was wrong with me, and I had to talk to the only other Nature guardian I knew of.

Finally, I got to the apartment door and knocked, standing there with my top drenched in sweat, and breathing heavily, trying to think clearly. Then when Terrence opened the door to greet me, a surge of emotions overwhelmed me because he didn't have a top on, and he looked like he had just finished a workout.

Oh – Frac Damn.

My eyes got distracted as I studied Terrence's excellent and well-defined features, and he just stood there smiling at me, excited to see me.

"Lila, I'm glad you're here . . . I wanted to . . . are you okay?" he asked with his incredibly amazing, sweet and sexy voice.

He was trying to tell me something about what I did last week and thanked me for not giving up on him. But I didn't care. I was trying so hard not to let my internal groan become an external groan as I bit my bottom lip.

Eventually, I lost all of my inhibitions, leaping into Terrence's arms, and wrapping my legs around him as I ran my hands through his hair, demanding him to just shut up and kiss me.

He held me up, cupping one hand on my butt and one pressed against my back, and did as I asked. But he hesitated for a second when he felt my phone vibrating in my pocket, trying to break away from the kiss.

I however didn't want him to and wouldn't let him go, forcing him to kind of mumble between our lip, "Aren't you going to get that?"

And No – I was very much disinclined to speak to anyone else with my thoughts focused on one thing and one thing only, so I pulled my phone out and threw on the couch all while continuing to kiss Terrence and remove my sweat-drenched shirt.

I then demanded him to take me to the bedroom but again, he hesitated, pulling his lips away from mine, "Lila, what's going on?"

I was so frustrated by his stall tactics and I wanted him so badly, that my eyes glowed gold as I breathed, "Take me to your bed . . . Now."

Then with an excited glimmer in him, Terrence did as he was told, carrying me into his bedroom and laying me down on the bed while kissing me. His soft lips were amazing and his hands knew exactly the right places to go, with his body nestled perfectly between my legs.

The downside was we still had pants on. But that was about to change as Terrence delicately unbuttoned my pants, and pulled them off me at superspeed.

He then leaned back over me as I lay beneath him in just my underwear, and I saw his eyes exploring my body. But they stopped at the scars on my chest, and I sensed his sadness.

So, I bit my bottom lip as I ran my fingers along one of the scars, and pouted a little as I pleaded, "Can you kiss them better?"

An eager smile appeared on Terrence as he did exactly as I asked gently pressing his lips against every scar he could see. And each time he did the memory of that scar faded away.

But again, we got interrupted by yet another phone call, and Terrence stopped making me feel better as he looked back at the door of his bedroom, causing me grunt.

"Don't worry about that. . . I'll deal with it later."

He stared back up at me confused, "Lila . . . what if it's important?"

And now even more frustrated, I locked my legs around his hips to stop him from moving and pulled him back up to meet my eyes as I sternly replied slightly breathless, "Terry . . . I'm important . . . and I need you . . . now."

## Journal entry insert by Alex Woods

I'm somewhat disappointed that Lila had volunteered me to train Katie today, in lieu of our training session. It left me really frustrated knowing that she was avoiding me, especially after she – and we almost – you know.

I also think Katie was starting to tire of being knocked to the ground over and over again, but she was letting her emotions lead her charges – which left her open for counters.

So while still pinning her to the ground, I tried to explain exactly that, but she paused, looking at me intensely and breathing heavily.

I then sensed her heart rate becoming erratic and her temperature had shot up, similar to Lila's.

"Katie, are you alright?" I asked, starting to get really worried.

Suddenly Katie's phone rang and I let her go, for her to pick up the call.

When she finished the phone call, she replied back to me, "That was my mum. She said that we may have all been exposed to a drug of some kind. And now I've been sent to my room. . . for my own protection."

It very quickly dawned on me as I whispered, "Lila," racing out of the room, almost knocking Shane to the ground as he stepped out of the elevator. – And that guy really needs to pick his timings around here.

I was going to go up to Lila's apartment but I picked up her scent heading towards my apartment instead. So, I raced into my apartment, trying so hard not to freak out, looking around and shouting Terrence's name.

My heart felt like it was ripping in two when I saw Lila's clothes lying on the floor leading into Terrence's bedroom, and next to it was Terrence's top and the sound of the shower running.

Awe – Crap.

I ran into the bathroom almost out of breath. And to be honest, I was both relieved and worried when I saw Lila in her bra and undies, unconscious being held by Terrence as he sat on the shower floor in his boxer shorts with only the cold water running.

"Alex, finally," Terrence gritted through shivering teeth, "I need your help. She's burning up."

I took my top off and jumped into the freezing cold shower as Terrence filled me in on the details of what happened and what was about to happen – but thankfully did not happen.

"So what do we do?" I asked.

He took a moment to think, and then looked back at me very concerned as he replied with frustration and hesitancy, "Well, if it's the drug I think it is, then nothing . . . this is a natural hormone which means the white lily won't work on it. The best we can hope for is that her body naturally breaks down the drug, and it passes through her system. All we need to do is keep her temperature down . . . if we can't, she'll die."

I disappeared out the room for a second, bringing back as many frozen vegetable bags as I could and questioned, "What if it doesn't work?"

I then held the frozen bags strategically on Lila's lower back and chest, and as I did that she shuddered at the shock of the ice-cold feeling, but then started to relax against them, taking a breath of relief.

Anxiety filled me as I stared back at Terrence waiting for his answer, but he looked back at me squeamishly, holding Lila even tighter. And he sounded so worried when he answered, "There's only one other way I know of to naturally force the body into a hormonal system reset. . . which is what her body was driving her to do before."

His eyes then tracked to the bed in the other room and then back at me, grimacing awkwardly, fully knowing that he was holding the woman both of us loved and respected.

So, we both persisted and worked through the night to help keep her temperature down. But to be honest, I was ready to do just about anything to save her life because I have no plans to ever lose her again.

## Original journal entry continued by Lila Winters

I woke up to a massive headache as the piercing bright moonlight shone through my bedroom window – or at least I thought it was my bedroom. Until I looked around to realise I was in Alex's room with both Terrence and Alex asleep, in just their boxers on either side of me.

They were holding defrosted bags of vegetables against my now cold naked body with nothing but a thin bed sheet to cover me, causing me to feel extremely cold. So I tried to quietly move the mushy bags of peas off me, but I unintentionally woke Alex up.

"Hey," he whispered, smiling at me.

I turned my head to meet his eyes and smiled, "Hey."

My eyes then casually peered down to the defrosted vegetable bags he was holding against me, and I grinned a little when he realised I was covered in goose-bumps and shivering.

He raced at half speed, taking all the vegetable bags off me, throwing them to the floor as he pulled a much warmer blanket up to cover me. He then sat next to me on the bed, handing one of his clean T-shirts and pyjama pants to me and looked away as I sat up to pull on his clothes.

Once I was covered, he turned back and lay down next to me offering to warm me up. And I happily accepted the offer, moving closer to him, and pressing my back up against his chest while using his arm as a pillow as they wrapped around me.

"How are you feeling?" he whispered still very nervous and worried about me.

I smiled and breathed deeply with relief, remembering everything Terrence and Alex did to try and keep my temperature down and keep me alive, then replied, "I'm better . . ."

But my eyes saddened and regret filled me as I breathlessly whimpered, turning a little to look at Alex and apologise.

"Alex, I am so sorry for doing that to you. . . and I definitely owe Terrence an apology because I think may have charmed him into doing something he didn't want to do."

My embarrassment was overwhelming, now with flushed cheeks, and it got worse when Alex smiled at me and brushed his fingers across my forehead to check my temperature, before he pulled me closer to him.

He chuckled a little as he explained, "First off. . .animal girl. That's not how charming works. We can only give suggestions. . . it's up to the animal to take it. And second. . . both me and Terrence do not hold anything against you . . . we know you weren't yourself . . . alright?"

Okay – I started to feel a little better about myself and my actions, and took another breath of relief, snuggling in closer to Alex.

Eventually I was able to relax as I stopped shivering, but I stayed in his arms as I drifted back off to sleep again, exhausted from the night. Then after a few moments of listening to the silence, I felt Alex's arms tighten around me and I heard him whisper, "I love you Lila."

# CHAPTER 25

# TIMING IS EVERYTHING

Personal observation notes collated
by Detective George Nell

Personal observation notes – by Officer Mark Davies

Day 12 – time: 06:00
Suspect's name: Lila Winters
Task orders: Report any suspicious behaviour
Results: So far all she likes to do is exercise

Daily notes— I was partnered with Jerry Higgins today and we've spent most of our morning standing in the Melbourne botanic gardens surveying from a distance as Lila and one of her colleagues Adela Eden were stretching and doing various yoga positions.

I started to question the purpose of this investigation. She seemed pretty normal to me.

"Does this chick do anything but exercise?" I grumbled, "She's been out here for hours."

However, Jerry, my partner, snapped back, most likely annoyed at my constant complaining, "We've only been watching her for two weeks, how can you possibly know if she's normal or not?"

Lila and Adela finished their stretches and started walking again.

"She's moving," I mumbled as I started to walk in a similar direction. "Nope, she's running," I stated quickly, bringing my walk into a run to keep up.

I heard Jerry complain this time as he struggled to keep a good running speed and seemed out of breath.

We ran a short distance behind the suspect, ensuring we were not noticed and stopped just shy of the hotel entrance when Lila and Adela somehow disappeared.

We walked through the lobby looking around with Jerry, struggling to breathe. I was worried he might be drawing too much attention to us.

"We lost them, didn't we?" Jerry wheezed.

I became frustrated, confirming his obvious statement, "Yep, we lost them," then I helped Jerry to stand and added, "Come on let's go get cleaned up. We're bound to run into her again."

Jerry was really struggling to stand as he gasped, "I've never seen anyone move so fast. What is she taking?"

As we got to the elevators to go up to our hotel room to recover, we found Lila again. She was standing in the elevator completely changed, showered, hair brushed and refreshed.

That was very strange and I believed to be not possible.

She greeted us with a big smile, "Hi, guys, how was your run this morning?"

I was confused and didn't know what to say as she gloated, "I saw you guys in the park this morning. It's a great day for a run."

She didn't even look tired from her run. And Jerry tried and failed to mask his fatigue and replied with a smile, "You bet."

Lila then wished us a pleasant stay as she walked towards Maxwell Eden—the owner of the hotel. And Jerry and I were both at a loss for words as to how she managed to move so quickly. Not only that, we also knew that we had to forgo our recovery moment in order to follow Ms Winters to her next destination at the Melbourne Myer shopping complex.

We observed from a distance again, watching as Adela and Lila both took their time looking at various clothing outfits in the shopping complex.

"They've been at this for three hours," Jerry snickered, "What could they possibly be doing?"

I handed him I cup of coffee in a takeaway cup and replied, "What everyone else does, browse around for hours and never buy anything."

We were strategic in where we stood and were able to hear just enough of the conversation. Adela seemed to be pressing Lila for answers and asked, "So do you want to tell me what we're doing here?'"

Lila looked cagey and replied, "I thought we were shopping?"

"You hate shopping," Adela suspiciously glared back, "now spill."

Lila seemed reluctant to respond, answering, "I just wanted to get out of the hotel that's all."

With a crooked smile, Adela groaned, "Ah, so you're avoiding someone, but the question is which someone?"

That statement for some reason rattled Lila, looking guilty as she tried to change the subject several times. But I did notice the subject also infuriated Jerry.

"Great now they're talking about guys. Will this day ever end?" Jerry grumbled, as he rubbed his legs in a bit of pain.

"Would you rather trade for the other assignment?" I snickered back, already knowing what the answer would be.

# Personal observation notes – by Officer Vicki Matthews

Day: 12 – Time: 11:30
Suspect's Name: Alex Woods
Task Orders: Report any suspicious behaviour
Results: None found

Daily Notes—My partner Lauren and I were sitting in the lobby, watching as Alex Woods walked in and out of the hotel, and Terrence Connors, his roommate, scurried around the ground floor promenade, looking in all the small stores and restaurants.

"Who do you think they're looking for?" I asked Lauren.

Lauren rolled her eyes, flicking through a magazine and scoffed, "Lila, obviously."

I nodded my head and commented, "It's like watching a love triangle on some TV show."

"You mean a square?" Lauren rebutted, "Your forgetting about her husband Matt."

We tried to act casual as they walked past us, completely oblivious to our observation, when I whispered to Lauren, "Oh, and don't forget that other guy. What's his name? Tyme or something."

As I said that, Tyme walked out of the elevator towards Alex and Terrence, also looking around for someone, and it was not difficult to guess who they were all looking for.

"Oh, here we go," I whispered, slightly excited, wishing I had popcorn.

"Have you seen Lila?" they all asked at the same time.

Tyme's brows furrowed, "Clearly not. Have you seen Adela?"

Alex shook his head, and Terrence queried, "Do you think she might be avoiding us?"

That's when both Tyme and Alex responded in unison, "Why?"

Unfortunately, the hotel owner's daughter and manager of the hotel, Jessica Eden, interrupted their odd conversation with the answer.

"Hey, guys. Max wants to see all of you in his office straight away. Oh, and yes, she's avoiding you."

Tyme, Alex and Terrence all looked at each other defensively and replied in unison, "Avoiding who?" as they all followed Jessica into the elevator.

Lauren and I waited a few moments and followed them in the adjacent elevator. We were both thinking the same thing, realising that something was just not right with the subjects we were investigating, especially Lila Winters.

We had quite a lot of questions that need answered.

Why did she have so many male interests?
Why did her spouse seem completely okay with the arrangement?
Why did the hotel have so many security staff on their payroll?
Why are only a few of the security team ever seen patrolling the hotel complex and actually doing their job?

These were just some of the questions we were struggling to find answers for.

We continued to tail the subjects and stopped one floor below them, standing in the hallway, while Lauren pulled her mobile phone out, opening a black box app. The team had planted several listening devices in various rooms, and this app helped us to listen and record when needed.

We listened as Alex, Terrence and Tyme were greeted by Mr Eden in his office and were asked to take a seat.

"Now, I've been thinking about last Monday's little incident involving a certain drug. To my knowledge, only the females were targeted, and no, I do not want to know any of the details regarding the fallout. The question I do want to ask is why were only the girls targeted? That's where you, boys, come in. I want you three to investigate what happened, who it was, and why."

Lauren looked at me and questioned, "What drug?"

I shrugged my shoulders and told her to shush as we listened to whom I think was Alex, reply, "If you don't mind me asking, why us? Isn't this Del and Jess's thing?"

"Yes, it is their thing," Mr Eden replied, "Unfortunately, Jess is heading off to the airport with me to pick up her mother, and Adela and Lila are busy."

"Busy, doing what?" I think Terrence asked with a high tone to his voice.

Max sounded like he was about to leave when he replied, "They said they were shopping. Whatever that's code for."

We then heard the office door open as Mr Eden spoke, "You can use my office for the day, and my assistant is on line 1 if you need any help. Good luck."

There was brief silence until Alex mumbled, "Lila hates shopping."

"We're in trouble, aren't we?" Terrence added.

We heard Tyme's phone receives a text message and, thankfully, we had the foresight to clone everyone's phones or at least the main six of the suspect pool.

Lauren shuffled through her bag to see which of the clone phones had sent a text; it was from Adela with a picture of Adela and Lila smiling with a text attached to the bottom reading: "Meet for Lunch."

We suddenly heard Alex ask, quite inquisitively, "Hot date?" and we both assumed that question was targeted at Tyme.

"Kind of," Tyme replied nervously.

"Give us a look then," Terrence said. The then room went quiet for a few seconds until Terrence asked, "Please tell me you're dating Adela."

Tyme started getting nervous, stuttering, "Yes . . . I mean no . . . I mean she's helping me with a Lila thing and—"

Alex then interrupted him, asking very defensively, "Wait. What Lila thing?"

"I'd really rather not talk about it," Tyme replied.

We suddenly heard the office door slam shut and I really wished we had managed to get a surveillance camera in there or something useful. As we listened to Alex rant,

"Nice try, buddy, but we know you can't leave while you're in that time rift. Not while the doors are closed anyway."

— Not quite sure what that meant.

Silence filled the room again for quite a few minutes and Lauren and I became worried that the subjects had left without our knowledge until Tyme quickly blurted out, "'Okay, okay. She's my sister."

"Adela's your sister?" Alex asked.

"No. Lila is. I came to Melbourne looking for my father, but instead, I found her," Tyme replied.

Terrence went to question him, asking in what way they were related and the answer revealed that Lila's biological father, William Knight, did not die in a car crash as the police report stated 26 years ago.

Tyme had also not yet revealed his biological relation to Lila either and was apparently waiting for the right time to tell her. And he thought that today might be the day.

Sounding either worried or desperate Alex tried to convince Tyme his idea was not well thought out. But Tyme just responded, "He'd never hurt her. He loves her."

Then the office door opened and slammed closed again.

Lauren looked at me again and murmured, "What did he mean when he said hurt her?"

Again, I didn't know the answers, but thinking back on Lila's many previous hospital admission reports and the recent disappearance, I was beginning to fear that this may well be part of a much larger criminal organisation.

Unfortunately, before we knew it, the room had gone silent, and we realised too late that they had all left the office. And we had lost them.

# Personal observation notes – by Jerry Higgins

Day: 12 – Time: 13:00
Suspect's Name: Lila Winters
Task Orders: Report any suspicious behaviour
Results: Seems normal. Exercises way too much

Daily Notes— Mark and I had been following the subject, Lila Winters, around the shopping centre for hours. And when they had finally decided to stop and sit, it was lunchtime, and they sat down at one of the cafés just off Burke Street Mall.

Thankfully, the café was crowded, and they didn't notice us sitting at the table behind them.

Adela looked nervous as she stared over at the door, slowly sipping her coffee. The waitress must have startled Adela, as she placed a toasted sandwich and Coke in front of Lila and a pastry pie in front of her.

"Are we expecting someone?" Lila enquired.

Adela looked back at her nervously before responding, "Um . . . no."

In disbelief, Lila scoffed, "Well, that's a lie," trying not to laugh as she ate.

So, Adela leaned forward and replied, "Okay, I invited Tyme to come meet us."

Lila pulled a very judgemental face, "I knew it. You are dating him now, aren't you?"

But Adela shook her head, unsure if she was or was not, and struggled to find her words when the man himself, Tyme, arrived, walking up to the table and interrupting their conversation.

"Tyme, you made it," Adela said, jumping to her feet, almost knocking the food off the table. "Have a seat. I'll go order for you," she mumbled rushing off to the registers to order.

Tyme sat down at the table, looking just as nervous, and Lila chuckled, "I hope she knows what you like."

He looked back at Adela then replied, "Yeah, toasted tomato and cheese. It's one of my favourites. My dad would have it all the time when I was little. I guess it just stuck with me."

With a sunny grin, Lila indicated that she had ordered the same, "Not my mum—I mean aunt. Hanna always complained that the cheese was too hot or that tomato should never be cooked in that way . . . I'm glad my taste in food wasn't genetic. Otherwise, I would have never eaten. That and I've been a vegetarian since . . . well all my life. Apparently when was young Hanna would try and feed me meat products like sausages and I would crinkle my nose and chuck a tantrum."

She then went silent in thought before she added, "Come to think of it. My real father might have been vegetarian or mother. I'm not sure which one was nature and which was the animal. It might have been both. But I never got a chance to ask them their eating preferences. So, it might be genetic."

Tyme just looked at Lila and smiled apprehensively at the odd train of thought she was voicing as Adela placed almost the exact same order as Lila on the table in front of Tyme then made some excuse, claiming that she had just spotted a sale in the store next door and wanted to go and have a quick look. Lila and Tyme seemed to have no other choice but to agree as she had already grabbed her bag and was out the door.

"Should we follow her?" Mark asked. But we both agreed the target was more important and stayed put.

"He looks nervous," Mark commented, looking at Tyme.

"Yeah. I think Adela just set them up on a date," I replied.

Mark looked at me, confused, stating that Lila was married. But does he honestly think, that a marriage stops people from looking around?

We got a bit more intrigued, listening to the awkward silence that Lila and Tyme were sitting in when Lila asked Tyme, "Why is your heart racing?"

How could she possibly know that?

But for some strange reason Tyme didn't question that, instead he apologised, explaining that he was nervous.

"About what?" Lila asked, slightly distracted by her cheese toasty.

"I was actually hoping to talk to you about your father," Tyme replied.

Lila sat back, almost defensive, and replied, "I didn't know you knew Richard?" then took a sip of her drink.

"No, I mean your real father. The nature one," Tyme replied.

Causing Lila to almost choke on her drink, struggling to recover as she spat out her Coke, covering her clothes and what was left of her lunch with the drink.

Tyme tried to help her by gently patting her back. "Are you alright?" he asked, "I'm sorry I didn't mean to . . ."

Standing to her feet, Lila grabbed the napkins, trying to dry her pants and excused herself, claiming she was just going to clean herself up as she walked to the back towards the toilets.

Tyme didn't look impressed and was slightly disillusioned as he slouched back into his chair, when Adela returned, holding yet another shopping bag, and questioned, "So did you talk to her?"

"I tried to, but she panicked the moment I mentioned William," he responded.

The conversation confused both Mark and myself, still under the assumption, based on previous department health records, that Lila's parents had died in a car crash when she was a baby. That and we have yet to understand what Lila meant by nature and animal in her brief conversation with Tyme.

But shortly after Adela arrived at the table, Tyme noticed Lila walking past the front of the café and getting onto the first city tram that went passed.

And we lost her again.

# Personal observation notes – by Lauren Chandler

Day: 12 – Time: 15:20.
Suspect's Name: Alex Woods
Task Orders: Report any suspicious behaviour
Results: Seems to have a thing for married women

Daily Notes—Vicki and I finally managed to sneak into Maxwell Eden's office and install a hidden camera on both his and the receptionist's desk. And we were back in the hallway, awaiting the return of pretty much anyone at this point, watching and listening on the phone. Eventually the elevator doors pulled open, and Alex and Terrence shuffled out, carrying a large and unusually shaped log with Alex whining, "I can't believe you locked him in a tree. I didn't even know that was possible."

Terrence just barked back, "It was the only thing I could think of," as they carried the enormous log into Mr Eden's office before closing the door.

We quickly switched to the office camera and heard Alex ask, "Where do you learn this stuff?"

Terrence responded, pointing down to the log, "From him," and then explained, "He was a guardian elder, and he used to mentor me. I'm not sure exactly what happened. I just remember William having a heated argument with Richard one day, and he quit. But because he knew too much about the many programs and organisations, he was never allowed to leave."

"Did you know that he was Lila's real father?" Alex asked, pointing back down to the log. "What if he still works for them?" he questioned further, almost sounding scared.

"Um. . . kind of," Terrence replied, grabbing a large metal object from one of the displays on the bookshelf then smashed it onto the log several times and commented, "That was always my favourite part."

The large log then shattered and fell to the floor, revealing an unconscious man trapped inside it. My first instinct was to rush in and help him, but Vicki stopped me and reminded me of the goal. So instead, I just watched the video, hoping the man would wake up.

Terrence seemed quite calm as he looked at the man and replied, "It should take about an hour for him to wake up."

That's when the office intercom buzzed as the receptionist alerted them, saying, "Mr Woods, Ms Winters has arrived back. Would you like me to contact her for you?"

Alex raced to the intercom and told the receptionist, not to contact Lila and to try and stall her. But suddenly, the unconscious man started to wake.

Alex looked at him then looked at Terrence and barked, "That was faster than an hour."

In a hurry, Terrence pulled the man to his feet and commented, "He's probably used to the side effects by now. We need to hide him and take him somewhere. We know Lila wouldn't go."

Alex began to help him, carry the man and replied, "Well, we know she's avoiding us, so she's less likely to go to—"

Before he could reveal their next location, Lila had opened the office door. She looked at them and then at the man they were holding as the man struggled to find his feet, almost drunk like, saying her name. Then with disappointment Lila shook her head and walked back out of the office.

We quickly switched to the receptionist's desk camera as we watched the drunk man stumble out after her, shouting her name again.

Alex chased after her as well and begged, "Lila, wait. Just let me explain. He's—"

"I know who he is!" Lila snapped interrupting Alex then pressed the elevator button.

Terrence walked into the hallway as well but remained silent, listening as both the drunk man and Alex questioned, "You do?"

"Please tell me you didn't know?" Lila asked Terrence demandingly.

Still Terrence remained quiet. So she repeated her question in more detail, "When he was talking with me back on the island, did you know he was my father?"

Again, Terrence didn't answer until Lila was just about to give up and walk down the stairs instead.

"Yes," he quickly responded.

Lila stopped and looked like she had been betrayed by Terrence, and she didn't seem too welcoming of the drunk man either, demanding that he leave.

The drunk man tried to regain his balance and replied, "Lila, please, I'm your father . . . I . . ." He tried to hold Lila's hand to gain her attention.

But she rebuked him in anger, "My father is dead after he tried to throw me off a building." She then wiped the tears from her face and yelled, "You are nothing but the stranger who abandoned me."

All of a sudden, and this is the most amazing part, the plants that were growing in the corner of the room grew faster, and the leaves wrapped around all three of the men and threw them into the elevator as the doors opened.

Adela and Tyme were already standing in the elevator when it happened, and Tyme looked down at the drunkard man, shocked and confused as he said, "Dad?"

Lila then watched as the elevator doors started to close and said, just as confused, "Dad?"

Now panicked, Tyme tried to rush out of the elevator, shouting, "No, Lila, wait . . . please," but it was too late. The doors had closed on him.

This was it. This was the evidence that we needed. We raced down to the lobby, luckily running into Mark and Jerry as we went. But before we got to the exit, we were greeted by one of the security guards named Chase accompanied by eight of his co-workers.

# Personal observation notes – by George Nell

Day: 12 – Time: 21:00
Suspect's Name: Lila Winters and Alex Woods
Task Orders: Report any suspicious behaviour
Results: Unusual and unexplained injuries and scars, disappearances, present at the scene of 2 fire incidents, and multiple visits to the ER, suspected victim of abuse

Daily Notes—I had received an urgent call from Ms Winters, requesting my presence at the Eden Hotel. I had also received an SOS signal from my undercover officers who were tailing Ms Winters, and I feared the worst.

I stormed through doors of Maxwell Eden's office where Lila was already waiting for me, and by the looks of it, she looked like she had just been crying. But I didn't care.

She offered me to take a seat, but I was infuriated and retorted, "I don't want a seat. I want my men back!"

Then standing to her feet to meet my level, Lila sneered through her tears, "And I want to go for a run without two men gawking at me, maybe even have lunch with my friends in peace. Or, and this is just an idea, the next time you of all people want to know something about me, you actually be upfront and ask me those pointed questions that you so desperately want to know."

I yelled back at her even angrier, "And like you'd ever tell the truth."

"I have always told you everything you need to know!" Lila replied.

"Well, that's not enough!" I bickered back and seemingly ended the shouting match.

Lila then took a breath and I noticed her eyes briefly change colour as she stepped away and pulled out a small USB from her pocket, placing it on the desk in front of me.

"I thought you'd say that," she said, sliding the USB towards me, "This has everything you need to know about me, my team, and what we really do at this hotel."

She looked at me very sternly, and was reluctant to let the USB go as she uttered, "But there's a condition to this, George. I am giving you this file because of the friendship we once had. And not an officer of the law, which means I am swearing you to the friendship code."

"Are you serious?" I asked, disbelieving that she would have the nerve to play that card.

-The friendship code is something our classmates came up with at school. The code was only ever called on when we knew the truth would incriminate and potentially expel one of our own, and we were then all sworn to secrecy-.

"Dead serious," Lila replied with such gravity in her voice, "I warn you now George, as my friend. This information could get you killed. Now swear the code or get out."

As I left the office, I demanded to be taken to where ever my officers were being detained, and Lila replied that they were all escorted home minus any photos or recordings. And that the next time I needed someone followed, I should maybe ask her team for some pointers first.

When I arrived back at the office, I inserted the USB into my computer to find—Nothing.

# CHAPTER 26

# TOMATO AND CHEESE TOASTY

*Journal entry by Lila Winters*

What a day I've had – what a week – what a month – and we've only just finished the last month – and January is not month I would want to revel in.

I really needed a moment to compose myself as I stood in the elevator on my way back to my apartment. And I was almost in disbelief at what I had just done, arguing with a detective and an old friend. I mean George and I had known each other since high school and sure, we weren't the best of friends – but our class knew how to take care of each other.

But swearing him to the friendship code—I hadn't done that in years. And I literally gave him everything he needed to arrest me and everyone else who worked with me.

Still, I trusted him and I knew that if I was going to keep doing this, I would need a friend on that side of the law, one I could count on. I also knew he wouldn't just let this go easily.

I guess, maybe I wasn't expecting to have to reveal my cards quite so early, but when I found the hidden camera in Max's offices and what was left of a shattered tree log, I definitely had to pull up the timeline.

I scrubbed my hands through my hair and crouched in the corner of the elevator – waiting for the metaphorical, fractastic crap to hit the fan.

And as the elevator doors opened on to my floor, the crap hit the fan when I peered up from my little corner of the elevator and saw Tyme sitting outside my apartment, waiting for me and crying.

Epic sigh – the day's not done yet.

I stood to my feet and hesitated for just a moment, but eventually, I stepped off the elevator. Part of me wanted to run away – but another part of me also knew that Tyme had done nothing wrong. He had also done nothing but try to help me since the day we met. And I was very much aware that he wanted to talk to me – but I just kept brushing him off. So, I knew his guilt was partly my fault.

The problem is – I have not had the best of luck with family over the years. I can't speak for anyone else, but for me – having your adoptive father turn out to be a deranged, power-hungry psychopath really pushed my limits for family drama.

Tyme quickly stood to his feet when he saw me walking towards him. And it probably didn't help, but I stayed silent, feeling very nervous, not really knowing what to say, and also feeling like the weight of the world was on my shoulders.

"Lila, please just let me explain," he sobbed with pleading eyes, "I swear I was going to tell you. I was just waiting for the right time. . . Please, please just give me a chance to--"

I know my action seem weird and spontaneous, but while he was trying to explain himself, I wrapped my arms around his torso and hugged him, trying so hard not to cry.

But honestly, after everything I've been through, it was actually really nice to know I had a family member who wasn't a deranged murderous bastard.

I must have caught him off guard though, as he stopped his rambling and stood silently, wrapping his arms around me and exhaled with a great sigh of relief.

We stood in the hall-way for a few minutes just hugging, and I won't lie—I did use my nifty abilities to check that he definitely wasn't a deranged murderous bastard—and he wasn't.

Then when I pulled away again, I sniffled a bit still holding back some nervous tears,

"I've never had a brother or a family member who didn't want to kill me or collect me. . . even Hanna has her moments. So I'm not really sure what to do here."

I'm not sure if he noticed, but I had started twiddling with my finger feeling overwhelmed with nerves, and I really hoped he didn't have the same nervous twitch because otherwise – it would totally give me away.

Either way, my nerves stayed with me as I stared at Tyme waiting for an answer and he gawped back at me just as confused, and for some reason guilt-ridden. – I don't think he was expecting any of that.

Oh Frac –What did you just do Lila – you're going to scare him away with all your family crap. – He probably isn't a hugger either. – You stupid idiot. – Say something not stupid.

But what the hell are you supposed to say to a long-lost brother who you've been ignoring for months? 'Hi, sorry I used you for your abilities, and welcome to the family, try not to die on your way out'.

Yeah coz that won't send him packing. – Crap he's staring at me. – I've clearly scared him – he's not saying anything – What is he thinking about? – Why hasn't he left yet?

– Fraccing, Frac, Fracs – My thoughts really hate me today.

Finally, he broke the tension that was building between us and wrapped his arms around me again, pulling me in for another hug. And I heard him whimper a bit as my face buried into his chest.

"I am so sorry Lila," he whispered, "I wanted to tell you the moment I saw you . . . But you were a little busy . . . dying and all."

Double Frac – first impressions really do matter, and he first met me lying in a pool of my own blood, and then I jumped off the bloody building and tore the damn street apart.

Double Fracs-with cherries on it. – Pull it together Lila, he's clearly not scared of you – even with everything that's happened. Okay – let's try and figure out a way to break the ice.

While still feeling extremely nervous, I pulled away from the hug again, clearing my throat and holding back some of my tears as I eventually spoke, "Um? We never did get to finish our lunch today. . . so . . . um . . . would you like to share a tomato and cheese toasty with me?"

I don't think Tyme knew what to say. And I think he was expecting a much different reaction from me as he just stood there, watching me open the apartment door, seeming stunned, but eventually, he replied, "I'd love to."

He then followed me in and sat in silence at the bench while I cooked the toasty and broke it in two, pulling two cans of Coke from the fridge and a bag of my favourite crisp chips from the cupboard.

It was pretty late at night and I didn't want to wake the kids or Shane and Matt, so Tyme quietly followed me into my bedroom. Then helped me to set up a makeshift picnic area on the floor in the corner, and we each sat leaning against a wall.

We stayed up all night and talked about everything we could think of, while we ate the food. He told me his story and I told him – well, a much lighter version of my story– again I didn't want to scare him.

I was having a lot of fun though, and we laughed, and he cried a bit, and then I cried a bit. Eventually, he asked me if I'd be willing to meet his dad – properly this time. But I shook my head, feeling like that was too much of a deep wound.

I mean I still felt so much anger towards him – and uncertainty. For 26 years I thought my father was dead – but now I have so many questions that I'm afraid to know the answers to. Like – why he didn't want me or fight for me or even come looking for me?

# CHAPTER 27

# FAMILY FIRST

## *Journal entry by Shane Winters*

I woke up to the prettiest sight, next to my new—whatever it is we are.

Katie Hooper, she and I have been almost inseparable for over a week now. And I just laid there staring at her as the morning sun gently warmed her face. I watched her stretching as she woke up then grinned when she realised I had been ogling her.

I was just about to ask if she wanted to stay and have breakfast with me when I heard the sounds of pots being loudly smacked around in the kitchen.

Now I know this is Matt's apartment, and if he wanted to bash pots and pans around in the morning, who was I to argue. But I just got that nagging feeling that something was up. So, I begged Katie not to move and to hold that beautiful pose she had going for her, as I backed slowly out of the guest room.

- It was technically Danny's bedroom that I was crashing in - 'til I figure out my life and all. But if Katie was willing to stay in it, I think I know exactly where my life was headed.

I walked out into the kitchen to see Matt, extremely agitated and taking it out on the pancakes that he always makes on the Saturdays. Not sure of his reasons, I thought it would help if I lighten the mood and I joked, "Look mate, whatever it is · · · the pancakes didn't deserve it."

He turned to me and didn't even chuckle as he greeted me with a "good morning" before offering me some half-mangled pancakes. I took one look at them and tried very hard not to pull the sour face that I usually pull when I'm faced with something – unpleasant and replied,

"Actually, I was thinking of going out for breakfast."

Matt grunted back at me as he returned to burning his pancakes and mumbled, "Yeah· · · okay."

And as his little brother I definitely knew that if Matt was burning pancakes then something had to be up. So I sat down at the kitchen bench and readied myself to be that great little brother, as I asked, "Is there something you wanted to get off your chest?"

I waited for his response and watched as Matt huffed, throwing the last burnt pancake onto the stack, "No—Yes—Maybe —I'm not sure."

Well, that's a definitive answer. Still leaving me confused, as I sat there trying to figure out which one he meant, and responded back, "You're gonna have to pick one, mate."

He then placed the pancake stack down on the bench and pulled a sour face, looking at his end results, clearly unhappy with it, and irked at the world, "It's Lila · · · I think she's sleeping with someone else."

"Ouch· · ·" I hissed, feeling a little tense, "· · · is it Alex or Terrence?"

It was obviously not the response he wanted because he stared back at me almost confused, shaking his head, "What? No it's not them."

Seriously – it's not them? They ogle her like she was a piece of delicious cake, and even I wanted a piece of that action when I was younger – and it's not them?

"Well, she does spend a lot of time with them," I rebutted, trying to get Matt to see reason. But that just caused more annoyance for Matt as he sighed, "No, it's her other friend, Tyme."

Okay, I still really thought that was stupid name and I sniggered jokingly, "Seriously, who names their son Tyme? · · · it's as if his parents hated him."

As I said that though Matt raced around the counter to shush me as he whispered, "Not too loud. He's here."

"What now?" I whispered back, waiting as Matt nodded his head, still staying quiet.

    Damn – What kind of man sleeps with another man's wife under his roof?

That is it, I had had it. And I marched into Lila's room like a man on a mission, and sure enough, there he was—the man with the stupid name, sitting next to Lila on her bed and laughing with her.

But honestly, I didn't care what he was doing with her. I wanted him out, and that's where he was gonna to go. So I grabbed Tyme by his collar and dragged him out of the bedroom towards the front door.

Now here's what I wasn't expecting — I wasn't expecting Lila to come chasing out after me, screaming, "Shane what are you doing?"

But I happily replied, "Saving your marriage. · · Trust me Sissy, it's for your own good," and continued dragging the homewrecker out of the apartment.

I was also not expecting – Lila to run at a ridiculous speed and appear in front of me, ripping Tyme out of my hands and pushing me to the ground as if I were an annoying fly she just swatted away.

I was also not expecting – Katie to run out of my room at a ridiculous speed as well, appearing in front of Lila and tackling her into the wall, creating a very large hole in the plaster, webbing up to the roof.

It was like I had pressed fast-forward on a reality TV show as I watched Tyme move at the same speed as Katie and Lila, pushing Katie backwards before she stood in front of me protectively. – Me – Katie was protecting Me.

All I could do was I stare in a shock, watching as Tyme helped Lila to stand and stood protectively in front of her.

What the? – was there something in Matt's pancakes that causes you to Hallucinate?

Things were getting way too intense, until Matt, stood between all of us, holding a spatula and yelled, "HEY! You're going to wake up the kids. Now, what the hell is going on?"

But he said that looking directly at me – as if this were all my fault. So, I stood up and defended my actions, pointing at Tyme, "That idiot won't take a hint. . . And I think your wife's on steroids."

I may have grunted a little, rubbing my now bruised butt cheek, still seriously confused. Then Lila shouted, "What are you doing here?" to Katie, completely ignoring my statement. "Protecting Shane!" Katie gritted through her teeth, then looked at Tyme and retorted, "What is he doing here?"

Tyme however, didn't shout but he continued to stand protectively in front of Lila, replying, "Obviously, protecting Lila."

Katie then snickered condescendingly at his comment, "And here I thought that was Alex's little perk."

Only causing Lila to get angry as she shouted back, "Katie that's enough."

But that's when I finally got the attention back and yelled, "So it is true, you two are sleeping together."

I think I might accidentally dob in Matt here, because Lila stood back and gasped in surprise, actually offended by my accusation and asked, "Why the frac would you think that?"

Um yep – I'm definitely dobbing in Matt here, and I casually glanced over at him, noticing he was still hoping to keep the peace as he replied, "Well, he has been spending a lot of nights here."

In disbelief, Lila shook her head, glaring at Matt. "I can't believe you, would think that of me."

To my surprise, Matt stood back and looked as if he was the guilty one, so I came to his defence and asked, "Then what were you doing with him that lasted all night?"

Tyme then relaxed a little, taking a breath of annoyance as he handed Matt a handful of photos that he had dropped to the floor during the—whatever that fast thingy was.

I anxiously and curiously stared at Matt as he quickly skimmed the pictures in his hands and asked, "Why were you looking at baby photos all night?"

And this is the next part I wasn't expecting – because Lila walked to the middle of the room and asked – me of all the people to give them some privacy.

"What?" I scoffed.

But thankfully, Matt jumped to my defence, "No, he's family. Whatever you have to say to me, you can say in front of him."

I stood a little taller after that and waited for some answers. But I don't think Lila was expecting that from Matt, and she just shook her again, chuckling a little. All while glaring at him as if she were warning him that he was going to regret making that choice·

Still, Matt stood his ground, so Lila took a deep breath and answered, "Okay, Matt · · · I would like to officially introduce you to Tyme Knight· · · my brother·"

Alrighty – I'm going to add now – that I also wasn't expecting that·

And neither was Matt as he took a few steps back, staring at Tyme and gasped, "I don't understand · · · How · · · How did you find out about William?"

He then glanced over at Lila, acting almost as if it had been this taboo secret that Lila wasn't supposed to know about· Only causing Lila to reply with frustration in her voice, "While I'm not surprised you know about him, I am surprised, you of all people, chose to keep it a secret from me · · · Either way, it doesn't matter· I found out about my father back on the island·"

Right – That comment threw me a little·

"Island? What island?" I asked, hoping Lila would respond·

But instead, I got her brother's response, speaking in the sense that this is something I should have already known about, as he explained, "It's the island that she was held captive on a few months back·"

I felt my gut twisting in knots as I glared back at Matt and then to Lila, and my voice trembled a bit when I fearfully asked, "What does he mean by held captive?"

It was then I noticed Lila wasn't wearing the long pants like she always does, today she was wearing pyjama shorts· So I took a quick glance down at Lila's leg, and saw the bite scars from the supposed 'animal attack', but that wasn't the only scar I saw on her leg· And when I looked closer, I could see I lot more scars then I wanted to see· They were all over her legs, and they looked like large puncture marks and cuts·

As my eyes studied her many scars, they wandered up to just above the top of her pyjama shorts and below her favourite yellow cardigan, that had ridden up in the scuffle – and I eyed a very prominent scar leading from her hip and disappearing under her buttoned-up cardigan·

I then held my breath, moving closer to her and lifted the base of the cardigan to get a better look· But as I did Lila looked away from me as if she were ashamed – I could feel her entire body tense·

My frustration and anger rose, as I kept finding more scars on her stomach and legs quickly realising it only got worse the more I looked· And I know I shouldn't have, but I wanted to know, So I very firmly demanded, "Take it off · · · now·"

She knew what I was talking about, and stared back at me hoping I'd change my mind but I didn't· So she took off her cardigan and stood in front of me in just her sports bra and pyjama bottoms, handing me her cardigan to hold·

And Damn – I wasn't expecting any of this· And poor Lila started crying just looking at my horrified reaction· Even her brother looked away at the sight of her mutilated skin·

There was more than just one scar· There were dozens all over her body – large cuts and punctures· It looked like someone had hacked away at her again and again, and again· And they were everywhere right down to where it looked like heated manacles were bound to her scarred wrist and ankles, causing the skin the blister and fade·

I began to realise that these scars were the reason why she always wore long sleeves and pants now, and why I always see her wearing make-up, even though she hates make-up, and believes that it only hides your true beauty·

*Oh shit – Lila doesn't believe she's beautiful anymore.*

*In shock, I stared into her teary eyes and finally let go of the breath I was holding on to.*

"Oh· · · Sissy," *I gasped and I was in tears when I questioned,* "Lila· · · where were you when you were supposedly dead?"

*Short of her own breath, Lila stepped away, pulling her yellow cardigan from my hand and put it back on to cover up the scars, yet stayed quiet needing a moment. Then in tears she glared at Matt, shaking her head,* "You happy Matt · · · now your brother · · · and mine · · · can't look at me anymore without seeing me as damaged and broken. I expected you · · · to have just that little bit of faith in me."

*She wiped the tears from her face and couldn't even look at me as she stormed out of the apartment with Tyme. Leaving me still waiting for an answer. So I turned to Matt and asked again,* "Matt · · · what island?"

*But he didn't answer either, instead he cradled his head in his hands with deep regret and groaned, before coming up with some lame attempt of an excuse,* "She meant the spa down on Phillip Island," *then glanced at me stupidly hoping I would buy that.*

*And No – I'm not blind, and I didn't buy it. Those are not the scars you get from being lost in the damn woods or at a spa.*

"Nice try brother," *I seethed glaring at him,* "But you and I both know where Lila's fears come from, and we both know she would never willingly stay on an island."

*It was clear to me that Matt didn't want to talk, and there was clearly something he wasn't telling me. Even Katie knew the secret, and she was trying to distract me from finding out, asking if I was still interested in having breakfast with her.*

No, I definitely wasn't interested in anything she had to offer. I was in tears and I wanted to know what happened to My Sissy - to My Friend.

So while continuing to glare at my brother, I snapped, "No · · · What I want is for my brother to stop feeding me a bunch of lies · · · Now I've seen a lot of weird crap in this hotel and never pushed for any answers. But Lila is someone I love and care about, and I want the damn truth."

Matt took a moment to breathe, leaning back on the kitchen bench before he glanced over at Katie, and hinted, "We're going to be here a while."'

Instantly Katie took that as her cue to leave, grabbing her jumper and rushing out the door. All while I continued to stand there angrily glaring at Matt as the door closed.

# Journal entry insert by Tyme Knight

I stood in the elevator, feeling like a complete idiot as Lila stood next to me in silence.

She had realised too late that she left the apartment in her pyjamas, and quickly raced into Alex's room to steal some of his gym clothes. They were long pants and a long-sleeved shirt, and they were very loose on her, but I think she wanted them to be loose to cover the scars – the scars she had not yet talked to me about. – The one she didn't want me to see.

But I knew they were there because I had heard some of the stories from Dad, when he went to rescue Lila from the island.

When we stepped back into the elevator, Lila took a brief moment, crouching to the floor and covering her face to muffle her scream. I knew that part of what had just happened was my fault, but I was afraid to ask for the clarification. But still had to know, and I asked timidly, "Lila, did I do something wrong?"

"No . . .," she instantly replied, but then grunted holding back tears, "I mean yes and no . . . You see, Shane didn't know about this particular part of my life yet."

Damn it – I felt like an even bigger idiot.

"I'm so sorry, Lila," I replied, now covering my face to hide my shame, "I just thought, since he lived with you, that he would have . . . I've screwed up, haven't I?"

I felt so much frustration building me that I took it out on the elevator, punching the wall slightly harder than expected, and I was really hating myself right now. I mean, I couldn't even last a damn week without screwing up Lila's life. – I am really sucking at this little brother thing.

The elevator started to shake when I hit the wall, causing Lila to leap her feet to calm me down, "Woah, Tyme. . . You haven't screwed up anything. He was bound to find out eventually."

She then looked really nervous and a little teary-eyed tucking the sleeves of her shirt in to her hand, as she whimpered, "There is one thing I do want to know from you. . . as you saw from Shane, I haven't had the best experiences when people see me . . . and I didn't want you to see them because . . . I didn't want to scare you away. . . but you're still here and I'm curious . . . why?"

While watching her nervous tears fall, I moved to stand in front of her and held her hands, pulling the crumpled cuffs of her sleeves from her fingers to look at the little scars on them. I then peeked back up to see her tears, and to also let her see my unwavering and caring smile as I spoke, "I am not going anywhere, and your scars don't scare me because when I look at you, all I see is my sister . . . and I promise I will never see as broken. . . Maybe a little trouble-prone. . . but never broken."

With a cute little sniffle, she wiped a tear from her eye, and whimpered, "Can I hold you to that promise."

And my response was to hug her, and make her feel better as I answered, "Absolutely."

But as the elevator doors opened, I got the slight impression Lila still wanted to keep hugging, and I was more than happy to keep a hold of her. So I slowly walked her out of the elevator into the lobby before I asked, "So, what do we do now. . . about the one who calls you Sissy? And I also want to add, that I don't like that name and I don't like him calling you that."

I heard her laugh as she pulled out of the hug, and looked up at me with a huge smile as she chortled, "Well he doesn't like your name either. . . but I get it . . . And as for what we do now. . . we continue as normal. Or did you forget we have a mission to prepare for?"

I happily nodded and accepted her gentle reminder – that I had somewhere I needed to be, and turned to walk back into the elevator. But as Lila turned to walk to the lobby desk, she saw her old friend, George, standing at the desk then very unexcitedly whispered, "Frac."

## Journal entry insert by Lila Winters

George arrived at the hotel today, and I won't lie, he really has the worst timing — especially after having to deal with Shane. But I needed to give George the opportunity to talk things through, and give him the chance to ask his questions, and hopefully not press charges on anyone.

I mean, we did unintentionally start a fire and a lot of other illegal things — like breaking and entering on multiple occasions, destroying a shopping centre, and lying about it, but who needs to go into specifics here.

We decided to walk through the park not far from the hotel, and I sat down and waited for George to eventually say something. He seemed to still be speechless, struggling to find the best way to start, pacing backwards and forwards in front of me.

So instead I broke the silence, "Is something wrong?"

George stopped in his tracks and glared at me, "Is something wrong? Everything is wrong. How can you keep this kind of thing a secret? How do I even know you're telling the truth? How many more people know about this? How many of you are out there? Why. . . I mean how do you not fear for your life every time you leave your apartment?"

He stared at me, waiting for an answer then blurted, "Proof . . . I want proof."

So, in being in a cooperative spirit, I pulled out one of the small seeds from my bracelet, which astonished George as he realised I had been carrying plant seeds this whole time.

I held the seed out in both hands being careful to shield it from other gawkers, then he stared up at my eyes as they glowed green, and the seed blossomed into a purple dahlia before I placed it in George's hand. I then picked up a small rock from the ground, crushing it with my hand, and held out the crumbs for George to see.

He looked at me in amazement and disbelief, and shuddered, "Why doesn't anyone know about this? I mean, you should be on TV. . . The whole world should know what you are. You could be using these gifts to help people."

I sat back down on the park bench and calmly replied, "I am helping people."

But George got more upset, and irked, "I mean helping real people like fighting crime and healing the sick."

With a slight chuckle, I shook my head, "George. . . Those people don't need my help."

"Why?" George snapped back, "Who are you to decide who gets your help and who doesn't?"

It was difficult to answer that question, especially to a police officer. But thankfully, my phone rang at the perfect time. It was Adela, letting me know that phase 2 was ready with the subjects. And that gave me the perfect opportunity to really show George why I choose to focus my talents on one area and not on his.

So, I invited George up to Adela's apartment, which was halfway through its repairs from the minor mishap with a certain USB.

I did find it a little funny as George looked around the empty apartment and commented, "Gees, it looks like a bomb's gone off in here."

He then looked at me, realising he was spot on the money, and gasped in shock. But before he could say anything I stood in the middle of the room and said, "We're ready when you are, Tyme."

George moved closer to me, watching in fright, not knowing where to stand as the room began to change, and Tyme, Adela, Terrence and Alex appeared standing next to me.

I also noticed William standing next to the three large waterlily pods, analysing their design and watching us. I wasn't overly happy with him being here, but he's Tyme's dad so I had to at least try not to let my frustration show. Instead I focused on George, hoping he wouldn't faint. And thankfully, he didn't. He just stood with his back against the door, seeming slightly freaked.

I very much wanted to laugh at him, as I remembered the kind of macho-man I'm not scared of anything attitude he had back in high school. – I guess he was wrong.

I didn't laugh at him though. I stayed nice and just kept smiling as I explained, "George, this is part of my team. . . Adela is a Water guardian, Alex is an Animal guardian, Terrence is a Nature guardian like me, and this is my brother Tyme, and he is a Time guardian."

I kept my focus on George as he looked around, trying to analyse the scene and glanced over to the oversized water lily pods.

"What about him. . . who's he?" he asked, pointing over to William.

I was reluctant to reveal who or what he was, so instead I replied in a brief remark, "That's just one of Terrence's old mentors, William. He's not part of the team. He's just consulting."

Unfortunately, by not acknowledging William, I hurt Tyme's feelings and could sense his disappointment from here. I knew he was hoping for one, big family-reunion moment, but it just wasn't going to happen.

I walked George over to the waterlily pods and waved my hand over the petals, causing it to roll down and reveal Zera, still asleep inside. And again, George jumped in fright.

"Holy Mother . . ." he gasped pulling out his gun, unsure what to do.

I tried to calm him, holding my hands out, praying he didn't shoot anything.

"It's alright . . . She's just asleep. This is a life pod. It keeps patients in a sleep state while the healing properties of the flower aid in their recovery."

I turned and waved my hand over the other two pods to reveal Jordan and Tora, and continued to clarify, "These pods contain the passengers from the New Year's Eve car fire. They're Guardians like us and they're under the influence of a drug called Neuritamine."

I then handed George the sample vial of Neuritamine, and explained how and why the drug was being used, and that we were trying to find an effective tonic to counteract the effects without creating any adverse reactions.

However, William decided to interrupt and grabbed hold of my arm, seeming nervous as he whispered, "Lila, are you sure he needs to know this?"

I didn't want to cause any alarm or suspicion to George, so I discreetly moved at full speed, stepping away from William, and thankfully, Tyme got the hint, pulling William to the side and whispering under his breath, "Dad not now."

George very carefully studied the Neuritamine vial then asked, "Why do you have it? And do you know who made it?"

I smiled a little and became excitedly confident, knowing that George wasn't totally freaking out and was approaching this with an open mind when I replied, "We retrieved this during one of our early investigations when Adela had gone missing. But as to who made it, we still haven't figured—"

"I created the Neuritamine. . ." William interrupted again as he stepped closer to me.

I couldn't believe what I had just heard as I glared at Tyme and shook my head. I was furious that Tyme had so casually left that crucial piece of information out when we had our very long catch-up sessions over the past <u>week</u>. He couldn't even look at me, he was so mortified.

Even Terrence was shocked when he demandingly asked, "Why?"

But that wasn't the worst fallout. George instantly jumped to the wrong conclusion.

"You made it," he said, then looked at me in fear, "How do I know you haven't been brainwashed yourself."

Again, William interrupted, "She can't. It's a fail-safe I designed to maintain the balance of power."

Unfortunately, that caused George to start backing towards the door again, struggling to hide his fear. "Power. What power?"

My body tensed with frustration and I was really starting to get ticked off because William just wasn't taking the hint to shut up as he answered, "To avoid The Board being in total control of the most powerful beings in the world. I designed the drug to be useless against Guardians of my kind. That way, there would always be one person who could fight back."

Yep – really ticked off. Especially when he looked back at me, smiling as if he were proud. Everything he said infuriated me.

But because George was there, I couldn't let my animal nature get the best of me.

My hair did start to streak white, but I managed to control it. And breathe calmly as I listened to George ask if William could fix the mess he made. But finally, William was speechless, shaking his head.

– Praise the Fracs.

"I can," I happily replied, holding up the glowing blue vial sitting next to a stack of blue roses and white lilies. I handed the white lily to George and explained, "This lily when used properly has the ability to remove any foreign toxins from the body and has been successful in every rescue we have done so far."

I then handed George the blue rose, "There is a catch though. Each person we've cured has ended up losing the memory's they had of the time of their abduction due to the trauma, which is where the blue rose comes in. This rose can heal almost anything in the body. From the common cold right up to knife wounds."

To prove its healing effectiveness, I lifted my shirt to show George the scars of the ice shard stabbing, and wolf incident and some of the others. I didn't want to because everyone else was in the room but most of them knew about them anyway.

He glanced at the wounds and sighed a little because they were the questions he wanted answered. But I stayed on topic and continued, "I believe if I increase the potency of both and combine them together, they should completely heal and restore the missing guardians to their former selves."

I then handed George the finished product in the glowing blue vial, and briefly glanced over to see William staring at me almost amazed that I had managed to fix his mess.

George stared at the vial, and the flowers, and the waterlily pods and then lifted my shirt to look at the scars again. But when he did, he scanned the room and notices the team saddened at the sight of the scars, even Alex and Terrence.

He then took little breaths and worryingly questioned, "These scars . . . When you were missing last year . . . did they. . ."

I nodded before he could finish that question. And George took a step back, almost in disbelief, "Why are you telling me all of this?"

—Well isn't that a twist — just one week ago he wanted to know all the answers and now he's regretting it — what a shock.

I kind of needed a moment to <u>not</u> laugh at the irony, before I replied, "Because these are the people who really need my help. . . They've had their free will stripped away from them all because they were different. . . And there's no one to fight for them because no one knows about them."

— It's actually pretty interesting for me — one of the things I learnt when I was a child was that — it's when you hide in the shadow that you find all the monsters — it's probably why humans tend to stay in the light and ignore the shadows.

I don't think George could take anymore though, and I could sense that he was close to tears – staring at me. And when he lifted the cuffs of my sleeves and ran his fingers across the discolouration of my wrist, he handed the flowers and vial back to me and replied,

"Enough, I can't take anymore – I'm done," then he walked out.

## Original journal entry continued
## by Shane Winters

I was fuming, after everything Matt told me about what was really going on in this hotel – and about where Lila really was before Christmas. So, I searched the hotel looking for Lila, wanting to talk to her about it, and when the elevator doors opened, I saw Detective Nell, looking a lot worse for wear as Lila rushed out of an apartment, calling his name.

But what really got me fired up was him, the man responsible for this whole mess – Terrence Connors is a dead man – because I'm going to kill him.

He stood next to Lila like there was nothing wrong which only infuriated me more, as I ran out of the elevator, tackling him to the ground, repeatedly punching him.

"You're a monster!" I shouted.

Within seconds, Detective Nell and Lila rushed to pull me off of him and held me back. So, I turned to Lila in a fury and shouted, "How could you do it? How could you be friends with the man who's caused you so much pain?"

Again, she didn't answer my question, instead she asked me to calm down. But I wouldn't, and she glared at me, shaking her head and glancing back at the detective, smiling as if everything was okay. – Looks like I wasn't the only one being kept in the dark.

"I know about the island!" I yelled, "where _he_ kept you, studied you, and used you!"

That gained the detective's interest as he relaxed his grip on me and asked, "What's he talking about? Did your friend do that to you?"

But again, Lila tried to shrug it off as if it were nothing.

"It's not nothing," I answered, pulling away from George. "And he's gonna pay... They're both going to pay,"

I then went to hit Alex this time because he was just as responsible for all the pain Lila's been through. And my fist was just about to collide with Alex's tiny little face when Lila grabbed hold of me again, this time pinning me to the wall with my arm twisted behind my back.

I shouted in frustration, "Why are you protecting them... You know this is their fault!" all while trying to push away from her, but Lila was too strong.

"Because I Love them..." she shouted but then stuttered, "...you. Because I Love you, and I don't want to see you hurt... If you know about the island, then you would know that both Alex and Terrence are a lot stronger than you. Getting them angry is not a good idea!"

Again, I tried to push away and failed as I grumbled, "I can take 'em."

"Shane, you can't even take me on," Lila sneered still holding me against the wall.

She then hauled me back into the elevator with her and escorted me back up to the apartment, sending me to my room as she gave me the death stare and scorned me, "Stay in there and be quiet. I have to deal with something important... Don't come out if you know what good for you."

In both fear and amazement, I watched as her hair turned white, and her eyes turned black.

I knew it – I knew I wasn't crazy – and I knew I wasn't seeing things – but the white hair is kind of cool and creepy at the same time.

Still, I wanted to argue back and tell her that she was crazy for ever bringing that monster back here, but before I could, Lila heard a knock at the front door and closed my bedroom door in a huff.

That's right – I got sent to my room. ME – a grown man sent to his room.

And damn that made me angry, but still curious at the same time. So I sat at the bedroom door and pulled the door ajar to peer out and listen. I saw Lila sitting on the coffee table in the lounge room in front of Adela and Matt, talking very quietly. Which meant I had to stay quiet.

Lila seemed very nervous when she spoke, "Adela · · · I have something for you · · · but you don't have to use it if you don't want to · · · and this is a decision that both of you should be aware of." She then handed Adela a small pinkish vial and added, "I've figured out a way for you to get your memory back· · · it's already been tested on Henry and he started remembering things within the first four hours of taking it."

Matt sounded really excited of the news but when he noticed Lila fidgeting with her fingers he questioned, "Lila that's great news · · · why are you so nervous?"

I noticed Lila's nose crinkle and she really struggled to get the next words out, "Adela would regain all of her memories· · · of everyone she hurt, betrayed, killed and · · · loved · · · She would remember everything."

It was really odd, because the room began to feel very tense, when Matt looked at Adela in a confused dread, unsure of what to say or how to react, and instead walked off into his room. All while Adela just sat there staring down at the floor, almost looking like she was about to cry. But she couldn't because there was another knock at the door.

Lila rushed to grab her beanie from the kitchen counter to cover her white hair before she opened the door to greet her mother. Hanna instantly greeted Lila with a hug then loudly expressed her concern, "Thank you darling. . . you know I'm so glad you called me. I was beginning to worry about you. I heard this dreadful rumour that you and Matt had separated because of some cheating scandal. Naturally, I didn't believe it."

She started walking into the lounge room to sit down, continuing, "You're a Willows and us Willows women would never let some cheap floozy hooker get in the way of our marriage . . . Oh hello, Adela. I didn't see you there . . . I'm sorry dear."

Okay that little piece of information was new. - and I wasn't expecting it.

While still in a bit of shock, I watched as Adela poured Hanna some tea, that for some reason, had the bud of a passion flower floating around in the tea pot, with the petals slowly disintegrating in the water. - And I don't think that's normal tea.

I sat at the door processing everything as all the pieces started to fit together, and it looked like Matt was still trying to keep me in the dark about all of this.

I was right though it wasn't tea because when Hanna took one sip of the <u>not</u> tea, she drifted off to sleep on the couch. So, while Lila and Adela were distracted trying to make Hanna comfortable, I took the opportunity to sneak into Matt's room to get some much-deserved answers.

Matt was lying on the bed, staring up at the ceiling, and I spoke quietly as I stood at the end of the bed, "You cheated on her· That's why she's mad all the time · · · isn't it?"

In a huff, Matt covered his face and mumbled, "Not now, Shane·"

"Lila's the best thing that could have ever happen to you · · · You've loved her since high school · · · Why would you cheat on her?" I asked quite frustratingly·

Matt sat up shaking his head and defensively grunted, "I don't know · · · I thought she was dead· I was sad and lonely and drunk, and I just wanted something to take the pain away·"

I was stunned at that answer and sat down on the end of the bed· "Well, how can Lila be angry about that? You have a valid excuse·"

"She's not angry about that· · ·," Matt mumbled hanging his head in embarrassment, "· · ·She's sad · · · Sad that when she came back from the island, I didn't tell her · · · but I also didn't stop sleeping with the other woman·"

Ah Right· – I sat in silence, listening to Matt cry and tried to think of some way to fix this·

"Well, what about her?" I questioned, "She spends a lot of time with those two guys· She even spends the night there sometimes, and I think she's wearing Alex's clothes right now · · · Surely, something's happened there?"

I know I shouldn't have but I really wanted it to be a yes, but it wasn't· And Matt responded through gritted teeth, "They haven't touched her · · · not intentionally anyway· And even when she was drugged and had lost all control of her inhibitions, they called me and told me what was happening to her · · · They have done nothing·"

Damn – I took a few more seconds to think then spoke even quieter, "But why don't you let them?"

My brother then glared at me in disbelief as I continued, "If you let Lila cheat on you, then that should even the score · · · She said she loved them, and it's obvious that both Alex and Terrence have the hots for her · · · So give her your blessing · · · even the score."

Still, Matt stared at me in disbelief, wiping the tears from his eyes, "She said what?"

So, I replied, trying to be as clear as possible, "She loves them · · · She let it slip, when she was yelling at me just before."

I quickly stopped my explanation when I saw Matt sitting on the side of the bed, looking as if his entire world had been shattered, and I very hesitantly asked, "You didn't know, did you?"

Right – Well I really put my foot in that one. And I thought, right now would be best time to disappear and let him think, so I stood up and mumbled, "Right, I'm gonna go for a walk · · · before I say anything else stupid."

I then rushed out of the room not hesitating to walk past Lila, who still seemed preoccupied with whatever was happening to her mother.

# Journal entry insert by Tyme Knight

I had just finished administering the last of the blue rose and lily tonic to the last unconscious patient, with my dad helping me pull them from the water lilies to place them gently on the couch to recover.

Dad looked back in amazement when he saw what was left of the water lilies as they started to shrivel and wilt away, "So you said Lila created these?"

"Yeah," I replied with a huge smile, "She's amazing, isn't she? You'd be really proud of her, Dad."

He then mopingly sat down on a dining chair and drifted in his thought, and I leaned on the back of the couch, crossing my arms, not entirely sure how to broach the next subject.

"So, I got a good look at the scars on her this morning . . . she was arguing with her brother-in-law and he demanded to see them. . . she looked so ashamed . . . the worst part was she didn't want me to see them because she was worried I'd see her as broken. . ."

I started crying and I could say anymore, so instead I sat there staring at dad.

He brushed his hands into his hair, holding them there while staring down at the ground shaking his head, "I still can't believe they did that to her . . . that Richard would do that to her."

He then sat back in his chair and he too had tears, but they were tears of anger and he sighed, "When I heard that they had her . . . I did everything I could to get to her. But when I found her on the island and saw her crying . . . I realised I was too late . . . They had already done so much damage. And I felt powerless because I knew it was my fault . . . I could have done more for her, but I didn't."

We sat in silence for a while, not knowing what to say, until Adela walked back into the apartment, excitedly rambling, "It worked . . . Lila's mum's going to be okay."

Those words caused Dad to jump to his feet in a panic, querying, "Katharine's here?"

The fright in his voice was horrifying and I got scared just watching him. But it also caused Adela to stop jumping and became very curious, staring back at Dad. "No, Hanna . . . Um . . . I thought Katherine was dead?"

I glared at Dad, discreetly shaking my head, trying to stop him from saying anything else, but Adela persisted and asked again, "Katherine is dead, isn't she?"

– Oh Crap.

Now feeling incredibly tense and worried, I very sternly glared at my dad again, hoping he wouldn't ruin this for me – or him, as he replied, "Yeah . . . sorry. Force of habit," then walked out of the apartment.

Oh Crap. Oh Crap. Oh Crap – this is not good.

Trying to distract the moment, I just casually smiled back at Adela and brought the attention back on to Jordan, who was thankfully beginning to wake up. And changed the subject entirely.

I know I wasn't being completely honest to Lila about what I knew – but I thought if we could build a relationship with her first and maybe even introduce her properly to Dad, start trusting each other and possibly create some family bonds. Then maybe after a while, Dad could sit her down and explain the real story to her – of how the family got torn apart.

# Original journal entry continued
## by Shane Winters

As I walked around Melbourne, trying to clear my head, I ran into Detective George Nell again· He was sitting on the park bench across the road from the hotel, holding some kind of purple flower·

I stood in front of him, creating a shadow, and commented, "They told you too, didn't they?"

He looked up at me in a confused shock as he nodded, "I don't know how I can keep this secret· · · When Lila was talking to me, all I could think about was how many laws she had broken and how many lies she had told· And then when I looked at those scars· · · Lila's been through so much· · · all I could think about was the danger and what kind of danger the world would be in if they knew·"

I thought back on those scars and the extent of them, and it wasn't hard to imagine the kind of danger Lila was in, and still is in· I then felt a surge of empathy and anger that raged through me, making me want to hurl·

"I think I need a drink," I murmured, "Do you want to join me?"

George looked up at me and nodded with sigh, "You took the words right out of my mouth"

He then followed me down the street towards one of the local bars that I had become a regular at· – We didn't really say much· – We just drank and tried process – Everything·

# CHAPTER 28

# WILL IT EVER STOP TRAINING?

*Journal entry by Lila Winters*

It was finally time to set off to Canada. And I felt really confident because I now had my mum in a good and safe place, and she was slowly starting to remember, and Chase promised me she would be safe while I was gone.

I was in my apartment, hurriedly packing my bags when I noticed the envelope – And when I got to the airport, my entire demeanour had changed. That envelope caused me to stay quiet the entire drive to the airport, and when I sat on the plane, all I wanted was space to process everything.

Zera and Jordan had successfully regained their memory and their free will, and were happy to join us on the rescue mission, so they sat with Adela and Katie going over the mission details.

I however, made it a point not to sit near Alex or Terrence because I didn't want either of them to sense the hurt and pain I was trying to control. Instead, they strategically sat in the bay of seats at the other end of the cabin, where they could still see me.

And while I stared out the window, watching the clouds brush over the wings of the plane I pretended I couldn't hear them as Alex whispered, "She hasn't said a word since we saw her this morning . . . Something's not right."

I knew they were worried about me, but I didn't want to talk. So I discreetly wiped a tear from my cheek, and tried to process everything that had happened just moment before I left for Canada.

I was all packed and ready to go when I read what was in the envelope, and in a confused fury I stormed into Matt's room while he was still sleeping.

"What the hell is this?" I barked, holding up the envelope.

It caused Matt to wake up in a daze, looking at me confusingly, "What's wrong?"

I almost hoped that this whole thing was just a hoax as I screeched, "You want a divorce . . . Are you out of your mind? I thought you wanted to fix our relationship."

He quickly got out of his bed and stood in front of me, trying to hold my hand and look at me lovingly as he replied, "We still can . . ."

But I pulled away from him struggling so badly to control my confused temper, "Then why the divorce papers?"

I was so confused, I mean I honestly thought Matt wanted to mend our relationship, not break it. This is the was the last thing I was expecting.

He moved closer to me again and looked into my eyes, trying to hold my hands. I tried to pull away, but he persisted and eventually I gave up, and listened to him.

"Do you remember the day after we got married?" he asked still holding tightly to my hands trying to get closer, "You were so worried that we might have rushed into the relationship."

I butted in there, tearfully snapping, "Yes, but that was just my nerves and the General getting to me."

Again, I tried to pull away, but Matt didn't let go and tried to keep eye contact with me as he continued, "But we also talked about what we would do if either one of us fell in love with another person." He then pulled my hand that was holding the divorce papers up and whispered, "Shane told me what you said."

I couldn't believe it. Again, Shane was messing everything up.

"I'm gonna kill that boy," I mumbled through my sniffles, "I didn't mean it."

"Yes, you did," Matt rebuked with so much sadness in him, "But it's okay. . . It doesn't mean we have to actually be separated. You don't have to sign it . . . I'm just giving you the opportunity to choose who you love."

I looked into Matt's eyes with tears streaming down my face, whimpering, "But I still love you."

He caringly smiled at me as he wiped my tears away and whispered, "I love you too, Lila. . . But I don't want us to stay together because of a legal piece of paper . . . I want you to choose."

My thoughts stopped there as I snapped back to reality, back on the plane flying away from him when Tyme walked up to stand next to me, and asked, "Hey, is everything okay?"

I wanted to distance him like everyone else but he was my little brother, and we were both still learning what it meant to be—family. So instead, I tried to just shrug it off and told him I was fine, but he could see through that, and sat down next to me, looking at me very sternly as he spoke, "Look, I know I'm new at this, and I know you don't like it when people try to push past those icy walls that you put up . . . But as your brother, I think I have the right to at least try to make you feel better . . . Now I won't ask you what's wrong, but I will offer you a hug."

He stayed staring at me in the hopes I would in some way reciprocate in a positive way, and it seemed like he had been practising what to say for a while. So, I turned and let him put his arm around me as I rested my head on his shoulder. He even brought a blanket up to keep me warm. — And as little brothers go, I think I scored a good one.

## Journal entry insert by Jessica Eden

My father had asked me to stay back and assist him with the hotel's operations instead of joining Adela on the mission. He even gave me the tedious task of making sure our newest resident had recovered, and to get her settled in her own room.

Tora was one of the guardians who was still recovering from the Neuritamine. Apparently, she had been working for The Board a lot longer than her other colleagues, and had seen a lot more things. — Personally, I think she would have preferred to forget.

My father stood at his office desk next to me, handing Tora the apartment key as he explained, "Okay, so we've organised for your own room, and Jessica is going to fill you in on hotels operations. We do request that guardian abilities are kept to a minimum . . . You know, so we don't scare the other guests."

Tora just smiled and nodded at that request. And my father again, offered to try and get in touch with one of her family members or arrange flights to anywhere she wanted. But she shook her head and replied, "No thank you. There's nothing for me at home . . . Thanks again, Mr Eden." Then followed me out of the office, so I could lead her to the assigned apartment.

While Tora and I were standing in the elevator, the doors opened to Matt's apartment floor where Matt was waiting, ready to go to work. He stepped in and greeted both of us with a smile. But just as the elevator doors were about to close, William ran up, shouting,

"Hold the elevator."

Instantly, Matt held the door and let William through, and awkwardly nodded to him.

"Hey . . . err Matt, right?" he asked.

Matt stayed quiet and nodded with a smile again then William held out his hand to introduce himself, "I'm William, Lila's—",

". . . I know who you are," Matt interrupted, seeming somewhat uncomfortable, but still trying to be nice, "Did you need anything?"

Obviously gaining a clear read of the room, William pulled his hand back as he responded, "I'm actually looking for Lila or Tyme, but I can't seem to find them anywhere."

Ah Right. – Matt needed a moment to think about his response. And considering Tyme did not tell his father where he was going, there's a strong assumption that William is not supposed to know, so eventually Matt replied, "They went on a holiday retreat."

Puzzled by Matt's answer, William asked, "Oh, how come you didn't go?"

Again, Matt seemed to be struggling with the pleasantries side of this moment and replied slightly agitated, "I have work and children to look after."

William's face then beamed with a smile as he eagerly replied, "You and Lila have children?"

You could definitely tell he was really interested, and probably excited to be a granddad. But it looked like Matt was ready to run out the door the first chance he got, as he tried to very nicely answer, "Yes . . . We have two children, and no . . . you can't meet them. Not without Lila's okay."

It seemed like a reasonable request and William was happy to oblige with it, stopping the conversation there. Then as soon as the elevator door opened, Matt stepped out and sighed, holding his head.

I was a little concerned for him, because something had clearly gotten to him, and I just had this gut feeling that it wasn't meeting Lila's real father for the first time that did it.

## Journal entry insert by Alex Woods

That was the longest plane ride I have ever been on.

When we finally landed on the ground again, Henry met us all at the private airstrip and drove us back to a large log cabin that he had acquired in the Northwest Territories of Canada. And as the weather forecaster so accurately predicted, it was raining. But all that was not what put me in a sour mood.

It was Lila – She's been giving me the cold shoulder for weeks, and it all started when I stupidly told her that I loved her while I was half asleep and cuddling her.

And what makes this all worse was that she accidentally blurted out that she loved me too, while protecting me and Terrence from Matt's little brother. – Not that we needed protection.

I mean, I honestly don't get it – she clearly feels comfortable enough to steal my clothes without asking me – not that I minded, I really like seeing her in my oversized T-shirts. – And I will leave that thought there before it goes too far.

I did have this idea that, maybe while we were up here, I would be able to talk to her, and confront her, maybe even ask her why she was pulling away. – It's not like she was oblivious to my feeling before this. – Deep down, she's always known that I loved her, ever since the moment we met. I've just never said it out loud before.

When we stepped out of the car and collected our bags from the boot, Lila handed her bag to Tyme then disappeared, running off at full speed into the woods.

"Where is she going?" Terrence asked.

And Tyme grinned back, replying, "She's doing a perimeter run," while carrying his and Lila's bags inside.

I felt a great wave of annoyance rush over me, and Terrence looked just as annoyed, staring out at the tree line and shrugged his shoulder. I suspect he was just as eager to talk to Lila as well.

Seeing how he was also noticing the distance, after the 'almost' moment they had as well.

I stood next to Terrence, as I stared out at the tree line where Lila had disappeared and asked, "Shouldn't someone go with her?"

I then looked back to see Tyme stop just at the door of the cabin, placing the bags down and replying with a slightly sarcastic tone, "I think you both already know the answer to that one."

We definitely did – Lila clearly wanted some space – and we should respect that.

When we went inside the log cabin, Henry stood at the stairs and explained, "Well, there's only 4 bedrooms left, so you will have to share. Pick your rooms and freshen up . . . We have a lot of work to do."

The log cabin was a pretty decent size, with a large kitchen and dining area, it even had a training room off to the side. Henry definitely knew what to look for when he was looking for potential real estate—large cottage, middle of no-where, surrounded by animals and trees, and constantly raining. And with an open log fire, it ticked all the elemental boxes for us.

It was quite interesting though, who in the team ended up bunking together, and it surprised me when Adela and Tyme didn't opt to sleep in the same room, given their current relational interactions. Instead, Adela bunked with Katie, and Tyme had already agreed to bunk with Lila.

Zera and Jordan were obvious, because they were life partners, which left me and Terrence with the last room. Which again sucked because it left me no opportunity to talk or spend time with Lila. And I was pretty sure Tyme wasn't planning to give up his sister to either of us.

## Journal entry insert by Matt Winters

This week had not started out as well as I had hoped. I continued as planned to go to work, knowing full well that I had a team of Lila's security guards keeping a general watch over me. And I was thankful that it was the school holidays for Danny and Ruby, because Max had agreed to stay with them and keep them entertained.

When I mean entertained – it was really code for spoil them rotten. But I didn't argue with it, because it kept the kids distracted from asking where their mother and the rest of her friends went.

The last thing I wanted to tell them was that their mother had gone to the other side of the world, on a dangerous and potentially deadly rescue mission. All to save some random people who have been missing for God knows how long, and may not even want to be rescued.

You could really tell that I wasn't 100% okay with this daring plan, and I especially wasn't okay with being left behind. But part me wanted to stay.

For the last few days, I've been having flash backs of the last mission Lila asked me to join her on, and it felt like I was reliving that horrid moment when she was shot and disappeared behind that wall of fire, over and over again.

The agony I felt, knowing that Lila wasn't coming home – just the thought of it was unbearable. And I don't ever want to do it again.

As I stepped out into the basement car park ready to go to work for the day, I tried to shake off those horrible worrying feelings, while walking towards my car. Unfortunately, I was completely oblivious to my surrounding when Vicki, one of the undercover police officers who had been tailing my wife and her team, snuck up behind me, and violently pinned me to the car.

"Where is she?" she shouted, quite angrily, holding a gun to my back.

I tried to break free but thought it unwise to aggravate her, so instead stalled for time and asked, "Where's who?"

I'm going to guess she knew I was playing dumb because she pushed the gun further into my back and irked, "Your wife, damn it. After George took us off this case, he went to go speak to your wife."

She then showed me her iPhone with a picture of Lila and George walking into the hotel together, explaining, "This was the last time he was seen or heard from, and now, all of a sudden, I get word that your wife has fled the country. . . Now I'll ask you again . . . where is your wife?"

Alright, I was out of ideas now and was struggling for stall tactics, so instead I answered, "I don't know where she is, but I can help you find him . . . George. I mean. . . please let me help."

Thankfully, Jessica and her security team ran around the corner, with Jessica holding up her favourite taser gun and yelled, "Put the gun down and place your hands flat on the ground . . . Now!"

Vicki just snickered back, seemingly unafraid, "Or what? You'll shoot a police officer?"

That caused Jessica to hesitate for a moment weighing her options, but it actually bought me the distraction I needed to pull my arm free. I then spun around, grabbing hold of the gun, and elbowing Vicki in the head, as I pushed her into the side of the car.

As she fell, I quickly grabbed hold of her again, before she lost consciousness, and softly placed her flat on the ground, to ensure no more damage was caused.

Once it was safe, Jessica rushed to my side to secure the gun, then demanded to her security team to call an ambulance, before she turned back to me and commented, "Nice moves."

I finally took a breath, and with relief I replied, "Thanks, Lila's an excellent teacher."

"Interesting, it's not like you to have a stalker . . ." Jessica stated in confusion, as she watched me rummage around Vicki's pockets for her iPhone.

I started looking through the photos on the phone and explained, "It isn't me she's after. She's looking for George."

"So why do you still look worried?" Jessica asked, kneeling down to my level.

I stopped and grunted a bit when I finally found the photo I was looking for. — I could tell by the tone in Vicki's voice when she said that it was the last photo she had of them, that it was a lie. There was one last photo of Shane and George walking along a Melbourne street at night, heading into a bar.

I was now filled with a lot of worry as I turned the phone to show Jessica, and explained, "Because Shane also hasn't been home in days. And I'm starting to fear the worst."

Jessica moved closer to look at the phone and questioned, "Why would anyone want to kidnap Shane and George?"

I then pointed to a small woman standing in the picture who, to the inexperienced eye was just an ordinary woman. But I've been around Lila long enough to I know — that the woman in the photo was tailing Shane and George. It's the same way Lila and her cadet friends would tail someone when they were training.

I stood to my feet, and sighed as I answered Jessica's question, "Because they were both told the hotels secret and disappeared the same day."

## Original journal entry continued by Lila Winters

Well, so far so good – the first stage was a success. We arrived in Canada without arousing any suspicion. Now, all we had to do was wait, and each take turns in recon.

I had so far managed to stay focused and in control, trying hard not to let my feelings get in the way of the mission. And my training helped me to stay focused, so every day, I would train.

Today I stood on one of the high branches of the tall trees just outside the log cabin. I was blindfolded, holding a sparring stick, and trying to fine-tune the bond I had with nature.

Every time I moved, the trees moved to catch my footing and keep me balanced. And I was putting a lot of the trust in the trees to make sure I didn't fall.

But the trees also helped me train my other senses as the higher branches of the trees played shoulder tag with me, and I had to listen and move at the right time. – And yes, I very much like the shoulder tag game.

It was a thrilling and exhilarating experience if it weren't for the fact that it is incredibly dangerous. And I could feel Tyme's anxious and worried nerves as he watched me train from the porch of the cabin.

After a good hour or so of training with the trees, I was caught off guard and was distracted when Alex appeared below me, yelling very sternly, "Lila, we need to talk."

Frac.

My emotions quickly got the best of me and overwhelmed me, which caused the trees to react in a similar motion. And as the trees retracted from beneath me, I fell, blindfolded, towards the ground.

But I didn't panic or scream, I didn't even squirm to take off my blindfold, as I fell into Alex's waiting arms. He then held onto me tightly, slightly shaking in fear as he pulled the blindfold off for me, and looked me over to see if I was injured.

"Are you okay? Are you hurt?" he asked.

With a cheeky grin, I looked into his steely and overprotective eyes, to reply, "Yes, Alex, I'm fine."

I wasn't scared at all. I was actually quite confident and somehow just knew that Alex would always be there to catch me. He did need a moment to calm his own nerves though, as his arms tightened around me. And I was happy to wait for a little while longer.

"Are you going to put me down?" I asked, still with a calm and cheeky smile.

But instead, he held me tighter. "Um, no . . .I think I'm gonna hold on to you for a little longer." He then began to walk slowly back to the cabin, still holding me in his arms.

"Did you need something, Alex?" I giggled, kind of already knowing the answer.

"A chance to talk to you would be nice," he replied, glancing down at me and clearly starting to take the long way back to the cabin. – Ah sneaky one, he is.

I didn't fight him or struggle to break free, and I had a very mild suspicion he was using his animal charming skills to keep me relaxed, so I got comfortable and kept smiling, "Well, it looks like I'm not going anywhere."

He took another breath and needed to work up the courage to start his long-awaited conversation that I knew he desperately wanted to have with me.

"Okay. We've known each other for a while now, right?" he asked and I nodded, allowing him to continue, "And I consider you to be my best friend, and I'm really hoping you consider me to be at least one of your best friends."

I could sense him becoming extremely nervous at this point, and interrupted gazing up at him, "Alex, after all we've been through, you're more than just a best friend."

But he then stopped walking and looked at me with his stare becoming glassy and sad, "So why have you been avoiding me? Have I done something wrong?"

Frac – Not now.

I started to feel the flurry of emotions rising within me, and I knew I was struggling to control it, and I grew desperate to move away from him, trying to hide one particular emotion I was feeling. So using all my will power, I broke through the charm hold he had on me, and landed back on the ground.

"I can't do this . . ." I responded a bit squeamishly, "I'm really sweaty, and I just . . . I need a shower."

I tried to slowly back away when Alex grabbed hold of my hand and begged, "Lila, don't do that. . . please."

As Alex's hand connected with mine, he instantly felt a swell of all my emotions stream through him. He felt my sadness, betrayal, love, loss, envy, fear, regret and a burst of other feelings that were just too hard for me to describe.

And now short of breath, he looked at me, muddled and terrified, feeling like all of this was his fault – but it wasn't and I wanted him to know that. So, I held back my tears, placing my hand on his chest while holding his hand to mine then stared into his eyes as I listened to the sound of his heart beating, and I whispered, "Alex, listen. Okay. . . Just listen."

He did as I asked, and he very slowly began to calm down as he listened to my heart beating, just as his did. Then I whispered again, "Alex, you could never do anything wrong to me, and none of these feelings are your fault. . . You are perfect . . . and I know in my heart that you will always be the person I trust to be there for me no matter what . . . But right now. . . I can't do this."

It felt like my heart was being held his hands as I pulled away from him again, and this time, he didn't stop me. He just remained silent and walked next to me back to the log cabin.

## Journal entry insert by Matt Winters

After I left Jessica to deal with the unconscious police officer and the ambulance's many questions, I raced back up to my apartment with a copy of the photo Vicki had of George and Shane. Then in a slightly panicked state, I rummaged through Lila's study, amongst the many stacks of files and papers she had on the missing guardians, mumbling to myself when Jessica walked in, asking if I was going to work today. My obvious answer was no. And thankfully I found it.

Lila had pulled a picture from the hotel security footage from the day she was drugged. It was an image of a young Asian woman who had glowing blue eye. Lila had even managed to ID the woman, and had attached the picture to her missing profile and labelled it: "Kim Black – Water Nymph – disguise used." It also had a last known address.

"It looks like Lila's done all the work for us," I commented, handing the photo to Jessica.

I didn't even realise what Jessica had found while in Lila's office when she started to read through the divorce papers.

"What's this?" she asked.

I moved quickly to take the papers from her, and bury it amongst the rest of the files on Lila's desk, briefly stating, "It's nothing. Just a bit of paperwork. . . Come on . . . We're wasting time."

Jessica agreed to help me on my new mission, and we decided to take one of the standard hotel-hire-cars to try and reduce recognition and suspicion as we drove towards Kim's last known address in the hopes of rescuing Shane – and George.

I drove and Jessica sat in the front passenger seat, struggling greatly to not ask any questions until she blurted out, "Why would you and Lila have divorce papers? Are you two getting a divorce?"

I rolled my eyes and continued to drive, following the GPS directions and muttered, "We're not getting a divorce."

She didn't believe me though and played up her sarcasm. "Oh, so Lila's married to another Matt who she wants to divorce."

And with that I retorted, "I asked for the divorce, not her."

"Are you nuts?" she shrieked, pulling a sour face, "You've said it yourself that Lila was your entire world. Why would you want to let her go?"

'Was' being the standout word there. –– I pulled the car over not far from our destination and turned to Jessica, trying to clear things up and explained, "I don't want to let her go. I just want to give Lila the option to leave . . . I know I was the one who cheated on her . . . and I understand that she would find it impossible to forgive me. But Lila loves me too much to ask for a divorce herself . . . So I asked for her . . . But I still have hope that she doesn't sign the papers, and she'll choose to stay with me."

Jessica stared back at me all doe-eyed, and sighed "That's both romantic and sad at the same time."

Great, so I'm a sad-romantic. –– Either way we still had a mission to complete. So getting back on topic I urged, "Now can we please focus on saving my brother."

As she nodded, I turned our attention to a closed-down bar on the St Kilda pier line, and I questioned, "Are you sure we're at the right place?"

Jessica briefly looked at the address on the back of the security photo then nodded, "This is it . . . So we'll need to stick together, go through the back, and check out the building room by room."

She then stared back at me under the assumption that I would just agree, as she handed me a gun. And I didn't have much of a choice to argue or counter anything she said, as she stepped out of the car ready to cross the road.

Okay – So we're doing this.

## Journal entry insert by Maxwell Eden

I was in the office, filling out paperwork for the hotel, and waiting for my daily check-in from the Canadian team when Jess knocked on the door.

"Hey, sweetie," I greeted, welcoming her in, "I thought you were out on an errand with Matt."

Jess walked in, seeming a little standoffish but I just put it down to her being emotional about being left behind and not going to Canada.

She stood at the desk and replied, "Yes, but I got called back. I just got a message from Lila . . . She asked that you please ensure the tree is safe."

I stood up, slightly suspicious, wondering how Jess knew I had the tree stone in my care. But this woman knows almost everything about this hotel, and I'm not totally surprised she knew about this.

"Well, I checked on it this morning, but it won't hurt to check again."

I then walked over to my bookcase and tilted two books forward, triggering the hidden door release, revealing my safe. All I needed to do was key in the code before I opened the safe door and looked inside to reveal a large green tree stone sitting amongst the many other artefacts and diamonds.

Suddenly, I felt a sharp, stabbing pain in the back of my neck, and I began to feel woozy and weak. Then as I fell to the ground, I watched my Jessica morph back into Tora and walk out with the tree stone in hand with me powerless to stop her.

## Journal entry insert by Matt Winters

As Jessica and I cautiously searched the old building, we eventually found George and Shane semiconscious, and looking a lot worse for wear. Both of them were handcuffed and dangling from a bar on the ceiling.

There were two men sitting at the table, playing cards, guarding them when Jessica spun around the corner and shot both of them with her tranquiliser gun then rushed over, cautiously watching as they fell asleep on the table.

"Well, that was easy," she said, scanning around the room.

But as she turned her back, a large puddle of water rose from the ground to take the shape of Kim Black, looking a lot more like a water nymph than before.

"Jess, look out!" I shouted, then quickly move to shoot at Kim with my gun. But Kim's body turned to water, and the bullets passed straight through her, hitting the wall behind. Still, I kept shooting, each time missing until the clip was empty.

And now realising that both our guns were empty, Kim retook solid form to punch Jessica to the ground.

Every time Jessica or I tried to fight her, she would phase from a fluidic to solid form, using it to her advantage. At one stage, I tried throwing a chair at her, but instead, it passed straight through her and hit my brother in the chest causing him to grunt from the pain.

"Sorry," I shouted, hoping Shane could hear me.

Kim then retook her solid form again to kick me in the face and chest, knocking me to the ground in front of George's weapons that had been placed just out of arm's reach from him, most likely to taunt him.

In seeing that, I rushed to pull out George's gun, only to realise it was a Taser. And finally, I knew my brains could win over brawn. I quickly shouted to Kim to get her attention, and naturally, she turned to a fluidic substance as I fired the weapon, and the electric nodes of the Taser landed inside her body of water, discharging an electrical current into it.

Kim screamed as her entire body coursed with electricity, causing her to return back into her solid form, with the electrical nodes inside her body.

Oh Damn Craps.

I dropped the Taser and shuddered at the sight as I yelled, "Oh crap . . . I just killed a woman."

Still in shock I stood over Kim's dead body and stared, struggling to move, as she broke into her fluidic form and dispersed, seeping in and among the floorboards.

I turned back to see Jessica cradling her stomach and grunting from the pain as she rushed for the handcuff keys sitting on the table next to the unconscious men. Then moved to un-cuff Shane and George as she demanded I call an ambulance, claiming officer down.

Oh Crap, Oh Crap – What have I done?

## Journal entry insert by Alex Woods

I finally got to talk to Lila today – well kind of. I at least found out that it wasn't me she was angry at, – and that gave me some comfort. But the emotions I sensed from her when I held her hand were very concerning for me. I understand that at the moment she's not ready to talk, but hopefully once the mission is done – she will be.

Tonight, the team all decided to sit down and take a break from planning, and instead had hot chocolate and sat by the fire. Except of course for Lila, who was sparring with Tyme in the training room, teaching him how to fight. And it was clear to all of us that Tyme had not had to fight anyone a day in his life, which in the end, made us all nervous for the success of this mission.

Everyone pretended not to be watching and judging as Tyme got thrown to the floor over and over again, but the comments from Adela and Katie probably didn't help.

"Something is seriously wrong," Katie muttered to Adela, "She hasn't stopped training since we got here."

"Do think something happened back in Melbourne?" Adela speculated, turning to me and demanding I spill the beans, but they didn't believe me when I told them that I was just as clueless about Lila as them.

Adela started getting cagey, lowering her voice to a whisper, "Look . . . I know we all agreed we'd never ask . . . but it's killing me. So, I need to know what happened between you and Lila . . . You know . . . on that night."

She acted all awkward, pulling the 'you know what I mean' face. But I still wasn't understanding the question until Katie chimed in, and Adela thankfully – for me anyway – received a phone call, distracting the conversation.

But Katie rolled her eyes, bringing the attention back to me again, "So everyone knows that me, Adela and Lila were all targeted and placed under the influence of a very powerful sex drug. . . Now I know how I fixed my issue, and Adela's fix is pretty obvious as well . . .,"

She then stopped to point at Tyme, giving the subtle hint of Adela's fix. But before she could say anything more, I interrupted her, knowing exactly where the question was leading, and made things clear as I very quietly explained.

"Yes, I was with Lila that night as was Terrence, but we spent most of the night in a cold shower with our underwear on. . . And once Lila's temperature had dropped, both Terrence and I stayed with her to keep an eye on her . . . I even called Matt to let him know what was happening."

I glanced back at Terrence, who nodded and agreed to everything I said, hoping Katie would drop the subject. But she didn't, she just got more annoyed. "Argh . . . Well, if nothing happened, then why has Lila been avoiding you and Terrence this whole trip?"

"I know. . .," Adela answered looking incredibly shocked and saddened as she hung up the phone.

We all stared at her and waited eagerly for her response – although, given the emotions that I picked up from Lila today, I wasn't sure I wanted the response.

Then taking a breath, Adela stated, "That was Jess. . . Matt asked Lila for a divorce just before we left for Canada . . . and Lila signed the papers . . . She's getting a divorce."

WHAT THE HELL!?!

## Original journal entry continued by Lila Winters

Once Tyme had called it quits for the night, I didn't hesitate in disappearing up into my room. I could definitely sense the vibe of the team had changed, and I was in no mood to deal with any fallout. — I guess they forget sometimes that I can multitask, being able to listen to their conversations about me while still kicking my bothers arse.

However, I did have other things on my mind when I raced up into my room. — I needed to return a missed phone call from Max. I was expecting his call though, as well as the security photo of Tora handing the tree stone seed to the Commander of the US Navy ship that we had escaped from last year. — Terrence was right. It was him. And this gave us the advantage we needed.

"Are you alright?" I asked Maxwell through the phone.

"Yeah . . . Nothing a goodnight sleep won't fix," he replied, "How did you know?"

I looked down at the security photo, and then reached into my luggage bag to pull out the real island tree stone as it glowed in my hand and replied, "It was just a hunch."

# CHAPTER 29

# LET'S PLAY A GAME

*Journal entry by Lila Winters*

The time had come to put our plan into action and I was nervously excited.

Terrence and I had agreed to do one more perimeter run around the large facility called Agronomique – Environmental Science Group Limited.

Their name was insulting, and their play on the truth was gut-churning. I mean, yes – The facility was a science base, and they did study the environmental factors – it just wasn't in the way anyone would usually expect.

Either way, I was planning on showing them just how powerful the environment can be –when used properly that is. So, I was pretty determined, and Terrence followed my lead, leaping through the tops of the trees along the facilities borders.

The entire building was surrounded by an ominous black wrought iron fence with decorative spikes at the top, separated by large brick pillars. And every time Terrence or I jumped to the next tree, we would drop a small cutting of creeping vines to the ground next to the fence. It would then slowly start growing, wrapping its tendrils around the iron fence and along the ground.

We eventually stopped and rested at the top of one of the tallest trees where a small white snowy owl sat waiting for us.

"Hello Alex," I greeted, gently stroking the wing of the owl.

Alex quickly became agitated, noticing that I wasn't wearing my seed bracelet for the mission and started to peck at the new bracelet Terrence made for me from the tendrils of the Morning Glory vine.

Terrence had specially designed the bracelet to grow and shrink as I did in order for me to morph into any animal without losing it, and in the centre of the bracelet nestled the remnants of an old tree stone that glowed in a swirl of purple and green. – My two second favourite colours – Yellow is still my favourite.

Agetha had gifted the stone to Terrence as an offering to help with our mission. So, he split what was left of the tree stone in two and created two matching bracelets, one for him and one for me.

Apparently, the stone gave the person who possessed it a heightened link to the flora surrounding them. It also had the added benefit, of linking the emotions of each stone.

And though Terrence would never admit it, I don't think he was totally on board with the plan and wanted a — let's just say, a back-up way of communicating. But I wasn't going to argue with him, if it helped to calm his nerves.

Still, the snowy owl was upset as it nestled up close to me, perching on my shoulder, then began chirping at Terrence. And Terrence shrugged his shoulders, looking at me in the hopes of a translation.

"Alex," I scowled with a slight chuckle, "Terrence is a Nature guardian and doesn't speak bird . . . and I am not going to translate that."

He also asked me why I wasn't wearing any shoes, so while biting my bottom lip I explained, "I left them back at the cottage. . . it's actually easier for me to run and climb with no shoes on."

The snowy owl chirped again and spread its wings in frustration, as he eyed me.

"Alright, alright . . . Just give me a minute," I sighed as I pulled out two small bamboo gift bags filled with a mix of seeds. I then held them out for the owl to claw into as he flew off.

And as he gained flight, I yelled to remind him, "Remember to do a guard count on your way back this time."

Terrence and I watched as the owl flew over the building and disappeared from sight when suddenly, a large wind blew through the trees as a helicopter flew over our heads, also causing a gust of leaves to race through the trees and hit both Terrence and I.

And because Terrence had perched closer to the trunk of the tree, he had something to grab hold of. I on the other hand, was out in the open, and lost my grip as I tried to shield myself from the razor-sharp leaves then fell backwards as one of the leaves slashed my cheek just below my eye.

As I fell, Terrence dove to catch me, locking his feet around the branch then swinging down and around, using a second branch to catch us. He then pulled me closer to the trunk of the tree as he noticed the helicopter turning around.

It grew obvious that the pilot had spotted something as he flew past again, slowly this time. So, Terrence pulled me to the other side of the tree and pressed me against the trunk, pushing his chest very close to mine. And as his eyes glowed green, the trunk of the tree created a second layer of bark that grew around us, encasing us on the inside.

It was a tight squeeze as we waited, listening to the helicopter circling around the trees, looking for something. And Terrence and I were so close that we could feel each other's breath.

Eventually, the helicopter gave up and continued on its flight path. So Terrence pulled back some of the bark to create a large enough opening for us to climb out. Then while still holding held me firmly against the tree he checked to see if the coast was clear. But instantly looked back at me when he saw both mine and his tree stones glowing brighter.

"Lila, what's wrong? Why are you nervous?"

I'm pretty sure that was a clear answer, but I wasn't going to tell him.

While we were in our little hidey-hole the owl had returned, perched on the original branch we found him on, and was staring at Terrence still pinning me to the trunk of the tree, and now chirping profusely.

Alex was trying to warn us about something, and demanded us to climb up to see the helicopter landing on the Agronomique's helipad. We then saw Commander Eric Peterson step out from the helicopter, escorted by several heavily armed marines and Matt in handcuffs, looking quite weary and distressed.

I crouched down next to the snowy owl and whispered, "Right on time. Now for phase 2."

Then with a cheeky smile, I stared at Alex and winked, beaming with excitement as my hair began to turn white and my eyes turned black. – I was getting damn good at this.

As I climbed down the tree, leaping from branch to branch, I slowly began to morph and landed on the ground, standing tall and growling as a large white wolf, shaking off what was left of my clothes. – Except for the bracelet of course, which actually did shrink to size.

I peered up and watched as the snowy owl swooped down next to me and morphed into a large grey wolf.

We both looked at each other with eager excitement and howled as we ran alongside each other, racing through the trees, and stopped just before the main road. Then waited in the cover of the bushes as Terrence leapt down from the trees to hide with us while we listened for the sound of a transport truck that routinely made its deliveries to Agronomique's at the exact same time each day.

When I heard the sound of the tyres race over a pothole full of water, the rain clouds began to form overhead. And that was the sign for me to start running – Phase 2 had begun.

Alex decided to give me a running head start as I left him standing next to Terrence, and it was really cool because he was almost the same height as him.

As wolves go, Alex looked like an alpha – but I wasn't much smaller than him.

## Journal entry insert by Alex Woods

I admit, I was having a lot of fun now that I had another animal guardian running alongside me, and she really knew how to make it a challenge.

I chased Lila through the trees as she ran as a beautiful, great white wolf. And I as a grey wolf, followed her shimmering white fur as she ducked in and out of the leaves and shrubs.

She ran towards the sound of the delivery truck, then without any hesitation, she stopped and waited for me to tackle her onto the road in front of the oncoming truck causing it to slam on its breaks.

The driver watched as we wrestled each other, fighting and growling. And our fight got quite heated and violent – with a lot of biting and scratching. The fight continued until one of the armed guards stepped out of the back of the truck and created a fireball in his hand, throwing it at my feet as a warning shot.

So, I gave up the fight and ran into the bushes to take cover, leaving my poor white wolf wounded and dazed on the ground in front of the truck, struggling to stand and make her escape.

I really started to worry, that maybe I was a bit too rough with her, and watched from the safety of the bushes as one of the guards stood in front of her, staring at the great white wolf as she collapsed to the ground and morphed back into Lila's human form. – Well almost.

She still had pointy elf-like ears and long white hair, and the hair was so long, that it almost acted as a blanket, covering her naked body. But she was also covered in bite marks and minor scratches caused by me, and I wasn't overly happy with this part of the plan – because it only adds more scars to that beautiful body of hers.

I sensed the pain Lila was in as she tried to crawl away from the guard but eventually, she had to give up, and looked back up at the guard in fear before she fainted.

I was really struggling to see any of the guard's insignia, to figure out who he was. All I could see was his dark skin until another voice yelled from the back of the truck, "Hey, Stephen. . . What's the hold-up?"

The guard yelled back, confirming his identity for me, and said with a very strong Texan accent, "Billy, ya gotta see this."

The next thing I saw was, I'm assuming Billy, step out of the truck with his arm covered in flames as if he were ready for a fight. And he very much looked like a military man – a Navy SEAL if I had to guess. But I still think if I had to fight him – I'd win.

I watched as Stephen knelt down next to Lila and pull the hair back, that was shielding her face. Then looking back up at Billy, he asked rhetorically, "Recognise her?"

Billy started scanning the trees around him and heard me, panting as I hid in the shadows of the trees. I think he could tell I was waiting for an opportunity to strike. So, he created a fireball in his hand, and stood protectively in front of Stephen as he ordered him to pick Lila up and put her in the truck.

As Stephen cradled Lila's unconscious body in his arms, I rushed out from the safety of the trees and tried to rescue her, but I failed when Billy created a wall of fire between me and the truck. Instead, all I could do was watch, growling at him as Lila was loaded into the back of the truck, and Billy sat next to her as the truck sped off towards the facility.

I paced back and forth along the wall of fire, glaring at Billy as he stared back at me. Then as soon as the truck was out of sight, I raced back into the shelter of the bushes and waited for Terrence to jump from one of the branches of the trees and hand me some clothes.

"Did you have to be so rough with her?" Terrence snickered while he waited for me to get dressed.

I stepped out from the bushes, back as my human self, pulling my top over my head then showed Terrence the many bites and scratches that I endured during that wonderfully staged fight of ours, and very annoyingly snapped, "She bit me first."

With a huff, Terrence handed me a vial of blue rose tonic, before we began to move again as he stated, "Hurry up . . . We need to regroup for phase 3."

Terrence and I then raced back to the cabin at full speed, both very competitive. I was winning, until Terrence cheated and used one of the branches of a nearby tree to throw himself towards the cottage, reaching the porch just seconds before me.

We began to bicker with each other about who the real winner was, until Jennifer walked out interrupting our squabble.

"I take it the drop offs were successful?" she asked quietly, being cautious not to be too loud and looking around at the trees.

I moved in closer and replied, "Everything went to plan. . . on our end anyway."

But then Jennifer noticed some of the wounds that I scored in the fight with Lila, and looked slightly disappointed when she realised they were still slowly healing. "Terrence, can you speed this up faster with a paste?"

Terrence looked over at the bite marks, now realising they were deeper than both of us originally thought, "Sure. . . I think I have some inside."

But as Terrence started to walk into the cabin, he suddenly fell to the ground, holding the back of his head, screaming in pain.

Awe – Crap.

"That not a good sign," Adela said, racing out of the cottage to assist him.

Jennifer watched Terrence as he tried to cope with the pain, stepping back nervously and fearfully asked, "What do we do now?"

She knew that Terrence's pain meant we had an unforeseen player on the playing field. But we weren't overly sure what to do, and we also couldn't change the plan because too many of our players were in the field – especially the most important one.

Eventually Terrence stood to his feet, taking slow breathes and trying to control the pain, "We stick to the plan . . . I can handle this. It just caught me off guard, that's all."

I wasn't totally convinced with that, but we had no other choice, we had to trust each other now, so we all got back to our assigned tasks.

## Original journal entry continued by Lila Winters

I pretended to be asleep as they carried me into their med bay, and chained me to the base of the medical bed with hand cuffs. And they definitely weren't taking my arrival lightly because these handcuffs were industrial, and twice the size and strength of ordinary handcuffs with a small electrical charge that released whenever I pulled too hard on the centre chains.

And if that wasn't enough, there were several armed guards babysitting me, including Billy and Stephen — the men who unwittingly put me in the truck and drove into the base that I wanted to get into. — Silly boys.

They were all standing at the end of my bed, just waiting for me to make the wrong move.

— And don't I feel popular again.

I could sense their nerves as they watched me sleep. And I really felt like opening my eyes and yelling 'Boo' at the top of my voice.

They even tensed up when one of their own medical staff — Anna, approached the bed to tend to the bite wounds and scratches that covered me. She carried with her a tray of black mud, and when she waved her hands over the mud it levitated above me, breaking up into small beads and landing gently on all of my wounds. — I think I like this one though, because she was careful to keep my nudity covered with the blanket, which I thought showed honour on her part.

I kept my eyes closed while receiving the treatment, just barely peering through the lashes to watch as Anna peeled away each of the mud stains to reveal my wounds starting to close up and scab. But I was also listening in as Billy whispered to his friend Stephen, "Are you sure she's the same girl from the island?"

"Positive" Stephen whispered sounding so sure of himself.

Gosh — are they really that daft thinking I can't hear them?

Still Billy was curious and stepped closer to me, pulling back my long white hair to reveal my elfish ears and studied my face, moving closer to me. "I thought she was a nature guardian. . . Why was she roaming around Canada as a white wolf?"

While he was still studying me, I opened my eyes to look into his, and answered his question with a wry grin, "Because I'm a hybrid."

Instantly he stepped back, staring at my eyes as I added, "I'm what your boss would call a very rare collector's item."

Billy and Stephen then created a fireball in their hands, raising them up, ready to torch me as my eyes flickered black and then back to normal blue. I know I didn't have to do that, but I was curious to see how jumpy they were.

Unfortunately, the nurse – Anna, jumped in front of them, demanding, "Whoa . . . Guys, calm down . . . I just started healing her."

Well damn, that fun was short lived. – But it was still beneficial, as glanced around at the guards. I couldn't see all of the them, but I could tell that at least two of them were Water guardians, and four of them were humans who instinctively reached for their guns instead of creating an elemental weapon.

"Sorry, Anna" Billy said, extinguishing his fireball, "But we have orders . . . If she moves, we shoot."

– It was very tempting to test that supposed 'order', seeing how I am 'rare'. And I cheekily grinned at Billy again, causing him to tense up, probably curious as to why I was so calm.

I mean, what was he expecting – I have been through this before, so I really wasn't surprised with the treatment I was receiving.

"It's alright, Anna. . . You can go if you want. I feel much better now," I cheeked, trying to sit up in the bed, still respecting the handcuffs range of motion.

Anna turned back to me, picking up what was left of her tray of mud, and irked, "Just try not to get shot . . . I am the one who has to clean it up if you do."

–Wow, I could just feel the sympathy oozing out of her – NOT.

"I'll try," I tittered with a smile, and yet still in a cheeky mood I added, "No promises though."

But my smile quickly disappeared when Odele walked into the med bay, deviously boasting, "My, my Ms Winters. This is a surprise . . . What brings you to my neck of the woods?"

It was clear she already suspected the answer, as she held Matt's phone in her hands. So, I tried not to let her get to me as I cleared my throat, "I was told this was a great place for a holiday . . . You know to get away from it all."

She walked closer to me, feigning her sincerity, "Hmm . . . Stephen tells me you were attacked by a wolf. . . That wouldn't be Alex by any chance?"

Again, she already knew that answer. But it seemed like she wanted to play the game too.

– So let's play.

With a cheeky smirk, I sighed and became slightly agitated as my eyes flickered black again, and I replied, "We had a . . . disagreement on which tourist attraction we should visit . . . there's actually a lot of interesting things to discover around here."

Odele walked around the bed, looking at my long white hair and pointed ears, and was just fascinated, watching my eyes change colour from black to normal blue. She then noticed the bracelet still on my wrist and gently ran her figures over the tree stone, almost entranced by it.

"Oh, you poor dear," she replied, trying to pull the stone from the vines and failing, ". . . and here I thought your men just follow you blindly, no questions asked."

I laughed as I snickered back at her, "I guess I haven't mastered the technique like you have." –– Clearly gesturing to the many men standing guard behind her.

I then focused all my effort to create a small spark of a flame at the tips of my fingers, singeing the cuff of Odele's sleeve, forcing her to give up tugging at my bracelet.

I was actually pretty chuffed I could muster that – I still hadn't fully figured out how to use that particular element. But it also sparked Billy's interest as Odele stood back and scowled at me, glaring down at the tree stone and patting out the flames on her sleeve. I guess she was agitated that yet again, she couldn't get what she wanted from me as the tree stone remained firmly in its rightful place on my wrist.

She glared at me for a mere few seconds, before she sneered, "The Commander wishes to see her . . . Prep her," then stormed out of the bay.

– Ooh now that was a fun game, let do it again.

I grinned and yelled back to Odele while she was still in the hallway, "It was nice seeing you again, Odele. I'll be sure to say hi to Terrence for you!"

– Yep that really stirred that pot.

I couldn't stop my giggles as I heard Odele frustratingly grunt from the hall way. But I could also tell that I was getting to Billy as he gawked back at me in a curious wonder.

Nature – Animal – and fire – What else does he think I can do? I guess he also wasn't used to seeing someone like us be so openly defiant like that before. That or he was beginning to suspect that I was playing them. Which I very much was — and I liked the game I was playing. Even though I knew it was going to hurt in the end.

Still, Billy remained guarded, as he helped me to out of the bed but I noticed he wrapped the blanket around me to keep me covered from the others as he led me behind a cloth partition.

I stayed smiling at him and stared at his typical short crew-cut black hair, and he was actually quite muscly and tall — I mean my eyes only just met his chin. And he had fascinating green eyes, that became a little puzzled as he uncuffed my restraints in order for me to dress into more appropriate attire. — I think Billy was expecting me to try and run — but I didn't.

It was also very interesting, because when he handed me a pair of knickers and bra, I had to drop the blanket to dress into them and his eyes stayed focused on mine until I was appropriately covered.

I then stood in front of him, waiting for pants and top but noticed him studying me, moving closer to me as he slowly brushed is fingers across some of the scars I had, focusing particularly on the three slashes across my abdomen.

Normally I'd feel very uncomfortable with — this. But it was like Billy was more curious than sad. And when he glanced up, noticing that I was watching him, he stepped back clearing his throat as he handed— what a surprise— the only thing they had spare in the clothes department— army pants and a singlet.

Again I had to giggle as I got dressed into them because now I looked like I was a cadet back in my training days. And I kept smiling at him as he put the handcuffs back on me. I was trying to get him to smile back, and it looked like he wanted to but he was being difficult and stubborn – Clearly not wanting to play my game.

He then turned me around to braid my unusually long hair and when he finished, the hair tie stopped and rested on the cheeks of my buttocks.

And wow – My hair is ridiculously long now.

But still this Billy guy is a very curious one. – He turned me back around and looked at me intensely as he clicked his fingers together, creating a small flame in the centre of his hand all while staring cautiously at me. – Ah so he did want to play, after all.

I remained perfectly still and obedient for him then copied him, slowly raising my cuffed hands and I snapped my fingers, creating a small flame in the centre of my hand, holding it next to his. But I wasn't planning on telling him that it was pretty much all I could do – I was going to bluff – and I over-confidently winked at him as I quenched my flame, which finally, caused him to smile – briefly, but he still did it.

He then slowly walked me back out towards the rest of my many escorts, and as they guided me towards the elevator,

I passed a room where Odele was talking to another Fire guardian. It looked like Terrence's brother, Keith. So, I listened in as I heard Odele snap at him, "Did you find them?"

"They're in a cottage about 12 miles out," he replied quietly.

"Do what you have to," Odele commanded then just before Keith stepped out of the room she added, "But if you hurt my son, I'll break your hands."

"Yes mother," he sighed with such disappointment in his voice. But as Keith walked back passed me and my escorts, waiting for the elevator, he scowled back at me and grinned. He knew of my ability to sense his desires – and he coveted a very painful and slow death for his brother.

Still I couldn't worry about that and had to trust Terrence could look after himself. So, I stayed the obedient one, standing next to Billy, waiting patiently for the elevator.

He occasionally glanced down at my handcuffs and then back at his friend, Stephen, in a curious astonishment. It was a very tense crowd, so I thought I'd break the silence and jested, "Well, this is awkward . . . Does anyone have any jokes?"

They stayed silent, so instead, I started us off, "Okay . . . I'll go first. What did the snow say to the Rocky Mountains?" I waited but again, got no response. And answered.

"I got you covered . . ."

But still the group remained silent, waiting for the elevator, so I tried again, "No . . . okay. . . oh, I got another one. . . Um . . . an Australian woman walks up to a Canadian man in a bar to introduce herself. She tells him she from Australia and he replies 'where a boots' to which the Australian replies 'No, I'm wearing runners.'"

It was a struggle, but I eagerly smiled as Stephen cracked and started laughing at my hilarious attempt at bad humour, which then caused the rest of the group to start laughing as well. I felt a bit victorious, in breaking the ice and giggled along with them when Stephen looked at me and asked through his laughter, "Can I ask you a question?".

"Fire away," I replied then looked at the many guns they were holding and joked, "Well, not literally I mean."

He laughed even more at that and tried to compose himself as he asked "What are you doing here?"

I looked around at the guards and the people passing us, and sarcastically replied, "From the looks of it, I'm waiting for an elevator."

Stephen's laughter then started to diminish as he became more serious and asked again – but still with a small grin on his face, "No, I mean . . . we've met before. I pulled you from the water after you destroyed The Village training facility. I know those handcuffs aren't going to stop you, and that you could probably take us all out in a second. So . . . what's stopping you?"

Before I could answer, Billy stepped in and rebuked, "Maybe knock you out in a second. But she hasn't taken me on yet."

"That sounds like a challenge . . ." I cheekily grinned turning to Billy as I held up my cuffed hands to show him the tree stone bracelet coming to life, growing tendrils in and around the handcuffs as I stood ready to fight him.

Suddenly, the group fell quiet and tense again as all of the guards stood back, drawing their weapons, and aiming them at me. – Wow, tough crowd.

Finally, and luckily, the elevator doors opened, and the tendrils of the bracelet retracted all while I continued to grin at Billy.

"Now wasn't that good timing," I commented, stepping backwards into the elevator and waited with a giggle, "Are you coming, boys?"

I stood in the middle of the elevator as the guards surrounded me, all still very tense and cautious. And I watched as Billy pressed the basement button then glanced back at me again, still very curious. So I thought I'd keep playing with him, and winked at him again as we started the long journey down.

I already knew, after studying the Agronomique facility blueprints, that most of their facility was several hundred feet underground, which is why I wasn't surprised that the elevator took so long.

We did however make a few stops on the other floors, and I became the talking point for a quiet a few levels.

Suddenly, a familiar face stepped into the elevator. It was Jordan and he had acquired an Agronomique's uniform while he was roaming around the grounds, dispersing seeds into the air vents and into all the nooks and crannies.

He rode the elevator down one level, then very briefly glanced back at me as he stepped out, leaving a nice full bag of seeds hidden in the corner of the elevator. I smiled back at him and winked as the doors closed. -- And I don't know about anyone else but I was having a lot of fun because so far, the plan was running perfectly. - That and Billy couldn't figure out why I was smiling at him.

# Journal entry insert by Keith Connors

Mission Report

It was pouring with rain by the time my team had approached the cabin where Terrence and the traitors resided.

My crew consisted of myself - a Fire guardian, Adam - an Animal guardian, Bryce - a Land guardian, and Joel - a Water guardian.

We hid in the bushes and peered in through the windows to see four shadows, confirming their presence. So I gave Joel the signal to fire the sleeping gas canister, and we watched as the white gas started to pour out the windows and dissipate.

"Move in," I whispered.

Joel and Bryce were the first through the door. They cased the first floor and found nothing but puddles of water. But as they walked over the puddles, they rose to take human shape and ambushed both of them from behind.

Bryce tried to fight back as his hands transformed into large rocks and swung to hit the water body. But the water was fast, dodging every punch and cartwheeling over the coffee table, grabbing what looked like an EpiPen.

It then somersaulted over Bryce and, while it was mid-air, injected Bryce with the EpiPen.

Joel quickly shouted for backup, running to the window to warn us that it was an ambush before his coms went dead.

Instantly, Adam transformed himself into a giant grizzly bear and stormed into the cottage, breaking through the window. I heard a struggle coming from inside the cabin, and by the time I had made it up to the window, there was a loud, screeching roar followed by the sound of the coffee table breaking.

As I peered through the window, I saw two water nymphs standing over my crew's unconscious bodies. And in following my training, I believed the team to be compromised and took action to prevent further casualties, throwing several fireballs in though the cottage windows on both levels in order to destroy any evidence.

The water nymphs chased after me, and I defended myself, throwing fireballs at them, causing them to burst into steam. But as I ran towards the tree line, several more water nymphs appeared, forming from the puddles caused by the rain. They had me surrounded.

I was quick and created a stream of fire that blazed along the ground, but I needed more fuel, so I aimed for the trees that surrounded the cottage. The flames engulfed the trees, creating a large enough distraction for me to disappear.

I didn't go far. Instead, I stayed and watched from a distance as I heard one of the nymph's shout, "We must protect the guardians," racing back into the blazing cottage and dragging my unconscious crew out, and working as a team to extinguish the fire.

As the fire dwindled, one of the water nymphs stood over Bryce to check if he was breathing then tapped her ear and said, "Sira to Del, the plan worked. We got all but one, a fire guardian . . He set fire to the cottage and ran. Should we pursue?"

"Negative," a soft voice replied through the nymphs hidden earpiece. "Take care of the agents you have and prepare for the next phase."

That's when I ran back to deliver my report.

Mission Failed.

# Journal entry insert by Terrence Connors

We stood waiting in the cover of the trees bordering the Agronomique's facility, with Adela just arriving on scene with Jennifer after receiving reports of the water nymph's success in the 4th phase. And Alex was getting a little impatient, worrying about Lila.

It especially didn't help the situation for either of our nerves when Adela said, "Everything is in place. The next phase is up to Lila."

Yeah — I was beginning to really regret letting Lila volunteer to be the distraction. I know her plan had worked before to rescue Alex and then rescue me. But this was more like taking down the island training camp — not springing me from the hospital.

And if Lila remembered correctly — last time we did that it almost killed her.

# CHAPTER 30

# OLD ENEMIES – NEW RULES

*Journal entry by Lila Winters*

As the elevator finally opened on to the basement floor, I walked out with a minor blood nose, still in handcuffs, along with quite a few confused yet still heavily armed escorts.

There was really no way of knowing if the blue rose and white lilies potency worked or if they were even under the influence of Neuritamine to begin with, so I continued the ruse and waited for my next phase to be in place.

I was escorted out into a large underground cavern. And it was beautiful, with green grassy running tracks, and floral shrubbery and trees that adorned the cave walls. There was also a waterfall that flowed into the centre of the cavern, filling a small glistening pond.

It was almost like déjà vu — if it weren't for the training mats and sparring soldiers, it would be just like the hidden underground cavern back in China.

I followed my escorts as they led me down a marble stone path that trailed down towards the training mat where Commander Peterson stood, berating and teaching his newest recruits.

But I noticed Stephen looking confused, as he walked alongside me. And both he and Billy looked like they had a small headache. — Hmm potentially a good sign for me.

"Is everything okay?" I asked, looking at Stephen with genuine concern.

He just shook it off and snapped back, "Yeah, I'm fine. Keep moving."

So I nodded and obeyed his orders, following him to stand at the edge of the training mat opposite the new recruits as we all watched the Commander sparring with one of the recruits, throwing him to the ground over and over again, to the point where the recruit could no longer stand.

The Commander walked over and offered to help him up, only to pull him halfway up and kick him back down to the ground. He then stood over the recruit and sneered, "What rule did you just break?"

But the recruit stared at the ground, ashamed to answer. So Instead, the Commander looked at the others and answered his own question, "Rule 9 — The enemy will take any opportunity to strike . . . as should you."

The recruit nodded then stood to his feet, walking to stand back in line, but as he did, the Commander grabbed one of his sparring sticks and hit the backs of the recruit's knees, forcing him back down to the ground.

"Who can tell me what rule he broke this time?" the Commander asked again, but he still got no response.

Until I answered, "Rule 3 – Never turn your back on the enemy.'"

He then turned to look at me and leered, now knowing who I was and who trained me, and I could just tell from the annoyed smugness in his voice, that the fallout for him losing me once did not go well for him. "Ah, the girl who was plucked from the ocean . . . Come to join our training session have you?"

Still with smug arrogance written all over him, he held out a sparring stick for me to grab. And with a smile I glanced down at my handcuffs before I sniped, "Not particularly, no."

But the Commander didn't want that answer and his lips tilted up slightly, as he started to swing the sparring stick repeatedly, trying to hit my shoulder or head – I'm not exactly sure what he was aiming for. Either way I wasn't in the mood to be hit, so each time he took a swing at me, I moved to avoid it – but never fought back.

"I did not come here to fight you," I shouted, between swings.

"Then tell me. . . Why are you here?" he bellowed back, becoming more and more frustrated, clearly breaking rule 8, which left him open.

And with that I raised my hand up and used the handcuffs to block his next strike, unintentionally triggering the handcuffs electric defences. – Oopsi-Frac.

I moved quickly, commanding the tendrils of my bracelet to grow in and around the handcuff to absorb the majority of the electrical currents, and grounded them back down along the ground. But I won't lie, the residual current of electricity that managed to course through me was – almost unbearable. – Ouch.

Still, I didn't let the pain get to me, instead I grabbed hold of the sparring stick, walking along to its centre, then used my entire body as I spun around, pulling the sparring stick out of the Commander's hands.

But before I completed my twirl, just as I was about to hit the Commander, I stopped just shy of his face. Then took a step sideways, spinning again, this time aiming low and hit the backs of his knees, forcing him to the ground – face first.

Alright that was definitely hilarious to watch, and I may have grinned as I stood over him, holding the sparring stick on his back and answered, "I'm here to give you a chance to surrender and leave peacefully."

I looked up at my armed escort, expecting repercussions, but instead, only four of them reacted – the humans.

The Guardians of my escort looked more confused and nervous than anything else, and I sensed few mixed emotions from them – Fear mostly.

However, the humans of my security escorts, drew their guns and aimed them at me, demanding me to step back. Even the new recruits jumped in on the action and stood ready to fight me.

But I, not willing to fight any of them, stood back, then handed the sparring stick to Billy, before returning to where I last stood, next to him and Stephen.

In a huff, the Commander rose to his feet, furious and embarrassed after being defeated by a woman in handcuffs. He stormed toward me and pulled the knife from his holster, pressing it against my cheek, just hard enough to pierce my skin and make me bleed, as he sneered, "And why would I do that?"

But before I could answer him a voice shouted from behind me, "Enough!!!!"

It was a voice I recognised and feared, making my stomach churn in rage.

Oh Frac.

In hearing that, the Commander stepped back, and I turned to face General Willows.

Frac Damn — he was alive and well with only one minor defect of a limp caused by a spinal injury from our previous conflict.

He grinned so arrogantly as he limped towards me with the aid of a walking stick, and following behind him was Matt, handcuffed as well with a black eye and a cut lip.

I stared back at Matt then to Richard, who greeted me with a doting and condescending, "Hello Pumpkin."

Frac, Frac, Crapitty, Frac, Crap – This was not who I was expecting.

## Journal entry insert by Terrence Connors

We were still hiding amongst the trees, watching for any sign of Lila's success, but we had been waiting for a while, well into the night. And I was starting to feel very nervous, and it got worse when I looked down to see my tree stone bracelet glowing brighter.

"Oh no," I fearfully whispered.

Alex turned to me and he too, grew nervous, looking at the tree stone, demanding, "What is it? What wrong?"

"It's Lila," I replied, "I can feel her emotions changing rapidly . . . She was confident just a minute ago. But now she's scared and confused and angry."

Without a second thought, Alex rushed out from the shadow of the trees and raced towards the iron fence. "We need to help her," he growled as he began to slowly morph into a wolf.

That is until I stopped him and pulled him back into reality. "No . . . We both promised Lila we'd stick to the plan . . . no matter what."

Alex scowled back at me and with a growling voice said, "The plans just changed." He then pulled away, taking a running jump over the fence, and used the darkness of the night to sneak up the facility.

And Yeah — this was not at all part of the plan.

I hesitated for just a moment, wanting to follow the plan but I also didn't want Alex to be on his own — and finding the wrong kind of trouble. So, I followed after him.

It was very unusual though because it seemed easy — too easy.

While staying in the cover of the night, Alex crept up to one of the building entrances, and almost made it until he walked through the facility doors, and into a finely woven electrified net draped from the roof to the floor. It wrapped around him as he fell to the ground, writhing in pain.

This was not a good sign — it was as if they knew he was going to react this way and come running in to save her.

I stopped just outside the door, watching Alex as he trembled trying to control the pain then quickly turned to me, staring at me in fear, listening to hundreds of heavy footsteps racing towards him.

"Run . . .," he shouted "Go!"

With reluctancy, I turned and raced at super speed across the grassy fields to escape, only to be trapped in a fiery circle of flames, and my brother — Keith standing on the other side, smiling at me.

I felt powerless, watching in the distance as Adela and Jenifer were found. They tried to put up a fight but inevitably failed, as they too were caught by electrified nets.

# Journal entry insert by Tyme Knight

Alright – I didn't like this at all. Today is literally the worst day of my life. Because I had to watch my sister – the one I had only just gotten to know and love, – walk into the belly of the beast and be greeted by a madman, with me not able to do anything – It was gut wrenching.

I had been given a separate mission to the others and Lila trusted me to not stray from the plan no matter what. Before I left to carry out my group's mission phase, Lila made me promise not to break this trust and urged me to understand that it was "A Life or Death promise."

And since I didn't want Lila's death on my hands or any of the others, I stood watching from the time rift as my sister took a beating from Richard's minion and didn't fight back – because that was her mission.

My mission was to sneak Jordan, Zera and Katie into the facility and leave them to carry out each of their tasks. With me ordered to stay hidden, out of their time but only just, and only ever step in if the mission went sideways or when Lila told me to.

It was very hard for me to do this, watching from the security room as the entire plan fell apart. And I don't know how she did, but Lila just knew this would happen.

She knew that the entire plan would fall apart, and she already had a back-up plan in the works.

Before we left a few nights ago, she muttered something to me about rule 5. But I didn't understand what it meant – until now.

## *Original journal entry continued by Lila Winters*

Well Frac Buckets – I could feel through the stone in my bracelet that the mission was starting to go wrong. I could read Terrence's emotion clearly and felt my heart ache for him when I sensed his feelings of failure, fear and guilt.

But I couldn't worry about them, because I had someone else I had to deal with. And while Richard's arrival was unexpected, it did not deter the plan – much.

Naturally, he arrived with his own entourage of soldiers who were ordered to – let's say, ensure I knew my place. I did dodge a few strikes and fists, mainly the ones that were aiming for my head. But I also knew that if the soldiers didn't fulfil their orders and give me the appropriate beating, then Richard definitely would have shot them for their incompetence and blamed me for their deaths. And I had no plans for anyone to die today – not because of me.

Once Richard was satisfied with the beating I received, he called his soldier's back, and they left me lying on the sparring mat, quite bloodied and sore.

Again, I didn't let the pain get to me, I just rose back up onto my feet and stood waiting for the next phase to be in place.

Richard then stared at me and started to applaud me before walking onto the sparring mat himself and contemptuously spoke, "Well, I have to admit, Pumpkin, your plan was bold and audacious. . . And if it weren't for the fact that you took on a giant that is a lot stronger, smarter, and darker than you . . . I probably would have been proud of the girl I raised you to be."

Ooh, I really hate this man.

With a smug grin, Richard used his walking stick and struck me across the face, then started to berate me, "I know I raised you to be smarter than this . . ."

He then began listing all the rules I had broken, and with each rule he struck me with his walking stick.

"Rule 2 – Never let down your defences. . . Rule 4 – Don't draw attention to yourself. . . Rule 7 – Do your homework and know your enemy. . . Rule 5 – If your mission is going well, it's most likely a trap . . . and finally, the most important rule of all . . . Rule 10 – Don't get caught."

That last rule angered Richard further as he struck me harder across the face and in the stomach, causing me to fall to my knees again.

I heard Matt call to me and he struggled to break free of the hold his guards had on him while they forced him to watch.

The pain I felt was severe as I spat out the blood that had accumulated in my mouth, and just knew I had some internal bleeding now. But I pushed through the pain and stood to my feet, determined to not give Richard any of the satisfaction.

Then shaking his head, he stood in front of me as if he were disappointed, and grunted, "My baby girl . . . My pumpkin . . . What in the hell were you thinking?"

I took a breath, and stood tall and confident, but I was pretty sure I didn't look too crash hot to anyone, as I felt the blood trickling down my face from the open gash above my eye. I also needed to spit out the blood that had accumulated in my mouth. But I stayed calm through it all, then cheekily and very sweetly answered, "I thought I would be a nice little Pumpkin and offer you a chance to surrender and leave peacefully."

He didn't go for it — instead he glared back at me and then turned to the Commander as they both broke into hysterical laughter.

"You think you still have the advantage here?" Richard chortled, "Oh, Pumpkin. . . You have no idea how to take us on. Because if you actually did do your homework . . . you would know that we have our claws in everything, every business, every country, every king, queen, president, politician and prime minister. . . Anyone that you think would come running to your rescue. . . We own them . . . they don't even sneeze without us knowing."

He then struck me again, across my back a lot harder than before, and kicked me to the ground.

And as I pulled myself back up onto my knees, I turned my head just a little to look at Billy and Stephen – who were still standing behind me, but now seemed very uneasy just watching me take a beating from an arrogant mad man.

"Your ignorance is pathetic," Richard sniggered.

Again, I took a few breaths then chuckled, bearing through the burning pain I felt in my ribs and back and various other places as I replied, "And your arrogance is sickening."

I then turned again to Billy and smiled when I saw him holding his hand out toward me, and I happily accepted his assistance as he reached down to help me to my feet. But as Billy held onto me – I realised whose side he was on.

So I quickly broke free from him, and turned to Richard to continue with a raspy voice, "You walk through life claiming power you do not deserve and authority you have not earned... You take things that don't belong to you... You ensnare the weak and innocent and fight only for yourself... And that... is why you will always lose."

Again, Richard laughed at me and walked toward me as he jeered, "You really think you can beat me?... I taught you everything you know."

He then raised his walking stick to deliver one final blow, but as he did Billy stepped in front of me, using the sparring stick I gave him, to protect me. So instead of my face getting hit, the walking stick collided with the sparring stick in Billy's hand and snapped in two.

Now in an angered shock, Richard glared back at him. And I cheekily grinned, looking over Billy's shoulder while discreetly leaning on him as well to stay standing as I very smugly but sweetly spoke. "You did teach me a lot of things, Richard. . . including rule 6 – never show all of your cards."

## Journal entry insert by Terrence Connors

Yeah — the plan had gone terribly wrong, and I was filled with fear as I sat in the holding cell feeling like a failure, staring at the tree stone bracelet as it continued to glow.

"Is she still alive?" Alex asked feeling just as miserable.

I broke my concentration away from the stone and glanced across to see Alex, Adela and Jennifer, all sitting in their separate holding cells, all waiting for the same confirmation.

That is until we heard a commotion coming from outside the holding cells main door, and one of the guards was thrown into the door, breaking the door down and sending him sliding through the narrow hallway.

We all watched in a slight confused shock as Jordan calmly followed him, walking in through the now non-existent door, holding an ice bat in his hand, and snickered, "You're late."

He moved at superspeed and rummaged around to find the cell door key card to free us as Alex stood to his feet, and joked, "Really . . . And here I thought we were early."

With a chuckle, Jordan looked back up at Alex as he smirked, "Your Lila knew you were not going to stick to her plan. . . and gave my team a counter plan. . . Lila's providing the distraction we need with the General and Commander both down in the basement . . . We tried to locate Ms Connors, but she has gone to radio silence."

Alex stared back at Jordan, in stunned fear when he repeated, "Richard's alive?"

I also stared at Jordan, fearfully waiting for that answer as he opened Alex's cell door and nodded, "Alive and furious at the girl he calls 'Pumpkin'. . . But no matter, we stick to plan."

Oh Crap — 'Pumpkin' — The General must have known she was coming, in order to be this cocky and resort to using the pet name he had for her.

I then looked down at my bracelet again, as I felt a slight change in Lila's emotions — there was faint glimmer of happiness amongst all of her anger, but still there was no fear. So, I told Alex not to worry and to trust Lila as I began to help Jordan free all prisoners being held in the other holding cells.

Jordan then demanded us to hurry as we followed him out into the corridor, and we all split up again with Adela and Jenifer going their way, and Alex and I on our own mission.

## Original journal entry continued by Lila Winters

I continued to lean on Billy as he stood protectively in front of me and surprisingly, he didn't mind. But I casually moved to stand next to him instead — when I glanced across to one of the air vents, and finally saw the long thorny rose stems and leafy branches overflowing from it.

Finally — the next phase was ready.

I smirked, leering back at Richard as he followed my gaze over to the air vent and panicked. But before he could do anything else, I used all the force I could muster and smashed my hands down, though the rocky soil, grabbing hold of the plant roots growing beneath the surface.

My eyes then glowed a vigorous green, and my nose began to bleed again as I used all of my concentration and energy to link with the roses and lilies. Then within seconds, the flowers released a blue sweaty pollen into every hallway and room of the facility.

The pollen landed on every worker, scientist, guardian, agent and creature in the building, causing them to become dazed and confused, and releasing all of them who were under the influence of the Neuritamine toxin.

*"DO IT NOW TYME!"* I screamed as loud as I could, giving Tyme the signal to pull the fire alarm, sounding the evacuation procedures.

And once the pollen started to settle, I pulled my hands from the soil to stand back up again, briefly looking down at the now shattered handcuffs as they fell away, freeing my movements.

"What have you done?" Richard shrieked, looking around at some of the new recruits as they became dazed and unsure of their environment.

The Commander also seemed a little unnerved and lost his patience, pushing Richard to the side of the sparring mat as he drew his gun to shoot me. But before he could Stephen and the new recruits stepped in, wrestling the gun from him, and holding him in a headlock.

And now we were in stand-off – It seems that not all of the recruits and guardians were under the influence of Neuritamine as they drew their guns and created weapons, readying themselves to fight each other.

"STOP!" I shouted, standing between everyone with my hands in the air.

They all stared at me, confused as to what I was doing and listened as I explained, "I did not come here for people to die. . . I came here to give people the freedom to choose."

I could sense that I was getting to some of the guardians as their need and want for revenge wavered. But Richard just had to open his big mouth as he stood to his feet and clapped mockingly, "There's the girl I was looking for . . . So what now? Do you honestly think we were just going to let them all leave? Did you think, you were just going to walk out the front door no questions asked?"

Ah – what an arrogant idiot. – I destroyed a Fraccing island and almost a Naval air carrier, and still he thinks a rock cavern is going to stop me.

I let out a long sigh and grinned at him, while pointing towards the roof of the cavern, which was now covered in creeping vines and replied, "I don't need a door."

The fear rose in him, as I pulled my arm down with one swoop, and the creeping vines reacted to my command, breaking apart the cavern roof and creating a rocky mounded staircase up to the surface – where my team was waiting and assisting with the evacuation.

The new recruits, who were now free, didn't hesitate to start making their escape. Even those who hadn't been affected by the Neuritamine started to waver in their loyalty to The Board. And Richard scrutinized them, as all of his loyal followers abandoned him. Then in a furious rage, he pulled out his gun and fired at me, almost emptying his clip.

At full speed, Billy raced to wrestle the gun from him, as I tried to dodge the bullets at the fastest speed I could gather through all the pain. But I wasn't fast enough, so Matt raced at full speed as well to pull me out of the firing line, getting shot in the back as we both fell to the ground.

It felt like I had been shot too, but I really didn't care. And to be honest, I probably wouldn't be able to tell, given all the blood on me already. I was more concerned about Matt and the others. As I looked up to see Billy towering over Richard and was just about to shoot him, until he heard me scream, "No Billy, Please!"

He stared back at me in angered confusion only to see me holding Matt in my arms as he started to bleed out.

"He's a monster . . . He deserves to die!" he shouted.

"Maybe. . .," I contested trying to speak loud enough though my pain, "But who are you to judge one man, over the sins of many. . . even your own. . . He is not the only monster on this earth, Billy . . . But right now you've all been given chance to choose what type of guardian you want to be. . . I won't stop you if you choose to kill him . . . but if you do this now . . . of your own free-will, you will only become the monster you hate."

All the guardians took a moment as they contemplated their actions, and thought about what they wanted of themselves. Then Stephen freed the Commander from the hold he had on him, and Billy lowered the gun then threw it into the cavern pond.

And while the Commander and the General tried to regain their bearing, Stephen rushed to help Matt to his feet, and Billy helped me to mine then at full speed we ran up the rocky mound on to the surface to join the others.

We were soon greeted by a very worried and panicked Jennifer as she pushed through the groups of confused scientists and guardians. She raced to grab hold of Matt as Stephen placed him gently on the ground.

Billy then helped me to kneel down next to Matt as he morphed back into Henry and I sniffled trying hard not to cry, "Henry, I'm so sorry. I can fix this just give me a minute."

I hurriedly looked around for a blue rose seed when he stopped me, grabbing hold of my hand, and wheezed, "I'm stronger than I look . . . Stick to the plan . . . Now is the time to send The Board a message. Don't waste it on me."

I wanted to help him but he was right. So I nodded, looking up to the skies knowing exactly what was to come next as several armed helicopters raced over the tree lines, dropping what looked like a dozen black ops units to the ground, moving to surround us.

"Down on the ground. . . Now!" they shouted.

In fear of their lives, all of the rescued scientist, and guardians, and creatures obeyed.

Everyone but me.

The General was a very predictable man, but so was Odele as she stood amongst the armed ground troops, waiting for us to make the wrong move.

I walked towards her, completely ignoring the black ops men, as they shouted at me.

"I said don't move!" one of them screamed as he loomed over me.

But still my focus stayed on Odele as I stood in front of her, watching her search through the crowd, looking for Terrence, while I replied to the demand, "Very well . . . I won't move."

Then with one blink of the eye, a swarm of Water nymphs and Wood nymphs appeared, surrounding the black ops units, along with the guardian elders Leeroy, Samuel, Leah and Broch. While Tyme, Zera, and Katie appeared standing next to me, ready to fight.

The beautiful sight to see – was from the rain when it formed into a ferocious water dragon that flew through the air, attacking the helicopters and throwing them into the trees, trapping them amongst branches.

I watched as Odele and her men looked around, instantly realising they were outnumbered and outgunned. And I wasn't entirely sure but I think I was grinning – I couldn't really feel my face, but I had enough in me to mock, "Your move, Mrs Connors"

She took a moment, sizing me up then wisely shouted, "Stand down!" calling for her troops to lower their weapons.

With I think still a grin on me – I stayed staring at Odele but spoke loud enough for all to hear, "To all guardians, humans, and creatures, who are wishing to leave this place . . . go now! . . . Follow the nymphs! They will lead you to safety!"

In seconds, the Wood nymphs and Water nymphs began to disappear, leading and carrying people away from this place. Billy and Stephen helped to carry Henry, following Jenifer to safety. All while I stayed, and watched as they all disappeared, until there was only me, surrounded by what was left of the men still loyal to The Board and to Odele.

Odele looked around and arrogantly croaked, "It will never work . . . we will simply collect them again."

I then moved at full speed to stand inches from of her – staring into her cold eyes, and with a sly grin, I whispered, "I know . . . but this time is different. This time, they remember everything. . . How to fight. How to hide. How to hunt . . . And while you're busy trying to regain your collection . . . I will pick apart your entire empire piece by piece."

As Odele sneered in anger, raising her hand to strike me, Alex and Terrence came running at full speed out of the Agronomique's building, seconds before it exploded.

The explosion was enough of a distraction for us to make our escape, but not before I left a small peace offering with Odele. – It was the antidote to make the nanobots in her body inert.

# CHAPTER 31

# THE SWEET SMELL OF VICTORY

## Journal entry by Alex Woods

It worked! I can't believe it worked – even though the plan went completely bonkers.

As soon the Agronomique's building went up in smokes, we high-tailed it out of there, and I picked up Lila in the process, carrying her in my arms, following Terrence as we raced at full speed though the trees towards one of the open tree portals.

"That was amazing!" I shouted, helping Lila to step through the tree portal into New York's Central Park.

We stood at the top of one of the large maple trees where Agatha and Wyala were waiting for us. And I was really happy that we had all survived – but Lila looked like she had been through a war, covered in blood, cuts, and bruises.

She did however manage to bring her wolf-like appearance back under control as her hair and ears returned to normal – And she didn't even need my help. She's getting damn good at it.

Lila looked so happy as she stared out through the foliage of the trees, to see the beautiful city of New York and smiled, "No Alex this is amazing."

Wyala moved to stand next to her, staring out at the skyline and commented, "This was my favourite place to visit before I met you."

Surprised by that, Lila looked back at her, asking, "And you've never been afraid of people seeing you?"

"No," Wyala replied peering down at the locals below, "That's the amazing thing about humans. Our kind have visited this town for hundreds of years. . . And I sit on this branch watching the humans walk straight past, always too busy to look up."

I followed her gaze, looking down to see the humans and remarked, "Huh. Their loss."

Agetha then turned to Lila and handed her a gift. She happily accepted the gift, but stared at Agetha confusingly as she pulled the leafy wrapping paper away. And the joy on Lila's face was amazing to see as she held in her hands a new journal with a wooden cover made from an old oak tree, and on the front of the cover, it had carvings of vines and leaves surrounding a white oak tree in the centre.

Lila flipped through to see the beautiful, soft pages that filled the book and gasped, "It's beautiful . . . but—"

"Because you give us hope . . ." Agetha interruptingly answered, ". . . Many of our kind had given up on the humans and their constant pursuit of power. . . But your courage, and determination to fight for what's right, no matter the odds, has inspired our kind again . . . and we want you to know how proud and thankful we are."

Awe Damn – that was inspiring – I mean even I'm proud of her.

While biting her bottom lip, Lila looked back up at Agetha and Wyala teary-eyed, thanking them both before she said goodbye, and helped them to step back through the tree portal, closing it behind them.

I was about to help Lila to the ground before she beat me to it, and jumped from the top of the tree to the ground. – Show off.

Terrence and I quickly followed, landing just in time to catch her as she stumbled from her pain. It was then we all realised that she was in shock still from a gunshot wound, and I pulled down the strap of her blood-covered singlet top to inspect the gaping hole in her shoulder.

Apparently, one of Richard's bullets had actually managed to hit Lila, and had embedded itself just below her collarbone.

"I'm okay. It's just a scratch," she said, trying to shrug it off.

Just a scratch – Is she out of her damn mind. She's got a bloody bullet in her body.

Terrence and I both stared at the many wounds Lila had endured and didn't know what to say, given everything she had been through all to rescue some strangers who she may never meet again. There really wasn't much to say. I mean, seriously – The fact that we all survived meant we couldn't really be mad at her.

Once she had regained what little strength she had, Lila looked at our gobsmacked faces and joked, "Come on. Max is waiting for us. Race you there . . . Loser buys Dinner."

Yep – She's lost her damn mind.

"No!" I screeched, grabbing hold of Lila's arm, "You can't run around New York in this condition."

Unfortunately, at the worst of possible timings, a mounted police officer approached us from behind. "Ma'am, are these men bothering you?"

Terrence turned to him, casually replying with a smile, "No Officer, we're fine."

The problem was – Lila definitely didn't look fine, so his statement was quickly dismissed.

"Is that a gunshot wound?" the officer asked staring back at Lila.

"Don't move," he demanded, then talked into his radio, "I've got a female GSW, Central Park North, requesting an Ambulance."

The problem was, he had also started to draw the attention of the other New York pedestrians and tourists. So, while the officer was distracted with his radio Terrence looked away and his eyes glowed, calling the leaves to flurry around us to create a distraction as we all ran at full speed out of Central Park. – Well, Terrence and I ran – Lila was scooped up into my arms and was smart enough not to argue with me.

We quickly appeared in the lobby of the NY-Eden Hotel where Max was already waiting for us with our room key. And he very excitedly gave us a quick briefing about all the rescued guardians and workers that safely arrived back at the hotel, and were either relocated or safely on their way back to their homes – via standard transportation or through the tree portals.

There were, however, some who chose to stay and had organised with Adela a freedom victory party that was a non-negotiable in attendance for us because Adela claimed it was a much-needed morale booster for the team. Which left Lila with only 2 hours to heal and get cleaned up. So we didn't waste any time as I carried her up to our room.

It took a while for Terrence to dig the bullet out of Lila's shoulder but she handled it with a brave face, and held my hand the whole way through.

Eventually Terrence managed to clean and stitch all of Lila wounds up. So by the time, we were due to go down to the party, Lila was –– not bleeding at least, and was mending slowly with the help of the blue rose paste and tonic.

When we arrived down at the hotel bar, the entire team was waiting, including what was left of the rescued Guardians, and the Guardian elders.

The best surprise of all, was when Lila was greeted by Danny and Ruby as they came racing out of the crowd from where Matt stood to give her the biggest cuddles.

She then made her rounds to greet everyone, and receive the many offers of thanks and praise. They were all so grateful and supportive, and several of them even asked to join our team, which was good because Jenifer and Henry had requested to set up their own New York-based team and operate out of this hotel.

There was a moment, however, I felt I spark of overprotective jealousy when Lila bumped into the man she called – Billy. He smiled at her differently and gently ran his fingers over the now stitched bullet wound, and the gash above her eye. She then winked at him with a cheeky grin – as if it was an in-joke between them. Which was just weird.

And yes – I acted on my emotions and quickly asked Lila to come keep me company, as we sat around the tables and celebrated, laughing with each other and getting to know the other guardian.

Max then got up onto the stage to give a toast.

"Can I have your attention, please . . . I would like to take this moment to express on behalf of. . . I think everyone here. . . of just how grateful we are for Lila and her amazing team. Because of her leadership, families have been reunited, our futures have been redefined, and we have all been given the opportunity and the freedom to choose what our future looks like . . . It is an amazing feeling to have. . . And together, I know and believe that we can bring freedom and hope to others who have yet to see the truth, and to be given that opportunity to choose."

And as everyone raised their drink, we toasted – "To Freedom."